THE CANNAWAY CONCERN

ALSO BY GRAHAM SHELBY

The Knights of Dark Renown

The Kings of Vain Intent

The Oath and the Sword

The Devil Is Loose

The Wolf at the Door

The Cannaways

THE
CANNAWAY
CONCERN

GRAHAM SHELBY

Doubleday & Company, Inc.
Garden City, New York
1980

With the exception of actual historical persons,
all of the characters in this book are fictitious,
and any resemblance to actual persons, living or dead,
is purely coincidental.

ISBN: 0-385-14113-0
Library of Congress Catalog Card Number 78–22355

*Dédié à mes chers amis
à l'Olmadel, La Bastide
et ailleurs.*

CONTENTS

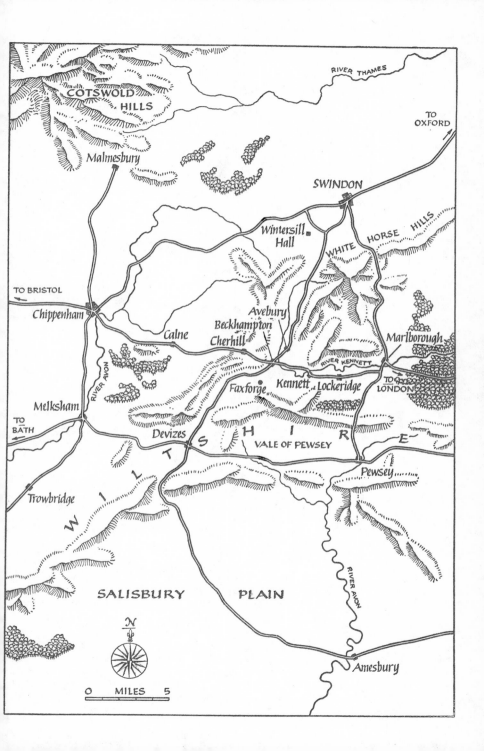

THE CANNAWAY CONCERN

PART ONE

BROOK

1719–1720

ONE

They had said between noon and nightfall. So any time now.

Waiting for them, the man's natural impatience had brought him from the fireside to stand near the mullioned window, brandy glass in hand, peering eastward along the drive. The heels of his turn-top boots rapped the flagged, uncarpeted floor. At the far end of the room—the hall of the Hall—the clock on the rosewood sideboard registered twenty minutes past four in the afternoon. The sky beyond the window was growing dark, the air filled with snow. The man's heel taps were erratic and he steadied himself before turning to refill his glass from a flask on the long central table. He blamed his clouded gaze on the smoke that gusted from the fireplace, though he had been drinking since midmorning and his hand now fumbled with this, his third flask of the day.

He walked back to the window and stood confused for a moment, then realised the tattered curtain was outside, the flakes of snow clinging to the leaded panes. He leaned forward as if to reach the window sash, thought better of it and struggled to regain his balance. He said, "Come on, blast you, if you're coming." By five o'clock it would be properly dark, yet his friends had assured him they would be here before nightfall. *So thrash along before this blizzard suffocates the roads! What else do you suppose, damn you, that I intend to share Christmas alone with the hedgerow bitch?*

He emptied his glass, veered away to stand it on the table, then strode from the long, panelled hall.

✳

The doxies had been eager enough, God knows; it was scarcely the fault of the girls. Yet one thing had led to another, as it will, and the young men had overstayed their time in Swindon. It was not until Eldon Sith shrilled the hour that they'd thought it advisable to get the women into the wagon, scramble aboard the benches and show their whips to the mounts.

They were less than halfway to the Hall when the sky had split along its seams. . . .

There were three vehicles in the party; the first, Eldon's light-wheeled curricle, now made lopsided by the presence of the portly, do-as-you-will Markis Mayman. Scion of a landowning family, and with lucrative business interests in the capital, Markis radiated a comfortable and cheery bonhomie. Stamp on his foot, someone had said, and you could be sure of a beaming apology. True or not, he had never been known to pick a squabble, raise his voice in anger, air any but the mildest opinions. Markis Mayman was what he wished to be—everybody's friend.

Beside him, and higher on the sloping bench seat, Eldon Sith bowed his thin, weasel's face against the snow. In common with Markis, he too was the wealthy son of wealthy parents, though the men were as different in character and temperament as in the set of their features, the poundage of flesh on their frames.

Eldon, for example, was terrified that the snow would prevent them from reaching the Hall tonight. Bad enough if they were stranded out here on the open road; the closed road if the snow continued to fall. But it wasn't the fear of freezing that made Eldon scowl and lash at the horses. It was fear of how things would go later, when they met the man who was waiting for them now. He would not take it kindly if his friends failed to get through. No, indeed, not kindly at all. There'd be the very devil to pay.

Shrilling his fear at the horses, Eldon laid about them with the whip. Markis said, "Be a while before we're impeded. I've the confidence we'll be safely there by dark." Then he settled his chin lower inside the high double collar of his redingote, whilst his nervous companion, his friend, punished the horses onward along the bleak downland road.

✳

He was out on the steps now, the snow swirling in his face. Yellow light spilled from the windows of the Hall, staining the flakes as they fell. His skirted coat seemed to age and discolour, the snow dampening the powder on his wig. He had forgotten to collect his tricorn hat from the rack in the entranceway, and it required too much effort to retrace his steps inside.

He leaned for support against one of the pillars that flanked the steps. The brandy soured within him, its heat rising in his throat. He expelled the fumes in a sudden roar of anger. "Come *on*, pox rot you, come *on!*" Then he listened, his own words smothered somewhere out there on the drive.

✳

Coming hard behind Eldon and Markis were the Taylor brothers, their single-horse gig jolted from ridge to rut along the track. It was the first time either Theo or Simeon had been invited to the Hall, and they viewed their inclusion in the Christmas festivities as a stroke of the greatest good fortune.

At nineteen, and thus senior to Simeon by a year, Theo Taylor had met his host just once, in October, at a ball-*cum*-banquet in the nearby wool town of Marlborough. Eldon Sith had been there, and Markis Mayman and the others, though it was not until the tail of the evening that Theo had been held in conversation by the man who now awaited his arrival.

"Unmannerly of me to have left things late as this, Master Taylor. You've a brother, so I believe, the two of you being the Taylors who, according to some wag or other, have most of England stitched up." Theo had frowned at that and the man had explained, "Tailors? Stitched up?" Then the nineteen-year-old had nodded and grinned at the joke, aware that the clever play on words was true. After all, he and Simeon *had* just inherited one eighth part of the county, together with other properties that extended northward into Gloucestershire, westward into Somerset, southward across the border into Dorset and Hampshire, eastward into Berkshire and, estate by farm by holding, most of the way to London. So it *could* be said that the Taylors had things stitched up.

"Care to spend Christmas? The two of you? There'll be most of what a gentleman would enjoy."

Theo had blurted his acceptance, for both he and Simeon had heard of their host and of the seasonal goings-on in *that* particular Hall. And, from the stories that were put about, there was *everything* a gentleman might enjoy.

So, flattered by the invitation, the youngest and wealthiest members of the party raced to keep up with the curricle ahead.

He blinked, as though to assist his hearing. The snowflakes spiralled, teasing his senses. He slashed at them with a hand, yet still retained his hold on the fluted pillar. He leaned forward, listening, listening. . . .

Mouth swathed, his voice muffled by the scarf, Lucas Ripnall said, "There's the wall of the estate. We'll be inside with the last of the light."

Hunched beside him, and more than seven feet above the snow- and mud-spattered road, Peter Seal grunted agreement, pleased that he would not now have to clamber about, sparking flints to light the lamps.

If Markis Mayman and Eldon Sith were as different as chalk from cheese, Lucas Ripnall and Peter Seal were as hard-edged bricks, fired in the same flaring kiln. Both of them stocky and well muscled, they might more easily have been cast in the mould of highwaymen than what they were, moneyed gentlemen of Wiltshire.

Not that they could do more than read and write, and only that with their tongues between their lips.

And not that they had money to throw around, though they would without hesitation throw some other member of the gentry around if the outcome of the contest earned them money.

They were, quite simply, gentlemen of the county because they did not need to work for their living. They had their houses, and property that was farmed by their tenants, and a dribble of income from investments and stock in the city. But they were not involved in commerce, as was Markis. Nor the darling of their parents, as was Eldon. Nor rich beyond accounting, as were the Taylor brothers, the guileless Theo and Simeon.

They were more like their host, gentlemen by continuance, and safe in the knowledge that no one dared challenge their title.

Nevertheless, they had all the bulk and thrust of highwaymen, and were driving a wagon that was quite beyond the requirements of the gentry.

Drawn by six plunging horses, the bench half concealed by black tarred side walls, the boxlike vehicle was pierced along its length by a row of small oval windows. The box itself stood five and a half feet high above its axles, extended twice that length from rear door to driving bench and closely resembled the type of conveyance used in the transport of felons to prison. This evening, however, it was carrying a more willing type of passenger; nine young ladies from Mistress De Rue's Seminary for Gentlewomen; nine doxies from the most expensive whorehouse in Swindon.

The massive black wagon lumbered beside the wall. Peter Seal jabbed a gauntleted finger ahead of him. "They're turning in through the lodge gate."

Lucas Ripnall nodded, a spray of snow tipping from his three-cornered hat. Then he snarled through his muffler, leading the horses wide toward the verge, before urging them past the deserted gatehouse and along the half-mile drive.

Eldon and Markis had already disappeared among the gloomy overhang of trees.

The Taylor brothers had turned their gig nicely, following the curricle through the gate.

High on the wagon bench, Lucas now shook away his scarf and grinned at Peter.

"Rabbits are in," Lucas said.

To which Peter Seal responded, "Snares are set."

✳

For a while he'd been shivering with the cold. Then the warming effects of the brandy had faded and he'd started to shake in earnest, his body jerking as though in the spasms of intercourse or pain. He'd retreated under the shelter of the portico, hugged himself until the shaking lessened, then eased the cold clean air into his mouth.

Resistant, and with a knowledge of what drink might do, he had shaken the snow from his coat, stamped his boots, wiped away the rivulets from his face.

And then—surely his reward, surely his recompense for having kept watch so long—he heard the distant dull drum of hoofbeats, the distant dull rumble of wheels.

He started down the steps, changed his mind, hurried back to the entranceway and lifted his hat from its peg. No need for them to know his wig was damp, or that he'd been waiting on the threshold. He *had* been expecting them, yes, of course, and had been crossing the entranceway when he'd heard the rumble and the drum. So he'd snatched his hat, kicked the snow from the topmost step and—

"Here we are, Brooksy! Doubted we'd make it, Brooksy? Snow came down thicker than we thought!" It was Eldon Sith, his voice as shrill as a blade on a cutler's wheel.

Struggling free of his collar, Markis said, "Glad to be here, Brooksy, and there's a fact. Brought you some little trinkets for the season." Then he reached behind him and raised a wickerbound bottle, shouting again as the curricle went past the steps, "Two dozen of port, m'dear Brooksy. Thought they might slip down."

The Taylor brothers took their gig in procession, the eighteen-year-old Simeon doffing his hat to his host. He had never before met the man, dared not address him on such familiar terms as Brooksy, so thought it best to say nothing. He'd wait until Theo made the proper introductions.

But young Simeon's problems were already swamped by the arrival of the massive, windowed wagon. Lucas Ripnall was bellowing from the bench, Peter Seal risking his limbs in a wild jump to the drive. Shrieks and laughter could be heard from within the wagon, though the girls would stay prisoner until the steps had been hooked in place below the door, the outside bolt slid back along its groove. The matter of a moment for the agile Peter, then the doxies were stepping like ladies from their carriage, though with their skirts and petticoats held high and their mouths open to squeal with excitement at the scene.

The vehicles were left to be led away by a servant. Stumbling together through the snow, Eldon Sith and Markis Mayman and the Taylor brothers and Lucas Ripnall and Peter Seal and the nine shrieking doxies converged on the pillared steps.

Not for a long time had their host felt himself to be so very much the centre of attention.

✳

His name was Brook Henry Wintersill. Twenty-six years old, he was the master of Wintersill Hall and its property, and so a gentleman of the county.

He had been married for eight months, almost nine, during which time he had gained some thirty pounds in weight.

Since his wedding he had revealed to his wife that his true height was elevated by the wearing of sliced leather heels. And that his hips and belly had been contained within a cross-laced restrainer. And that his wig was not settled over his natural hair but on the stubble that sprouted from his skull.

His wife had learned that he drank brandy for as long as his eyes would stay open. That the violence of his temper could be matched by the force of his blows. And that he had lied to her, consummately and consistently, throughout all the time of their wooing.

She had learned—and Brook Wintersill no longer denied her knowledge—that he was deeper in debt than in credit, that the splendid clothes he had worn when he wooed her had been hired for the occasion, and that the bill had yet to be paid.

His wife had also learned of his sexual predilections, fought against them and been beaten to the ground. He had ceased to call her "my wife" or "my sweet" or "my beloved". Instead, as he struck her, teaching her the truth of her marriage, he'd accorded her his own invented title—my silly hedgerow bitch.

Her married name, though Brook preferred his invention, was Charlotte Wintersill. But the name she'd been born with, the name she now whispered or mouthed in silence, was Cannaway, Charlotte Cannaway, a name like many that can, so it seems, come to grief by being changed. . . .

TWO

If the trap had not been ready on that particular April morning, Charlotte Wintersill would still have been Charlotte Cannaway, married and living in Melksham. She would have been the wife of her cousin Waylen, a man as dull as buried copper.

It had long been supposed, at least by her parents, Brydd and Elizabeth, and by Waylen's parents, William and Margaret, that the cousins would one day be wed. No one had pressed the union. It was simply understood that when Charlotte turned seventeen in May the families would make their preparations and the wedding would take place in the autumn, most likely in the local church in Kennett.

Charlotte had confided to her mother that she felt no affection whatsoever for Master Waylen. "He is humourless and stuffy and, in my opinion, greatly in need of a shaking. He is altogether too well pleased with himself, that young man. I doubt if I, or any other woman, could add much to his stock of satisfaction. He also scratches a lot, have you noticed?"

"He wears unseasonal clothes," Elizabeth had reasoned. "He's a businessman, after all."

"Believes he is, perhaps, though what is he really but a deskbound clerk in a corner of my uncle's yard? It's William who's the businessman. Waylen just dresses the part—and badly."

Elizabeth had remained non-committal. It was true that Waylen lacked humour and held himself in unwarranted high regard. Yet Charlotte was unfair to describe him as no more than a deskbound clerk; he had an excellent head for figures and did much to drum up business for his father. Originally no more than a stoneyard, the Cannaway establishment at Melksham was now a building concern of some repute, twenty or more houses in the area bearing witness to William's skill.

Even so, Charlotte was right when she said Waylen scratched a lot. Maybe, Elizabeth thought, a determined wife could break him of the habit.

And then, in April, Charlotte had taken a brand-new trap for a test run on the downs. After that she'd no longer cared if Waylen chose to scratch himself clear to the bone.

✳

The vehicle bounced across the desolate road that led northward from Devizes. These first few yards were an important part of the test, subjecting the trap to the dry mud ruts, then the hump of the verge, then the grass-covered shale that littered the foot of the slope. If a bolt had been badly fixed, an axle pin left loose, it was here that the fault would show.

Not that Charlotte expected it to, since the light, varnished trap bore the hallmark of Faxforge and thus the personal assurance of her father, Brydd Cannaway.

Some eighty miles west of London and thirty miles east of Bristol, the coachmaking yard of Faxforge was among the best between the capital and the busy city-port. Go elsewhere for a cart made more quickly, a carriage knocked together on the cheap. But if a farmer wanted a wagon that would serve him for years he'd be well advised to come here to Faxforge and discuss his requirements with the lean and ambitious Brydd Cannaway. Likewise, if a doctor or magistrate thought to equip himself with a carriage, he'd find it worth the journey to this isolated coachyard—so long as he was prepared to accept Brydd's price.

Attempt to haggle, and Brydd would produce two sturdy planks of wood, identical in appearance, chestnut perhaps or oak. He would then suggest the customer make a choice.

"Well, now," the man would say, "that's rather more your affair than mine, Master Cannaway. I'm eager to keep the price down, is all. See it from my point of view, sir, if you will."

"Then from your point of view, sir, which is the better of these?"

"At a glance they're the same."

"So the slight oozing of resin? The fissure that runs with the grain? The trough in this one? The beginnings of a cast in that?"

"I do not doubt you know your timbers, sir. I merely expressed the desire to keep the expenditure within bounds."

"Very well. Then shall we strike a nice cheap bargain, so I may use both these planks in your gig?"

After which, if the man had any sense, he would agree to Brydd's price. If not he'd be bade good day. There was, of course, no question of the unfit timbers being used, except in lengths of fencing, or for a sheep pen on the hills.

So Charlotte did not expect the bolts to spring as she took the trap across the road and up the long, treeless slope. . . .

✻

Since the age of fourteen she had been allowed to test the lightweight carts and gigs. She had taken the task seriously, reporting back to her father or one of his craftsmen, then standing firm beside her report. If a creak or a squeal seemed out of place she said so. If the vehicle felt sluggish on the turn, one shaft twitching more than the other, the seat not properly balanced, then she said so. From the very first she said exactly what she thought of the runner's performance, and her views were soon regarded as both strict and impartial. "Let young

Mistress Charlotte try it out," became the growled consensus in the yard. "She'll give us her opinion straight enough."

As she would today, on this cool April morning, once she'd clicked the horse to the crest of the slope, then along its two-mile circuit on the downs.

A month short of her seventeenth birthday, the pale-haired Charlotte Cannaway wore an outfit that might well have earned Cousin Waylen's disapproval. High-laced boots, crimson riding skirt, shirt trimmed with lace at the cuffs and bodice, buttoned jacket that matched the skirt, tricorn hat to which she had pinned an extravagant spray of feathers. Waylen would have called the outfit "unnecessary garish," a remark with which Charlotte would have readily agreed. "Isn't it, though? And I should hope it would be; I worked on it half the winter." He'd have frowned at that, or shaken his head with regret at her rather showy ways. His wife to be. It wouldn't do for her to dress like that when they were married. It wouldn't go well with the business. However, she was young, and the phase would pass. She'd grow out of it, *have* to grow out of it, when they were married and settled at Melksham.

Waylen Cannaway was then eighteen years old.

Had Charlotte cared to glance back from the crest of the slope she'd have seen the paths and yard and house and outbuildings that were Faxforge. She'd have seen the road gate and the pond, the fringe of trees around it, the vegetable garden and the orchard, and the hill that climbed away to the east, the ridge dominated by the drooping stand of trees called the Bellringers. But today she preferred to ride onward, putting the horse and trap through its paces, sending the mount at a canter down the opposite side of the slope.

The bark of a pistol made her wince and duck on the bench. The sound came from her left, close by, the flat toneless blast making the animal run askew. She caught at the reins, quieted the horse, then glared in the direction of the sound.

For an instant she was too incensed to accept that it might be brigands. The village of Cherhill was nearby, its name made infamous by the gang who resided there; a forty-strong group of highwaymen who preyed on the coaches that ran between London and Bristol, especially upon those that risked the journey after dark.

Yet this was midmorning. Bald downland and a high-sailing sun. Not at all the time or place to attract the likes of the Cherhill gang.

Similar in character to her father, Charlotte Cannaway turned the horse, then rode directly toward the mouth of the pistol. She rose from her seat on the bench, the point of her tricorn shading her eyes, her slender features drawn with indignation. By God, she'd have a word to say to whoever had let loose. What a damned stupid performance. Not a word of warning, just the pointing of a muzzle and the careless squeeze of a trigger.

"You! Behind the ridge there! Declare yourself before you kill me or my mount!" Then she reined in, now standing on the footboard of the trap, hidden from Faxforge by the rise of ground to the east, and from the shooter by the mound that lay ahead.

A murmur of voices and then two frock-coated riders came around the base of the hill. The first of them, with his pinched, weasel's face and high-pitched voice, said, "Sorry you got in the line there, mistress. Best you should take your outings on the common road."

Ignoring his companion, Charlotte snapped, "And you would do better, sir, than to offer me advice. These downs are as much common property as the highway. It is you, perhaps, who should limit your shooting to whatever private grounds you might possess. Your behaviour is irresponsible. Worse, it's downright dangerous. What on earth were you shooting at, or did you bang away by mistake?"

It was the man's turn to be startled. He blinked vacantly, then said, "It so happens I'd set eyes on a rabbit. And would've taken him, if your horse hadn't whinnied and put me off my aim."

"My horse did nothing of the—"

"Still, since you're clearly upset, how's a coin to settle the issue? How's a shilling? Or seeing as you're an attractive young thing, how's two?"

Charlotte Cannaway resumed her seat and urged her mount a few yards forward. The second rider said nothing, staying back and away to the right. She rode alongside the weasel, reached as if to take the money he offered, then pulled the pistol from the holster strapped beside his saddle. Made even more furious by the insult of his offer, she said, "This for your coins, sir," and sent the weapon spinning away. It struck a stone, tumbled aside and was lost amid the bracken. The man blinked again, then opened his mouth to shrill.

But before he could do so the second rider came close. "You really are the finest of fools, my dear Eldon. The young lady is correct in everything she says. And did you really suppose she'd be bought off with your shillings?" He turned to Charlotte, doffed his hat in a slow, courteous greeting, then asked in what manner he might set things to rights. "If you wish to banish us from this stretch of the downs, so be it. I can understand your displeasure, Mistress, ah—"

"Cannaway. And it's not a bad idea. I have reason to be here, sir, though it won't much help if my life's put at risk when I come." She gazed at him, approving of his long green jacket, the tumble of his three-curl russet wig, the authority with which he sat his saddle and addressed his quick-fingered friend. She compared him to his companion, then to her cousin Waylen, her dour and scratching future husband. Better, she thought, he is very much better than they. "And now you have the advantage, sir, for you've yet to say who you are."

"Did I not? It's Brook Wintersill. I've a place some ten miles north of here. As for my rabbit-hunting companion, he's Eldon Sith, and I'll see to it he doesn't let loose again this side of the London road."

Charlotte nodded, then glanced at Eldon, who seemed to

twitch in obedience. She said, "Good," and was turning the trap away from the riders when she heard herself add, "I am here most mornings at this time, testing vehicles for my father. So I'll thank you both to do your shooting elsewhere. You must have your share of rabbits *north* of the London road."

Then all the way down the slope to Faxforge she kept the remembered fragments in her mind. Her memories of the plum-featured Waylen, with his lack of humour and his need to scratch and fidget, his monotonous voice reminding her that he and his father—in that order, *he and his father*—were doing better than ever, fresh orders coming in from as far as fifteen miles away. . . . And then the arrogant Eldon Sith, his screechy tone suggesting he might settle her fears for a shilling, though seeing as she was an attractive young thing he'd make it two. . . .

It was not until she'd neared the road gate that the sixteen-year-old Charlotte Cannaway found a place in her mind for Brook Wintersill, regarding him as a man of authority, smiling at the way he'd called his companion the finest of fools. . . . He was more attractive by far than her cousin or the weasel. . . . A gentleman most likely, with his place ten miles to the north. . . .

She was glad she'd let slip she'd be there on the downs most mornings at this hour.

❋

Brydd Cannaway's craftsmen listened in silence as Charlotte told them there was something not quite right about it, she would need to test it again tomorrow to be sure.

"Anythin' special as worries you, Mistress Charlotte? Might just be a matter of tightenin'—"

"I'm sure it's not serious. I'll take it for another run in the morning." She smiled at the men, Ben Waite and Matthew Ives, then left the yard as they led the trap back to the coach house. They probably *would* check the bolts and pins, couplings and trace rings, if only to satisfy themselves there was nothing obviously amiss. She felt guilty at having deceived them, though there were things she too had to verify tomorrow.

THREE

He was waiting alone near the base of the hill below the crest. He'd expected some pretence on her part, a stammered "Oh, it's you, Master Wintersill. A coincidence we should meet again so soon." But she spared him any feigned and wide-eyed greeting, merely nodding in recognition, then waiting for him to dismount and assist her from the bench.

She did not for a moment *need* his help; she'd been climbing on and off horses, on and off carts and wagons, all her life. What she needed—what she wished for anyway—was the grasp of his hand as she alighted from the trap.

His skin was softer than she'd imagined. Though it would be, she told herself, Master Wintersill being a gentleman. One would scarcely expect him to have the calloused palms of a farmer, or a coachmaker like her father.

They walked within sight of the horses, the animals unwitting chaperones. Charlotte and Brook did not again clasp hands, their sideways glances infrequent, their conversation overly polite. They agreed it was as clement an April as either could remember. "Though I've no doubt I can recollect a good few more than you, Mistress Cannaway."

"A half dozen," she finished, silently guessing the figure was closer to ten. A reasonable difference in age between—well, a man and a woman.

They agreed the downs made a pretty carpet of flowers in the spring. And that the Cannaway trap was an essay in elegance. And that somebody really *should* do something to smoke the Cherhill gang from their lair.

They raised topics like flags to the masthead, dutifully admired them, then replaced them with others, equally pastel in colour. They agreed for the moment on everything, laughing where a smile would have sufficed.

The moment of proper relaxation came when Brook said, "I must tell you, my friend Eldon's as displeased as can be, what with missing his rabbit, then having his pistol snatched away."

"I'm sorry for that," Charlotte answered, "but he should not have banged off as he did. Nor thought to buy me with his coins."

Brook laughed, eyes on the sky. "No more he should, Mistress Cannaway. And you'd not need a stranger's two shillings, now would you? The daughter of such a well-known man as Brydd Cannaway of Faxforge?"

Missing the point of his remark, she said, "I am pleased my father's been heard of, so far north of the London–Bristol road."

"You're too modest on his behalf. The Cannaway reputation stretches wide, don't you know. I myself have had it in mind for a while to order up a carriage from his yard. Something rather more splendid than I'm used to."

Again ignorant of his meaning, pleased only that she might combine the Cannaway business with a chance to see Brook at Faxforge, she said, "Present yourself at the yard, Master Wintersill, and my father will do his best to meet your needs. He went to France in his youth, and to Austria, to study the making of coaches. Your vehicle would be as splendid as you wished."

"Well," Brook smiled, "let's see how things go. It's anyway lodged in my mind."

They continued walking within the incurious gaze of the mounts. Charlotte was convinced the man liked her, else why would he have been waiting here today? She heard him remark on the vibrance of her outfit, felt his hand touch her arm as he guided her past an outcrop of dull grey rock. She said, "I was looking elsewhere," the words both an apology and a lie. She had seen the rock, knew this part of the downs well enough to avoid every stone in the dark. Yet why be so sure-footed, when she'd a gentleman of the county to escort her?

It was with genuine regret that she regained her seat on the bench. Brook suggested he might ride that way tomorrow, leaving Charlotte to say, "As might I, Master Wintersill, depending on how things go."

"In your favour, I hope, Mistress Cannaway. Unlike Eldon, I'd not ride ten miles for a rabbit." Then he laughed at the sky again whilst Charlotte took the trap across the crest.

He had a square, masculine face, she decided. And stood taller than she by a clear couple of inches. And had been schooled, by his accent. And was certainly no more than ten years older than she was—a perfectly acceptable difference in age between a husband and his wife.

So it came as a stick in the wheels when Cousin Waylen arrived at Faxforge that afternoon. He carried a letter from William, a business matter that required Brydd's attention, though ensuring that Waylen would stay the night and most of the following day.

Excited by her meeting with Brook, Charlotte was in no mood to sit opposite her cousin at the table, or to suffer the jokes of her younger brother Giles, the tooth-and-claw remarks of her sister, the thirteen-year-old Hester.

Yet that's how things were; Brydd Cannaway at the head of

the table, Charlotte to his right across from Waylen; then Giles and Hester opposite each other, with Elizabeth at the other end, near the range in the red-tiled kitchen.

No sooner were they seated than Waylen observed, "You're gaudily dressed for a family dinner, my dear Charlotte. Is there something I should know about, some village dance we'll be going to later? If I'd known of it I'd have brought a change of linen. D'you suppose these working clothes will do?"

"Be calm," Charlotte said wearily. "There's no festivity on the calendar. Your outfit is perfect for what you are." Then under her breath she murmured, "Drab."

Diagonally across from her was her sister, the shrewd and merciless Hester. Adoring Charlotte, the young girl loathed Cousin Waylen and never missed the chance to sprinkle misery on his life. The thought that Waylen might one day marry Charlotte kept her awake at night, plotting his downfall, or better yet his demise. He really was a puff-throated toad, and young Hester spent much of her time planning his disgrace and death and burial in an unmarked grave.

Now she said, "It may not be festive, though Ben Waite did tell me there's a meeting of builders this evening in the Wool Hall in Marlborough. It's rather more sober than a dance, eh, Cousin, though maybe of value to you." Then she frowned and nodded, showing Waylen how well she understood.

He opened his mouth and snatched the bait, talking with the hook through his tongue.

"It's odd I didn't hear of this in Melksham. Builders' conference, you say? Then I'd best be off there; might scare up some business, never know." He glanced at Elizabeth, then indicated his plate. "Would you mind seeing me served first, Mistress Elizabeth, on account of my having to leave?" He looked sideways and asked, "Is that right, young Hester? An assemblage of builders in the Wool Hall?"

Hester frowned again and murmured, "Something of the kind," though she avoided her parents' gaze.

The easygoing, fifteen-year-old Giles looked askance at Way-

len, then made a study of his own empty plate. Rarely outspo-
ken, Giles was content to keep his opinions to himself. Even
so, he had long ago accepted that Waylen Cannaway was the
joke within the family; how did the school book put it, the
jester at the court?

Charlotte said nothing, showed nothing in her expression.
Yet, sitting across the scrubbed boards of the kitchen table at
Faxforge, she thought, So this is to be my husband. Critical of
my dress, and a fish that flounders on Hester's hook, is this to
be the man with whom I'm to live my life and die? Am I truly
to bear the children of such a dull, insensitive creature? Is
this—is he—what the Cannaways of Faxforge and Melksham
have in store for me, and suppose my future to be? Mistress
Charlotte Cannaway of Melksham, beloved wife of Waylen
Cannaway, with a bonnet to hide the colour of her hair, a
shapeless outfit to conceal her body, her fingers stained with
the ink of her husband's accounts?

She then thought no, imagining instead the rider in his long
green coat, who'd been waiting there this morning near the
base of the hill below the crest. . . .

Brydd Cannaway cut in to question Hester. "You say it was
Ben Waite who told you there'd be a meeting of builders in
Marlborough?" The depth of his tone made her falter. She de-
cided to dodge the directness of his gaze.

"He said something about builders. Maybe I misheard it. I
was busy in the garden. Anyway, that's what it *sounded* to be.
Though, come to think of it, he didn't say Marlborough, not
outright. And perhaps I assumed it was the Wool Hall. I was
some way off, in the garden. I thought Cousin Waylen might
have heard of it, that's all."

Fearing the growled disapproval of her father, Hester
flinched as her mother leaned close to say, "Enough of your
misheard inventions, young lady. You've a talent for stirring up
trouble. Now, if you please, stir something worth while and
ladle out the soup."

They might then have settled to their dinner, the Cannaways of Faxforge and their visitor from Melksham. But Waylen had swallowed Hester's lure, hook and bait, and was now on his feet, excusing himself from the table, telling them he'd best get to Marlborough—"Just in case young Hester heard right."

There was no way of stopping him. And frankly no one was much inclined to do so. Brydd and Giles saw him off from the yard, returned to the table and mixed the hardness of their expressions with the edgings of a smile. Hester really had no right to mislead him. Though how easily Master Waylen was misled.

Throughout the evening Elizabeth Cannaway had kept her eyes on Charlotte. Not knowing what had happened on the downs, the intuitive Elizabeth sensed a fresh surge of impatience in her already headstrong daughter. Measure and weigh it how one might, Charlotte seemed more than ever determined to alienate her cousin. The question was not so much why, but why now?

He waited, each midmorning, near the base below the crest. For the first few days they walked the same perimeter. If anyone came upon them, Charlotte would say she had been recognised as Brydd Cannaway's daughter and that this gentleman —"Master Wintersill, is that the name?"—wished to discuss with her the purchase of a carriage. The intruder might ask himself why Master Wintersill did not go directly to Faxforge, though Brook would defuse his suspicions by declaring aloud, "Well, Mistress Cannaway, I'll not detain you further. The next step is to talk things over with the master of the yard." Then he'd doff his hat to Charlotte and the intruder and ride away.

But no one discovered them.

They became more emboldened; not touching, though addressing each other as Mistress Charlotte, Master Brook. Then simply as Charlotte, my dear Charlotte, and as Brook.

She eventually asked if he'd care to visit Faxforge. "We could say we all but collided today. You might even order that carriage you want, then ask my father's permission to call on me."

She did not tell him of the understanding between the Cannaways of Faxforge and the Cannaways of Melksham.

Nor did Brook Wintersill tell Charlotte what he had in mind.

"I'll come tomorrow," he said. "We'll meet here in the morning—collide, as you put it—then ride on down together to the yard." He watched as she smiled. Then, as was his habit, he raised his square face to the sky, where a flock of clouds was being shepherded by the breeze.

✻

Dressed in his usual garb of leather boots, deerhide leggings, jerkin and workaday coat, the master of Faxforge showed his client around the yard. For an hour or more they discussed what the customer wanted, Brook suggesting, Brydd amending, a sheaf of sketches brought out and studied, a dozen charcoal details drawn to illustrate this point or that.

"You've some talent as an artist, Master Cannaway. You could sell the sketches, and no need to make the gigs."

Brydd ignored the remark, continued to jot measurements, notes on the materials to be used, sources of supply. The frame, wheels and bodywork could be fashioned from the stocks at Faxforge. The leather for the doors and canopy would have to be ordered from Bristol. The special paints would come from London, the ornate and expensive studding sent from Swindon.

"The cost will be high, Master Wintersill."

"I expect it to be, Master Cannaway. One usually ends up paying the most for the best." Then, choosing his words carefully, Brook Wintersill said, "Shall I leave sufficient coins with you now, sir, so you can purchase what you need?" It was a bald and insulting suggestion, since anyone who knew of Faxforge also knew that payment took place on the day of delivery, a sign of Brydd's confidence in his work. Brook was not surprised when Master Cannaway glanced at him, again ignoring the remark.

It was late afternoon before the men emerged from the yard. The carriage would be delivered in July. The cost was in keeping with Brook Wintersill's expectations. The men shook hands, the physical seal witnessed by Ben Waite and Matthew Ives.

And by Charlotte, who happened to be approaching them, her hair brushed to a gleam.

"Well? Was I right to guide Master Wintersill down here? It seems so, from the handshake." Her long-legged stride took her close to them, her glance moving from Brydd—*Is he not the best customer ever to have come here?*—to Brook— *Have you asked him yet if you might call on me?* She was aware her father thought Waylen insufferable, a doughy, self-satisfied clerk. All Brook Wintersill had to do was ask permission to call on her, and Brydd would hesitate, as a father must, then say he saw nothing special against it.

And with that, Cousin Waylen would be out. Word would be sent to the Cannaways at Melksham, or more likely Brydd would explain things to William, and Charlotte would be free to be wooed by Master Brook Wintersill, gentleman of the county. . . .

She heard Brook say, "The business done with, Master Cannaway, I've a more personal request to make. I came near to colliding with your daughter this morning; my own blinkered riding; my thoughts were off the leash. Yet she forgave my clumsiness and—well, sir, I'd regard it as an honour if I might call on Mistress Cannaway—"

Then Charlotte heard her father say, "No." The shock made her lapse behind his words, and she gaped and gazed in an effort to keep up. He again said no, then went on, "I have heard too much about you, sir, and am not much impressed by what I've heard. Come here for a carriage and I'll see you get full value for your coins. But the way you conduct your life is beyond my approval, and I would rather you kept your visits to Faxforge to the minimum. You are known, sir, as something of a reprobate. You shall have your runner, though not the company of my daughter."

Charlotte turned her gaze on Brook. Disloyal or not, she silently begged him to speak out in his own defence. Tell him you are not a reprobate, and that whatever my father has heard of you is wrong. Tell him he has no cause to accuse you, my dear Brook. Tell him he does not know you, so cannot know what you are! Speak up for yourself, else, don't you see, you'll leave me stranded here at the mercy of my clerkish, plum-faced cousin!

But the master of Wintersill Hall preferred to be hurt, more than angered. He said he had come with the best intentions, to order up a carriage and ask permission to visit Brydd's daughter.

"However, since you think so ill of me, Master Cannaway, I've no choice but to abandon both my plans. My regrets if I've wasted your time. Your servant, Master Cannaway. *Au revoir*, Mistress Charlotte. I'll know better now, and stay north of the London road." Then he strode to his horse, mounted and rode past the tree-fringed pond to the road gate, taking care to close it behind him, though not once glancing back along the path.

✳

Charlotte committed herself to immediate battle with her father. She demanded an explanation of the term he'd used, reprobate, since in her mind it meant a man given up to depravity, a creature beyond redemption. "And you dare call him that, on the basis of hearsay chatter, some unpaid grocer's gossip? I think I know his behaviour better than you. Not once when we met did Master Wintersill show any of the vices you award him. He is a gentleman! He is the best client who ever came down here—"

"Not once," Brydd measured, "when you met? But didn't you tell me you'd all but collided for the first time today beyond the crest of the slope?" Then he gazed at her, his expression nailed even, and all she could do was shrug and turn away from him, claiming he'd misheard what she'd said—"And most likely what you've been told of Master Brook by a few disgruntled tradesmen."

Brydd Cannaway waited, then reached out to catch his daughter by the arm. He put no strength behind it, merely the control that would bring her around to face him whilst he queried, "A single collision, and you already call him Master Brook?"

They no longer walked in the hollow below the crest, unafraid of being observed. Their meetings were now carefully prearranged, this latest rendezvous near a clump of elms that stood two miles south of Faxforge, well away from the road. Here— touching now, Charlotte allowing Brook to draw her close— they declared a passionate love for each other, the need for secrecy adding spice to their embrace.

Charlotte saw them as victims of her father's prejudice, the maligned young squire and the pale-haired country girl, innocent lovers whom neither Brydd nor the world would ever part. She remembered snatches of song in which love such as theirs prevailed. Mawkish ditties she had thought them once, smiling at silly women who dabbed their eyes. Yet now the popular melodies seemed sweet, the commonplace phrases fresh and finely turned.

She asked, "Is my father correct when he calls you a reprobate? Are you truly beyond redemption, my dear Brook?"

Stretched full length on the grass, his face shadowed by the point of his tricorn, his turn-top boots crossed at the ankle, he murmured, "If so, I'd be bound to deny it. The only way you could be sure would be to risk the depravity of my house. Though I imagine you would first insist upon the services of a cleric."

Willing her voice not to tremble, she said, "You are going the long way around the square. What particular service would I ask this churchman to perform?" *Say it, my dearest. Make light of it if you will, but then, oh, please . . .*

Brook Wintersill moved his shoulders in a shrug. "What service? Why, the marriage one, most likely." He raised his head and tipped back his hat, gazing at her, studying her almost, as he told her he had waited all his life to find her, half his life given over to the search. She slipped easily against him, whispering that she too had waited for such a man as he.

She agreed when he said they should be married soon, though at a distance from Faxforge. "However, you must not announce it to your family, for fear your father will step between us. I'll have everything arranged for, let's see, the Thursday of this week. Bring your possessions from Faxforge to the tavern at Avebury sometime on Wednesday night. I know a cleric who will marry us in a church nearby, no matter at what hour we call. You have little to concern you, my dear Charlotte. Three days from now you'll be my wife, the mistress of Wintersill Hall."

Seeing no single blemish in him, she agreed to everything. This was, she believed, the happiest moment of her life. And with the promise of happier months and years to come.

She was also rid forever of Cousin Waylen.

✳

She resisted all temptation to tell her parents, Giles or Hester, the craftsmen whom she knew as lifelong friends. She did not venture far from the house, unless it was to join Brydd or Giles in the coachyard, or spend an idle hour with Hester in the orchard. If she seemed unusually attentive toward her family, they did not remark upon it, at least not then. It was enough that the squabbles were over and, Brydd supposed, his daughter's flirtation with Master Wintersill.

It was hard for Charlotte to contain her deceit, to blanket the honesty and openness with which she had always conducted her life. The thing she most wanted to say she could not now voice; the delight she wished to share with her family was now something to be locked away, a pleasure she dared not divulge. They were hard, these final days, the elder daughter concealing her happiness from those she most wished to make happy.

Against that it was easy to escape from Faxforge. She left a letter on the table in the kitchen, in which she wrote of her unbounded love for Brook—"Though even this, perhaps, is surpassed by the hope that you will see it in your hearts to forgive me. It is not we who truly choose our love, but Heaven itself directing from above."

Then the sixteen-year-old Charlotte made her way from the house, saddled a horse and led the animal quietly to the road gate, all she possessed contained within two leather-strapped bags. She believed her parents would understand. And that the last line of her letter—borrowed from a song—explained it all.

⁕

She met Brook as arranged in the tavern at Avebury, a few miles north of the London–Bristol road. A number of his friends were with him; the shrilling Eldon Sith, whose pistol Charlotte had snatched from his holster on the downs; the benign and portly Markis Mayman, busy topping glasses to the brim; the hard-edged pair, Peter Seal and Lucas Ripnall, each of whom kissed Charlotte as if they had met before and were now on intimate terms. She did not enjoy their fondlings but said nothing, aware that friends of the groom took liberties with any bride to be.

No one thought to give Charlotte any flowers, or any talisman or token of good luck. Peter Seal recounted a number of ribald stories, women invariably the object of some grotesque sexual advance. Brook and Lucas roared in unison, Eldon shrilling, Markis wreathed in smiles. The drinking continued until dawn.

Then Brook and Charlotte, hemmed around by the others, clattered through the greyness to a nearby church, where the ceremony of marriage was performed.

Again, there were no flowers in evidence, no carillon of bells. There was no music, no singing, the service over and done with in the time it would take a farrier to shoe a horse.

Charlotte watched as her husband paid the cleric, turning away as she heard the churchman whine, "You'd have me be ready half the night, and this is the best you offer?"

Outside, near the porch, Markis Mayman uncapped a silver flask, handing it around.

Eldon Sith said, "I hope you won't go snatching at Brooksy's pistol too fiercely, eh, Mistress Wintersill," then screeched at the humour of his joke.

Lucas Ripnall and Peter Seal stood impatient, near their mounts. Then Lucas said, "Have done with Master Church and let's get back." He glanced at Peter and the two men swung into their saddles.

Brook Wintersill emerged from the porch. He jerked his head at Eldon and Markis, then found time to see Charlotte to her horse. They rode from the church as from the tavern, Brook and Charlotte in the lead, though crowded by the others all the way north on the homeward journey along the bleak dawn roads to the Hall.

Deriving what comfort she could from the ceremony, Charlotte told herself it was the way things were done by the gentlemen of the county. What need had a couple for flowers, after all? They'd not even survive the jostling of the long ride home. And as for the pealing of bells, it was just a noise to be carried away on the wind. All that mattered was that Brook had kept his promise. He had made her his wife. She was Charlotte Wintersill now, the mistress of his Hall—and hers.

Yet she kept her head low, not wishing her husband or his friends to see the faint shimmer of tears. It suddenly did not seem enough to have gained what she was after, the taste of victory salt upon her tongue.

FOUR

Hidden behind the gauze of snow that curtained the window, the eight-month bride watched the visitors swarm below her toward the steps. She recognised all but two of the men; Theo and Simeon Taylor hanging back, waiting to be presented to their host. She could not say for certain that she recognised the doxies; they were just nine shrieking women, some of whom, all of whom, might have been to the Hall before.

She saw Markis and Eldon return to their carriage, lifting from it a crate of wickerbound bottles. She heard her husband bellowing in the entranceway, his shouts chorused by others. Markis stumbled, the mishap greeted with roars of derision. Then the crate was brought safely inside, the double doors slammed shut, the noise now swirling upward, vaulting the stairs, hammering for attention on the door of Charlotte Wintersill's corner room.

Brook would send for her soon, to join the party.

She had already displeased him by staying up here today. "Between noon and nightfall," he had told her, "that's when they'll be arriving, and I trust you will be at the door to greet them. I know what you think of them, you've told me often enough. God knows, I could compile a dictionary from your descriptions. Brutal, caterwauling, witless, stupid, foul-headed —*and* foul-tongued, so you tell me. Crass and insensitive and —oh yes, I have a very fair knowledge of my wife's opinions of my friends. But they *are* my friends, do you see, which is why I shall have them properly welcomed when they come."

She had said something then about making ready and going down to join him later. Instead, she had chosen to stay in her room, leaving Brook to do his waiting and drinking alone.

Even so, she acknowledged, there was little to be gained by further inciting his wrath. He had proved himself both quick-tempered and violent during these past eight months, his former swagger become the staggering of a drunkard, the cut and dash of his wooing reduced to the clumsiness of a brute. His demands upon her were indecent, his own capabilities more often than not beyond him. If he thought to make love he must first maltreat her, heightening his excitement as he bruised her with his heavy, fleshy fists.

And then if, dulled by drink, he failed to satisfy his needs? Charlotte's fault, he accused; she was unresponsive, willingly cold to his touch. He claimed that she mocked him—well, if not with her tongue, then with her eyes. She was by no means at all what he'd expected of her. By no means was she worthy of being his wife.

Throughout the entirety of their marriage they had never once slept together. Brook Wintersill had his own rooms, larger than hers, on the opposite side of the high, railed gallery. He did not pass his nights in Charlotte's bed. He simply used it, as he used its occupant.

✳

Hearing the shrieks and laughter swirl from below, Charlotte collected a tasselled silk shawl, settled it around her shoulders and made her way downstairs to join the guests.

She was dressed this evening in a hooped grey skirt, frilled bodice and square-toed, horn buckle shoes. She might in addition have worn a stiff lace cap, carried a fan of chicken skin or paper, sported black velvet patches on her face. She might also have doused herself with perfume, rubbed circles of rouge on her cheekbones, arched her eyebrows and choked her neck with beads. These were all in fashion, as were garters embroidered with mottoes, some of them faithful—"My heart is fixt, I cannot range; I like my choice too well to change"—others provocative—"Only from a distance gaze; reach not the parting of the ways."

For women it was the age of extravagant footwear, of damask shoes with lacquered wooden heels, buttoned boots or Turkish slippers. It was acceptable to wear earrings, a gold watch around the throat, elbow-length gloves soaked in musk or amber, any of a score of pungent scents. It was fun for young women to follow these fashions, greater fun still to set them.

But for whom would Charlotte be parading tonight? Not for Brook, or the shrilling weasel Eldon, or the beaming Markis, or for Lucas or Peter Seal. She had no need of cap or fan, garter or choker, patches of velvet or rubbed-in circles of rouge. Instead, her fine pale hair was brushed and left unadorned, her face free of powders or paints. She had after all been a clear-skinned country girl far longer than she had been the mistress of the Hall.

At the foot of the stairs she hesitated, then crossed the entranceway and entered the long, panelled room. The buffets of noise made her hesitate again, pipe smoke mingling with the smoke of the fire, the liberated fumes of port and brandy wafting amid the smell of the men in their snow-damp clothes, the cloying scent of the doxies.

Brook Wintersill lurched toward her, a glass in one hand, bottle in the other, the bottle employed to make sure the glass remained full. Coming close to his wife, he slurred, "Christmas Eve . . . Time for the festivities. . . . Someone's thought us up a game. . . ." Then he ushered her in, a spray of brandy flicked from his glass as he turned. The sounds and smells enveloped her, whilst Lucas Ripnall and Peter Seal came forward to smear her with their greetings.

✳

A while later and coats had been thrown aside, cravats unpinned, travelling boots exchanged for buckled shoes. Dishes of food had been arrayed on the sideboard, the guests preferring to pick and choose their refreshments through the night. The long central table was swept clear, Eldon using his sleeve to wipe it dry. The doxies had already been told their part in the game and they now allowed themselves to be herded together at one end of the table, where they tugged at their bodices, loosening the crisscross ribbons.

Grouped at the other end of the broad, twenty-foot plank, the men emptied their glasses, dried their fingers, dug in their pockets for two- and five-guinea coins. No gambler worth his salt would play with less.

Some way between the men and the doxies, Charlotte moved to stand beside Theo and Simeon Taylor. She wondered what such clear-featured young men were doing here— Scarcely the type my husband seeks for his friends. They glanced at her, smiled nervously, aware she was neither of nor with the girls.

Waiting for a lull in the raucous storm of sound, Charlotte then introduced herself, in response to which Theo Taylor bowed deeply from the waist. "My profound apologies, Mistress Wintersill. I assure you, I had no idea as to your identity, though I should indeed have declared my own. Master Theo Taylor. Your servant, Mistress Wintersill. I trust you will forgive my ill manners."

Squeals from one end of the table, the shouting of wagers from the other. The noises surged and ebbed.

Charlotte smiled at the man and said, "Forgive you, Master Taylor? But no, sir, I will not, since your self-reproach is unfounded. Bow as nicely as that, and I'd say you'd be welcome anywhere." Then she thought, I commend him for his courtesy, yet he is probably older than I. However, it's not me he's bowing to. It's to Mistress Wintersill, wife of the man who's invited him here to play games.

Theo stood aside, whilst his brother matched the depth and sincerity of his greeting. "Master Simeon Taylor, Mistress Wintersill. I too had no idea you were—well, I realised you were not one of the—well, that's to say I—Oh, Lord, I seem to be drowning in my wells." He shrugged at his own incompetence, though Charlotte tilted her head and laughed with pleasure. "I shall not let you drown, Master Taylor. Dig as many wells as you care to, sir, whilst you and your brother tell me where you're from." She leaned forward as they answered her, their words then smothered by a further gale of sound.

The game of shove-guinea was on.

Wagers were still being offered, the last of the glasses set carelessly on the sideboard. Brook yelled at Lucas, "Your suggestion, so you take the privilege! Now then, who's to say he can do it?" Further bets, for or against, with Eldon screeching his excitement.

At the far end of the table a girl edged the others away. She smiled at Lucas, leaned against the edge of the plank, her hips prominent, her powdered, unlaced bosoms pressed to the wood. "Do the best you can," she enticed him. "Won't it all be later for the best?"

King George's head was sent sliding along the table. The heavy silver coin struck the girl on the inner swell of her left breast, turning to be lodged in the frills of her bodice. She shrieked with delight, then came strutting around the board, whilst Ripnall collected his winnings from his friends. He told the girl she had earned the coin, then stooped to murmur something in her ear. She nodded and clung to him, the doxy aware that this outing from Swindon might prove in every way as profitable as she'd hoped.

Peter Seal took his place at the table, singled out one of the women and called to her, "You!" Then he sent his coin skidding, saw it tumble between her unrestricted breasts. Wagers were settled, food picked at random from the sideboard, port and brandy tipped into glasses, the ruby and gold splashing to mix with the scraps that soiled the floor.

The doxies yelped for attention. The easygoing Markis made six attempts, at a cost of thirty guineas, before his coin toppled wearily into place. The girl hurried to embrace him, knowing she would be well rewarded and that Master Mayman's demands would be slight.

It was close to midnight when the nineteen-year-old Theo Taylor took his turn. Brook Wintersill had been at the table all evening, winning or losing, pounding backs and swallowing brandy, the perfect copy-me host. Busy encouraging Theo, and watching a girl who had stripped away her bodice at the far end of the board, Brook did not see Lucas Ripnall amble around to Charlotte. So he did not notice his friend lean down and murmur something to her, Ripnall's mouth still beaded with jewels of port.

But he did turn his head in time to see Charlotte step back, raise her hand and deliver Lucas Ripnall a full stinging slap across the face. Others had witnessed the incident, though the sound alone was enough to halt the progress of the game. A coin fell and spun and rattled to stillness on the flagstones. A glass was knocked over, its contents drip, drip, dripping until someone thought to stand it firm. There was the shuffle of feet, the creak of shoes, the rustle of garments as the men and women turned their attention to Charlotte. Who knows, they thought, she might prove a better diversion than the game.

Lucas Ripnall ran a palm across his jaw. "You have faulty hearing," he told her. "It's the only thing as could give you cause to strike me, Mistress Charlotte. Faulty hearing and too damn quick a temper."

"Let me tell you," Charlotte measured. "If things were different, Master Ripnall, I would not have struck you—I would have shot you where you stand. You come here, a so-called gentleman in this house, then hiss in my ear that I too should join the game. Better the women, isn't that what you

said? Move down there and better the women?" She started
suddenly, as if to strike him again. Then she wheeled away and
stood rigid, head lowered, wishing no further part of Ripnall or
his cronies or their half-dressed whores, or of the boorish festivities with which her husband marked Christmas in this
house. She had tried hard enough to find some merit in their
ways, but it was too far beyond her. She had not married
Brook so that one of his friends could suggest she bare her
bosoms for a coin.

Lucas turned to grin easily at his host. They had known
each other since childhood and Brook was willing to accept
that Lucas had said *something*, though no doubt blown to a
pigskin bladder by Charlotte. From the very first she had
thought ill of Lucas Ripnall. It would suit her to exaggerate—

"Mistress Wintersill heard aright. I was standing close by,
near the fireplace. It was not my intention to listen, but, well
. . ." He came forward, the timid and hesitant Simeon Taylor,
to be joined by Theo, the brothers watching to see what Brook
would do. Charlotte moved to stand with them, wondering if,
even now, a vestige of decency might be salvaged from her
marriage. If Brook, for example, demanded that Lucas—

"You have not yet had a turn at the table, Master Simeon.
Then along with you, sir. Unless, of course, you've been holding back for a purpose. Are you ignorant of women, innocent
of the pleasures they can bring? Or did you lurk near the fireplace out of choice, preferring the less intimate warmth of
logs?"

The challenge, as Brook Wintersill had intended, brought
Simeon hurrying to the table. Innocent though he was and,
yes, still ignorant of much that women might offer, he would
not have it said that he lurked out of choice near the fire.

Eldon Sith and Peter Seal yelled their wagers. Lucas Ripnall
let his grin rest on Charlotte for an instant, then strode across
to watch the game. The doxies were once again squealing and
jostling, Brook moving to stand with Lucas, to nod at what
Lucas told him, to clap his friend on the back.

There would be no reprimand for Master Ripnall; no apology offered to Charlotte.

She managed a smile for Theo Taylor, then walked from the panelled chamber, turning left in the entranceway and along the passage beside the staircase, seeking now the sanctuary of the kitchen and the decencies of ordinary folk.

❋

She closed the door with relief against the sounds. For a while the odours of tobacco smoke, brandy fumes and the doxies' pungent scents stayed with her, though these were gradually overcome by the more wholesome smells of bread and crushed spices, roasting meat, bubbling candlewax. She greeted the cook-*cum*-housekeeper, the usually close-mouthed Mistress Dench. Tonight, however, the woman asked, "You been out in the weather, Mis' Win'sill? Seems to me you're all of a shiver."

Charlotte wanted to say, "I am not shivering, I am trembling; there's a difference." She wanted to recount what had happened between her and Lucas Ripnall, between her husband and Simeon Taylor. She very much wanted to earn the sympathy of this dour and uncommunicative woman. Instead she lied, "I am weary, that's all, Mistress Dench. With your permission I shall sit here a moment before going up to my room."

"It be your house to sit where you please," the cook acknowledged. "Stay long as you wish, I'm sure." She turned to a clay-built oven beside the hearth and drew out several maslin loaves, the grey bread made of compounded wheat and rye. Setting them to cool, she moved away to ladle milk from a churn, tipped the milk into a pan, spooned grated black chocolate onto the fresh, frothy liquid. She set the pan on a trivet near the fire, then continued working, as it seemed to Charlotte, at a dozen concurrent tasks.

Much as Elizabeth Cannaway worked in the red-tiled kitchen at Faxforge . . .

As always, when she entered this room, Charlotte marvelled at its contents, at the wealth of its equipment. It was, she accepted, a perfect manufactory for meals. She understood most of it—the spice boxes, pickling vats, pestles and mortars, grooved boards, chopping boards, edged boards, moulding boards; the testing forks and spearing forks, the salt box and mustard quern, the dredgers and colanders, drainers and slicers; the rows of herb jars, earthenware containers, wooden barrels, churns and pails and pans and kettles—these and an array of things that were beyond her culinary knowledge. She had long wanted to enquire of Mistress Dench what *this* was for, and *that*. But the woman, who was never less than respectful, seemed never more than merely tolerant of Charlotte's presence in the room. "It be your house," she had said, though seemed as yet unwilling to let her mistress know its workings or its ways.

As if warned by a bell, the cook interrupted the mixing of various herbs, lifted the pan from the trivet, then handed Charlotte a mug of chocolate-flavoured milk. "Bein' weary don't mean you'll slip easy into sleep. Drink this if you've a mind to. Sweetens the dreams, so they say."

Surprised by her solicitude, Charlotte thanked her. She started to ask what Mistress Dench was concocting—"Why such a variety of herbs?"—but the rear door of the kitchen swung open and she glanced across at the ushering of snow.

The servant girl, the skivvy, the slavey of the Hall, came giggling into the warmth.

Lank-haired, dressed in cotton and threadbare wool, the simple-minded child-woman that was Fern halted near the doorway, blinked uncertainly, then twisted about to be sure her companion was with her.

Charlotte said gently, "Hello, Fern. Mistress Dench has had a pan of chocolate on the boil. Won't you share some with me?" She smiled encouragement at the retarded servant, not realising yet why Fern's expression should become distorted, her body writhing as she gaped in appeal at her companion.

The cook said abruptly, "It's an understanding we have at night, Mis' Win'sill. There's something the girl enjoys more by way of refreshment." She might again have added, "It be your house, though you've not yet learned how it's run."

Charlotte cupped her hands around the chocolate and stayed silent. Eight unending months, she thought, and I am still more the visitor here than Lucas or Peter, Markis or Eldon Sith. I wish to God I could say how things are between Brook and me; how they've always been since that night in the tavern at Avebury. But that would be disloyal, would it not? The mistress running tattletale to the cook. Can't have Brooksy's young wife admitting her fears to the commonplace, ten-a-penny staff. Oh no. Not when for all this time I've stayed clear of Faxforge, allowing my mother and father, Giles and Hester to believe I'm well married, happy in the conviction that I was right to defy them. To deceive them and leave silently, in the dark.

The image of Brydd and Elizabeth, of her brother and sister in her mind, she curled her fingers around the hot stone mug of chocolate and watched Fern's companion enter the low-beamed kitchen.

A liver-spotted hand on the girl to comfort her, the spare and aged coachman Ephram Toll put his shoulder to the door, closing it against the inquisitive flurries of snow. "Don't you go frettin'," he murmured. "Everythin's fine. Get your cloak off, girl, that's the way. In with you now, and see what work's to be done. Don't concern yourself. I'll see things go right."

Aware of Charlotte's presence, and so desperately uncertain, the servant girl edged beside the table, presented herself before Mistress Dench and gabbled in a tongue only she herself could understand. There was neither form nor cadence to the words; just a garbled outpouring of sound, a language unknown to anyone else upon the earth.

Yet the cook knew Fern well enough to tell her, "Over there in the corner, if you please. There's a block of salt as needs shaving. Fine as you can do it. Slow as you like—but careful."

The girl stared and waited, then ducked away to her task.

Ephram Toll came to stand before Charlotte, his speckled hand pushed through his chopped grey hair. In appearance he reminded her of her father's craftsmen, Ben Waite and Matthew Ives; quiet and courteous men who asked for nothing, knowing they already possessed a lifetime of skills, and with it the pride in their knowledge. They were not the type who'd need to skim coins along a table, or whisper that a woman should bare her breasts and compete with the harlots of Swindon.

"You mustn't be upset by Fern, Mis' Win'sill. It's a harmless little game we have. An' it does so seem to please 'er."

"Then you must go along with it, Master Ephram. Though perhaps you'd feel more at ease if I—"

"If you left us? Not a bit of it. D'you see 'er now? She's forgotten all but shavin' the salt." He nodded politely and made his way around the table.

Charlotte watched as the second game of the day—this an innocent, affectionate pantomime—unfolded.

Again as if summoned by a bell, Mistress Dench had drawn beer from a barrel, warmed it in a shallow copper bowl, continued with her tasks, then edged aside and lifted the rising froth from the trivet. She topped a mug with the dark, foaming brew and told Ephram, " 'Ere it be. Might do something to still your aches."

Stooped as he was with age and the dampness of his life in the open, the coachman grunted his thanks. He collected the mug, passed the heated stone from hand to hand and wandered incuriously to where Fern was cutting slivers from the salt. She was working in a corner of the kitchen, in the shadows.

Anticipating Ephram's arrival, she glanced at him and put a hand to her face and giggled. He frowned at her, his expression stern, a finger raised in caution. She stifled her excitement, though her gaze implored him to do as he'd said, to see that things went right.

The unsmiling Mistress Dench busied herself at the hearth, her black-dressed back to the corner.

The coachman looked across to make sure the cook was occupied with her tasks. Then he nodded at Fern, nodded at the foam-topped mug. He gestured as if to say, Now! Quick! Spirited as you can be!

The girl awarded him a lingering, secret grin. She pressed a clenched fist to her lower lip, peered past him to check the coast was clear, then stooped to suck the froth from the head of the dark, warm ale.

She made a noise doing it and the cook turned, as if finished with her business at the hearth. Ephram stood ready as Fern thrust the mug at him, the girl hastily wiping the evidence from her lips. Loving the victory, she gazed at the coachman, her eyes made sly by both the triumph and the taste.

She did not remember that she had stood in that corner, noisily sucking froth from the beer, every night for the past two years. For the simple-minded Fern each time was the first time, her secret undiscovered, the treat as fresh as ever it had been. . . .

✳

Charlotte bade good night to Mistress Dench, Ephram Toll, the grinning Fern. She returned along the corridor, then made her way up the staircase past the heavy-framed portraits of earlier Wintersills; undated portraits, though by the style of their dress going back two hundred years. She walked the length of the railed gallery, pausing as she reached her room to gaze down at the entranceway, sound and smoke billowing from the hall. Whatever game they were playing now, the gentlemen of Wiltshire and their hired ladies from Swindon, it called for an even greater cacophony of noise.

She entered her room, latched the door, then crossed the chamber to take a few split logs from a basket and lay them on the glowing eye of the fire. Touching a twist of paper to the embers, she blew on the spill and held the flame to a three-branch candelabrum. One by one the wicks blossomed into light.

She moved to the window, opened it sharply to dislodge the snow, then left it open as the air sighed inward, fine dry flakes caressing her, the fire stirred by the draught. She undressed where she stood, not knowing if it was for the pleasure the snow brought her as it touched and melted on her breasts, her. stomach, the shadowed length of her legs. Perhaps for that, or perhaps that the flakes might chill her and ease her toward death.

It was not the first time since her marriage to Brook Winter-sill that she had entertained such thoughts. Death, as an escape from his brutality; from the consequences of her own foolishness, from the shame of having deserted her family on that clear-moon April night. Death, the final evasion of all problems, the end of the search for solutions.

Yet these thoughts came unwelcome to her mind. True she had allowed them to linger, silky-tongued guests who chorused her unhappiness, beckoning her to have done with it, the concerns and distress of her life. Better to rest at ease, freed from disappointment, safe forever from the cruelties of—

She banged the window shut, leaving the soft-spoken demons to swoop and flutter with the snow. They might one day lay claim to her, but not yet. There were other avenues of escape to be explored before she allowed herself to be led along the darkest one of all.

She moved through the pool of candlelight to her bed, standing for a moment near the fire, the warmth of it drying the trickles of snow on her body. She murmured something in weary condemnation of her weakness, then slowly lowered a lace-trimmed shift over her pale hair, her slender, naked form. That done, she settled herself beneath the coverlets, her eyes open, the candles guttering, firelight chasing shadows across the low, boarded ceiling.

She wondered if her parents were asleep yet at Faxforge. Most likely they were, for it was now past midnight, and both

Brydd and Elizabeth would be up and about by five. No matter that it was now Christmas morning. There'd be the horses to attend to, the livestock to be fed, the dolphin pump to be unwrapped and thawed out, the snow to be shovelled from the paths and the coachyard, a dozen jobs to be done before the day itself began.

Though perhaps they had stayed up later than usual, talking quietly together in the kitchen. And who knows but that I might have been the upsetting subject of their talk.

She thought of her elder brother, Jarvis, Dr. Mabbott's assistant in Marlborough. As with the rest of her family, eight months had passed since she had last seen the thin, dedicated Jarvis. And what discontent have I brought you this Christmas, my dear Jarvis? Have you been thinking how much I worshipped you, demanding that you one day become the foremost surgeon in England? As you will, or at least as you very well might.

Turning to Faxforge again, she thought of Giles and Hester. They were doubtless asleep, Giles regaining his strength for work in the yard, Hester most probably dreaming up mischief for the morning. God bless you in your sleep, my dear Giles, my sweet Hester. And may you never be so foolish with your affections as—

The latch was thumbed down, the door swung open, the wood banging back against the wall. Brook Wintersill lurched in, then steadied himself to roar, "I've had time to dwell on what Lucas told me of you and Master Taylor! You pressed your body close to him, and that's why he defended you, did our spavined young Simeon! That's why you dared to say Lucas had insulted you! Because you offered yourself to Simeon and found him receptive to your touch! Now get out of bed and be dealt with, you wide-eyed hedgerow bitch!"

※

Shocked from her reverie and startled by Brook's intrusion, Charlotte was indeed wide-eyed at the vehemence of his charge. She fought to understand what he was saying—that she had pressed physically close to young Simeon Taylor? Excited him to the point whereby he'd accused Lucas Ripnall of saying things that Lucas had never really said? That the brick-hard Master Ripnall was the victim of a conspiracy between the courteous Simeon and the mistress of Wintersill Hall?

In short, that Brook's wife was promiscuous, his youngest guest a wilful liar? No more for Charlotte the insipid thoughts of death. She came from her bed and went around it and made straight for her lurching husband. Fury ran from her mind to her tongue and the things she would say to him were in readiness when he struck her, the knuckles of his fist against her head.

She fell against the bed, snatched at the coverlet and forced herself to her feet.

Before she could speak he struck her again, sending her now against the dry plaster wall, the flakes falling as snow within the room.

She lay there for a while, blood on her mouth, her shift in disarray. Brook was standing—leaning and swaying—above her, shouting down at her, his voice as thick and heavy as the brandy he'd consumed, as thick and heavy as his fists. "You don't seem to know what you are! You are my wife, you bloody bitch, though you don't seem to know it! You are what I say you are, all the things I say you are, and that is all you will ever be! Don't you know that yet? That you are mine, to be what I want?"

She twisted to her feet, her words prepared, aware that her time was spent. "Oh yes, I know better than ever the things I am! And how far I hope they will lead me away from you! As far as any star I can see in the sky! As far as—"

He struck her a third time, sending her now, as he'd intended, across the bed. He was upon her like an animal, his prey half stifled by the wide flock bolster. It suited him to take his pleasure in this fashion, the hound pinning its victim to the earth.

And then he abandoned her, stumbling across the gallery to his own suite of rooms, though leaving her door to swing open on its offset hinges, the sounds of her weeping drowned by the festive noises that issued now from every level of the house.

FIVE

Guided by the sweep of a lantern, Brydd Cannaway followed the ice-encrusted path to the coachyard. Another hour would elapse before the first faint wash of daylight cleared the hills to the east, silhouetting the Bellringers, though by then the yard would be alive and dinning with activity. Here at Faxforge, as elsewhere, work in winter began and ended within the yellow glow of lamplight.

Elizabeth was already in the kitchen, preparing a breakfast of ale and chocolate, bread and beef and cheese. Hester would be down to help her before long, whilst Giles went to join his father in the yard. For the moment however these younger Cannaways were struggling to stay awake. It was hard to believe that by dawn the girl would be as mischievous as ever, Giles a millrace of energy. He in his small bedroom, she in hers, it was all they could do to find their shoes.

Meanwhile, Brydd made his circuit of the yard. As he moved from smithy to workshop, barn to tackroom, he lifted lanterns from their niches in the walls, lighted them with a taper, then suspended them from nails. Slowly, as though it were a small town square, the cobbled yard took shape.

In the ten days since Christmas the snow had fallen infrequently, each fall seemingly lighter than the last. There was no trace of it underfoot today, just a brittle shell of ice. Crazing a sheet of it with his heel, Brydd grunted his thanks that the roads were again passable. It meant that Ben Waite and Matthew Ives could trudge the two miles from their cottages at Beckhampton, and that the yard could continue producing carts and wagons, traps and runners, these and the vehicle with which Brydd had established his reputation—the widely sought "Cannaway Carrier". Built originally for the conveyance of passengers between a number of the Wiltshire wool towns, the four-horse Carrier was now in service in the surrounding counties, among the flat expanses of East Anglia, as far abroad as the Netherlands and northern France. It pleased Brydd to think that the design of the coach had remained unaltered in the close on twenty years of its existence.

His breath now visible, he extinguished the taper and started in the direction of the stables. As he neared them he heard a sudden sharp crack, a flurry of noise and then a practised catalogue of oaths. Grinning to himself, he called ahead, "Do I find you maltreating the animals, Master Step?" There was further confusion, a more speedy issue of curses before an impish jockey of a man emerged from the stables, slapping straw and mud from his clothes.

"I tell you, Master Brydd, that roan's been corrupted by the Devil. Give me the very 'ell of a kick, she did. Like to 'ave knocked me through the boards. It'd please me greatly if you was to let me go back in there with a pistol." He turned and shouted into the barn, "You 'ear what I'm plannin' for you? A good lead ball 'tween the eyes!" Then he nodded vehemently, in case the horse still doubted his word.

Brydd grinned again and waited for Step to calm down. The men had been friends since their youth, Step Cotter destined to become a master driver, unequalled in his knowledge of the country tracks and coach roads. He had been in Brydd's employ since the founding of Faxforge, happy to live in the one-room cottage that stood a coin's spin from the Cannaways' own house. Short and wiry, his volatile nature was made all the more colourful by his appearance, the left side of his face scarred between the edge of his eye and his ear. Brydd had been with him on the night a highwayman's snapped-out shot had torn its ugly furrow, and it was Brydd who had taken the coach on through the ambush, the impish driver lying wounded beside him on the bench.

They had reached the safety of Sam Gilmore's tavern, the "Blazing Rag" at Beckhampton. There, dulled by brandy, Step Cotter had sat silent whilst one of Sam's customers stitched the flaps of skin across the wound. It was a brave effort, but crudely done, leaving Step with a hooded left eye and an expression men thought demonic, though women found rather dashing.

He had never married, preferring, as he put it, "Crops in the fields to what goes stale in the larder."

His argument with the roan now forgotten, he accompanied Brydd toward the coach house. They were joined by Giles, the young man stamping his boots against the cold. Ben Waite and Matthew Ives arrived, courteous as always, insisting that proper greetings be exchanged. Only then, when hats had been doffed and hands shaken, did the craftsmen fill their pipes and wait to hear what Brydd expected of the long day's toil.

If the December weather had been less severe than usual in the county, it remained the bleakest Christmastide Elizabeth Cannaway could remember. True, the anguish of Charlotte's springtime elopement had dulled to an ache, though as Christmas approached, so Elizabeth had allowed herself to believe she would hear from her daughter. God willing, even see her. Surely, in the season of kindness and reunion, He would grant the return, if only for a day, of the mistress of Wintersill Hall.

But nothing had happened. William and Margaret had chosen to stay at Melksham. Jarvis Cannaway had been invited to spend Christmas with a group of doctors and their assistants in Oxford. And Charlotte? Well, it could only be supposed that Charlotte preferred the company of Brook Wintersill and whoever they'd invited to the Hall.

Brydd had worked hard to make things cheerful at Faxforge, though it was Brydd who'd refused to break the silence between the Cannaways and Charlotte. As he had told Elizabeth in May, one month after their daughter's marriage to Brook, "She left this house of her own free will, choosing to do so at night. She married Master Wintersill within hours of her departure, and with all the gaiety of a murderer's funeral. And since then she has neither paid us a visit, nor penned a letter, nor entrusted so much as a phrase to a passing pedlar.

"She may indeed, as you suggest, Elizabeth, feel shamed into silence, though I'd rather she felt shamed into facing us again. Like you, I hope to hear from her, or better yet to see her turn in at the road gate. But until I do I shall not be the one to break the silence she's imposed."

In the months since then Elizabeth had appealed to Brydd, but in vain. "Will you not at least send our well-wishes? Give the letter to Giles; to Step Cotter if you'll not have your own son go there. Is it too much to ask, my dear Brydd, that we let our daugher know she is loved and in our thoughts?"

"She is aware of it," he'd retorted. "Seventeen years of life here at Faxforge have ensured her awareness of that. But if by love you mean I must address her as Mistress Wintersill, wife of a man who also chooses to ignore us, then the answer is no. As it was when that ill-reputed gentleman asked if he might call on her, regarding it, he said, as an honour. Charlotte will have to do with us when it suits her. Until then I shall assume it does not."

Obedient to his decision, Elizabeth knew her husband's feelings encompassed more than the stiffness of pride. He had shared her concern, suffered his own anxieties, more than once been tempted to ride the ten miles north to the Hall. She was unaware that he'd already written to Charlotte, before crumpling the letter in his fist. But she might have guessed he had done so; and that afterward he had bitten against the sudden desire to weep.

So the table in the kitchen had been sparsely set this Christmas. Step Cotter had been with one of his many lady friends, Sam Gilmore busy behind the plank-and-barrel bar of the "Blazing Rag." Ben Waite and Matthew Ives had spent the holiday with sisters or cousins in the district, leaving Faxforge to Brydd and Elizabeth, a pensive Giles, an openly sorrowing Hester. "It's the first time ever in my life that Charlotte has not been here. I don't care much about the others, I mean Cousins Waylen or Louisa, but it seems empty somehow to be sat here without Charlotte. Well, there's no need to scowl at me, Giles! It does!"

Giles had sighed, whilst Elizabeth had set about serving the Christmas meal. Glancing at her father, Hester had watched him nod in agreement. "Yes, my girl, it does seem empty. Though maybe she'll come by before year's end."

But she had not come by, and it was now the fourth day of January, the men crossing the lamplit yard to take their breakfast in the kitchen, Elizabeth and Hester setting plates and mugs around the table. Step Cotter ate breakfast with the family, as did Ben and Matthew. If someone was to tell a catchy joke this morning, they might yet recapture the atmosphere that had so often meant Christmas in the heart of the Cannaway house.

✳

At Wintersill Hall the joking was over. The guests had stayed until New Year's Day, the week-long festivities becoming ever more raucous, tempers turning sour.

Competitions were held, to see who could tell the best lascivious tales. It surprised the men to discover that the doxies were clearly the winners, recounting their experiences in Mistress De Rue's Seminary for Gentlewomen. Cheerfully indecent, they left Markis Mayman blanching, Eldon fidgeting in discomfort, Lucas Ripnall and Peter Seal hungry to hear more. The Taylor brothers, invited for no other reason than the weight of coins in their purse, hovered on the fringe of the proceedings, appalled by the behaviour of their host and his long-time friends. They were not so naïve as to suppose they had come here to kneel on a hassock. But neither had they expected to be the butt of Brook Wintersill's jibes, Simeon constantly nudged by Lucas Ripnall, the latter not forgetting that it was Simeon who'd sided with Charlotte on the night of the shove-guinea game.

Tiring of the women, the men played cards: Catch Jack and piquet and Wheat. It did nothing for Brook's humour when Theo Taylor won hand after hand; even less when he claimed ignorance of the game. "It's beginner's luck, Master Brook. I assure you, sir, I am not at all adept at the cards."

"So you say," Brook grated, "yet you seem to know more than is natural. I'll double this hand. Let's see how the tide runs now."

It ran fast in Theo's favour. Brook Wintersill lost more than six hundred guineas in an evening, Eldon Sith and Peter Seal close on four hundred guineas each. The losers told Theo they'd sign markers, then settle with him later.

Young though he was, he knew he would never see his money.

As New Year's Day approached, Brook Wintersill rounded on his friends. He picked arguments with Markis, sneered at the sycophantic Eldon, even squared off against his mirror image, Lucas.

Charlotte was present on that occasion, her fervent wish being that somehow Ripnall and her husband would beat each other to the ground. They did not, of course, for Brook cursed and stormed away, thus sparing himself the thrashing he might have received.

Theo and Simeon left early, with only Charlotte to bid them

farewell. They stood together for a moment on the steps, where Theo said quietly, "I would lie to you, Mistress Wintersill, if I were to say this week has been well spent. But I will say this. Master Simeon and I live a half day's ride away. Our place is called Grand Park. It's a mile or so beyond Marlborough, and it will always be open to you. Always, Mistress Wintersill, no matter the season, or the indication of the clock." Then he bowed as deeply as when Charlotte had first spoken to him. Simeon followed suit.

She watched them climb aboard their gig, gazed after them as the vehicle rattled along the drive and out of sight. In silence she asked, "And why did those two never come riding across the hills near Faxforge?"

✳

Once started, the exodus was soon over. Peter Seal was bound for an indefinite stay in Paris, Markis for a month or so in London. Eldon Sith and Lucas Ripnall would return to their estates, the doxies to their trade in Swindon. They all professed to have enjoyed themselves hugely, though Brook Wintersill's soured humour made the leave-taking a strained, uncomfortable affair. By unspoken consent they kept it short, the curricle and the great, six-horse conveyance rolling fast to disappear among the trees. But even before they'd gone, their host had re-entered the Hall.

By midafternoon he was stupefied with drink, his body slumped in a high-backed chair beside the fire. At his feet lay a scattering of papers, an inkwell overturned on the flagstones, quill pens lying as if freshly plucked from a bird. Several of the papers bore his scarcely legible scrawl—his attempts to assess what the festivities had cost him.

A fortune in outlay, what with the food and drink, the week-long company of the doxies, the money paid over at Catch Jack and shove-guinea and a dozen brandywise wagers.

But worse was the lack of income, the blame for which Brook laid squarely upon Theo and Simeon Taylor. They had been invited to the Hall for the express purpose of footing the bills. Why else would the angelic pair have been brought along? For the pleasure of seeing them bow? As companions for the hedgerow bitch? Oh no. They'd been expected to sit at the card table and there to lose. To accept Brook's wagers and to lose. To roll dice, spin coins, test their marksmanship, but to lose! Instead of which they had all but gutted the other players, leaving Brook to pay off the doxies, and with a sheaf of accounts he could not afford to settle.

It was time to get away from the place, he decided, though first he must talk with Keeper Venn.

✳

Rarely seen within the confines of the Hall, Brook's game-keeper fitted uneasily into his role. He was not a Wiltshire man but an offspring of London's dockside, coarse-grained and with an insolent manner that, if challenged, turned to bewilderment, his calloused hands spread wide. Charlotte guessed him to be about the same age as her husband, though where Brook was paunchy, his stomach laced in its restrainer, Keeper Venn was muscular, and fond of parading his strength.

He lived in a ramshackle cottage set in deep woodland, a quarter of a mile from the Hall. The only approach to it was through a maze of briars, the path so indistinct that no stranger could ever hope to find it. Disliking him on sight, it had occurred to Charlotte that if a man was on the run from the law he could do worse than dwell in the depths of a private estate. She could prove nothing, and was content to keep her distance from him. But the thought was there, the suspicion that Brook had not merely hired the Londoner but harboured him.

During the first days of January the men walked the grounds together, each armed with a long-barrelled fowling piece, Venn carrying a satchel packed with spare flints, powder and shot. The pockets of their frock coats bulged with tobacco pouches and hammered metal flasks. Impervious to the cold, or shelter-

ing perhaps in Venn's cottage, Brook did not return to the
Hall before dusk.

Exactly one week after his guests and their women had left,
Brook came to Charlotte's room. He forced himself upon her,
his actions as careless and brutal as before. This time he
wrenched her head back by the hair, groaning his satisfaction
whilst she wept with the pain of his attack.

A moment later and he twisted away, his short-lived pleasure
forgotten. Clambering to his feet, he turned and looked down
at her. "I shall depart for London in the morning. I'll be gone
some time, though I don't know for certain how long."

"Where will you—"

"Round and about. It doesn't matter. Keeper Venn knows
how to run the place. If there's anything to be done, you'll ask
him. And, Charlotte?"

Her eyes misted with tears of pain, she gazed at the stocky
shape that loomed above her. "Yes," she said dully. "What?"

"Just this. And bear it in mind. Keeper Venn is loyal to me.
I approve of his being here. So I hope I'll not learn you've
stirred up disagreement in my absence. You leave the manag-
ing of things to him. He'll be close at hand if he's needed."

"Close?" she murmured. "In the Hall itself?"

His image blurred, she did not see the gesture Brook made.
But she understood well enough when he said, "Across there.
I've installed him in my rooms."

Then without another word he was gone, latching the door
heavily behind him. He left Charlotte sprawled in disarray, for
all the world like a country harlot, though one denied even the
comfort of a coin.

❋

Venn's insolence turned to open effrontery, the man safe in
the knowledge that Brook Wintersill was a long way off. And
better than that; when the master returned he'd be as willing
to accept the keeper's version of things as he would the complaints of his wife. He had said as much when the men walked

the grounds. Quite the talker was Master Brook, with brandy
in his belly and his companion's broad shoulders to lean on.
Quite the unwitting fount of information . . .

So the Londoner made himself at home in the Hall. He con-
tradicted Charlotte's wishes, demanded his favourite meals of
Mistress Dench, amused himself by mocking the witless Fern.
He explored Brook's cellar, searching out a flask of port or
brandy, then sitting with it before an extravagant fire in the
long, panelled room. It was a pity, he thought, that he'd the
accents of the dockside. Otherwise he'd be as much at ease as
any so-called gentleman. What were they anyway but ordinary
persons with a few extra guineas to their names?

Charlotte did her best to stay clear of him. She had already
accepted that she was no match for the likes of Victor Venn.
He was altogether too slippery, with his cocksure smile, his
hands ready to touch her, his fingers closing too tight upon her
arm. If they met she forced herself to acknowledge him,
swallowing the distaste she felt at his grasp. "Goin' out
walkin', are yer, mistress? Lonely, I s'pose, the master bein'
away. Well, you jus' say if you needs company. Out there. Or
down 'ere. Or upstairs." As she hurried from his presence she
thought of him as but a roughhewn version of Peter Seal,
Lucas Ripnall, her own brutal husband, each of them cut from
the stained and muddied cloth of highwaymen, no matter that
they called themselves gentlemen of the county or keeper of
the estate.

✳

Fleeing Venn's grasp, Charlotte ventured from the building.
She crossed the driveway, climbed the slope that rose from the
gravel path to the southern wall of trees, then turned westward
toward the lake and the Moorish Palace.

Some twenty years old now, the wood and plaster folly had
been built by Brook's father, Sir Henry Wintersill, as a birthday gift for his wife. Derelict now, the structure comprised a

series of domes and minarets, a foursquare wall around a tiled courtyard, an arched entrance and a flight of steps that led up to a wall walk, from where one could view the fist-shaped lake and the Hall, and all the southward sweep of the property.

Lady Wintersill had seen a picture of the palace in a book. She had shown it to Sir Henry, not knowing that he'd bring architects from France, carpenters from Bath and London, painters he could trust from within the county. Amused by his secret, she had agreed to stay away from the lake for half the year. Meanwhile, the French and English worked together to recapture the delicate curves of this odd, foreign building, the local painters puzzling over its intricate designs.

On the day it was completed Sir Henry Wintersill and his wife had decked themselves out in sheets and shawls and played host to some two hundred guests. Sir Henry had rightly awarded himself the title of Sultan al-Wintersill, his wife the Queen of the Deserts of Araby.

Charlotte had learned none of this from Brook but from the coachman, Ephram Toll. It was he who'd told her that Lady Wintersill had skirted the lake to the Moorish Palace, where she'd spent her days painting scenes and landscapes, portraits of dogs and deer. "She'd a talent for it, had Sir Henry's gentle wife. I never saw anyone better at paintin'. than her ladyship, nor anyone more at home in that fragile house."

"So where is the result of her work, Master Toll? Where might I find some evidence of—"

"You won't," he had told her. "The pictures were all sold off." And then, avoiding further questions, the coachman had left to continue his work in the yard.

✳

Alone now near the lakeside, Charlotte stood huddled in her long, flared cloak, its hood pulled forward, shadowing her face. Slanted pockets were cut in the lining of the garment, though the cold air had already penetrated the cloth. Ice rimmed the water, the leafless trees as gaunt and skeletal as men left too long on the gallows.

Her thoughts directing her, she turned to gaze unblinking at the house. Then away from it, southward, toward the woodland and the high, red brick wall that surrounded the estate. Beyond it lay the downs and a few scattered villages, then Avebury, and beyond that the London–Bristol road.

And on the far side of the coach road, two miles below the Beckhampton Crossing, was the house and orchard, the pond and cobbled enclosure that was Faxforge. . . .

She had already decided she would go there and face her family. The visit might end in acrimony; God knew, her parents had reason enough to turn her away. But perhaps when they heard the truth they'd allow she had suffered enough, her foolishness repaid a hundredfold by the pains exacted at the Hall.

She might also be brought face to face with Cousin Waylen, a gloomy prospect indeed. Remembering his pomposity and the way he'd criticised the spirit and style of his future wife, she feared he'd be as righteous as a deacon. But that too was a penalty to be paid.

In truth, Charlotte was prepared to suffer whatever reprimands her family thought fitting. Her father's aversion to Brook Wintersill had been well founded, though not even Brydd Cannaway had guessed the depths of the man's depravity. He had said his piece, and his daughter had chosen to think him prejudiced, planting himself in the path of unbounded love. She knew better now, of course; her lips set in an ironic smile as she mused, I know better, since I now know the worst.

Retracing her steps from the lake, she made her way around the side of the Hall to the stables. The coachman was there, stooped as he polished brasswork on a bench.

"Mis' Win'sill?"

"Would you be game to take me for an outing, Master Ephram? Ten miles or so down the road?"

"Game to take you as far as a gig would run, Mis' Win'sill."

"Even if it was past Beckhampton, to Faxforge? It would be known you had run me there. Keeper Venn would know of it and tell my husband. It might very well cause you trouble."

The coachman thought it over and nodded. "Aye," he muttered, "so it might." Then he said he'd have a trap ready for her when it suited her to leave, nodding again as she asked, "Within the hour?"

They were stopped, as she'd suspected they would be, by the keeper. He emerged from the trees that flanked the drive, a number of snared rabbits swinging dead from a loop in his hand. "'Eard you on the path," he told them, pausing as if to be commended. "'Ardly the weather for jauntin', eh, mistress? Best you stay out of the cold." By then he had directed a warning glance at Ephram Toll and noticed the leather valise that had been placed in the well of the trap. He moved to catch the bridle of the horse. "Goin' off somewhere special, mistress, seein' as 'ow you've got baggage aboard the trap?"

"Take your hand from the traces, Master Venn. The horse is peaceable, without needing you as a drag."

"I asked if you was goin' off somewhere special. Master Brook 'olds me responsible for—"

"I said get your hand from the horse!" She leaned forward, rapped the coachman on the shoulder, then snapped at him, "Pass me the whip! I may need it to clear the path!"

Keeper Venn stood aside, the rabbits again set swinging from their loop. "The master won't be pleased by this, an' there's a fact. I'll 'ave to tell 'im as 'ow you went against my advice. An' threatened me with the crop. You do see where it puts me, eh, mistress, you bein' so blasted difficult with 'im away!" Then he glared at her, including Ephram within the frame of his anger.

Charlotte rapped the coachman harder than before. "You were difficult enough, Master Toll, when it came to getting this carriage hitched and running. Now, if you please, get along with it, for I am damned if I'll have you both bar my way!" She sat back, her head tipped in arrogance, whilst Ephram Toll clucked the horse toward the gatehouse.

It was only when they were clear of the estate that he turned on the bench and thanked her for the effort she had made to absolve him.

"Did I bruise you, Master Ephram, rapping you with my fist?"

"Not too bad, Mis' Win'sill. Not bad enough to stop me drivin' you past Beckhampton and—where is it you're goin'?"

"Faxforge," she murmured, then added, as if she was not quite certain, "I'm going home."

SIX

Hester was the first to see the trap turn in through the road gate. She squealed with delight, waved in frantic greeting at Charlotte, changed her mind and ran instead to tell her parents. Elizabeth emerged from the kitchen, shaded her eyes against the sun, then watched as Hester dashed past her in search of Brydd and Giles.

The Cannaways were repairing a ladder-back wagon in the coachyard. They were assisted in this by the newly engaged apprentice, Lewis Plant, whilst elsewhere in the yard Ben Waite and Matthew Ives worked on a damaged curricle. It had been overturned when its driver mistook a milestone for a buck in the moonlight. "Thought to run it down an' get me dinner for the morrow. But it did occur to me, as the cart went over—'e's got ruddy good bones on 'im, this deer!"

Farther away, a space had been cleared on the cobbles and Step Cotter was turning a dogcart in a circle, urging the single horse onward, then reining in, his scarred face tilted as he listened for unwarranted creaks from the axle.

Hester knew better than to interrupt her father, though there was nothing to stop her fidgeting and squirming for attention. When she'd caught Brydd's eye and he'd said, "What is it, Hester?" she blurted that Charlotte had arrived. "She's out there in a trap with some old man aside her on the bench."

Giles said, "Please go ahead, Father. Lewis and I can see to this. Tell Charlotte I'll be along when it's done." Then he gazed imperiously at his younger sister and said, "So? You've delivered your message. The yard's not a playground, you know."

Hester awarded him a furious glance, smiled prettily at Lewis, delayed her departure until Brydd was ready to leave. He grows more intolerable by the day, does that Giles! What a shame he's so hideous, else a girl might be encouraged to marry him and take him far away!

Blessed in fact with a sturdy build and a firm, open face, Giles Cannaway grinned at the gangling Lewis Plant. "Think yourself fortunate, Master Lewis, you're not burdened with a sister like that. Did you see the look she gave me? Enough to split a sizeable granite block. Ah well, it's my misfortune, not yours. Let's lift together, then I'll hammer the pin in place."

A year or so older than Giles, Lewis kept his thoughts to himself. The truth was, he'd be proud to count Hester as his sister; just as proud to have Giles for a brother. In the moments before he slept at night, Lewis Plant thanked God in His heaven—and the innkeeper of the "Blazing Rag"—for directing him here to Faxforge. It had been an erratic journey, begun amid the memory of smoke and flames. . . .

He'd spent the first sixteen years of his life in an isolated dwelling on the Somerset hills above Taunton. His mother's strength had failed her when he was eight, her death coming suddenly, her last faint words, "Such a weariness this morning." Deprived of her maternal protection, Lewis had fallen victim to a father whose work as a hurdle maker was as slipshod as his tongue. The man's complaints were endless, his hand ever ready to be curled and swung as a fist. It was written in their life together that the blows would one day be returned.

It happened in the winter, a week or so after Lewis Plant's uncelebrated sixteenth birthday. Goaded beyond endurance by his father's accusations, the gangling, long-boned Lewis had rounded on him, shouting that he was nothing so much as a slothful, ill-minded sot. "Let's have *you* take a turn with the stew pans! Let's see *you* cut the logs, eh, Father? Why not? It might help you work off your miseries and taunts!" But Aaron's efforts were restricted to a furious attack on Lewis, an attack that was halted as the young man struck back. If his blows were less powerful, they were more accurately delivered and Aaron retreated, flopping down in his chair. His earlier moans now carried the whine of self-pity.

Lewis snatched his hat and sheepskin jerkin from a peg, strode from the house and set off in the snow and darkness, not caring in which direction he walked, so long as he put some distance between himself and the man he hated.

There was no one to witness Aaron Plant's behaviour after that. A fresh outburst of anger? A bout of drinking followed by a clumsy mishap with a candle or lantern? A mindless stupor, the hem of his coat near the fire? Whatever it was, it brought Lewis floundering homeward to find the shabby building ablaze from end to end. Part of the roof had already collapsed. Flames were poking their malevolent tongues from the windows. Smoke squeezed and billowed around the edges of the doors.

For an hour the young man fought to gain entry, his hands burned raw, his face scorched and blackened, the snow-laden wind sharpening the appetite of the fire. The harder the wind blew from the hilltops, the more greedily the house was devoured. Then, as end wall of the building fell inward, Lewis retreated, choking, to the far side of the yard. He cupped snow between his hands, pressed the melting coolness to his face, then stood dazed and undecided as the house settled slowly upon itself. He had known from the start that Aaron could not have survived and that so insubstantial a structure would burn as readily as kindling in the hearth.

He scooped more snow and made his leaden way to the stables, releasing the horses and collecting a worn leather saddlebag from a shelf. Then, wishing nothing more of the place, he started on the long downhill path, the glow of the fire behind him, the snowflakes dabbing at his burns.

Three weeks later he was on the road, his destination London. Aaron's death had aroused the interest of several local creditors, and between them they'd laid claim to the land, the horses, even the stock of finished and unfinished hurdles. One of these men, a mite more generous than the others, had given Lewis a shallow handful of pennies and a fare-thee-well slap on the back. "Now get along with you, boy. There's few as can walk away chinking into life."

Lewis let the sermon go uncontested. He was grateful enough for the coins, though they'd purchase less than a halfway ticket to the capital.

And so, unable to afford the bouncing progress of a stagecoach, the jarring advance of a wagon, he started for London on foot. The coins, whilst they lasted, bought him meals and a bed, but of greater value were the contents of his dull green saddlebag. It rested easily on his shoulder, as well it might since the balanced pouches were filled with nothing more than whittled puppets and toys. How Aaron would have sneered at that; his son a secret carver of children's playthings!

Lewis Plant's journey was, of necessity, erratic. He zigzagged from Radstock to Trowbridge, north to Chippenham, then eastward past Calne and Cherhill and down to the Kennett Vale. And thus, one evening, he entered the low-beamed public parlour of the "Blazing Rag", bought a mug of ale, then asked the landlord Sam Gilmore if there were any fairs or markets on the calendar.

"Aye," Sam told him, "there'll be a market in Marlborough

come Saturday." Then he waited, allowing his customer to grunt or nod or further the conversation if he would.

"There's nothing doing until then? I was hoping, well, do you have any children, sir?"

"None as I know of," Sam Gilmore declared, "though that's not to say it ain't possible."

Lewis hurried, "Yes, quite," and thought it wise to clarify his question. "It's just that I, ah, chip out toys and that and sell them where I can. Maybe you'd care to see—"

By then he'd opened a pouch of the saddlebag and tipped out a selection of horses and clowns, a cart with wheels that would turn if one pushed it, a bandsman with drum and drumsticks. They cascaded across the plank-and-barrel bar. Sam Gilmore glowered. Lewis Plant reached to scoop them up. Other occupants of the "Blazing Rag" craned their necks or leaned across to see.

He felt the landlord's hand on his arm. "Leave them be if you will," Sam told him. Then, muttering in part to himself, in part to Lewis, he inspected the carvings, nodding as the bandsman's drumsticks struck the drum, pleased to see that the cartwheels turned, shaking the horse so the animal seemed to trot. "You've a skill for this, Master—"

"Plant. Lewis Plant."

Sam nodded, put the horse through a final canter, then glared about him in case anyone imagined he'd done it just for the fun. "There's a place down the road a way," he said obliquely. "A coachmaking yard. It's perhaps of no interest to you, Master Plant, though I've heard the owner's looking to take on an apprentice." He moved aside to serve one of his customers, leaving Lewis to repack his saddlebag.

Confused by the suggestion—the offer, if that's what it was —the young man took his mug of ale and went to sit at a table by the window. From there he could see a tall wooden post topped by an iron bowl; the beacon that burned each evening and gave the country tavern its name. Below it, in the yard, were a number of farm carts, and he gazed at them, wondering if his abilities would extend beyond the making of hurdles and toys.

Well, he thought, there's one certain way to find out.

He waited until he saw the landlord swabbing the counter, then went over to him and said quietly, "The place you spoke of, sir. Might I walk to it before dark?"

"Tall young fellow like you? You'd be there in no time. It's less than two miles toward Devizes. You'd best ask for Master Cannaway. Tell him Sam Gilmore thinks it worth his going through your bags."

And so, that January evening, Lewis Plant's journey had ended. He had stopped far short of London, though that city had never been more to him than a dream. What mattered was that Brydd Cannaway had accepted him, and that he'd earned the friendship of Giles and Step Cotter and the craftsmen. And, not least, the adoration of young Hester.

If he was not kin to the Cannaways by birth or blood, he was as close a member of their family as any who shared the life and fortunes of Faxforge.

As Giles and Lewis struggled to fix the axle pin of their wagon, Brydd joined Elizabeth near the wall that shielded the coach-yard from the drive. They waited in silence, Hester fidgeting beside them as Ephram Toll brought the trap along the drive from the road gate. He reined in, looped the traces around the curved metal guider, then stayed where he was, impassive on the bench. He had done what was asked of him and brought Mis' Win'sill home.

Charlotte also remained seated, gazing at her parents, aware that Hester was flagging a hand in secretive greeting. Brydd's level expression made her falter and she looked away for a moment. Then, slowly, she turned to meet his gaze again, ready to accept his judgement of her, to hear him ask what she was doing here, so far from the world she had chosen.

Instead he stepped forward, a hand extended to help her from the trap. "You bring good weather with you, my dear Charlotte. Prolong your visit, if you will. We need all the fine days we can get." Then he embraced her, relinquishing his hold so Elizabeth might in turn kiss her daughter, the air now noisy with Hester's squeals of welcome.

It was an effort for Charlotte to fight back her tears and keep her voice steady as she introduced the elderly Ephram Toll. He climbed stiffly from the bench, pulled his weather-worn hat from his head, then bowed and admitted, "Comes a time in life when it aches to sit quiet, or 'urts to move about."

"A jug of warmed ale is as good a remedy as most," Brydd observed. "Have you the time, sir, to sit in our kitchen and voice an opinion of the brew?"

"I 'ave, Master Cannaway, though I should warn you, sir, I'm not given to quick decisions."

"You'll not be hurried," Brydd assured him, turning to Charlotte as he added, "No one is encouraged to leave before they will."

A moment later and Giles came striding from the coachyard. He grinned at Charlotte, for an instant pretending to be in awe of his high-married sister. Then he hugged her and said she was very much missed about the place. "I mean, who else is there to test the gigs and jaunters?"

✳

She had feared the worst, believing she deserved it. Yet neither Brydd nor Elizabeth made any mention of her clear-moon flight from Faxforge. They spoke of the past nine months as though Charlotte had been with them—the August storm that left a tree in the orchard split and blackened by lightning; the day Step Cotter had been attacked by a swan; the night Sam Gilmore's tavern had been invaded by footpads, the brawny innkeeper going among them with a bung mallet in one hand, a thick stone bottle in the other. "Three of the brigands laid out on the floor, another in the yard, the rest sent scampering for the trees. Sam has never had a moment's trouble since then. We've told him he ought to change the name from the 'Blazing Rag' to the 'Shroud'."

She had waited, expecting to be called to the parlour by Brydd. But he had demanded nothing of her, and no word had passed between them concerning the church at Avebury or her life at Wintersill Hall. As for Elizabeth, she seemed unaware that her daughter had ever left.

So, gradually, in the days that followed, Charlotte recaptured the rhythms of Faxforge. She slept in the room she had occupied as a young, unmarried woman, remembering how narrow the stairs were here, how pleasantly cramped the kitchen. She awoke to the ring of hammers on hoops, on bars and nails, on pins and strappings and leaf springs. She dressed to the rasp of saws and chafers, the shouts of the craftsmen, the clopping of hooves in the yard. And then, although the bedroom enticed her to stay, she would leave it early, knowing she'd be welcome downstairs.

Below there was no panelled hall, no drunken guests, no sickening debris from the previous night's festivities. Instead there was Hester, idling in the kitchen, ready to plague her sister with a thousand thought-up questions. And there was Giles, wolfing his breakfast, a hand raised in greeting, his mouth too full to speak. And on occasion there was Brydd, though more often than not he had finished his meal and was already in the yard.

And there was always, praise God, Elizabeth; always the chance to sit with her when Giles and Hester had been sent about their business, mother and elder daughter left to sip chocolate and talk quietly together.

Their first exchanges had been halting, Elizabeth determined not to pry. Charlotte could not say precisely how long she'd be staying, though yes, she hoped it would be for a while.

Then hesitantly she had volunteered brief descriptions of her life at Wintersill Hall. It wasn't quite as splendid as she'd imagined. . . . There were still a few problems to be ironed out, a few differences to be aired. . . . It was not as easy a thing as she'd supposed, being married to a gentleman of the county. . . .

January flicked its tail, February strolling through the cool, clear days. Charlotte's painful memories diminished, and she wondered if Brook would ever return to Wiltshire, preferring perhaps to make his abode in London, the paunchy companion for a thousand eager doxies. Oh, God, that he would do so, dismissing his hedgerow bitch.

And then, quicker than seemed possible, February had gone its way, the breeze warmed by a springtime sun. Elizabeth and Charlotte were alone in the kitchen, Hester weeding and whistling in the garden. There was no sound reason for what happened; a surge of memory in Charlotte's mind, an explosion of images, a nightmare left lurking in the day. Whatever it was, it made the girl turn from her work, her head bowed forward, tears streaming from her eyes.

Elizabeth let the ladle she'd been using drown in the deep copper pan. She assisted her daughter to a bench, settled herself quietly in a chair and waited for what she had feared must come—the truth of Charlotte's marriage to Master Brook.

She heard of the ceremony itself, the bride-to-be jostled by Brook's cronies, the cleric whining at the meanness of his reward. Then she heard of her son-in-law's predilections, the way he slapped and fisted her daughter, the way he took his pleasure within her body. She heard of the Christmas festivities; of Lucas and Eldon, Peter and Markis, of the harlots who'd been brought in the oval-windowed wagon from Swindon.

Hester came in, a basket of vegetables in her hand. "Not now," Elizabeth told her, her gaze enough to send the girl backing silently from the room.

She heard more, her teeth clenched tight at the description of the boorish Keeper Venn. She wanted to ask her daughter why—"Why have you suffered all this, my sweet Charlotte?

Why have you let them do these things to you, these offences they commit? Your own husband? A gentleman, as he'd have us all believe? Oh, why, Charlotte, in the name of God why?"

But she clenched her teeth harder, knowing deep within her why the girl had permitted such indignities, why her own spirited daughter had accepted such insults and such pain.

Charlotte Cannaway—Wintersill—had done so because she was a married woman, and thus tied by her vows to her husband, forever at the mercy of the winds and currents that directed their fortunes, pleasurable or painful as they might be.

It was not Elizabeth's part to blame Charlotte for what she herself would have done. But it was her part to comfort her daughter, and to ask that Charlotte say none of this to Brydd. "If he ever learns how you've been treated by Master Wintersill, you can imagine how your father will respond. You may choose to tell him, but you know as well as I where things will end. In the killing of your husband, or of mine."

Clinging to her mother, Charlotte then wiped the tears from her eyes and gazed across the room. "The ladle's rising in the bowl," she warned. "I think the soup has come to the boil."

SEVEN

A letter arrived from William Cannaway, requesting to know if his brother and Elizabeth "would countenance a visit by me and mine. I have business to transact with a person of some standing in Devizes, and thought to travel on from there and inflict my family upon you for the night of Friday next. My dear wife Margaret enjoys the best of health. Waylen has a firm grasp of things here at Melksham. His sister Louisa bubbles as prettily as ever. I am to tell you she has prepared some delicacies. Meanwhile, our fondness and affection for you all precedes us."

Brydd shook his head at the stilted phrases, as foreign as French to the direct and down-to-earth William. It's Waylen's doing, he thought, remembering the last time he'd seen his nephew. Ah, yes, the words have all the satisfied smack of Master Waylen.

And then there was Louisa. Tapping the relevant passage in the letter, Brydd said, "I have fallen victim to Louisa's so-called delicacies before. Is she still, I wonder, as spoiled and hard to swallow as the sweetmeats she provides?"

"That is overharsh," Elizabeth protested, her voice lacking conviction. "The girl is unsure of herself—"

"She should borrow some sureness from Waylen."

"—and because of it she tends to be somewhat excitable—"

"An emotion he might borrow from her."

"—but there's no real harm in Louisa, none at all."

"As you say," he agreed cheerfully. "She reserves that for the cakes."

Her protest made, Elizabeth was of the same mind as Brydd. They welcomed the arrival of William and Margaret, not only as Cannaways but for the pleasurable company they provided. Although Brydd and William were brothers, they were unalike in their calling, different in character, yet willing beyond question to serve each other, support each other, save each other if the need should ever arise. And in many ways Elizabeth and Margaret were as close; firm, reliable women who loved their husbands and families, worked for the advancement of the coachyard, the stoneyard. Elizabeth had been a farmer's daughter, Margaret the daughter of a quarryman, so hardship and reversals were as known to them as the bitter downland winters, the cold damp stones of a quarry.

They also had a weakness for gossip, a shared sense of what was amusing, a belief that each had a shrewder eye for a bargain than the other.

So Brydd and Elizabeth looked forward to the Friday arrival of William and Margaret—somewhat less so to Waylen and Louisa.

Yet the youngsters at Faxforge could be as difficult as their Melksham cousins. Giles tended to cause trouble with Waylen, whilst Hester took a malicious delight in taunting the flouncy Louisa.

But more important than these tiresome squabbles was the risk of what might happen between Waylen and Charlotte, the former incensed that the girl he'd not thought worthy of him had supposed him not worthy of her.

Waylen would be a fool, of course, if he dared to cross swords with Charlotte. She was quicker than he would ever be, and he'd need to put balm on the scratches her words would inscribe. Even so, both Brydd and Elizabeth hoped William's son would steer clear of Charlotte's marriage, the young man doing what he'd always done best, flaunting and flouting his success.

❋

They travelled in a Cannaway carriage, an anniversary gift from Brydd to his brother and Margaret. The vehicle turned in at the road gate, dipped and rocked to a halt. The evening sun slipped downward, drawing its light beyond the humps and ridges of the hills. The yellow first, then the gold, the pink blooming crimson, the azure stained to mauve and darkened, the purple spreading as a coverlet for the night.

Hester had seen them rattling northward, and had as usual run shouting the alarm. Brydd and Giles sluiced their faces and necks at the dolphin pump, washed soot and rust and wood chips from their arms, scoured their hands and wiped them dry on their rough collarless shirts.

"A ha'penny wager," Giles offered. "Cousin Waylen will ask if my hair's wet from honest toil, or did I fall in the trough near the smithy?" Then he glanced grinning at his father.

"I'll better that," Brydd told him, his expression banishing the grin. "A whole penny says you cannot be civil to Master Waylen between your meeting him and the kitchen. He may not be your type, sir, but he *is* your cousin and I'll thank you to show him some respect."

They walked on in silence, Giles knowing he'd already lost the penny. A penny, a pound, a fortune in gold, it would all be lost between Waylen's descent from the carriage and the latch of the kitchen door. How could he, how could *anyone*, be civil to a shiny-shoe, lace-cuff character like that? He might as well pay up now and have done with it, defeated at the start.

They reached the drive, where Brydd caught Giles by the arm. "Between your meeting him and—halfway to the kitchen?"

The young man thought it over, then nodded slowly. "That's as far as I could manage it, I reckon."

"Very well. Then do so."

The women of Faxforge had already appeared and the first squeals were rising as Louisa spotted Charlotte, her heroine, now Mistress Charlotte Wintersill, lady of the Hall!

"Oh, Charlotte! Whoo-ee, Charlotte! I never imagined to see *you* down here. *Help me alight, Waylen, for heaven's sake, help me off these steps.* Whoo-ee, Cousin! *You have my hand, Waylen, you have my hand!* Charlotte! What are you doing down *here?*"

The Melksham Cannaways debouched from the carriage, whilst the Faxforge Cannaways came to greet them.

Elizabeth and Margaret embraced and stood together, their arms linked comfortably tight.

Brydd and William embraced, slapped shoulders and shook hands, neither—now the moment was here—needing to do more than smile, their greetings achieved by their grasp.

Louisa nodded absently at Giles and Hester, pinned her hatbrim with a finger, hurried onward to be with Elizabeth and Charlotte—Elizabeth and her own elegant cousin, weren't they born in the selfsame year—she and Mistress Charlotte Wintersill! "It's a pleasure to meet you again, Mistress Cannaway—Oh, Charlotte, what are you *doing* here? Is your husband, is Master Brook with you, for heaven's sake, where *is* he?"

The spindly apprentice, Lewis Plant, emerged from the yard, took the reins of the carriage and led the two-horse team inside.

Waylen checked the set of his tricorn, turned to shake the creases of travel from his coat, then gazed at his cousin, the split-knuckled cartmaker Giles. "You look soaked through, so you do, my dear Cousin. All work, or have you been in the pond?"

That's close enough, Giles thought. It's close enough for the winning of my ha'penny wager.

Then, honesty the rule, always the rule with Giles Cannaway, he determined to win the other bet, the whole penny. His father was close by, though with William. But no matter where Brydd was, he'd believe his son's account of the meeting, knowing full well it was not in Giles's character to lie for the profit of a penny.

So the husky young coachmaker offered his hand and surprised himself with the courtesy of his answer. "It was work until Hester alerted us to your coming, Cousin Waylen. Then I thought I should wash and be presentable. You'll excuse the workaday clothes—"

"Certainly," Waylen nodded, taking the offered hand, touching it, letting it go, "yes, by all means, certainly, of course." Then he thought, Here's a polish to Giles I've not seen before. Washed and made presentable for our arrival? Forgive the workaday garb?

"We'll celebrate tonight," Waylen pressed. "My father, he and I, we've written up an agreement for the building of twenty new houses near Devizes. Quite the most profitable deal my father—he and I have ever penned. What d'you say to that!"

Walking beside him, shorter in height, broader in the shoulder, thicker in the arms and thighs and with a brimming desire to strangle his cousin, Giles managed, "I have always admired your father's achievements, Waylen. His and yours. Though one wonders how Master William achieved anything before you brought *your* special skills to bear." He continued walking, again surprised by the ease of his response. Good God, he thought, I've a better tongue in my head than I supposed. Meanwhile, beside him, Waylen was saying, "Damn generous of you to remark it, Cousin. And I can't deny it, the business prospers more than ever."

By now they had left the drive and were turning along the narrow, flagged path to the kitchen. Giles heard his cousin droning on with praise for his perception. It was right, Waylen commended, that the young cart—the young *coach*maker should admire the things they'd achieved at Melksham, William and Waylen, "he and I."

Giles nodded and looked across at Brydd, leaving no doubt in his father's mind that both the ha'penny and the whole penny wagers had been won.

✳

Hester fired her first broadside. "Such a stylish hat, my dear Louisa. You must tell me, is it French?"

"I really couldn't say. Quite likely it is."

"Or Italian?"

"Well, perhaps."

"Brought into England by smugglers, along with bolts of silk and ribbons and that? The dark of the moon? A hooded lantern? Horses waiting on the clifftop?" Her eyes shone with the romance of it all, and Louisa agreed that yes, it was possible, the hat *did* have a certain foreign style.

"Then it must have been a galleon that brought it," Hester beamed. "I've seen three others, identical, in Marlborough."

Louisa blushed, but rallied. "When we've dined," she said, "you must once again show me your room. I remember your fine collection of dolls—"

"That was years ago. *Years*."

"Oh, surely not. I always think of you as a child who cossets her dolls."

"A child, you say! I am *thirteen*! I gave away such silly playthings—"

"Thirteen? My, you're a diminutive little thing for thirteen. Still, you'll find a man one day. There's short men, too, after all."

Decorating their dislike with their smiles, they settled themselves at the table in the warm, red-tiled kitchen. . . .

Waylen addressed the gathering. Raising his rough stone mug, he said, "I would offer a toast—to you, Mistress Elizabeth; to you, sir, Master Brydd; to my dear Charlotte or should

I say Mistress Wintersill; to Cousin Giles and our sweet young
Hester. I propose we drink to the best agreement my father
and I have ever written up in business. As I was telling Giles,
twenty houses and maybe more if—"

"Best you sit down," William murmured. "We've not come
here to start boasting." He glanced at Brydd, blessing his
brother for his evenness of expression. Elizabeth and Margaret
made conversation, passed around the dishes, kept a clatter
going while Waylen blustered, "I assure you, Father—I had no
intention—" then sat down.

"Even so," Brydd nodded, "our congratulations to you,
William. Shall you begin building them this year?"

Embarrassed by Waylen's trumpetings, William said, "Hope
to, yes," then busied himself with the mutton and larded potatoes. He managed somehow to see that his son was served last.

"Now then," from Louisa. "I pray you, dear Charlotte, tell
me how life has treated you since your marriage to Master
Wintersill, you'll not mind if I call him Master Brook. Have
you been happy with him, well, of course you have, who
wouldn't be with a gentleman at their every beck and call! It's
odd to think, though, that here we were, all believing you'd
one day marry Waylen. In a way it's a shame you didn't, eh,
Charlotte, though at least I can say I'm related to the master
of Wintersill Hall. A distant relation perhaps, but still the
cousin of his wife." She wriggled in her chair, then asked when
she might meet him, the words spilling over as she demanded
to know if they ate from silver platters and drank from silver
goblets—"it being what I've heard they do, the aristocracy of
England."

Charlotte leaned forward and said, "Your questions are so
intrusive, Cousin, I feel behoven to offer a response."

Louisa cleared her throat and smiled and said yes, not quite
knowing what she'd been told.

"As to whether or not you may call my husband Master
Brook, you may not. As to whether or not I've been happy
with him, no, Louisa, I've been dismal from the day I took his

name. And in the matter of silver tableware I would only say you're deluded, a victim perhaps of fairy tales and fables. I have left him, Cousin. Our marriage is in abeyance. And you, so it seems, are in danger of losing food from your fork."

Not wasting an instant, Hester leaned across, smiled sweetly at Louisa and in an overloud whisper said, "Pity I didn't know you intended to tilt at my sister. Never mind. We all regret the silly things we say."

By then William Cannaway was telling Brydd he had something to discuss with him, something he thought would be much to his brother's advantage. And Charlotte was listening politely as Waylen insisted it was no easy matter, whatever the world might suppose, to balance the books of as thriving a business as the building concern at Melksham. For example, did she realise . . .

And Giles was saying nothing, content in the knowledge that, if he chose to, he could practise his new-found ability and match Waylen word for word. Perhaps he'd subject the book-keeper to a nut and bolt description of the making of a long-board wagon. A complicated business, the making of a wagon. . . .

Not that he chose to for the moment, with a second helping of mutton and potatoes on his plate.

*

William said, "There's a story I'd pass on to you, brother. One with the happiest of endings, you'll agree."

The evening meal over, Brydd and William had retired to the cluttered room that, even after twenty years, defied the precision of a name. It was sometimes referred to as the parlour, at other times as the study, the office, "the room by the kitchen." Littered with papers, with Brydd's own sketched-out ideas for improvements to his vehicles, with timetables and handbills, it was a chaotic yet indispensable corner of the Cannaway business.

The story was told in William's deep-pitched voice, the

phrases not his own. "It concerns a party of English surgeons who recently had cause to travel the Spanish Peninsula. Whilst there they occasioned upon a remote mountain village and were astonished by the uniform vigour of its inhabitants."

"The uniform vigour of its inhabitants?"

"That's right." William nodded, ignoring Brydd's quizzical smile. "Anyway, in due course these medical gentlemen inquired as to the reason for the uncommon good condition of the people. Much favoured by the local families, the surgeons were conducted to a fissure in the rocks from whence bubbled a spring. They were informed—"

"Was this ever one of Waylen's stories?" Brydd asked, then saw William frown as though he had lost his place in a book.

"Waylen's? No, it has nothing to do with Waylen. Why should you think—"

"No matter. I apologise. Please continue."

Seated well back in his chair, William retained his frown until, so it seemed, he had once again found his place. "They were informed, these surgeons, that the, ah, effluvient waters were the source of the villagers' health and, ah, longevity. Samples were brought back to England. Tests were undertaken at considerable expense, resulting in the most heartening good news for all. It can be safely claimed that these—effluvient waters will cure"—and here William struggled in earnest—"surfeit, chrisomes, pleurisy, the light plague, the spotted fever, inflammations, tisick . . . and the rest I cannot pronounce."

Brydd nodded, not quite knowing why. "This is all very impressive, William."

"They have founded a society."

"Indeed? Even more impressive. But, William, why are you telling me—"

"The Curative and Medicinal Essence Society." And then, with a complete change of tack, the shambling builder said, "You remember my brother-in-law, Nathan Reed."

Brydd decided to let William keep the reins. Whatever the point of his oddly phrased story—had it already reached the happiest of endings?—it was better to let him make it in his own roundabout way. So Brydd contented himself with "Yes, a decent fellow, Nathan. And a damn good quarry master." Could that be the link, perhaps; a quarry master in England, a mountainside spring in Spain?

"He is all you say," William confirmed, "and with a steady head for business. You'll not find Nathan taking foolish risks, however attractive the prize. So, when he told me he'd bought stock in the Curative and Medicinal Essence Society, suggesting that I do the same, I knew it was advice I could trust."

"May I ask how much he—you—invested in this effluvient spring?"

"You sound doubtful, brother."

"Frankly, I am."

"Well, you just listen," William encouraged. "I went and bought sixty of their shares. Thirty-five pounds each they were when I signed for them, so they cost me in all two thousand one hundred pounds."

"That," Brydd said quietly, "is quite an outlay, even for a fellow who's just agreed up the building of twenty houses. How long ago did you buy them?"

"A month."

"And since then?"

William smiled, and immediately shrugged it away. He had no wish to crow, yet neither could he deny the truth that—

"Since then they've gone up to six thousand!"

Brydd gazed at him and said quietly, "Well now, brother, that's a spring-heeled jump to your fortunes."

"I regret I did not tell you sooner. It is such a chance, my dear Brydd, and by no means too late! Raise as much as you possibly can—"

"Assuredly not two thousand one hundred pounds. The profits here at Faxforge go back into Faxforge—"

"And can stay here! Who, tell me, is better thought of the length of the Kennett Vale? You go to a bank! Yes! As I did! You borrow against your own thriving business, Brydd, and with all the certainty that you can pay them back when you will. Borrow soon, buy quickly, sell when it suits you best. The Curative and—they need money for pumping equipment which they intend to install below the spring—"

"William."

"—and for a bottling and corking—yes, brother, what?"

"I have three things in mind. The first is that I never before heard you talk like a fairground barker. Borrow soon? Buy quick? Sell when it suits me best? If any man had said that to *you* more than a month ago . . . And anyway, you've long been chary of banks. For many years, as I well remember, you preferred to keep your money in an oilskin pouch under a flagstone in your house."

Made awkward by the reminder, William countered, "I did not then know of the advantages they offered."

"Well," Brydd said, "that aside, I've a question that needs your answer. Now that you've bought your stock and made three times your investment, will you sell it again?"

"As for that, it depends."

"On what? Will you sell if the value dips down?"

"That's generally the way."

"Though shares have been known to dip and then rise again, to falter, so to speak."

"Quite often they do."

"So might you not hold on?"

"It's conceivable. It depends on, well, the advice I get. Circumstances and so forth."

"For the moment, then, you have no intention of selling."

William shifted with discomfort. He had, in all honesty, expected his brother to leap at the opportunity, not sit across from him, casting doubts and suspicions. "You said you had three things in mind. You might care to impart the third."

"Yes," Brydd nodded, "the third. You are right about many things, my dear William; half the people I know are purchasing stock in such-and-such a company, this-and-that society, ventures and syndicates and schemes. Merchants with a weight of coins, farmers with next to nothing. It seems to be the common madness or, as you would have it, the chance of a lifetime. Yet if *all* the stocks are rising, if *everyone* is growing rich, who in God's name is footing this incalculable bill? Is it not, simply, that none of you wish to sell what you've purchased? That no one has yet called in?"

Saddened by Brydd's reaction, William Cannaway muttered, "I've told you how things are. I can only pass on the advice I've been given. You should buy yourself some stock."

"It's well-meant advice, I know it is, William. But I fear, if I took it, I would also keep my hands cupped open, whilst all this invisible fortune tumbled in. Reach across with your glass, sir. At least one can see and taste a full-bodied port."

Louisa's squeals were still worrying the morning air as the Melksham Cannaways departed around the low-hedged curve of the road. "You'll come to see us soon!" she cried. "Brook will regret your absence, Charlotte, so he will! You'll see! He will! You'll see!"

•And then, with the Faxforge Cannaways standing at the gate, Hester said, "She might have hidden her purse to pretend she's forgotten it. She might bring them back. I'll make sure they're on their way." She darted out and along the rutted coach track, leaving Brydd and Elizabeth, Charlotte and Giles to turn wearily from the entrance. The men would go back to their work in the yard, the women to the garden and the house. Later, they would talk and gossip as a family around the table, though not before dusk had fallen on the pond and forging fire, the flagged pathways and dolphin pump, and on the road that ran between the Beckhampton Crossing and Devizes.

Not that much traffic came along it after dark.

And so, that evening, with the plates and bowls cleared from the table, and the Cannaways relaxed around it, they were surprised to hear what they took to be a late-passing stage wagon. These massive, dish-wheeled vehicles were built to carry as many as twenty passengers, the wagons lumbering their way from wool town to wool town at a speed of two miles an hour.

Yet something was missing. There was something incomplete about the sound. Brydd and Giles sensed it together and the young man said, "There's all the horses," and Brydd remarked, "So there are, though no disturbance of a wagon." Then he lifted a hand a little above the table and the family listened and heard the creak as the road gate was pushed open.

EIGHT

Elizabeth Cannaway said quietly, "You're let off the dishes tonight, Hester. Do some reading in your room." The girl opened her mouth to protest, thought better of it, and bobbed her head. Giles had meanwhile left the table.

There were horses on the drive, four at a guess, maybe five. Brydd grunted approval of Elizabeth's command, eased himself from his chair, then glanced across at Charlotte. "I've a letter, it's addressed to old Flowerdewe in Swindon. Somewhere on my desk in the study. You've a sharp pair of eyes."

She nodded, turned to kiss her sulky sister good night, then waited for Hester to stamp noisily from the kitchen. "Who could it be?" she asked, and thought, Surely not now, after all this time.

Giles emerged from a corner of the room, a pistol in one hand, a fowling piece under his arm. He laid the weapons on the table, moved away again, returned with powder and shot. Quietly and efficiently, humming beneath his breath, he loaded and primed the pistol, jammed shot and a cotton wad down the barrel of the fowling piece. Then he screwed the flints in place and sprinkled powder on the pans.

The trampling of horses drew nearer.

Brydd repeated, "It's addressed to Edward Flowerdewe in Swindon." *Five horses.* He took the pistol from the table, closed the cover to keep the powder in its pan, then collected his greatcoat and thrust the weapon in a pocket. He told his son, "You will stay here, Giles, if you please, sir, and only level that piece when I say so." Then, with a proper courtesy for Charlotte, he ushered her into the parlour, closed the door behind her and went out through the steep-tiled porch.

The riders—*yes, five*—were waiting where path and drive converged. Brydd could only recognise one of them in the moonlight: Brook Wintersill, drunk and glaring, steadying himself in the saddle. Beside him was his keeper, Victor Venn. The others, Eldon Sith and Lucas Ripnall, and an uncomfortable Markis Mayman.

Brydd approached them along the path, stopped and acknowledged their presence with a nod. His voice nailed flat, he said, "Master Wintersill. It's been a while since we met."

"We both know that for a hard stone fact," Brook responded. "And we'd not be meeting now, Cannaway, if you'd not enticed my wife. Taken her under your wing, is that it? Guarding her 'gainst her desires?" He reached forward, as if to underscore the questions, his hand slipping on the pommel of his saddle.

"She is not being held by any restraint, Master Wintersill, though she is certainly under our roof. And now, may I ask you why our family matters need the audience of your friends?"

Brook had regained his balance in the saddle. Venn leaned across and mouthed something to him. He nodded, lurching again, and the keeper tapped heels to his horse; the step-forward bully in the service of his master. He let the animal crowd against Brydd.

His accent of the dockside, his voice raw with menace, he said, "Best give 'er back now, Cannaway, else we'll see this yard burned down." His words were followed by the sudden jab of a cudgel end aimed at Brydd Cannaway's face. If the club missed nose, mouth, eyes, it left its mark on the side of Brydd's forehead and sent him backward across the small summer garden that Hester claimed as her own.

From the very first sound of the horses, the realisation that they did not draw a late-passing wagon, Brydd had been suspicious of the callers. They might have been highwaymen, though none had yet dared venture within the confines of Faxforge. They might have been deserters from the Army or the Navy, desperate men on stolen horses, who must rob in order to eat. They might have been vagabonds, gypsies, aimless unsheltered riders who descended on outlying farmsteads like owls on their downland prey.

Recognising Brook, he'd left the pistol untouched in his pocket. The man's unannounced arrival had surprised him. Why had he come in darkness; and why with an escort? But at least, Brydd had supposed, there'd be talk, argument even, an arrangement finally reached.

What the master of Faxforge had not anticipated was this sudden attack by Venn; the running of blood that blinded him in one eye, the weakness that left him sprawling on the ground.

But he accepted now, as Charlotte had for long accepted, that Master Brook Wintersill and his henchmen were well practised in the art of revenge.

※

He heard the chink of metal, creak of leather, thud of heels on the path. Two of the men reached down, dragging him erect. They forced him onward, his arms pinioned, in the direction of the porch. He blinked in an effort to clear his sight, failed and turned his head, wiping blood along the collar of his coat.

The house door was wrenched open. An instant later he heard Venn bark, "Touch that piece, boy, and I'll snap you apart." Brydd echoed, "Yes, Giles, leave it be," then gasped as someone propelled him forward with a violent blow in the spine. He glimpsed Elizabeth, her face ashen with shock, and thanked God she had the sense not to scream.

Lucas Ripnall found the pistol in Brydd's pocket. The discovery was followed by another violent shove and this time, his arms released, Brydd was sent stumbling across the kitchen. He would have fallen had not Giles moved to catch him. As it was, he swayed for a moment before standing beside Elizabeth.

There was a flurry of words—Giles raging at the attackers, Brydd commanding him to be silent, Venn warning, "For the last time, boy, or be broken!" Elizabeth was doing what she could to dab blood from her husband's eye, whilst Lucas Ripnall made some grinning remark to Brook Wintersill. Brook himself snapped orders at Eldon and Markis, the former shrill with excitement, the latter flushed and unhappy. He really would not have come down here had he known things would turn so ugly.

Nevertheless, the portly Markis went through to the parlour whilst Eldon ascended the narrow stairs to check the upper rooms. Brydd and Elizabeth and Giles fell silent, their only weapons the disgust with which they stared at Brook and his keeper and his crony Lucas Ripnall. There was little the Cannaways could do as yet, faced with Venn's cudgel, the pistol Lucas had taken, the fowling piece Brook lifted from the table.

"Not much of a welcome this, eh, Cannaway. Almost as if you had something—or someone—to hide." Then he murmured an aside to Ripnall, turned to repeat it to Venn and seemed encouraged by their laughter.

From above they heard sounds of a struggle; a slap, a scream, Hester's voice raised in fury, faltering to tears. From the sounds that followed it was clear she was being hauled downstairs, kicking and fighting every step of the way.

The Cannaways hoped she'd delivered a damn good slap to Eldon. But that brief, cheering thought was dashed when they saw her all but flung into the kitchen, her own face marked by the imprint of a hand. Giles caught his sister to him and put an arm around her, telling her it was all right now, it was all right, be calm, it would not happen again.

At any other time he'd have thought young Hester an irritant, a nuisance, a mischief to be endured. Though not one to be slapped or dragged about, least of all by a spiny, embroidered creature who scuttled in obedience to Brook.

Raising his head, Giles asked, "You, sir, who are so freehanded with young women. What is your name? I shall need it, in order to trace you." He glared unswerving at Eldon, saw the man's eyes dart across to Brook, and realised—*Yes, that slapping gentleman is timid from heel to hair piece!* So it pleased Giles to add, "Trace you or, if need be, track you down."

But before he could identify Hester's assailant Charlotte entered the kitchen.

She did so by choice, having heard the kicks and shouting on the stairs. Until then, the parlour door and window shutters closed, she had been unaware of the disturbance outside, and even the bullied invasion of the house. Then Markis Mayman had entered, surprising her, and made his feeble attempt to draw her from the room. Unhappy in his task, his face still ruddy with embarrassment, he had not dared tell her Brydd Cannaway had been clubbed by Venn, only that her husband was here and had sent him to fetch her—request her to join him if she would.

But she'd then heard her sister and had left the rear of the parlour. Concealing her fears, she'd brushed past Markis, and hurried into the kitchen. He'd followed her, politely closing the doors.

And now Charlotte saw Elizabeth, her face drained grey, and Brydd with the blood wiped wide of his eye, and Hester held sobbing against Giles. And across from them Brook and Venn and Lucas, each man armed and in his own way smiling a welcome. Behind them stood Eldon Sith, knowing his place as Brook Wintersill's skeletal shadow.

"Well," Brook slurred, "my own precious Charlotte. And looking pinched as ever with contempt."

She went straight to her family, heard Elizabeth murmur what had happened, leaned forward and kissed her father, reached across to show support for Giles and Hester. Then she swung round, her eyes only for her husband.

Words rose scalding to her tongue, as she told him, "You've surprised my family tonight, sir, and from all I can see done them harm. You were excessive enough in your behaviour at the Hall, but now it seems you are widening your net, drumming down here with your servant and friends, and showing all the violence of a felon.

"I believed in my ignorance—my stupidity—that you might come here with some final honest intent. I beg you to shelve your smile, Master Brook; it *is* what I believed.

"However, since all you *will* do is smile, I shall tell you this, and trust it might shrink your lips. You've been a damnably sorry husband, are deluded to suppose yourself a gentleman and could not, I think, find your way through the days without the aid of your brutish Master Venn. No matter the shame you've brought on the Cannaways—you *and* I, since I thought you such a wondrous, sparkling find—but you'd do well to leave us now, Brook Wintersill. Go away, sir. Limit the spread of your disease. The act of marriage binds us as husband and wife, though I should most certainly try to kill you, or have you kill me, before letting you close again."

There was silence for a moment, Brook's smile at last losing ground. And then, tragically, Giles Cannaway launched an outburst of his own. "Yes, you bastard, why don't you leave! Or better yet, be assisted!" The challenge made, he stormed forward, fists clenched, ready to send Brook Wintersill on his way.

But the young man's threat served also as a warning. Venn had time to heft his cudgel and lash out with it, aiming at Giles's right knee. The sound of the blow was sickening, its victim going down on the dark red tiles. Fabric and skin were torn apart by the eruptive shards of bone. Giles screamed in agony. Hester screamed with him and vomited on her clothes. Elizabeth and Charlotte swooped together beside the ruined Giles, their skirts raised carelessly as they tore cambric for his wound.

Brook and Lucas were themselves shaken by the measured cruelty of Venn's act. Eldon Sith giggled uncontrollably. Markis Mayman retreated to the doorway, bile in his throat, his hat across his face.

Then Brydd roared to deafen the household and charged. The ugly, savage howl sped from wall to wall, a primitive animal in the maddened defence of its offspring.

He caught Eldon flat-footed, hurling the man against a dresser. Venn ducked aside, deserting his master, leaving Brook with the fowling piece, his fingers scrabbling for the trigger. But Brydd was already on him, and Wintersill sagged as he was pounded below the ribs. He lost his grip on the long-barrelled weapon and it clattered to the floor.

Lucas Ripnall had also edged away, though not far enough to avoid the backswing of Brydd's left arm. Lucas stumbled, his head jolted by the blow, while Brydd pressed his attack against Brook. It pleased the master of Faxforge to see his son-in-law wince from a second solid punch, this drawing blood from his nostrils. And by God there'd be a third and a fourth and—

But there weren't, for the keeper had again raised his club and now swept it downward, catching Brydd between his shoulder blades and the collared nape of his neck. The heavy knotted cudgel sent him flat, a side of his face skinned by the tiles, the only mercy that his senses were lost to him.

Recovered from Brydd's earlier jolting blow, Lucas Ripnall drew the confiscated pistol. Without hesitation he extended his arm, squinted along it, past the cocking piece and along the barrel and down at the coachmaker's skull.

Elizabeth, on her knees beside Giles, screamed fully in Ripnall's face. The pistol gouted flame and shot and Brydd lurched, already unconscious, part of his collar shredded by the ball, fresh blood darkening his hair. Giles squirmed toward him, the agony of his shattered knee no greater than the fears for his father. He cried openly with the pain and horror of the night, willing himself to crawl forward, yet wishing in part that Venn would thrash down again and spare him from his hell.

Charlotte rose like a wildcat from the floor. She threw herself at Lucas, raked him deeply along his jawbone, then gasped as Eldon slapped at her with spite. She gasped again as the keeper barged her away, a rhythm to his shoving. She was sent across the room to the doorway and through it and out onto the porch. Eldon was also pushed aside, Victor Venn unwilling to share the mistress with anyone. For the moment at least she was *his* to crowd, *his* to handle, *his* to smack onward, back and hip and buttock. He regarded it as only fair, his deserved reward for the high-chinned way she'd treated him at the Hall. Master Brook could have her back in a while, but just between here and the horses she could learn how a Londoner dealt with attractive, troublesome women.

Markis Mayman had already left the house. The downing of young Cannaway had appalled him and he stood near the horses, his podgy arms wrapped across his stomach, his lips moving as he told himself in silence, Not a bit what I'd expected. . . . Why did he have to . . . Where's the appeal in doing that . . . ?

Eldon Sith emerged, having snatched the fowling piece from the floor. Bruised by his collision with the dresser, and relieved that the coachmaker had spared him a second attack, he was already convincing himself he'd eluded the man's clumsy, floundering blows. Anyway, Sith thought, I gave old Brooksy's bitch a slap to remember.

Lucas and Brook walked with studied care from the house. Ripnall's head still dinned, blood seeping from the scratches on his face. Beside him, Brook held a wet, stained handkerchief to his nose. Drunk on his arrival at Faxforge, the exchange of violence had sobered him, and he now told Lucas the family deserved what they'd got. "There'll be no more running away by Charlotte. And as for her oafish brother, he should be hobbling for a good few years. It was rough treatment by Venn, I'll say that, though no more than they had coming. Hiding a wife from her husband! Christ, they should count themselves lucky they've a house still standing around them! Tell Markis to give his horse over to Charlotte. He and Eldon can ride double. I believe my nose is healed; let's leave this rag as a reminder." Then he threw aside the handkerchief and followed Lucas along the moon-pale path.

NINE

Elizabeth felt for the pulse of life in her husband. Giles lay
twisted on the floor, a woollen sleeve crammed in his mouth as
a silencer for his moans. Hester knelt near him, embarrassed by
the mess on her clothes, sobbing to herself and rocking with
the futility of shock. She herself needed comforting. After all,
she was the youngest, the most frightened of all, so why didn't
someone sit with her and cradle her and help her wipe the—
  "Hester? Do I have your attention!"
  "Oh, Mother! D'you see what I've done? Do you see—"
  "I see our men injured, girl, that's what! I see it's time you
behaved above your years. There's blankets and cushions you
can fetch, hot water to ladle out, Step Cotter and Lewis Plant
to be roused, though God knows why they're not here yet.
Well, girl?" And Elizabeth allowed her own tears to spill.
"Shall you be above your age, or shan't you? Shall you do what
you can for the men of this house? Oh, please, Hester, please! I
must have your help in this!"
  And by then the girl was climbing to her feet and saying yes,
she'd do whatever was needed, of course she would—"though
don't cry, for how can I leave you if you cry?"

"I am not," Elizabeth concealed, one hand on Brydd's blood-soaked collar, the other within reach of Giles. She said again, "I am not," setting the lie to it as Hester went upstairs to snatch the bedding from the beds.

❋

There was reason enough for Step Cotter's absence.

He'd kept it a secret from the Cannaways, from his friend Sam Gilmore, from the craftsmen Ben and Matthew. And then, a month ago, he'd let slip the secret to someone who'd blushed and assured him he'd *never* tell, not to anyone, Master Step had his promised word.

"So I should hope," the scarred and stunted Cotter had warned, "else you'll not reach the ground between here and Devizes."

❋

There was reason enough for Lewis Plant's absence.

Quartered in a neatly made hut in the northeast corner of the coachyard, the skinny apprentice wheelwright had eaten with the Cannaways, all but fallen asleep at their table, mumbled his apologies and gone wearily to his bed. The day's work had exhausted him and, as on many other occasions, he'd envied Master Giles his seemingly boundless energy. But then, Lewis had reasoned, he is of quite a different build. Maybe that's the cause of it; my limbs are too long; my strength is used up in travelling through my bones.

So, in bed and asleep, he had scarcely stirred at the trample of approaching horses, failed to hear Brydd Cannaway's savage roar, and only come awake—partially awake—at the distant bark of the pistol.

Even then he'd thought to haul the covers over his head. The sound might have been the split of unseasoned timber, a loose slate falling to the cobbles, the snap of a rusted nail. Such noises were commonplace in and around the yard. Pull up the covers again. It was probably just a slate.

Lewis turned in search of sleep.

Then he opened his eyes and sighed and swung his long bare legs to the floor. Much as he wished it, it was not the splitting of wood, the snapping of iron. Nor would a slate land on the cobbles with such a positive report.

Fumbling about him, the apprentice struck sparks to a lantern, pulled on boots and breeches and made his way, yawning, from the hut. He did not know what to look for, or what he expected to find. The moonlit yard was empty save for half-finished curricles, gigs awaiting a wheel or shaft, stacks of timber and piles of shavings, the body and ladder back of a heavy Wiltshire wagon.

Lewis peered about him and yawned again. Then, on the point of returning to the hut, he heard the sound of voices, the restive snorting of mounts. Visitors, he thought wearily. I've hauled myself out here for the going away of visitors.

Though visitors who suddenly cursed, a visiting lady who cried out?

Wide awake now and uncertain, Lewis Plant walked cautiously to the drive. There, made pallid by the moon, were several horsemen, two of them straddling the same tethered animal, the riders' faces shadowed by their tricorn hats. And, if Lewis could believe his eyes, there too was Charlotte Wintersill, her hair in disarray, a sleeve of her dress torn at the elbow, her head turned in anger toward a man who shook her and growled at her to keep shut. The man was Venn, though it was Lucas Ripnall who first caught sight of the apprentice. He muttered an aside to Brook, who nodded quickly, and Lewis was still gaping, his lantern held innocently high, as Ripnall spurred forward with the aim of charging him down.

The attack succeeded in that the lantern was sent flying, Lewis hurled against the wall. Black oil spilled from the lamp and ignited, the flames scorching the ground. A few feet away and spared the splash of the burning liquid, Lewis Plant lay near the base of the wall, his chest bruised by the charge of Ripnall's horse, his head bleeding where he'd struck the side-laid bricks. He heard Charlotte emit the beginnings of a scream but did not see Venn clap a hand across her mouth. Nor did he see Brook Wintersill gag her with a scarf, the horsemen then taking her onward, down to the road gate and north along the coach road. It was all Lewis could do to drag breath into his chest, and the riders were half a mile away before he could stand without falling.

Reason enough then why he came late to the scene in the kitchen.

*

Aching from Brydd's punches, Brook could nevertheless begin to enjoy what had happened. He'd reclaimed his wife, that was the thing, and with it his self-respect. And what could the Cannaways do about it? In a quick word, nothing. From dawn to dusk they could mouth their complaints, though what they could *do* was nothing.

Did marriage give a man control of his wife? The answer to that was yes. Was he therefore permitted to wrest her from her parents? The answer to *that* was yes. And what if the parents —not gentlemen, but carters—what if they stood in his way? Was he, the husband, then allowed to disarm them of their pistol and fowling piece and recoup to himself what was his? But certainly. Beyond question. A loud and resounding yes!

Oh, the Cannaways could wail and moan, dream in their beds and pray to heaven, clutch at a sympathetic sleeve. They could plot and scheme from now till doomsday, but there was nothing within the high, spiked fence of the law that they could do. Damn them to destruction, not a thing.

Eldon Sith pointed ahead and the riders saw the faint glow of the beacon that marked Sam Gilmore's tavern. It was here, at the Beckhampton Crossing, that Charlotte would squirm and seek help. Here, where the road from Devizes to Swindon crossed the road linking Bristol with London. But more important, where the innkeeper of the "Blazing Rag" leaned his muscular arms on the bar.

So Brook and Venn held Charlotte tight between them, urging their horses past the inn and up the slope to Avebury. Only then did the cavalcade relax, Brook Wintersill unknotting the scarf with which he had gagged his own wife. "Shout away now all you will. Though they'll just be words in the wind. But before you do, hear this, my sweet Charlotte. Leave my house again and I shall raise a regiment of friends. Then, together, we'll set your father's yard at the level of summer grass. Is that clear to you, you damn bitch, how completely Faxforge will be burned?"

Charlotte thought what to say, a hundred things, then chose to say none of them. Instead, knowing full well the price, she turned and spat in Brook's face. It was no more than a gesture, her mouth dry from the horrors of the night. But her husband took it for the insult it was and laid plans for the way he'd reward her when they were once again safe home.

✳

Meanwhile, Lewis had stumbled to the kitchen to be met by a woman transformed. No more the amusing, tiresome, attention-demanding child, Hester Cannaway now addressed him with all the authority of her mother. "You can see what's occurred here, Master Lewis. Sit down. I'll tend your wound while I tell you what's to do."

"My God, Mistress Hester, is Master Cannaway—"

"Alive and will stay so. One of Brook Wintersill's—lean your head forward—one of his gang fired a pistol—"

"So that was it. I thought I heard—"

"Lean forward, I say. Here's a paste to stanch the bleeding. Now listen to me, Lewis. Is Step Cotter still absent from the yard?"

The apprentice nodded and was glad that Hester failed to press her question. Filling the silence, he hastened, "You'll need someone to reach Marlborough and summon your brother Jarvis or Dr. Mabbott. I'm sure I can get there. Let me stand. D'you see; you've quite patched me up. I'll take the short cut past the Bellringers and—" He swayed for a moment, then felt his senses again come level. He cast a final anguished glance at Brydd and Giles, at Elizabeth crouched between them. "There'll be help here soon," Lewis blurted. "I'll make sure there is. You may count on it." Then all he could think of was, "Yes, I will, you may count on it, I'll go by the Bellringers," and he plunged from the house, along the path and across the yard to the stables.

He rode bareback, his heels curled under the barrelled belly of the mount. The short cut led north by east across the Cannaway meadows, then beside the clump of trees in the far corner of the property. Lewis slapped and shouted the horse up the incline, taking it so near the trees that both animal and rider were whipped by the low-hanging branches.

He felt blood on his neck, the paste dissolving around the wound.

The ground levelled, then dipped, levelled, then rose, the next half mile a seesaw that made the horse stamp or lurch, no longer sure of its footing.

Lewis fought to rein in, his promises forgotten amid the blur of pain in his head. He knew now that he'd not reach Marlborough. Yet where else could he go for help, when every uncertain hoofbeat took him farther toward the east?

He approached the village of Kennett and remembered a name, a place, a door he might knock on, though God knew what would happen if he did. The horse missed its step, recovered, yet caused the rider to gasp with pain. The impact decided him and he turned his mount across the fields that flanked the village, then along an alleyway and beside the Kennett River to a tall, wooden-clad flour mill and the house that stood against it.

By now the pain was chiselling at his skull. It seemed to match the stride of his horse, the beat of his heart, the quickening intake of his breath. As he neared the millhouse the darkness itself blurred before him. He reached down to lift the hook catch on the gate, misjudged the distance and fell awkwardly to the ground. He waited until he could once again see his way, knew he must make a final effort and staggered forward amid a nightmare of shapes and sounds. Somewhere to the left was the mill wheel, its broad blades thrashing in the water. The river itself bubbled along its deep-cut path. A rosebush clutched at him like a beggar in the shadows, then scratched him with its thorns, the beggar denied his coin.

Lewis tore himself free, his hands outstretched, feeling for the house, the door, *God, that I might soon reach the door.* As his head was cut deeper by the sharp tool of agony, he tripped against the threshold and sank downward, hammering, hammering, though not knowing if the blows were just the invention of his mind.

The darkness was turned to brilliance. He heard a man's voice, and then a woman's, felt himself being lifted, heard his name, sensed the glow of other, gentler lights. Then the welcome comfort of a fire, the fumes and taste of brandy, the touch of the woman's hand on his head.

He opened his eyes to see Step Cotter and—Step's slipped-out secret—the widow the impish driver had been wooing.

The exchange that followed was fractured, Lewis supposing it to last hours, the reality counted in moments. Questions were asked, answers given or twitched aside, Step Cotter extracting as much of the story as Lewis himself could recount. Brook Wintersill and a gang of his cronies had burst in upon Faxforge. Brydd and Giles Cannaway had been injured. Charlotte had been taken. Mistress Elizabeth was on her knees on the floor with blood around her and on her dress and on her hands. Hester had been magnificent. But help was needed from Marlborough, and that was why—

"—why I had to invade your privacy, Master Step. I'd have kept your secret, you know I would, but that knock I took reduced me—"

"You did right, young Lewis. You'll stay here now with Mistress Reece. As for me, I'll be off to get Dr. Mabbott or Jarvis Cannaway from town." Not much taller standing than was

Lewis in his chair, Step leaned forward and said, "It's still a secret to be kept, Master Lewis, 'less you wish to be ground in with the flour."

"Yes," Lewis managed. Then in case he'd said the wrong thing, "No."

✳

A pity the inhabitants of the Kennett Vale were asleep, else they might have seen Step Cotter put a lifetime's experience to the test.

Valuable minutes were spent saddling the horse, murmuring in its high-pricked ears, leading it out from the millhouse stable, letting it grow accustomed to the patchwork of clouds and moonlight.

Another precious moment, further encouragement, the gentle easing of the rider in the saddle.

And then, neither whipping nor goading, Step took the horse across the river bridge and turned eastward and settled for the eight-mile ride along the coach road to Marlborough. Whenever the moon was curtained by clouds, he held the mount to a jog. But on the level, with the clouds dispersed and the track turned white, Brydd Cannaway's friend and driver sent the animal thundering onward, guiding it to this side or that, his skinny hips raised clear of the leather, his head down, the reins bunched close to his chin. A pity indeed there was no one to see, for the miles between Kennett and Marlborough had never been swallowed so fast. The horse itself seemed to frisk at the challenge and gather its strength for the long upward incline into the town.

Dr. Mabbott's house was a fine bow-fronted dwelling at the western extremity of Marlborough. Once up the slope and Step could urge his blowing animal to the right and across the road and against the tethering rings in the wall.

He slid quickly from the saddle, looped the reins through a ring and pounded on the heavy black-painted door.

Above him lantern light bloomed in a window. Then it

faded and he heard the reluctant slap of slippers on the stairs. A moment later the door bolt was withdrawn, the door itself pulled open.

A tall, spare-framed young man turned to smother a yawn, mumbled an apology, then said, "Dr. Mabbott is away tonight in Swindon. I'm his assistant, Jarvis Cannaway. If there's anything—" and with a start of recognition, "—Step Cotter! Now why should *you* wish to ruin my sleep, Master Step?"

"I would not, sir," the man told him. "But you're needed at Faxforge. Your father's been injured, so I hear. And Giles as bad or worse. Shall I harness up a gig?"

His words brought Jarvis awake. Wasting no time with questions, he said, "No, though saddle me a horse if you will. The grey's our best runner." Then, unaware of Step's approval, he hurried inside in search of his clothes and bag and, should it be needed, an opiate to stifle pain.

✳

In the same hour that Step Cotter roused Jarvis in the doctor's house at Marlborough, Brook Wintersill, his keeper and cronies escorted Charlotte into the Hall.

Twisting in Brook's grasp, she was forced upstairs and herded into her room. He snatched the key from the inner face of the lock, seemed about to address her, then contented himself with a brief, humourless smile. However violently he might have raged at his errant mistress, whatever abuse he might have hurled at the hedgerow bitch, his parting expression was as eloquent and ominous a warning.

He locked the door from the outside, then made his way downstairs. He was eager to celebrate the night's success and relive it, again and again, with those who'd helped him in his task.

✳

In the millhouse at Kennett, the exhausted Lewis Plant was being made much of by Widow Reece. She had bandaged his head, wincing in sympathy with his groans. She'd fussed with the blanket that covered him, allowed him a second glass of brandy, cautioned him as to its potency, then later poured out a third. And with it—if he felt strong enough, though she would not be the slightest bit offended if he didn't—some simple sugared cake she'd made that morning.

Basking in the widow's attentions, Lewis murmured agreement with her that yes, Step Cotter was without doubt the most expert driver of coaches in the county. And every whit as accomplished a horseman. And yes, he'd a sharp sense of humour, once one got to know him. Altogether a remarkable and kindly fellow, Master Cotter.

※

The atmosphere at Faxforge was far different.

There were injured men and attentive women, the blankets that Hester had dragged from the beds, brandy in a flask on the table. But it was not the time for cake or cosseting; Brydd and Giles lay where they'd fallen, the women moving in silence, praying that Lewis had completed his journey and that someone, Mabbott or Jarvis, was even now on the moonlit valley road.

From time to time they heard Giles cry out with pain. Brydd had recovered his senses and he now placed a hand on Giles's shoulder, the only support he could offer his crippled son.

They knew, all four of them, that their world had tilted and, on this single terrible evening, sent them sliding toward the edge. . . .

PART TWO

CHARLOTTE

1720

TEN

For almost two weeks she was kept locked in her room, deprived of both firewood and candles. Her food was brought once a day by Mistress Dench, the woman forbidden to address her, the deliveries watched over by Keeper Venn.

From time to time Brook himself would visit her, assaulting his wife with a sudden wordless ferocity. She pleaded with him for news of Faxforge, her mind haunted by the nightmare images of her family, the remembered crack of the pistol, her father's body jerked by the impact of the ball. "Oh, please," she begged, "send someone to discover how they are. That my father is alive at least. You are not so inhuman as to deny me even that."

But Brook's response was to strike her. He'd tell her how things were later, perhaps. When she'd learned her place. There was time enough to satisfy her curiosity. Once she herself behaved more satisfactorily toward him.

Then, on the thirteenth morning, Keeper Venn unlocked the door and handed her the key. "Free as a bird you'll be now, mistress." He offered no further explanation, though it amused him to see her frown with mistrust.

She did not for a moment suppose her punishment was over, or that what Venn told her was true. So why had the cell been opened? And why did the gaoler think it worthy of a smirk?

Hesitant and suspicious, Charlotte waited for the man to leave. A wave of dizziness made her clutch at a chair back and she stood bowed over, her hair hanging lank about her face. Weakened by the meagre diet Brook had prescribed, and by the violence of his attacks, it was a while before she ventured from the room. She was not yet eighteen years old, yet looked as pinched and bruised as an inmate of a county poorhouse.

When the dizziness had passed, she made her way slowly along the gallery and down the stairs. As she descended to the entranceway she asked again, Why have I been released, when he knows I'm unrepentant?

❋

Outside on the steps and on the drive and near the lake she saw the truth repeated in the bulky presence of armed men. Brook was waiting for her, eager to tell her why.

"You badger me for news of your family, my loving young Charlotte. Well, this much will ease you; they are all alive and licking away at their wounds. Brydd Cannaway recovers from the pistol ball, and I hear that your brother Giles lies strapped and splinted. But word's leaked out of a plan to attack this place and spirit you away. I look forward to their efforts, Cannaway and—Cotter, is that his name? And the landlord of the 'Blazing Rag' and the men your father employs in his yard and others of his riffraff friends. I welcome their invasion, their criminal trespass on my property, for I shall then have every right to let loose at them, as I would at wild dogs that came snarling round the door.

"That is why I've hired a few more keepers, do you see. To stop my house being overrun by dogs."

Wishing to believe what he had told her about Brydd and Giles, yet frightened by his talk of invasion, Charlotte asked, "Am I permitted to walk in the grounds?"

"By all means," Brook nodded, "why not? Though I'd advise against trotting out a horse. Anyone seen riding—I've told the keepers—anyone out there on horseback and they've likely sneaked up from the valley. But of course you may stroll about, my dear Charlotte. So long as you don't go too deep among the trees."

His words were framed by an everted smile of triumph. The hiring of the keepers had rekindled his humour, and it pleased him to see Charlotte swallow his lie.

Not that all he'd told her was a lie; he *had* heard the Cannaways were on the mend and there *had* been rumours of unrest in the Kennett Vale. But his talk of a planned attack was pure invention. He had not recruited the guards as a deterrent against the stirrings of some country mob but in the expectation that Brydd Cannaway would, this week or next, come alone to seek him out. So be it. Let him try.

✳

Although Brook Wintersill had been quick to take precautions, Brydd's first outing—a few days later—was to Marlborough and Dr. Mabbott. He rode slowly through the valley toward the wool town, his neck still bruised by Venn's cudgel blow, his face marked by its skinning on the tiles. However, the real pain was centred in his left shoulder, the muscles torn by Lucas Ripnall's distracted shot. Each sharp spasm was a reminder to Brydd that, unexpected though the attack on Faxforge had been, he had failed to defend his wife, his family, his home. . . .

Young Hester had been slapped and terrified and was now prey to nightmares that shook her screaming awake. By day she was grimly obedient to her mother, the girl's once mischievous attitude to life gone, as it seemed, forever. She did her best to cheer Giles, though her chatter was forced, her jokes ineffectual. She feared he was crippled and would remain so.

Dr. Mabbott and Jarvis had made regular visits to see him, agreeing in their more sanguine fashion that Giles was fortunate; infection had failed to set in; they'd not needed to take off his leg. Naturally, for the first few months, a year perhaps, he would walk with the aid of a stick, but with patience and practice he might one day discard it and—

"And what?" he had shouted. "Climb ladders and the Wiltshire hills? Jump from a carriage bench again, or run to snatch at the bridle of a horse? Is limping about with a leg as rigid as a fence post enough that I should think myself fortunate?"

"No," Dr. Mabbott admitted. "I employed the word by way of comparison, that's all, Master Giles. Most broken limbs invite infection, after which there's no choice but the table."

"You would be strapped down," Jarvis said quietly, "flaps cut on either side of your knee, the ligamentum patella cut through, the muscles then sawn and the condyles tied off to stop the bleeding. Whatever you'd been given to dull your senses, laudanum or the like, your only true escape would be to faint from the intolerable pain. If not—well, the amputation of a limb can take six or seven minutes, more if the patient tears free."

Afterward, outside the room, James Mabbott had asked his assistant, "Why so descriptive, Master Jarvis? You've left your brother as pale as paper."

"So I have," Jarvis nodded, "though I believe it's for the best. Until Brook Wintersill and his henchmen—until the one called Venn laid about him with his club, Giles was the most energetic of us Cannaways. Robbed of that, there's a chance he'll grow sullen and embittered. I sought to show him that he *is* in fact fortunate to be spared the losing of his leg. He's pale as paper now, I agree. But later, when he thinks on it, he'll realise how much worse things might have been." He nodded again, this time to himself, and said, "If I know Giles, he'll find an answer to those questions. We shall yet see him on a ladder and a carriage bench and out there walking the downs."

"Give as much thought to your other patients," Mabbott

murmured dryly, "and even I might trust myself to you when I'm ill."

※

Jarred by the movement of his horse on the spring-dry track, Brydd Cannaway felt a flare of pain in his shoulder, the physical hurt reminding him of others he'd failed to defend. . . .

Lewis Plant—the young man's face bearing traces of the lashing he'd received from the Bellringers and the scratches of the beggarlike thorns. Still afflicted by bouts of dizziness, he was nevertheless back working in the yard. There, a few days ago, Brydd had asked him where he'd found Step Cotter on the night he had ridden for help. Intentionally vague, Lewis had replied, "In Kennett village, not far from the river," then hurried on with talk of repair work to a cart. His sigh of relief went unnoticed. Step Cotter's secret was safe.

The apprentice spent his evenings with Giles, straddling a rail-back chair beside the patient's bed. The two of them schemed of what they'd do to Brook and Venn and Eldon and Lucas, or shared their faulty knowledge of Somerset lasses, pretty young Wiltshire girls. From time to time Giles would sink back, his teeth clenched against the pain of his ruined knee. Whenever that happened, Lewis Plant would launch into some farfetched story of his adventures on the road from Taunton, as often as not drawing a grin from Giles. He was a welcome companion, very much now a part of the Cannaway family.

Brydd's thoughts turned for the hundredth time to Elizabeth and Charlotte, to the deep core of his failure. Elizabeth, crouched on the floor, the tiles smeared with blood and littered with fragments of the dishes shaken from the dresser, strips of her petticoats torn in readiness. His wife Elizabeth, brought that night to her knees.

And Charlotte—what now of Charlotte? Reclaimed by force, Faxforge proving as insubstantial a refuge as a tent.

What special treatment had Brook meted out to Charlotte? And what, if anything, could be done to prise her free?

I should not have gone out there with the pistol buried in my pocket. I should not have let Venn get so close. I should not—dear God, I should not have been so trusting, so ignorant, so slow.

As if in punishment for that, Brydd jabbed inward with his boot heels and drummed along the valley road to Marlborough.

*

That same morning Charlotte Wintersill tested the ground. Dressed in high-laced boots, flared skirt and jacket, frilled cravat and scarlet, feather-trimmed tricorn, she left the Hall and made her way down to the lake. Her course was apparently aimless; around the edge of the water, past the willows that dipped along the western bank, then southward among the trees.

A half mile of woodland and she'd reach the wall of the estate.

Brook's talk of a planned invasion by Brydd, Step, Sam Gilmore and others had done more than just alarm her. Not knowing it was a lie, a cover for his own protection, Charlotte had imagined what would happen. The would-be rescuers shot down by her husband's hired keepers, Brook claiming the slaughter as an act of self-defence.

The rescue, trespass, invasion, whatever it was, must be avoided. And it could be, Charlotte accepted, if she herself had already fled from the Hall. Had she known the truth, her courage might have weakened, the irony being that Brook had fed her the lie. It was this—his invented story of wild dogs from the valley—that stiffened her resolve. She'd escape, and as soon as possible. Today would do nicely. And with only a red brick wall to climb . . .

She continued unhurried among the trees. Then a man came toward her, a brace of pistols in his belt. His sleeveless leather jerkin was stained and patched over, sweat on the stubble of his face.

"Mis' Wintersill? Thought it was you. Saw you in the grounds the other day. Got lost, is that it? Easy enough to do, I'll own. But don't you worry, Mis' Wintersill, I'll guide you back, I've quite a knowledge of—"

"You are one of my husband's hired men, are you not?"

"One of his keepers, that's the term." He smiled at her, pleased that she'd been corrected. His tone could well have been in mimicry of Venn's, and Charlotte wondered if Brook had sent to London for his swarthy private army. Victor Venn would know where dross like this could be found.

"Well," she told him, "I am neither lost nor in need of a guide. I too have quite a knowledge of these grounds." She started forward, as though pursuing her aimless stroll.

Aware of the risk, she was nevertheless startled when the man barred her path, his fingers on her jacket. "You *are* lost," he measured, "and I'm here to guide you home."

"Keep your hands to yourself, sir! I shall walk where I please, and it's none of your affair where I go."

"Not unless you're lost, Mis' Wintersill. And you *are*. And you *will* be guided home." Again happy to correct her, he pressed the full imprint of his palm against her jacket, leaving her no choice but to retreat.

Escape, Charlotte realised, would be more than just a walk to the wall.

※

The men were separated by a desk and a difference of views. The desk seemed ready to collapse beneath piles of print and leather, pieces of bone—animal? human?—other substantial towers of paper and, as callers at the castles, quill pens and ink-stands, boxes and jars, trays and containers, two glasses of Spanish sherry. Inexplicably, there was also a lady's striped stocking, a six-pound weight—brass by the look of it—a riding crop and an ornate pocket watch showing the hour, the day and, if Brydd's glance was accurate, the Week When the World Would End. So far as he could tell the week was in August, the year 1810.

That, anyway, was something of a relief.

But the rest of it, the things he and James Mabbott were discussing, brought Brydd Cannaway no comfort at all. And now James was leaning forward between his unsteady towers of knowledge, a finger stiff in admonition, his normally gentle voice made harsher for the purpose.

"You say it's what you have in mind, and I'd oblige you with my views? Well, my dear friend, I'll tell you what I have in mind, though it won't oblige you at all. You're a damn fool, Brydd, and so's your idea, the damnedest damn fool idea I ever heard! Now then. Shall you jump up and leave? If not, I warn you, there's more reproach to come."

"You don't see me stirring," Brydd told him. "Finish with your damns and damnedests, then say why you think I'm wrong."

"Very well. So I will. And you're sensible to listen." He stopped to clutch at a pile of his books, brought the tower vertical, then again leaned forward, his finger pointing or tapping or fanning the odd-scented air. Only a doctor, Brydd thought, could suffer this mixture of smells. There's herbs here, and acids, perfumes and unguents and—

"Are you listening, or not?"

"Yes, James, I'm listening. Now for God's sake tell me why I'm wrong."

"Because you'll not succeed, that's why. You'll ride up there —isn't that your plan?—and you imagine you'll get yourself through the gate and along the drive and into the Hall. And then what? Find Wintersill unarmed, happy to take the beating you'll give him, willing to surrender his wife? No, Brydd, no, that is *not* how it will be. But rather this—that you'll be stopped at the gate itself—"

"There's other ways in."

"Very well, there's other ways in and you'll find them. And after that? You'll be shot as an intruder by Venn or Wintersill, or arrested and held for the magistrates. And think of the charges, *list* them, Brydd, the things your fine young son-in-law will delight to level against you. Common assault, trespass and forcing an entry; malicious intent to wound, malicious damage, armed robbery, attempted murder, interference with a marriage. Write it out for yourself, my dear Brydd. Choose from any lawbook you can find. Don't you see? Don't you *see?* The weight of the gentry will swing behind every parchment power of the law! You *cannot* intrude on Brook Wintersill's marriage. It is *not* your affair. And another thing—no, wait. I've talked myself dry. I must have a sip of sherry."

The force of James Mabbott's outburst surprised Brydd Cannaway, and he respected his friend's concern. There was sense in what he said. So he waited, as the doctor had asked, and reached for his own stemmed glass.

"Another thing, yes. Once the magistrates have done with you, you'll be hanged, if Wintersill gets his way. And he will, be sure of that. He'll have the trial held in Swindon, Venn swearing you went in with a fowling piece or pistols, aiming at his master, missing by a hair's breadth. You'll be hanged, and Charlotte's torment made worse. But beyond all that you'll lose Faxforge, for the county will appropriate your ownings as a felon, and how will that serve Elizabeth or Giles or Hester, or the men you employ? You'll not be there to see them, my dear friend, though would you wish them turned out on the road?"

There was silence then, the glasses no longer lifted, the men gazing at each other across the desk. Finally Brydd said, "I *am* obliged for your views, James," and Mabbott retorted, "Yes, though will you accept them?" Brydd shrugged, since all the while it had been his intention to even the score with Brook Wintersill and rescue his daughter. And the hell with what it might cost.

✳

Having escorted Charlotte to within sight of the Hall, the keeper had resumed his patrol among the trees. He'd report

the incident to Victor Venn, claiming that Mis' Wintersill
had seemed intent on reaching the wall. There might be a
bonus in it: a coin or a jar of gin.

Furious and humiliated, Charlotte began a slow, unchal-
lenged circuit of the lake. More than ever now she believed her
husband's talk of a planned invasion, realising that his hired
louts—how many of them were there? ten? a dozen?—served
as both guards and gaolers.

She must escape, and quickly. But first she must think the
thing through.

She'd need help, someone to act as a decoy perhaps, though
how could anyone clear the grounds of Brook's men, and in
whom could she confide?

The brutish, coarse-grained Venn? The thought was enough
to make her shudder. And yet . . . Might he not be bribed? A
handsome reward promised him if he enabled her to escape,
the promise written out and signed by Charlotte, the reward to
be paid at some agreed meeting place by her father. Surely, if
the amount was high enough—

But Venn would want the money first, then pocket it before
running to alert her husband. The keeper would agree to anything, one hand on a prayer book, the other on a Bible. So, no,
she would not confide in Keeper Victor Venn.

There were some among the hired louts who might be
approached, though they would also demand payment in advance, and it would take too long to woo them. And, since
they seemed to model themselves so carefully on Venn, there
was every chance they'd turn her in, cry loyalty and hope to be
rewarded by Master Brook. So, no, she would not take her troubles to the gaolers.

Nor would she call on the help of Mistress Dench. It was
not because she mistrusted the woman, but because the cook-
cum-housekeeper was the sole guardian of the innocent, backward Fern. To involve Mistress Dench in her plans would be
to place both the woman and the girl in jeopardy. So, again, reluctantly, no.

She stopped for a time among the willows, the sunlight dappling her clothes, brilliant shards reflected on the water. It was a place where a husband and wife might sit, the edge of their problems brushed smooth by the stirring of the leaves, their murmured dreams encouraged, their disappointments softened amid the shelter of the trees. It was, at the same time, a cheering and compassionate place.

She wondered how often Sir Henry and his wife had lingered here. Had Lady Wintersill set her easel at the lakeside, painting the view across the water, the ground that sloped gently upward to the Hall?

Charlotte gazed at the building and in doing so saw one of the hired keepers staring at her from the crest of the grassy slope. She turned abruptly, the reverie shattered, and continued her solitary walk around the lake.

She must escape, and quickly; that much was decided. But not with the help of Venn or her husband's hired louts; not if it meant involving Mistress Dench or the simple-minded Fern. So who else could she turn to? Who else dare she count on? Who else *was* there but the man who had already risked Brook's wrath by driving her the ten miles south to Faxforge? Might he be the one to help her, she wondered, the elderly Ephram Toll?

She had often spent time with him in the stables, her knowledge of horses not much less than his, her knowledge of vehicles as good and sometimes better. And she had never addressed him as merely a servant, she the mistress, he the slow-boned coachman.

Even so, she thought, I'd do well to go carefully. Both for Ephram's sake and mine.

ELEVEN

She waited until the coachman was alone, then made her way to the stables. Earlier, she had shut herself in her room, crossed to a wardrobe and lifted from it a single, long-tongued shoe. Grasping the shoe in one hand, she had wrenched at the tongue, tearing the stitches from the leather.

Charlotte carried the shoe with her as she went to see Ephram Toll. It was part of his job as coachman to repair the saddlery and bridles, the straps and trimmings of the gigs. If Brook or Venn intercepted Charlotte, demanding to know what she was doing in the stables, she could show them the broken stitches and say she was calling on Master Toll to mend the shoe. They might doubt her story but could not disprove it—unless, of course, Ephram chose to betray her.

Interrupted in his polishing of brass and trace rings, the old man nodded as Charlotte joined him near the tack room. Handing him the shoe, she said, "The stitching has come away, Master Ephram. Might you find the time to sew it?"

"Leave it on the bench there, Mis' Win'sill. I'll get around to it afore long." He continued polishing, then muttered as though to himself, "Bad business that, down at Faxforge. Worthy of better treatment, Master Cannaway and his folk."

Her voice as quiet as his, Charlotte said, "I've a mind to take out a trap, Master Ephram. Not now, but sometime soon."

"Wouldn't advise it," he droned, frowning with concentration as he worked. "Master Win'sill's made a rule 'gainst hitchin' up runners. Says no one's allowed to ride out of 'ere, without they first gets permission from 'im. I don't suppose you—"

"No," she told him, "I've neither gained nor sought his permission."

Ephram grunted, then worked on in silence for a while, the cloth bringing a lustre to the brass. Charlotte felt her hopes drain away. She could not blame Ephram Toll for his unwillingness to help her. Why should he, when by doing so he'd risk his livelihood? And, with Brook and Venn against him, maybe his life.

She was turning to leave when the coachman growled, "'Course, I'm allowed to ride out of 'ere, takin' messages an' suchlike. Which is why I keep a mount saddled in the back." He glanced at the rear of the stables, then added, "Just imagine, if a thief got in, say at dusk, an' me away at old Sir Henry's palace, puffin' as I like to on a pipe.

"Worse than that, think what'd 'appen if I was to fall asleep there, an' the palace was to catch alight accidental. There'd be keepers runnin' to the lake with buckets, Master Venn shoutin' his blasted head off—the best time of all, I'd say, for a thief to take old Muster from the stables and ride 'im away.

"Not that he'd get past the gatehouse, what with the other keepers on duty there, night and day. Still, I suppose if he knew which horse to steal, he'd also know there's bricks missing in the southeast corner of the wall." He shook his head as if appalled by the picture. "Me, scramblin' awake to find the Moorish Palace all in flames. The lake 'alf emptied of water.

An' dear old Muster ridden away an' gone. Lord in 'is raiment, that *would* be a time to remember."

"I think," Charlotte measured, "my husband would very likely kill you."

"So he would," Ephram nodded, "unless Venn 'ad killed me first."

"If, as you say, the palace were ever to catch fire, you know you could always find a home at Faxforge. You would be of great value to the yard, Master Ephram. My father would have a special cause to treat you well."

"Can't see why," the man told her. "All I've done is refuse to hitch you up a trap." But the stiff half bow he made was acknowledgement enough. "Anyway," he continued, "I believe I'd see my time out in Lincoln. I've a sister there. Terrible house-proud woman she is. No chance of enjoyin' a pipe, 'less it be in a tavern." He gazed in the direction of the yard, again muttering in an undertone. "You come 'ere an' see me one evenin', Mis' Win'sill. Like as not you'll find me leavin' for the palace. The times I like special are when there's clouds across the moon."

*

Excited by what Ephram had told her—what he had *not* directly told her—Charlotte pretended obedience to her husband, and all the while prayed for bad weather.

Her eighteenth birthday came and was forgotten. She stayed clear of the trees that fringed the lawn, allowing the keepers to see her near the lakeside, nodding at them as they trod their prearranged paths. She hated each and all of them, yet smiled when they passed, earning nothing more than a blank, unyielding stare.

If I was to spit at them and run, she thought, they would see it as their duty to plant a pistol ball in my back. Dear God, but I hope my father stays away from this place. And that the clouds Ephram spoke of close in.

A few days later Brook beckoned his wife aside. "Lucas and

Eldon are coming tomorrow, and with a fresh set of friends. You will be at the door to greet them, and stay by for as long as is needed."

"You make no mention of the Taylor brothers, Theo and Simeon. Surely you've invited them again, in the hopes of recouping what you lost."

"As it happens, I lost little," Brook lied, "though you, I think, miss the bob-and-bow of their company."

"And Peter Seal?"

"He's still in Paris."

"And Markis Mayman?"

Brook approached her then, his face suffused with anger. "You are here," he thrust, "to welcome the guests I invite. It is not your job to ask after fat and frightened creatures such as Markis. He has gone, and good riddance; a squeamish fellow at the best of times—"

"Because he thought ill of you for attacking my family like —what was it you said—like maddened dogs? He was happy enough at Christmas, your fat and frightened companion. Yet now you claim you're well rid of him, disturbed perhaps to find a vestige of decency in his blood? You should not exclude him so fast, Master Brook. You should instead crouch at his feet and learn."

Charlotte's taunts cost her dear. She was struck by his fleshy palm, driven against the banisters, roared at as she climbed the stairs to her room. She heard Brook's voice booming within the plaster shell of the roof. "You *will* be here to greet them, else I'll see you locked away until you starve! Damn your insolence! You'll be where it suits me, upstairs or down! And the worse for you if you're not at the door tomorrow, offering a welcome to my guests! Do you hear me, Charlotte? Do you hear me, you—"

The heavy oak door muffled his shouts. Charlotte moved to the window, searching for the moon, then around it to find the nearest fringes of cloud. If only God's lantern could be shielded . . . the light hidden by the running of His flock . . .

But the springtime sky remained clear, the clouds shepherded away.

So Charlotte Wintersill turned and reached for her cotton shift, aware that tomorrow she would again come face to face with the shrilling Eldon Sith, the brick-hard Lucas Ripnall. And with their friends. And with the keepers. And with Victor Venn and her husband, both of whom took such delight in seeing the mistress brought to misery, a Cannaway held in contempt.

✳

Next morning the sky was a brilliant blue, nailed like cloth to the heavens.   •

Brook's guests arrived in the afternoon, some with the same heavy shoulders as Lucas Ripnall, others as mincing as the neatly tailored Sith. Charlotte was there to meet them, offering her hand for their rough or insipid kisses, laughing where a smile would have done. She listened attentively to their talk of shares and politics and profits, nodding at them to continue; even, from time to time, topping their glasses.

Her performance was convincing. She remained with the guests until Brook called them to the card table, then quietly left the hall.

With the hiring of the extra keepers, Victor Venn had moved from his woodland cottage and was now quartered in a room below the main stairs of the house. He had taken on the dual role of bodyguard and butler, though his hands were better suited to the hefting of a cudgel than the handing around of drink. Nevertheless, he positioned himself near the table, bottles of port and brandy at his elbow, a brace of pistols in his belt.

Meanwhile, upstairs, Charlotte stood by the south-facing window, watching the sky grow ragged as clouds scudded in from the west. Soon, she thought, please God, soon.

She turned to glance at a small cord-wound clock, one of the few objects she admired within the sparsely furnished Hall. Below the bevelled window of the timepiece were engraved the initials J.L.W. and the date 1692. She guessed the clock to have been the property of Lady Wintersill, the date commemorating the year of her marriage to Sir Henry.

The arrow-point hands registered seventeen minutes past seven. Clouds continued to darken the May sky.

She knew now was the moment she'd been waiting for.

❋

She knew where she would go, where she'd stay tonight, where she hoped to be tomorrow. Among the first things she must do was send warning to Faxforge. Brook would expect her to flee there, and this time he'd come after her in force.

She was clutched by a sudden spasm of fear. Not only for herself but for those her escape would put at risk. Oh, God, what right have I to involve them? What real concern is it to others if a husband is deserted by his wife?

But there was more than that to it of course, and she recognised that those who helped her would do so willingly. She was not merely a wife fleeing from her husband. She was the woman they'd known as Charlotte Cannaway, a member of the close-knit Kennett Vale. She'd been the prettiest and most spirited girl in the district, and it did indeed concern them that Brook Wintersill thought her no more than a hedgerow bitch. Who was *he* to ride roughshod into Faxforge, leaving Brydd and Giles sprawled bleeding on the floor?

The spasm passed. She took a cloak and plain grey tricorn from her wardrobe. Then, reluctantly leaving the cord-wound clock on its shelf, she eased the door open and looked down across the entranceway to the hall.

She heard Lucas and her husband roaring in disagreement over the cards. Good, she thought, it'll hold the attention of the others. But it won't last long. If I'm to go, *I must go now!*

Spurred by the fear that Keeper Venn might emerge, perhaps on his way to the cellars, Charlotte hurried along the gallery. She kept close to the wall, avoiding the boards that had lifted and would creak. She carried her cloak, the tricorn hidden under its folds. If caught she would say the clothes were a gift for the servant girl—"Fern has eyed them with longing for some time." But no one saw her, and she hastened her way downstairs.

A dozen steps from the entranceway and she heard Eldon Sith say, "I must needs get some air in me chest. I'm more delicate than some of you. Count me out for the next hand, Brooksy, whilst I cough out this smoke in the garden."

Charlotte whirled toward the shadowed upper stairs. She knew she could get there in time, believed she'd be unseen if she crouched beneath the portraits, as still and silent as the figures they portrayed.

But to hunch like a thief from Eldon? To squirm shrinking into the darkness for fear I'll be discovered by Master Sith? Oh no. Not when there's an instant left, and the chance to elude him forever!

She dashed to the foot of the flight, snatching at the lowest pillar of the rail. Her hand slipped as she turned beside the staircase. Eldon came coughing from the hall. And then, as his own thin shadow flickered across the entranceway, Charlotte's vanished in the gloom beside the stairs.

An instant later and she was out through a side door of the building. The cloak swirled as she settled it around her shoulders, the tricorn tipped by the wind. She glanced in the direction of the arch, then at the rear wall of the yard. None of the keepers was about, thank God, though she had seen them before, using the yard as a short cut between their dormitory and the grounds.

A fresh spasm of fear clawed at her, leaving her mouth as dry as salted sand. But she knew she had come too far to go back now. If she failed in this she would never again find the strength, for with every day that passed she grew weaker,

Brook draining her, a leech that engorged itself on blood. Now was the moment. Now or never.

She crossed the open yard and entered the stables.

✳

Midway along, the light of an overhead lantern turned the air to a thin yellow mist.

Charlotte called softly, "Master Ephram, are you about?" She heard movement beyond the lamplight and the old man approached her, a currycomb in his hand. "I likes to keep Muster groomed," he told her, "afore I goes off for a pipe."

"He's a fine horse, Master Ephram."

"There's better and there's worse." He shrugged. Squinting past her, he asked, "Was there anythin' special you wanted of me, Mis' Win'sill, or was you just enjoyin' a stroll?"

"Just a stroll. Yes. Though the sky's clouding over."

"Aye, so it is. Best not go too far then, on foot." He patted the pockets of his coat, making sure he had pipe and tinderbox and pouch. "Well now," he said, "if there's nothin' you need of me I'll be off to sit quiet in the palace. I just 'ope as I don't fall asleep, that's all." He tossed the currycomb on a bench, then made his slow, stooped way toward the yard.

He will do it, Charlotte thought. He has told me all I need to know. And now, God protect that excellent old man, he will play the part he has chosen.

✳

In the hall they were playing their ninth hand of Wheat. Four had been won by a cheerful Brook Wintersill, two by Lucas, the rest by Brook's new-found friends. The atmosphere was noisy, the insults suitably coarse. Keeper Venn's thick fingers fumbled with bottles and glasses, the floor sticky with slopped-over drink. The men Eldon Sith had brought along shrilled as he took the ninth hand. Lucas Ripnall led his own friends in a derisive chorus. "Stop twittering your victory, blast you! Well, who's to pass out the cards?"

"Keep the thing running!"

"I've won the ninth and I'll win the nine to come!"

"Pox get you!"

"It got him years ago!"

"He's been sulphured twice, don't you know!"

Brook slumped at ease, revelling in the scene. *This was more like it! This was more the way of it by a damnsight!*

He told Venn to prepare a new pack, then watched as the keeper slit the soft leather case that held the cards. Expensive cards, sealed under supervision by Dowlers of Piccadilly. But only the best was good enough tonight. Only the best for my friends.

"There we are, Master Brook, sir. Neat as can be. An' a nice brimming glass, 'ow's that?"

The game stormed on.

* * *

Ephram emerged from among the sagging towers, the twisted minarets. The colours had long since faded and flaked, the inner staircase fallen away, the tiles vanished beneath the years of grass and weeds.

In the base of one of the towers he had left the tapped-out contents of his pipe, the ashes glowing as the west wind edged between the boards.

He had already murmured his apologies to the ghosts of Sir Henry and his wife. Needless apologies, perhaps, since they more than anyone would accept what he was doing, and why it had to be done.

Awaiting his moment, a clouding of the light, the coachman hurried across the open ground and into the trees. Even as he did so the wind puffed the glowing flakes against the debris of wood and straw.

* * *

There were, at any one time, six or seven keepers in the grounds. Two men kept watch near the gatehouse, their patrols extending along the eastern boundary and some way back along the drive. The others formed a protective circle around the Hall, the lake, the derelict Moorish Palace. Their route was marked by lanterns, though no one could say precisely where the men were stationed: within arm's stretch of one of the lamps, or midway between them, silent and alert.

And then, as the darkness closed in, the straw in the tower was fanned by the wind and crackled alive into flames. A small enough fire at first, but growing in strength and igniting the wood; chips and twigs and the remnants of a nest. Then a splinter of the wall itself, the end of a board, the flames funnelled up through the high, tinder-dry tower. The structure seemed almost to explode with the draught.

It roared for attention, splashed colour on the grass, sent curved planks springing to the ground. Flames swept along the wall walk, racing to capture a second tower, a leaning minaret. The sound and stain spread wider, not just calling for attention but demanding it!

Ill-disciplined men who'd been lured to the Hall by the promise of easy money, several of the keepers ran from cover. They knew nothing of the Moorish Palace, but supposed it to be of value to Brook Wintersill. So they swerved in their running to warn Venn or the master that the odd-looking building in the grounds—the castle, or whatever it was—was alight.

Converging on the wide main steps, two of them slammed shoulders in an effort to be first with the news. There might be a bonus in it, why not, their quick-made report worth a shilling, a barrel of ale. That other guard, he'd got something for reporting how he'd caught Mistress Wintersill near the wall. *So shove aside, blast you!*

They were met by Venn, who snapped at them to get buckets from the stables.

❋

Charlotte heard the stamp of their boot heels on the drive. It had not occurred to her that the men would come here, and she ran back between the stalls, then through to the tack room at the rear. Feeling her way blindly in the darkness, she moved among the web of bridles and traces, softly chinking harnesses, straps that swung as she disturbed them. She heard one of the men growl, "Where's the store 'ere? They must 'ave a proper bloody store."

She reached a corner of the tack room, turned and waited. She knew she was partly concealed, her presence unsuspected, though if the men came in with lanterns—

"These'll do." The clatter of wooden buckets, then the pounding of footsteps as the keepers ran from the stables.

Charlotte reached forward to brush her way back through the web.

The half-open door of the tack room was kicked wide and Victor Venn said, "I do 'ope as you're not crouched in there, else I'll see you suffer, so I will. But you wouldn't be, would you? You'd not dare to, would you? You'd not be be'ind them saddles, now, would you, else I'd 'ear you squeakin' with fright.

"Even so, I'll be back with a lantern when I've done, and we'll talk about 'ow that building out there got itself set on fire. What say you to that, eh—my miserable Master Toll?"

He stood listening for a moment, Charlotte less than a dozen feet from him, her lips pressed tight, her heart thudding with the shock of what he'd said. Then he swung round and strode off through the stables. There'd be time enough later for that talk with Ephram Toll. Unless of course the old fool was trapped in the palace.

Charlotte waited, ashamed to find herself quivering uncontrollably. Dear God, but until he said—until he named Ephram I believed he was speaking to me. Another threat, a step beyond the doorway and I'd have whimpered my presence like a child. . . .

The temptation now was to cross the yard and hurry upstairs to her room. She could then call from the south-facing window, or down from the landing, curious as to the glow beyond the lake. Someone would tell her the palace was alight and—

What? Pretend I'm not part of it? Let Ephram's efforts go for nothing? Let Venn continue smirking, Brook doing all the things he— Oh no. Not when there's a saddled horse in its stall, the one that might carry me ten miles distant before I could ever rein in.

Oh no, Mistress Wintersill; no, Charlotte Cannaway; no, my girl, there'll be no more backing away. You'll make your own efforts now and succeed. You have to succeed. You cannot afford to fail.

She brushed aside the bridles and halters and crept to the high, arched entrance of the stables. The yard was deserted. She hurried back inside.

A tug at the reins and the slipknot came free. Then Charlotte was in the saddle and riding the horse out and across the drive and south by east, her ears straining for sounds of alarm. It would only need someone to emerge from the Hall; one of the keepers to come running from the gate; a keen-sighted man to turn his back on the fire. She crouched low and murmured, "Yes, that's the spirit, Muster, go quiet and we can do it. Look there, do you see? Once we're among the trees we'll be—"

"You! Rider! Whoa up!" A shape moved ahead of her. The voice was hard and insistent, though Charlotte sensed that the challenge might have been louder. The man seemed unwilling to shout out his orders, for fear perhaps that the rider was Brook or Venn. So Charlotte said nothing, judged the man's position, then urged the horse to a gallop. There was a solid thud as the keeper was knocked aside. His pistol was triggered, the sound of it muffled by the undergrowth.

And then she was clear, the man left groaning, the wall of the estate looming up, and over to the left the gap where the shallow red bricks had fallen away.

Charlotte Wintersill—Charlotte Cannaway as she much preferred to be—set her mount at the easy hurdle. And with no one to stop her it was safe to call out, her words garbled in the sheer exhilaration of escape.

Not that by gaining her freedom from the grounds could she yet account herself free. The injured guard might even now be heaving himself to his feet, gasping for breath, determined to raise the alarm. And the moment he did so, Brook and Venn, the cronies and keepers would organize their pursuit. The prisoner was clear of the prison, though her flight had scarcely begun.

TWELVE

The destruction of the Moorish Palace meant nothing to Brook, except as a damned inconvenience, a break in his luck at cards. He was far and away the best winner to date, richer by a thousand guineas. But now this; his friends deserting the table, pouring from the house as though the fire was in place of fireworks.

He sighed with resignation and watched the keepers haul water from the lake. Ah well, a few more buckets and the flames'll be doused and we can then go back to the game. I must ask Venn what caused it, though frankly I'm glad to be rid of the thing, my father's lovelorn folly.

One of the onlookers, a friend of Eldon's, asked what it had been—"I mean, what did it represent?"

"Simple, my dear fellow. It represented the squandering of good money for the purchase of a lady's smile. It was something my father had built, so his wife could daub away to her heart's content. It seems fitting the building's done with, since I already sold off—"

"Someone's comin' across." The voice was Venn's, his long arm extended, a thick-knuckled finger pointing toward the trees. Brook glanced around to see one of the keepers staggering forward, shouting words torn away by the wind.

Lucas and Eldon and the others drew close, the men surrounding the keeper as he reached them. They heard him gasp, "There's a rider's charged me down, Master Wintersill! I've a broken bone in me chest, sir, I can feel it!" He hunched over, then sank to his knees, battered anew by their questions.

"Could you recognise the rider?"

"No, 'e was on me afore—"

"Well, was he entering the grounds or—"

"No, sir, 'e was bound for that gap in—"

"Alone? Was he alone?"

"I've a bone snapped inside me, sir! I can feel it!"

"*Was he alone?*"

"Maybe 'e was. Yes. I didn't see no others. Slim, from the glimpse I got of 'im. Youngish-looking. God, Master Wintersill, this chest bone's loose inside me!"

Leaning forward to watch and listen, Eldon Sith said, "Clear as glass what's happened, Brooksy. Someone from the Kennett Vale's got in here, fired the palace as a decoy, then charged out to summon the rest. There's an invasion been launched, that's the way of it! An invasion coming whilst we're all out here, lit and in the open! It's their plan to catch us defenceless, Brooksy! Come on, sir! All of you! Let's get back to the house and prime up!" Obedient to his own advice, he fled in the direction of the Hall. The friends he had brought fled with him, leaving Brook and Venn, Lucas and his companions peering with suspicion at the trees.

"I see it different," Venn growled. "It's that blasted Toll what set the fire, and 'im as run down the keeper. Any real invasion and they'd 'ave come at us by now. It's Toll's doing, all of this, though what he thinks to gain by it—"

"Oh, you blind and bloody fools!"

"Master Brook? I don't see as 'ow you've cause to—"

"Don't you?" Brook snarled. "Don't you, Keeper? Don't any of you see what's happened or hear what was said, what this man here's just told us? Slim and youngish; don't you see beyond the talk of invasion or your private dislikes of Toll? Blind and bloody fools the lot of you!" Then he ran toward the Hall and up the staircase and along the gallery to the corner room—empty as he knew it would be, *as I should have suspected when first I was called from the table.*

✳

The keepers who had been fighting the fire were summoned back to the Hall.

Brook's friends were busy in the long, panelled room, loading and priming their weapons.

The other hired guards—the off-duty shift—came yawning from their quarters in the attic.

A few moments later there were eighteen men armed and milling in the entranceway. Venn reported that a search of the outbuildings had failed to unearth Ephram Toll.

"Christ, man," Brook shouted, "he's of no concern to me now! He's part of it, and I'll kill him for his part, but not until my wife's back here to see it! That'll be her special reward, watching as I deal with Toll. Now get your men mounted. We've a ten-mile ride ahead of us. And this time . . ."

"Master Brook?"

". . . Yes, this time we'll teach the Cannaways the real meaning of invasion." He turned to Lucas and Eldon. "Are you and your friends in the mood for this? A ride and a little rough sport?"

Their roars of approval filled the entranceway, then the stables, then flew above them like pennants as they drummed toward the gatehouse.

✳

Brydd and Elizabeth sat silent in the kitchen at Faxforge. Several days had elapsed since Brydd sought the advice of his friend James Mabbott in Marlborough.

In that time the master of the coachyard had declared to his wife his intention to visit the Hall. He had also told her what Mabbott had said—how he, Brydd, would be shot if he failed and hanged if he succeeded. Then, as he'd known, Elizabeth had respected him for his honesty, sided with Mabbott and told her husband he was indeed the damnedest of damn fools.

Echoing the doctor, she'd pleaded with him to see sense and to think of his children. Not once had she spoken of what might happen to her—turned out on the road—though she'd asked what the others would do. "An answer here and now, my dear Brydd; tell me, what of the future of Faxforge?"

He'd offered no answer then, and he'd none to offer now. He weighed and reweighed the problem, brooding on it, made sleepless by it, yet knowing in himself what he must do.

For the moment, however, he kept silent, seated across from Elizabeth, yet almost ready now to tell her that their life together and the lives of others were outbalanced by his own sense of failure. And his need, his consuming need, to level the scales.

✳

No one knew it, but the burly landlord of the "Blazing Rag" slept in a nightcap trimmed with pale grey fur. It had been made for him by a woman who'd presented it to him there in his room; if the truth be told, in his bed. She had insisted he wear it. "Promise me, Sam." "Very well, if it'll please you." "That's no promise! I want your promise!" "I've said I will! Yes! I promise!" "And you'll dream of me? You will, Sam, won't you, you'll wear it and dream of me?"

Three days later the woman had left with a passing tinker bound for London.

Sam Gilmore still wore the nightcap—not that he wished to dream of the frivolous woman but because he'd grown used to wearing it and, well, yes, it was comfortable and warm.

If ever he was awoken in the night, he tore it from his head. In the daytime he kept it hidden under his pillow. Every man, he told himself, is allowed a weakness, though I'll murder anyone as catches me in me cap.

And now, with the sound of tapping on the outside door, he sat up in bed, concealed the cap and only then struck sparks to a lantern.

It was not the dull, insistent pounding of a drunkard, come to plead for more ale.

Nor was it the uncertain knock of a traveller, the brisk tattoo of a magistrate, the imperious rap of an army man, demanding bed and board for himself and a dozen fusiliers.

This was the light yet urgent sound of a woman, the door latch rattled in support of her stinging knuckles. Only women, it seemed to Sam, had the sense to rattle the latch.

He slung his greatcoat around his shoulders, held his lantern ahead of him and was met on the landing by his potboy, John Whitten. A reliable young man, John Whitten. For one thing, he could stop a fight in mid-swing. Employing his own methods, he would simply step around the bar, amble across to the bloodied and fisting protagonists, then insert himself between them, his skinny hands raised, palms outward, as though to protect his ears. "This," he would tell them, looking straight ahead, "is the finest tavern between Bristol and London, and known to be so by all as travel the road. There are places in Marlborough you can go to for a fight. There's places in Chipp'nam, so I've heard, as'll lend you staves to fight with. But any more of your fisticuffs, gen'lemen, and I'll have to see you out!" Then he'd indicate the door, his finger no thicker than a chalk stick, and turn to face the pugilists.

Heavy-set, hard-breathing men, they'd gape at the twiglike John Whitten. Then—and it had never yet failed—they'd curse or laugh and reach to shake his hands. They'd tell him how close he'd come to being murdered, slaughtered, crushed or maimed for life. They'd assure him he was mad, a fellow with a seeking for pain, a youngster who yearned to be killed. But he certainly had some spine, some bottom, some damn good gravel in his blood. And they'd grant him the "Rag" was the best place for miles. He'd no need to show them the door again; they'd done with fighting; they'd be over there in the corner if he cared to bring them some ale. . . .

Alerted by the noise downstairs, John Whitten said, "Shall I see who it is, Master Gilmore? We 'ad those 'ighwaymen come by, you remember that, last year?"

"I remember," Sam smiled, shaking his head as he did so. "And you were first down to meet them, and told them the house was closed for the night, then shut the door in their face. But you get back to bed if you will. I'll give you a shout if you're needed."

The potboy said, "Be sure you do, Master Gilmore. It's good to get the trade, an' that, but us fellows is entitled to our sleep."

John Whitten was fifteen years old, five feet in height, and the weight of a grain sack from which some of the grain had spilled out.

＊

No sooner had the bolts been slipped than Charlotte edged inside. "God bless you, Sam. Now listen to me. I've escaped from Wintersill Hall. For good and ever. It has to be. But, Sam—yes, I'm shivering, I'm frightened, though listen—they'll know I've gone by now and they'll be coming in pursuit. Sixteen of them, twenty, God knows the number. And Brook, he'll believe I've ridden on to Faxforge. But I can't—you see that, don't you, Sam?—you see why I dare not go there. If I do —if I'm there when Brook and his cronies— If he finds me there he'll have every right to reclaim me. So please, my dear Sam, let me stay here the night and I'll take the dawn stage to Bristol."

"Aye, Mistress Charlotte, if that's what—"

"But more than that, you must raise some help for Faxforge! They're coming after me, Master Gilmore, my husband and his friends and all the men they've— Oh, Sam, I'm shaking fit to break! Please God, Sam, help my family!"

The courage that had brought her this far now failed. She'd carried through her conspiracy with Ephram Toll. She'd kept silent in the face of Venn's unwitting inquisition in the tack room. She'd charged down the guard and escaped from the grounds and covered eight of the ten miles to Faxforge, all of them with the moonlight scarred by clouds. And she'd ridden with her eyes wide in expectation of an ambush, her ears strained for the drumming of pursuit. Luck or Heaven had seen to it that no highwaymen halted her flight. But how far could she stretch this taut and fragile cord?

She leaned against Sam Gilmore's greatcoated chest. "I beg you, Sam! *There'll be nothing to see of Faxforge by morning!*"

He held her gently away, turned his head and bellowed up the stairs. "Master Whitten! Get you down 'ere! Lady to be guarded. Pistols in the sacking on the shelf behind the bar. Check that the doors and windows are bolted. Three clear knocks from me when I return, and I'll thank you to level at anyone else who comes. Is that clear to you, John? Are you there to tell me it's clear?"

Again stepping quietly from his room, a lantern in his hand, the potboy gazed down the stairs. Charlotte saw him and could not help letting slip to Sam, "Do you think he—I mean, he doesn't look the type to—"

"Don't look it, I agree," Sam murmured. "But d'you know of Dan Rayden, the liftin' champion of these parts? And the one they call 'Stone' Smith? Master Whitten knows 'em, since the day he stopped 'em brawlin' and sat 'em down in their seats. He don't look much at all, I'll admit, though I'd leave you with him, Mistress Charlotte, sure as I'd leave you with me."

Then, in the boots he'd pulled on upstairs and the greatcoat he'd draped around him, Sam Gilmore strode away to the kitchen, scarcely breaking stride as he took a blunderbuss from its hooks on the wall, a long-barrelled musket from a shelf, flint and ball and powder from a drawer.

He borrowed the horse on which Charlotte had ridden to the "Rag." The stirrups were set too high for him, so he let his legs hang free. He urged the animal across the yard and past the beacon. As he did so he recited the names of the men he knew who lived beside the coach road in the cluster of dwellings that made up the Beckhampton Crossing.

✳

Charlotte followed the light of John's lantern to the upper floor and Sam Gilmore's deserted room.

"I'll build us up a fire, Mistress, ah—"

"Wint—" the habit still there, but easy to shake—"Cannaway. Mistress Cannaway. Please do so, Master Whitten."

He went to the log box, looked down at its contents and tutted. "Would you mind, Mistress Cannaway, givin' me a hand? I cain't no way lift a log like that. But maybe, the two of us, doin' it together . . ."

Her ears attuned to the approach of Brook and his army, Charlotte frowned at the potboy. Was it really possible that this makeweight assistant had intervened between a local champion and the man called "Stone"? Quite frankly, she thought, he looks incapable of sorting day-old chicks from ducklings.

She helped him settle the log on the fire, then reminded him, "There's the pistols to be collected from the bar."

"You're right," he said cheerfully, "so 'ere's what we'll do. You get the fire goin', an' I'll run down for 'em. Though you'll 'ave to 'elp me prepare 'em, Mistress Cannaway. I ain't *never* mastered the fillin' and flintin' of shooters."

✳

The pursuers had reined in twice since leaving the Hall. Once to question a lone rider and hear him blurt, "That's correct, yes, a young lady, attractive from the glimpse I got of her. Yes, riding south—*You've no call to shove me!*—I've told you in which direction she was headed."

He'd waited, furious, as the riders thundered past, then told himself that the next time someone questioned him he'd direct them to the first place he thought of, the county of Kent or the kingdom of Sweden, and let them find their own damned way from there!

The second time they halted was to drag a tramp from the ditch. Brook's query was repaid with a crenellated smile and the jerk of a filthy thumb. "Gone past, an' not long since. 'Eard the mount go through Avebury an' down the slope to Beck'ampton. Spare me a coin, sir? You've a generous look about you, sir. Spare a poor old fellow—"

Brook had thrust him aside, and the horsemen had ridden on.

And now they had reached the "Blazing Rag" and Venn was pointing at the light in Sam Gilmore's room.

"We've delayed enough," Brook told him. "If she's come this far, she'll have carried on to Faxforge."

"I'm not saying she won't. But if she'd 'ad somewhere else in mind, Marlborough maybe or Chippenham, this is where she'd 'ave turned. Leave it to me if you like, sir. I'll just ask if they saw 'er go by." He drew aside and the riders stamped to a halt. Brook Wintersill waited, rapping his heavy-gloved fist on the pommel of his saddle. Victor Venn dismounted and hammered on the tavern door.

There was silence, the sound of the bolts dragged back, then the lightweight figure of John Whitten in the doorway. He peered ahead, raised his eyes and gazed at the overbearing keeper.

"A rider came past," Venn started, "not more than an hour ago. You'll 'ave 'eard it, I think, and—"

"There's clocks, do you know," the potboy told him. "There's church clocks an' town clocks an' no one's far from a timepiece. Taverns keep their hours like anywheres else, an' a clock would tell you you're well past disturbing us 'ere."

Venn's oath blew stale breath around the entrance. He stepped forward to lift the feeble young potboy from his feet. Then he faltered, and rocked back on his heels as John Whitten swung a brace of pistols from concealment and aimed them, one at the keeper's body, the other tipped up at his face.

The boy said, "There's riders an' travellers an' such as pass 'ere at all unearthly hours. But they don't come bangin' us up with their questions, nor threatenin' us with oaths. So I'll bid you good night, sir, an' tell you they've a church clock in Kennett an' a prettier one in Avebury."

Then the fifteen-year-old guardian of the "Blazing Rag" pushed the door shut and slid the bolts across.

Venn stood there cursing until Brook and Lucas encouraged him back to his horse.

"It's what I said," Brook told him. "If she's come this far she has carried on to Faxforge. That's where she's gone, Keeper, and that's where we can both burn off our anger."

✳

John Whitten rejoined Charlotte, the pistols still in his hands. "I 'ope I done right," he said. "Don't know if you 'eard 'im; big, stocky fellow 'e was; deep voice an'—"

"Yes," she smiled, "I heard him, Master Whitten. I know the man, and I now see why Sam entrusted me to your care. You are quite the thing, sir, may I say. Quite the most extraordinary young man I ever met. But weren't you frightened of him, that monster?"

"Frightened? What? I should say I wasn't frightened. Why should I be frightened of 'im, great lumpen creature like that?"

Ashamed of the thought, Charlotte almost disbelieved him. Then, remembering what Sam had told her of Dan Rayden and his opponent "Stone" Smith, she asked, "Is there anything that scares you, Master Whitten? I'd be hard put to imagine it, but—"

"Spiders," he responded darkly. "Cain't abide spiders, never could. Dreadful, 'orrid beasts they be. Set me skin a-crawl."

"Well," she said. "There's a surprise. I don't mind them a
bit."

"Don't you, Mistress Cannaway? You really don't? Well, tell
you what we'll do then. You sit 'ere by the fire an' keep an eye
out for spiders, an' I'll stand guard 'gainst anyone what comes.
Will that suit you, Mistress Cannaway? *I'll* keep me pistols
ready an' *you'll* deal with anything as runs across the floor. Is
that a fair arrangement, would you say?"

Amused by the potboy's fear and courage, Charlotte said yes,
that would suit her, the arrangement seemed eminently fair.
And with that John Whitten set his back to the fire, his head
moving from time to time as he heard the wind gust around
the tavern, the beat of a bird's wing, the crackle of embers in
the beacon.

✳

"We're near it," Brook warned them. "We'll go on from here
in silence. I want the road gate eased open—Eldon, you'll see
to it—then we'll file through and regroup. Cautious now, it's
somewhere ahead on the left."

His eighteen-man army hauled their mounts back to a trot.
Clouds blinded the moon as the riders jostled south to Faxforge.

THIRTEEN

Ephram Toll had come quietly from hiding to see the horse-men stampede along the drive. He'd waited for the shouts to fade, the riders to drum away toward the gatehouse. Then he'd refilled his pipe, glanced one last time at the smouldering Moorish Palace and made his way to the kitchen.

Mistress Dench had nodded her usual dour greeting. Fern had smiled shyly, chattered to herself and giggled at something only she could understand. The cook had asked, "Come around for your ale, Master Toll?"

"You'd oblige me with a mug of it, aye, Mistress Dench, though it ain't my real purpose for callin'. Truth is, I'm all set to leave."

"Thought you might be, what with the fire, an' the mistress gone missin'. Not that I care to be told of it. If the ear ain't filled, the tale ain't spilled. Take your drink."

Ephram had done so, then clasped the woman's hand in his. Just for a moment. Just long enough for Mistress Dench to gaze at him and let him see she understood.

"Now then," she snapped, "finish and get away with you. An' don't go sayin' no good-byes to Fern. I don't want the girl confused." She turned to the stove and said nothing more until Ephram opened the door.

"You'll be missed, old man."

"Did you call to me, Mistress Dench?"

"I told you to get along, Master Toll, that's what I told you to do."

"Aye," he nodded, "an' you'll also be missed, the both of you."

He collected his possessions—clothes and candles, an unreliable pistol, razor and whetstone, the coverlet and bolster from his bed. These, together with the oddments of thirty years, were left in a pile near the stables whilst he made a final tour of the coach house.

Puffing at his pipe, he inspected the rows of gigs and carriages, curricles and jaunters, some of them the property of Brook Wintersill, others belonging to his friends. Fine vehicles, most of them, the best being Lucas Ripnall's polished and tight-sprung carriage.

Without a moment's hesitation or the slightest nagging of guilt, Ephram stole it and with it a pair of Brook's horses. Then, his possessions piled in the well between the seats, he hauled himself onto the driving bench and rattled along to the gatehouse.

He was challenged by the two men who'd been left on guard. One of them said, "You're the Wintersill coachman, ain't you? An' doin' what out 'ere at this hour?"

"My, my," Ephram told him, "you 'ave been kept in the dark. Don't you know the mistress 'as run off?"

"So we've 'eard."

"Well, then, what do you think this carriage is for, if not to bring her back? Or do you imagine I've filched it—"

"Never said that."

"—an' am off to see me sister?"

"Never said that. An' now you've explained it—well, you'd best get on then! Only, don't you go tellin' Master Wintersill we slowed you."

"I shan't tell him a thing," Ephram promised. "Though why don't you remind him how easy you let me through? Who knows what he might do for you in return?" Then he wheeled through the gate arch and the guards nodded across at each other. Why not, if it meant a bonus from the master?

✳

The riders stilled their horses, waiting as Eldon raised the hook and inched the road gate open. The five-bar frame creaked softly as it swung, the sound covered by the rustle of trees around the pond.

Eldon Sith remounted and the horsemen filed through.

A smudge of light spilled from the kitchen window. That's where they'll be, Brook nodded, my sweet, hard-done-by Charlotte with the Cannaways clustered around her. "*Oh, you cannot know how I've suffered up there in the hell that is the Hall!*" The piteous image made Brook Wintersill grin in the darkness. He allowed the riders time to regroup on the drive. Then he drew his pistols and turned in the saddle, impatient to order the attack.

A spark was struck among the trees beside the pond, a pile of pitch-soaked straw ignited, then another pile near the gate, another by the coachyard wall, another beside the house. Other fires sprang up between them, encircling the riders. They milled and collided, shouting at Brook for guidance, the man himself all but choking on the words that crowded his tongue. Too late now to give orders or bellow commands. Too late now to charge onward, surround the house and burst in on the Cannaways. Too late now—and the realisation contorted Wintersill's face. . . .

He heard the level tones of his father-in-law, in every sense now the master of the yard. "You're done for, Brook Wintersill, though I don't want you left in any doubt. So listen hard and you'll know you're ringed around. Will you, Master Lewis, start the knock?"

Concealed in the shadows, the apprentice tapped the barrel

of his pistol. The signal was repeated by a man from Beck-hampton, by Matthew Ives, by another Beckhampton neigh-bour, by Sam Gilmore, Step Cotter, another from the coach-road crossing, by Ben Waite and Brydd Cannaway himself. Nine solid signals, knuckle to barrel or knuckle to stock, the men well hidden beyond the circle of fires.

"Now you listen to me!" Brook shouted. "I have every right to be here, and by God—"

"By God, if we're both to make free with His name, your rights have long since been forfeit. Reverse your weapons. All of you. We've a thing or two to talk about, Master Wintersill, though first we'll take up a collection. Sam? Matthew? Will you see who's not yet reversed, then shoot them in the leg?"

A moment's scrutiny and the disappointed Sam Gilmore said, "Seems they're all in the mood to surrender."

Brydd grunted, then asked Lewis Plant and Matthew Ives to collect the offered pieces. They passed their own weapons to those beside them and came forward from the shadows, pro-tected by their friends.

Matthew filled his arms with Brook's shooters, then Lucas Ripnall's, and two or three blunderbusses, all of which he piled at a distance from the riders. Lewis took a pretty, enamelled weapon from Eldon, a fowling piece from a guard. Then he grinned up at Venn and relieved the keeper of his pistols. "Many thanks," he said impudently. "All donations is grate-fully received."

He turned away, still grinning, and Venn pulled a butcher's knife from its sheath in his boot and rammed it in Lewis Plant's spine.

The young man's grin sagged and slipped away. His arms fell open, the weapons tumbling loose. He managed to say, "I'm killed, Master Brydd," but by then he was sinking downward, his dying fall interrupted as Venn reclaimed the knife.

For all Lewis Plant's intelligence and bravery . . . For all his abilities at carving toys and shaping the wood for coaches . . . For all his friendship with the Cannaways, the brightness of his future in the yard . . . For all his gangling ways and the hours he'd spent with Giles, joking and telling stories and adding inventions if the tales would then sound better . . . For all that, his spine had been severed by a madman's need for revenge. . . .

Brydd Cannaway raised a pistol and took aim. Eldon Sith squealed with terror, his delicate fingers in a net across his face. The landlord of the "Blazing Rag" squinted along the barrel of his musket, his teeth clamped shut with fury. Brook howled, "No! This wasn't intended!" Those riders who still held their weapons scattered them on the ground. Lucas Ripnall shook visibly in the firelight.

And then—but all part of it—the murderous keeper lashed at his horse and the animal bucked forward. As he did so, an impish figure sprang yelling from the shadows.

"Nobody touch him! It's Lewis and me shared a secret! So it's me who'll—*nobody touch him, I say!*—it's me who'll settle this score!"

Step Cotter, braced in the animal's path, and Venn driving onward, the knife ahead of him as a bloody extension of his arm.

"You stunted man! What makes you think you—"

But Step said, "This!" and raised the trumpet mouth of a blunderbuss and squeezed his finger white against the trigger.

The weapon jerked, vomiting shards and splinters of metal, rusted nails, the ugly scraps with which such weapons were fed. The left side of Victor Venn's face was blown away, the right side torn apart. His head was snapped back, the night wind stealing his hat as though for a trophy. Step Cotter moved nimbly aside as the wild-eyed animal plunged past.

Dead and disfigured in the saddle, the Londoner's fingers curled tighter than ever round the handle of his knife. . . .

No one moved. The horse turned and swung back toward the riders. The attackers and defenders of Faxforge stayed silent, watching as the body tipped and swayed.

The animal frisked with discomfort and Venn fell sideways, his boots tearing loose from the stirrups. He crashed to the ground and lay there, a dozen feet from Lewis, the knife at last jarred free.

※

Brydd strode forward, caught Brook by the arm and wrenched the man from the saddle. No sooner had he fallen than he was hauled to his knees, dragged by coat and collar to his feet.

"So you've let Lewis Plant be murdered! You've come here with your rabble and told me of your rights and we've all seen Venn's prowess with a knife! You look ready to speak, sir. Well, don't! You've had your chance, yet thought to creep in in silence. So now you'll say nothing whilst I take you on a tour of this place.

"You believe I am harbouring my daughter tonight? Well, sir, let's see. Let's visit every shed and hut and room on the property. Let's take you up every staircase and ladder, then through every loft we possess. I said to you before, your rights were forfeit, though you shouldn't be left in doubt. And you'll not be, God damn you! By the time we've finished you'll have no doubts at all. Nor, if I can manage it, the strength to do more than draw breath!

"Matthew, will you accompany us on our tour? Sam, may I leave you in charge of the prisoners? And will you, Ben, see Lewis laid gently in the yard, then watch over him? It's the place he'd best like to be now, I think, among the vehicles he helped us put together.

"As for you, Master Wintersill, I am about to take you around." He shoved his son-in-law toward the light that streamed from the kitchen. Matthew Ives went with them, a lantern in one hand, a long-barrelled pistol in the other. He, too, had thought Lewis Plant a credit to Faxforge, and hoped the so-called gentleman of Wiltshire would twist from Brydd's grasp and make a run for it. Five paces, ten at the most, and the craftsman would see to it that a bullet was firmly lodged in the gentleman's skull.

✳

The tour lasted the better part of the night.

Brook Wintersill was taken first to the kitchen and confronted there by Elizabeth and Hester—and by Giles, who'd insisted on being carried down from his room. The young man remembered all too clearly the previous visit by Wintersill and Venn; his own angry charge and the slash of Venn's cudgel; the agony of his shattered knee and the wave of helplessness that had swamped him as Charlotte was hustled from the room.

But tonight was different. He'd been told of Charlotte's escape to the "Rag"; heard the hurried preparations as Brydd and Sam and their neighbours set the ambush. He'd shouted then that he'd not be left out of it, and Brydd had agreed to install him in the kitchen, as protector of the women. And with a brace of shooters to lay across his lap.

So he managed a smile as Brook was marched in, delighted to see Master Wintersill bowed by the grasp of Brydd's hand.

"Heard the hell of a blast just now," Giles said. "Blunderbuss by the sound of it. Anyone get damaged?"

Before he replied, Brydd had a word for Brook. "Is she *here*, would you say? Shall you wish to check the larder?" The captive shook his head as best he could, and Brydd thrust him aside to be guarded by Matthew Ives.

Stepping forward, he reached for Elizabeth, including his wife and Hester in the answer he gave to Giles.

"Yes," he said gently, "there's been damage done and you'll be saddened to hear what it was. There've been two men killed, and one of them—it distresses me to tell you—was Master Lewis Plant come from Taunton. The other"—and his voice grew hard—"the other was the man who killed him, Keeper Venn."

Elizabeth tightened the grip of her hand on Brydd's arm.

Hester stared straight ahead, tears welling to run uneven down her cheeks. She attempted to say the apprentice's name and mouthed, "Lewis—" then turned away, her body racked by her anguish.

Giles took a pistol from his lap, pointed it at Brook and grated, "Him? Was he to do with it? Was he to do with the killing of Master Plant?"

Before Brydd could speak, Brook Wintersill shouted for himself. "*I was not!* And I'll not be called to account for the doings of my servants! How was I to know he carried a knife and would—"

"With a knife! Lewis was killed with a knife?" And now Giles Cannaway's weapon was centred above the bridge of Wintersill's nose.

Brook recoiled and was instantly pinioned by the craftsman Matthew Ives. Brydd allowed himself a fleeting thought: So what if he's killed, he deserves to be killed, and there's few with as much right to kill him as my son.

Yet he knew things could not be like that here, among the Cannaways of Faxforge. He told Giles to put up his pistol and keep his finger clear of the trigger.

Elizabeth turned to comfort Hester.

Giles glared, though was pleased to see his father snatch Brook by the collar and tell him, "If you've no wish to check the larder, there's a hundred places yet to be inspected. Are you with us, Matthew?"

"With you, Master Brydd, though eager as ever to see this gentleman run."

❋

That's how it went through the night, Brook dragged without mercy into every shed and barn and byre.

"Is my daughter *here?*" Brydd would ask. "Is she *there*, do you think, hiding in the gloom? Or has she taken refuge in the cellar? Or maybe under the eaves? You keep shaking your head, Master Wintersill, though I'd not want you left in any

doubt. So get up, sir; climb the ladder! Go down, sir; tramp
the stairs!"

Time and again Brydd slammed the man onward, and time
and again Brook said he accepted that his wife was far from
Faxforge.

And each time Brook tried to cry off the search Brydd would
remind him there were other sheds, other workshops, half a
hundred crannies and corners yet to be inspected.

The darkness was turning to dawn as Brydd and Matthew
marched their captive along the western face of the coachyard.
They were met by Sam Gilmore, who said he'd tucked the in-
vaders in an outhouse. "Not so well furnished, though they're
close enough to keep each other warm."

Brydd said, "Good," and left it at that, uncaring that the
outhouse measured less than six feet by four.

However, the tour at last over, he told Sam to let the men
out, then barged Brook onward to the drive. The others stumbled to join him, willingly herded by those who'd staged the
ambush.

When Brook and his companions were grouped in sullen silence, Brydd Cannaway addressed them, his voice kept level,
harnessing his wish to fist them past the gate.

"You are a mixed and motley collection. Hired skulkers and
wellborn men of this county. Your lodestone has been the
strutting Master Wintersill, or the unlamented Venn. You can
now see the one who stands with you, and the other who lies
over there beside the path.

"This is the second time my house and family have been the
subject of your attack. The first was made successful by its
force and brutality, and our own unawareness of your power.
You, Master Wintersill, came in then and let your keeper
swing at my son, whilst your friend—Lucas Ripnall? Oh yes, sir,
I recognise *you*—took my very own pistol to shoot me when I
was down.

"So you cannot be surprised that we were this time ready to
receive you. Once again, Master Wintersill, I address myself to

you. It's you who hired these bodyguards and licked along your friends. It's you who claimed the right to be here, convinced that Charlotte was in hiding. But she's not, d'you see, so why did Master Plant have to die, and because of that Keeper Venn? Your outing has been fruitless, and before I send you back, I'd tell you this.

"You have been the instrument of a double death, failed in your intentions and—I am glad to say—lost hours in the pursuit of your wife. I shall not forgive you for the way you deceived us with your rigged and imitation charm. Nor that, by doing so, you cheated my daughter into marriage. Nor for the miseries you've caused my family and myself. Indeed, sir, I regard you as wholly unpardonable, a disgrace and a reprobate and—but your presence here is sickening. Start off and take your rabble with you. And all the way back, remind yourself of this: if I ever see you at Faxforge or within sight of the property, I shall shoot you, or call on a friend to shoot you, or have that friend call on someone else to shoot you for us all." He turned to Sam Gilmore. "A single horse for Venn's body. The rest can walk their way home."

The attackers were prodded toward the gate. Two of Brook's keepers lifted Venn's faceless corpse, draping it across the saddle. Then, accompanied by the mounted Sam Gilmore and the others who'd rallied to Faxforge, Brook Wintersill and his army shuffled from the scene of their defeat.

Brydd Cannaway watched them go. He was joined by Step Cotter, the men standing in silence as the hoofbeats, the footfalls died away. Only then, and still silent, did they tip the powder from their weapons and walk slowly back to the house.

The red-faced passenger clicked the lid of his hunter and said, "If they keep this up we'll be ahead of ourselves at Bristol!" He gestured at the pitch-sealed canopy of the coach, forward of which were the driver and guard on their high hammercloth bench. Beaming with pleasure at his own remark, the man pulled in his stomach and tucked the watch in the pocket of his waistband.

There were four other passengers in the vehicle. Beside him sat a mother and her infant child, though boy or girl it was impossible to tell. The child was dressed in a miniature wig, a man's cravat, a tailored jacket and long, beribboned skirt. It held a picture book on its knees, mother and child both staring intently at the pages.

The third traveller was equally bizarre; an actor wearing the robes and regalia of a cardinal, or maybe a genuine emissary from Rome. Whichever he was, he slept with his mouth open, his breath reeking of gin.

The fourth passenger on the coach was Charlotte, staring now through the dusty side window as the vehicle rattled westward among the hills. She felt drained by the night-long vigil in Sam Gilmore's room, and by the imagined horrors that Brook and his cronies might have inflicted upon her family. From time to time she'd talked quietly with the potboy, their conversations ceasing whenever he raised a hand. He would listen then, his pistols at the ready, until he'd identified the sound beyond the tavern. "Fox most likely. Nothin' to worry about, Mistress Charlotte."

Soon after dawn he rocked forward in his chair. Again listening hard, he said, "Crowd comin' up to the Crossin'." He moved to the window, the pistols dragging at his wrists. Charlotte watched as he peered around the edge of the frame. She heard the boy murmur, "Well, now, if that don't beat it all. It's the gentlemen and keepers you've been tellin' me of. Only they ain't no longer mounted."

She had taken her place at the other side of the window, gazing down as Brook and Eldon, Lucas and the others stumbled past. She had seen the single horse and the body slung across it, the man in a crimson cap. Then she'd gasped with revulsion, the potboy whistling as they realised the cap was but a dripping mask of blood.

The defenders of Faxforge had reined in near the beacon,

their weapons held level as Brook and his companions toiled away. A few moments later and the horsemen dispersed, Sam Gilmore swinging wearily from his saddle. John Whitten hurried downstairs to let him in, leaving Charlotte alone with the knowledge that Faxforge had triumphed, though unaware at what cost to Lewis Plant.

She thought of him now, as the stagecoach jolted the final miles to Bristol. And of her family; alive, praise God, yet once more forced to defend themselves against her husband's craving for revenge. She thought of Step and Ephram, Sam Gilmore and the potboy who feared nothing but the scuttle of spiders. All these and others were part of the bloodstained fabric Brook Wintersill had woven. Though would he have stitched such a tapestry, Charlotte wondered, unless I had first inspired in him the pattern?

The red-faced passenger again consulted his watch. "Speediest journey in a twelvemonth," he announced. "Much faster than this, and the horses will take to the air!" The idea amused him, but he looked in vain for a response. The mother and child continued to stare at the picture book, whilst the real or invented cardinal slept on.

Charlotte gazed from the window, mourning the past, yet steeling herself to face her uncertain future.

FOURTEEN

Lewis Plant lay buried in the churchyard at Kennett. The service had been attended by the Cannaways of Faxforge, by Step and Ben and Matthew, by Sam Gilmore and John Whitten and the men from Beckhampton who'd rallied in defence of the coachyard.

And by Step Cotter's lady friend, Widow Reece, who stood a little apart from the mourners, remembering the night the dizzy and thorn-raked young man had hammered on the millhouse door. That was the night Step Cotter had ridden to Marlborough, leaving Lewis to be cared for and kept going with brandy and cake. It was a terrible thing, the murder of Master Plant. It made a person wonder at the way the world was turning, ever more violent, with precious lives held cheap.

She did not acknowledge Step's presence at the graveside, though she could see his shoulders were trembling, his bony hand dashing summer dust from his eyes. It was rumoured—though quietly, and well beyond earshot of the magistrates—that the impish Step Cotter had killed the man who'd murdered Lewis Plant. The news of it had shocked Widow Reece. Then other rumours had reached her, telling of how things

had happened. The knife in the back. The treacherous, cow-
ardly killing. And the shock had faded and she'd thought it
right that *someone* had seen to Keeper Venn, and who better
than Lewis Plant's dwarflike friend, jumping out to avenge his
murder?

If the case was ever investigated, the gentle Widow Reece
would say Step Cotter had been in *her* house that night, and
yes, they'd been alone together, and yes, upstairs in her bedroom. And so what if her reputation was sullied? *Someone* had
to protect the man who'd dealt with Keeper Venn.

A few days on and there'd been other rumours, other events, a
further turning of the world. Brook Wintersill, it was said,
spent his days and nights in the Hall, cursing the wife who'd
escaped him, the coachman who'd fled, the keeper who'd
stabbed so stupidly and been shot. The Kennett Vale enjoyed
these rumours, adding fringes and tassels to the tales. Brook
had sunk into madness and floundered naked in his lake. He'd
offered a thousand guineas to learn the whereabouts of Charlotte. He'd renounced his former way of life and invited clerics
of every persuasion to take room and board at the Hall. He'd
set fire to the unburned portions of the Moorish Palace. He'd
rebuilt the gap in the wall through which Charlotte had escaped. He'd chained the gates shut across the drive. He stalked
the grounds howling like a wolf.

These were just some of the embellishments, all of them invented, though pleasing to the ear. And then, with Lewis
buried and his grave heaped high with flowers, the occupants
of the valley continued on with their lives. Whenever they met
Brydd or Elizabeth they asked if young Giles was a-mending.
Whenever they saw Step Cotter they touched their hats in admiration for what he'd done. And whenever they were in the
vicinity of the "Blazing Rag" they found an excuse to stop by.
After all, it was Sam Gilmore who'd alerted the Cannaways
and helped send Wintersill packing.

Besides, as his potboy kept saying, it *was* the best tavern on
the London–Bristol road.

❋

Meanwhile, at Faxforge the wounds continued to heal.

By early June Brydd had fully recovered from Lucas Ripnall's shot. The muscles and tendons of his shoulder had knit
and he was again sketching details of coaches, his work begin-
ning before the sun had skirted the Bellringers. And later,
when the light had dipped below the bald western hills, he
would return from a day's work in the yard, ink his pen and
continue with the outlines of wagon beds or bearings, the
ratchet brake for a carriage.

The younger Cannaway was also at work, forcing his leg to
respond.

He'd had first to master the simple acts of dressing and hobbling from his room. That done, he'd been halted, needing
Brydd or Elizabeth or the willing Hester to assist him down
the stairs.

Then there'd come the day when he'd warned them off, slipping and scrabbling, yet descending by himself. Hester had
shouted and hugged him, and was distressed that he'd pushed
her aside.

"He's pleased to be hugged," Elizabeth had told her, "but
we mustn't make milestones of his progress. If he wants our
applause he'll seek it, and we'll clap to turn him deaf. But otherwise, my dear, we'll take his achievements for granted, and
wait for the day when he hurls his crutches in the pond."

"But I wish to encourage him," Hester protested. "He tries
so hard. I do so want to cheer him on."

"So you can, my girl. And by offering no quarter. He's as
much the man now as before he was injured, and deserving the
same respect. Or, in your case"—and Elizabeth smiled—"the
lack of it."

From then on Giles Cannaway was allowed to slip and curse

and get himself to his feet. He mastered the stairs and swung his way out and insisted on touring the yard. He fell there, the tips of his crutches skidding on the straw or the stones. And whenever he did so he found Ben Waite and Matthew Ives and Step Cotter busy at what they were doing, seemingly careless of his struggles and strains.

He loved them for it.

*

The nightmares had come with her, unseen passengers on the coach from the "Blazing Rag." Her aunt's house in Bristol was thirty-two miles from the Beckhampton Crossing, no more than forty from Wintersill Hall. Yet Charlotte was now a world away from the life she had known with her husband, from the earlier and happier days at Faxforge.

Exhausted by her flight from the Hall, the sleepless night in Sam Gilmore's room and her day-long journey across Wiltshire, she had stood lost and undecided as her fellow travellers left the coach and went their ways. The gin-steeped cardinal had raised the hem of his robes, then veered unsteadily into the tavern that marked the Bristol end of the coach route. The mother and her boy-or-girl child were met by a man and a second infant, this one also dressed in a magistrate's wig and a skirt. The other passenger, the timekeeper, had consulted his watch, glared at Charlotte and snapped, "You see? They can do it when they want to."

The city-port of Bristol snarled and roared, jounced and rattled around her. The late afternoon cacophony had left her blinking. Fatigue dulled her limbs like an opiate; yet the noise, the incredible force and variety of noise, thrashed and screamed at her, a thousand sounds yelling to be heard and understood.

She had staggered and felt someone catch her by the arm. "It's the filthy smoke from the kilns and the glass-cones. Lord bear me witness, I've petitioned against it enough times, though d'you suppose the City Council's inclined to listen? What are fumes and stench to them when there's profits to be made and pockets to be lined with—"

"Please," she said, gazing dully at the man who supported her. "Please can you direct me to The Biss? It fronts the river Frome, I believe. Near where the Frome meets the Avon?"

"It does, young lady, though I'll do better than direct you. You've need of a post chaise and—that's it, take my arm—out onto the street we—there! Driver! Haul in for a delicate fare!"

The man had then opened the side door of a light, one-horse trap. He had reached to help her aboard and told the driver to take her gently to The Biss. The last Charlotte had seen of her Samaritan was the flash of his smile below the shadow of his ordinary hat. The post chaise had rolled forward and she'd closed her eyes, telling herself she had come this far and would not give in to her exhaustion before she'd met Sophia and explained her presence on the step.

It was only when the post chaise had halted and the driver called back to her, "The Biss it was? An' The Biss it is!" that she realised the Samaritan had stolen her purse.

She remembered little of what had followed. A losing fight against tears; the driver's demand for payment cut short by a voice that thrummed with authority. The warmth and colour of Sophia's house. The inner warmth of fine mellow brandy. The dark polished glow of a staircase and the sound of her own drained murmurings as she'd tried to explain, tried to apologise, tried to give reasons for why she was here uninvited without a farthing to her name. And with the name itself, the Wintersill name made worthless by her failings and . . . She could tell her story better tomorrow. . . . Would Aunt Sophia object if . . . The story was . . . If it was . . . Tomorrow . . .

✳

The nightmares had hopped from the stagecoach, scrambled aboard the post chaise and sneaked into the house. They'd waited, impatient, until Charlotte seemed ready to wake from her first exhausted sleep. Then they'd skittered forward, eager to distort and deceive.

She heard Brook and Lucas, Eldon and others roaring below the gallery. Brook's cronies were urging him to go up to her, "though carefully, step by step. Pretend you're a servant. Knock lightly on her door. Let her think it's Mistress Dench or the idiot Fern. Though she'll know, old Brooksy, in her pretty, trembling body she will know!"

A light tapping on the door and it was opened. Charlotte flinched awake, her lips parted to emit her scream. "No! No! I will not!" She shook her head violently, her wide-stretched gaze seeing nothing beyond the horror of her fears. No longer screaming, she again said, "I will not." Then she stared at the figure standing silent in the doorway.

It was Aunt Sophia, tall and too much like Brydd Cannaway to be attractive, yet with presence enough to bring a regiment to the salute. Sophia Biss, Brydd's elder sister, sharing his level gaze, the length and narrowness of his features, the length and leanness of his limbs. The despair of convention, she was a bony, rakish, pepper-haired woman, and no one would call her beautiful unless paid, and paid well, to do so. But they'd say she was elegant, and not charge a penny. They'd remark her as witty, and feel privileged to do so. And they, the men who'd met her and knew her, would willingly set her against the prettiest biscuit-box ladies of the city, then wager heavily on the outcome. Invitations to the house of Sophia Biss were displayed in a prominent place.

"No need for such upset, young Charlotte. You're in my own best room in Bristol. The lanterns on the quay are kept burning all night, and my butler Chapman would not, without my knowledge, let a cockroach through the door. I shall inflict the city's gossip on you when you've more of a mind to enjoy it. Meanwhile, rest easy, my dear. You are in safe, if spindly, hands."

With that she withdrew from the room, leaving Charlotte to sink back on the pillows.

*

She was in many ways a remarkable woman, Sophia Biss. Three years older than Brydd, she had married a gentle-spoken merchant, Master Joseph Biss of Bristol. A forward-thinking man in his time, Joseph had invested his mercantile profits in the furnishings of a fine house and in the purchase of the quayside he'd called The Biss. The best stretch, as was often said, with the best moorings in the port.

Six years ago a storm had ripped apart the sea and sky around the southwest corner of England. The mild-mannered Joseph had been out in it, and his ship had been one of seventeen to founder in the space of that single night. It was reported that more than three hundred men were drowned— sailors, fishermen, smugglers, ferrymen and passengers—whilst less than a dozen survived the coldly boiling waves.

Sophia waited to hear if Joseph had been saved. Then, when she realised all further hope was meaningless, a self-inflicted evasion of the truth, she retired to her room and sorted through her jewellery. It took her a long time to select the objects she loved the most—all of them gifts from her husband. But eventually she was satisfied, this favourite and that wrapped in velvet, the beautiful and cherished creations laid carefully in a silk-lined box.

The next day she took them into Bristol and sold them for the best price she could get.

She was a wealthy woman, not needing to sell her possessions. Joseph would have been horrified. Though only at first. Only until she'd told him why she'd done it. Of course, she would not have done it if he'd been among the dozen to survive.

In her mind, though, she could tell him why she'd sold off the things she held precious. And, knowing Joseph, he'd manage a rueful smile and say, "You *should* have held them. They *were* precious." But he'd listen then and nod and his smile would brighten. "Reason enough," he'd tell her. "There were, as you say, quite a few of us as got wet-through that night."

So, knowing her husband for the fine man he was, the fine man he had been, Sophia had toured the quays and wharves of Bristol, visiting the port offices, questioning anyone who could help her. Finally, she had drawn up a list of some one hundred and twenty names. The widows and daughters and dependents of those who had drowned.

All who could be traced were invited to call at a bank in Bristol where, as the message phrased it, "they would be made privy to information of advantage." Most of them did, and came away with a sum that—well, could be lost in a month of gambling, or buy food and clothes for quite a few years to come.

But it wasn't the money; Joseph would have understood that. Nor even the giving of it, by the wealthy, anonymous Sophia. It was not, God forbid, it was not that she wished to play Lady Bounteous, else she'd have drawn the sum from her account. It was not the money, but simply that food and clothes for a widowed family seemed a better memorial to Joseph than the displaying of a necklace or a brooch. Though Joseph would probably have managed another wry smile and asked, "What if I'd been in the Navy, and half the British fleet had gone down in that storm?"

Indirectly the death of Lewis Plant threatened the future of Faxforge.

Brydd and his craftsmen worked harder than ever, though Giles, for all his determination, could do little more than paint or varnish, stretch leather or shave wheel spokes. He was first in the yard in the mornings, the last to leave it at night, but he knew—as did Brydd and the others—that he and the yard itself were limping along. Delivery dates were weeks and months overdue. The latest passenger coach, a "Cannaway Carrier," was not yet finished. Though it should now have been in service with a transport company in Norwich. Simple repair work took days instead of hours. Ben Waite and Matthew Ives, neither of them young, were showing the signs of strain.

The problem was not just that Giles was on crutches, young Lewis laid in his grave. Damage and death had left a gap to be filled—though by someone worthy of his hire.

Brydd had already travelled to Marlborough and Devizes, in the hopes of finding an apprentice, and a labourer with a willingness to lift.

The apprentice he'd hired lasted exactly six days. Then, with a show of stupidity that left Brydd poised between fury and laughter, the young man had stolen a pocketful of tools and fled. Had he waited one more day he'd have collected his wages for the week.

As for the labourer, he had suddenly declared himself a member of the Disciples of Eden on Earth, a sect who saw fit to chant prayers a dozen times a day, abandoning their work to do so. This included the letting down of a coach wheel—Matthew saving his fingers by inches—and the jettisoning of seasoned planks that split as they crashed to the cobbles.

Brydd Cannaway had dismissed the man, stood silent in the face of the labourer's ranting curses, then given the member of the Disciples of Eden on Earth a blow to jar every rotting tooth in its socket.

"You are a menace and a danger, and God help you if you ever meet the true disciples. They would not, I am sure, want the likes of *you* around their boats and nets and workshops."

The labourer had stamped away, a hand to his puffed-up mouth. And, watching him go, Brydd Cannaway wondered yet again how the gap left by Lewis and Giles might be filled.

✳

He made another fruitless journey to Devizes. Then, desperate for help, he appealed to Sam Gilmore; after all, it was Sam who'd recommended Lewis. But the landlord could only shrug and say he'd keep it in mind. There weren't so many reliable fellows around these days. He was lucky to have the likes of John Whitten to help him. "And he's been offered work in most of the taverns in the district."

And then, in the latter half of June, the latch of the road gate at Faxforge was lifted and young Hester glanced up from the garden, gaping at the extraordinary creature who strode in. She threw aside her trowel and fled in excitement to her father. He listened to her outburst, decided it needed a hefty pinch of salt and went to meet the visitor.

"Oy!" the man addressed him. "Be you the master 'ere? Be you Brydd Cannaway of Faxforge?"

I've misjudged her, Brydd acknowledged. My daughter's description did not need salt.

He nodded in reply to the questions, then gazed as the caller strutted close. A young man of what—eighteen perhaps— dressed in high, turn-top boots, a silk or satin waistcoat, a moleskin tricorn, an embroidered and encrusted greatcoat of the type one might purchase with half a year's saved-up earnings. He had a square, broad-boned face, the evidence of muscles in his shoulders and in the swell of his thighs inside his tight, buckled breeches.

"That right, then? You're the one what runs this place?"

"I am. And you?"

"The name's Jones," the young man said, then turned it to a question as he added, "Jonas Jones?"

No, Brydd thought, you are not Jonas Jones, nor ever were, and you're not even keen to deceive me. He turned to see Hester lurking near the entrance to the yard. Her expression implored him to bring her out, to effect an introduction, at least to let her meet this glorious oddity.

He beckoned her with the merest twitch of his hand. "My daughter Hester, Master Jones."

They waited for him to doff his moleskin hat, to smile perhaps or bow. They waited for a nod or phrase, for *something* to match the splendour of his dress.

" 'Ester, is it?" he said. "Known lots of 'Esters in me time. Though I will say you're pretty as any of 'em. Now why don't you just leave us, 'Ester, an' let me an' Master Cannaway 'ave a chat?" Brydd made as if to rebuke him for his impertinence, then stopped as he heard the girl say, "Yes, Master Jones. Will you please go ahead, sir. I've all sorts of things to do. I hope I shall see you again, Master Jones. Good day to you, sir. Good day."

By God, Brydd told himself, she's been smitten. *Yes, Master Jones? I hope I shall see you again, Master Jones? Good day to you, sir, and good day?*

His daughter gone, he said, "You've some business here at Faxforge?"

"That's the way of it, Master Cannaway. Come lookin' for a job. For a spell of work, you might say."

"And as what, dressed as you are?"

The impudent young man roared with laughter. "Well, I wouldn't get much done in this 'ere garb, now would I? I didn't come dressed for workin', you can see that. I come dressed to get the job, that's all. It's what me father and me uncles said I should wear, so—"

Glowering down at him, the lean and impatient Brydd Cannaway asked, "And what is your father's trade, Master Jones? His and all your uncles?"

"Oh yes, I was supposed to 'ave told you. They're the Cherhill gang. You know? The highwaymen of Cherhill, a few miles west of 'ere? That's where I got these garments, from our store."

Measuring his words, Brydd enquired, "You're the son, the nephew of the ambushers who've had their lair in Cherhill for these past thirty years? You're the offspring of those who prey on the London-to-Bristol route? And the clothes you're wearing have all been stolen from passengers you've waylaid? Am I right in this, Master Jones? Master Jonas Jones? And you've now come here for a job?"

"Deadeye," the young man told him. "Me father thinks I should learn a proper trade. There's no future in arrestin' coaches, none at all, an' he knows it. So do me uncles. By the way, we 'eard 'ow you dealt with Squire Wintersill. Nice that. Ever so clever the trap you all laid for 'im. Serve the strutter right."

For the first time in the conversation, Brydd felt the sparkings of a grin. The episode was unreal; the young man's name, his flamboyant apparel, his being sent down here from the highwaymen's nest at Cherhill, in search of a job as—

"What in hell do you have to recommend you, Master Jones? Are you practised in the making and mending of vehicles, or simply halting them on the road?"

"I learn quick," he said cheerfully, "and I've a memory as can't be beat. Why don't you just test me, then we'll see how I shape in your yard. Describe the work to me and I'll echo it word for word. It's a gift I've got." Without further ado, he recited, "'My daughter 'Ester, Master Jones.' ''Ester, is it? Known lots of 'Esters in me time. Though I will say you're pretty as any of 'em. Now why don't you just leave us, 'Ester, an' let me an' Master Cannaway 'ave a chat?'

"''Yes, Master Jones. Will you please go ahead, sir. I've all sorts of things to do. I 'ope I shall see you again, Master Jones. Good day to you, sir. Good day.'

"Then you said, 'You've some business 'ere at Faxforge?' An' I said—"

"That'll do," Brydd told him. "Your memory is prodigious. It's beyond me why you've come here, and I've a deep suspicion of your presence. But you've a strapping build, and it is, I suppose, just possible you're speaking the truth. You'll have a room to yourself in a corner of the yard. I'll find some workaday clothes to fit you. You'll be paid a fortnight hence. Though let me add this, Master Jonas Jones. If I sense any

trickery in your being here, I shall heave you off the property."
Then he gazed at the hard and decorated young highwayman
and asked point-blank, "Or do you think I won't?"

"Oh, I think it's likely you *will*"—the young man nodded
agreeably—"'knowing as 'ow you done for Wintersill and 'is
friends."

FIFTEEN

In the foursquare house at Melksham, the bearlike William Cannaway sucked the last of his chocolate from the bowl. His wife had already finished her breakfast and sat waiting for Waylen and Louisa to leave the table.

The young man had also done with his meal of bread and chocolate. He was now crouched forward, an account book open in front of him, his face furrowed with an early morning scowl.

The scowl deepened as his sister edged from the bench and sidled around the table to sweet-talk William. "You know I told you, my dearest Father, how I went into Melksham last week? And saw those crimping scissors and lace they've got in stock? You remember, I'm sure you do, for I told you that very same night. Well . . ." Then she stroked his shoulder and batted her lashes, careful to avoid her mother's gaze.

"So you're looking for finance, is that it?" William asked. "They are all the world to you, Louisa, these scissors and laces—"

"Not laces, my dearest Father—*lace!* And yes, they are, they really are, and you'd not want me disappointed because someone else had been first to proffer a coin. It's such attractive lacework, and the scissors will last me for an *age!*" She hugged him then, though withheld her kiss until he'd sighed and stumped up a shilling. "Oh, you *are* the dearest father! The sweetest and kindest—"

"Don't overplay the role," Margaret said tartly. "You've got what you were after, so now go and dress for the street." She watched as Louisa pouted and flounced away. A tiresome daughter at the best of times, her moods dependent on the chink of William's pocket. I wish he wasn't so indulgent of her. Or at least that she'd act with some restraint.

Waylen rapped the account book and frowned across at his father. "There's discrepancies here, sir, as'll need our attention. I'm not naming names and I'm not pointing fingers, but there's a certain man who's been advanced a rack of bricks and claims he's paid us, though there's not a trace of his settling to be found."

"How much is it?" William asked, happy to bask for a moment in the warmth of the kitchen, the warmth of the chocolate in his belly, the warmth of the sunlight that streamed through the open window. "Is it something we should chase him for, or can we leave it until we—"

"Leave it, Father? Leave two pounds and nine shillings unaccounted? And what then, may I ask, is the point of my keeping the books? I'll check, of course, I always check when discrepancies arise, though I'm sure we've been cheated and I'm certain I know by whom." A dissatisfied nod to William and a mumbled "With your permission," then he hurried out, the account book clutched to his chest. William gazed after him—an efficient and conscientious young man. Yet if only he'd make a joke or take a drink. Or at least shed his self-righteousness once in a while.

Their children gone, William and Margaret Cannaway exchanged a smile and the vestige of a shrug, then settled to enjoy those moments together before the day swept them apart. "There's some chocolate left in the pan," Margaret told him—as she'd told him for twenty years. "In that case," William said, and extended his bowl—as he'd done since the day they were married.

She filled it, the measure as constant as their words. William was sipping the beverage, Margaret rinsing the pan, when the quarry master Nathan Reed burst in, a sheet of newsprint flapping in his hand.

He did not apologise for the manner of his intrusion. He did not bid his sister or brother-in-law good day. He did not expect to be seated or offered a breakfast, but moved so the newsprint would catch the light from the window and said, "Listen to this, William Cannaway. Hark to this, for we've both been plunged to disaster."

William set his bowl on the table, then turned to face Nathan. "I am," he said evenly. "I am listening to you hard."

"This is now the fourteenth of June. I have here a copy of the *Weekly Journal*, dated and dispatched from London on the tenth. There are two things in it; I'll read them as I found them. The first is a letter—wait, here it is—a letter from numerous bishops and surgeons and members of the Parliament. Now listen, my dear Margaret, listen to me, William, this is what they say."

He paused and looked at them to be sure of their attention. He felt suddenly awkward, embarrassed at the way he'd charged in. He'd been William Cannaway's friend for many a long year, Nathan smiling as William smiled, the two men in easy agreement as to what they liked and what they had little time for. Steady, undemonstrative men who'd not charge in anywhere without reason.

"They say, and it's *their* heavy wording, not mine—" Another pause and William said, "You'd best just read it aloud." Peering at the small, close-set characters, Nathan began:

"Rampant in the Cause of Verity and Justice, we who claim Some Dignity as Servants of this City, are Aroused and Angered by the presence of an OUTFIT calling itself

The Curative and Medicinal Essence Society.

"An OUTFIT which professes to Treat and Cure all manner of Illness WITH WATER!

"Water is in itself God-Given and of proven Rejuvenative Value. England has for long been the guardian of Spas and Hotwells, Springs and Health-giving Fountains. There is little the World can teach England about the Efficacies of Water!

"Yet this OUTFIT dares to import Foreign Water, even Spanish Water, when its rivers are Notorious as the breeding ground of Serpents and Evil Humours.

"We say to our own Countrymen—BEWARE! You stand to be Duped by this IMAGINATIVE OUTFIT! What need have we of Tricksters with their jars of FOREIGN LIQUIDS! The purest water in all the World is HERE!"

Nathan stopped, then murmured apologetically, "As I said, the signatories are churchmen and politicians, and surgeons, I suppose of some repute."

Margaret turned from her brother to her husband, William still gazing at Nathan.

"So a letter of dissent has been published. But that's not why you've hurried here, is it? It's the other thing you've found, eh, my dear Nathan? And I can half guess what it is."

"God knows," the quarry master told him, "in a way I hope you can. If not, then you must either let me tell you, or read for yourself, what this letter has done to our shares."

Aware of his brother-in-law's awkwardness, William took the initiative and said, "They have fallen. On account of this pompous and partisan letter, our stock has taken a tumble."

Nathan Reed nodded. "That is so, William, though it's been more injurious than just a tumble."

The stonemason smiled to encourage him. "Well now, let's see. I'll admit I don't follow the fortunes of my shares day by day, but I do know I have sixty of 'em, and that they've risen from thirty-five pounds apiece to a hundred and twenty, where they've hovered throughout the spring. And now comes this letter, its viewpoint made weighty by a group of men who were probably vexed to discover the stock had all been sold.

"I don't even pretend a knowledge of what sends shares up or down. You say they've taken a tumble, Nathan—"

"No, William, it was you as said a tumble. I said a plunge."

"The one," William Cannaway acknowledged, "or the other. The letter's been published and they've plunged or tumbled and what are they down to now?" He glanced at Margaret and asked, "A levelled-off hundred?" She said nothing, was not expected to, and he looked again at Nathan. "Even less, if that's possible? Down to ninety?"

"Lower still," the quarry master started. "Down, I must tell you—" But he couldn't, and thrust the thumbed and ink-smudged copy of the *Weekly Journal* at William. "Near the foot of the column. And the quote is now four days old."

William Cannaway tipped the sheet toward the light. Fifty, he read, the value of each share was fifty; his stock in the Curative and Medicinal Essence Society had sunk and tumbled and plunged to fifty—and that, as Nathan had reminded him, was of four days ago. . . .

He looked at the newspaper longer than was necessary. Then he raised his head and asked, "How is it possible that the value has dropped on the very day, in the very edition in which this letter appears?"

Nathan shrugged. "It was probably circulated in the City of London before it was ever set in print. The stockjobbers would be the first to know of it."

William glanced at the paper again, pushed it away and remarked, "Wouldn't think much of an angling rod that snapped if the line got tangled. Wouldn't think much of a dog as couldn't hold firm with its teeth. Down to fifty, are we, this week? So now's the time to bend and bite. We'll see how things are in a while." He reached forward to tap the newspaper. "There'll be another letter in there next week, extolling the virtues of that selfsame water."

"But what," Nathan queried, "if the stock continues to fall? I know you for a sensible fellow, William, and if you're determined to hold on a while, so be it. But as for me, I'm off to the bank to learn the latest price they're quoting. And if it's sunk much lower than fifty, I'll put my stock up for sale and be rid of it."

Margaret voiced no opinion as to which of them was right: the firm, unexcitable Nathan, the steadfast William Cannaway. She did not understand, or wish to learn, about stock and shares, bank loans or rates of interest at such-and-such a percentage by the month. Nathan had done well with his quarries, cutting and selling a wide variety of stone. And her husband had done well, of course, with his houses in Melksham and the outlying areas, and his recent agreement to build a crescent of porticoed dwellings in Devizes.

She was content to leave business and the talk of business to the men. Whichever of them was right, she thought, the other would not be far wrong.

※

Safe though she was now—and in her aunt's own best room—Charlotte was nevertheless still prey to the nightmares and memories that had ridden with her on the stagecoach and slipped into the house.

Sophia came to sit with her, gently drawing the story from her, as poison from a wound. The women both realised that Charlotte would suffer further nights of twisting and torment before the memories could be expiated, the sounds of the quay divorced forever from the remembered activities of the Hall.

Almost three weeks had passed since she arrived, penniless and incoherent, at The Biss. She had not yet left her room, staring hour upon hour from the window, as often as not unaware that Sophia or the servant girl, Tilly, was present.

Then, slowly, she had responded to Sophia's questions, the woman's voice like gravel between the hands. Charlotte spoke of her treatment by Brook and of the shame she had felt at deceiving and deserting her family. "Your family too, Aunt Sophia. Yours and mine."

Little by little the cruelties and humiliations had been aired. Not all of them, for many were beyond explaining, and Sophia accepted that Charlotte alone must bear the burden of these, her most intimate sufferings.

Sensibly, Sophia Biss did not probe too deep at the wounds. Instead, deciding that what Charlotte most needed was a freshness of outlook, a different voice in her ear, she left her niece at the mercy of the bubbling, tireless mill wheel that was Tilly.

✳

She was a sparrow of a girl, Tilly Cross, chirpy and single-minded and not at all sympathetic toward the exhausted, fugitive Charlotte. The weary and pale-haired young lady was no more than a captive audience, a perfect target for Tilly's own troubles. And when better to spill her woes than now, with the patient weak and obedient in the bed?

"Oh yes, Mistress Charlotte, I'll tell you all you want to know about Bristol, but the thing as worries *me* most is me future with Broadrip. Master Broadrip Ness. Apprenticed to a butcher in Castle Street, out by the city wall. I can say this to you, I know I can, woman to woman as we are. I mean, how I feel a strong affection toward him. But I can't find much to talk about, 'less it's to tell 'im to keep 'is 'ands to 'imself."

"Trade," Charlotte murmured. "You might think to discuss with him his trade. My own experience is limited, Tilly, though there's few men born who cannot be approached via talk of their work or trade, craftsmanship or profession. A man spends half the hours of his life amid the problems and progress of his work. You might think to show an interest in that, Mistress Tilly; in how Master Ness stores his mutton and beef, how he sharpens his knives, how he hopes, perhaps, to set up a

shop and where it might be in the city. It's merely a suggestion. And now, if you'll not too much mind, I shall sleep."

Gradually, by remark and reply, question and comment,
Sophia's matter-of-fact approach and Tilly's lovelorn demands,
Charlotte recovered her senses and her strength. Even so she
lacked the desire to do more than sit and let the world turn
about her.

And then, a few days later, Tilly scurried in to say she had
taken Charlotte's advice and asked Broadrip how he stored his
meats and honed his knives and, yes, where *would* he set up
shop within the city? "And, on account of what you said, I
stitched him up an apron. I'll 'ave 'im yet, so I will. My word,
but we'll be married by Christmas! Then you just call by, Mistress Charlotte, and I'll see you fed for free. Talk to a man of
'is trade or professing? Oh yes. Oh, that's what counts all right.
You knew what you was doin' there. My word, so you did!"

Charlotte said she was pleased, though could not tell Tilly
how hard it was to follow the random paths of men like Brook
Wintersill: men without a trade or profession, a craft or
calling or the beckonings of a skill. Easy enough to give the servant girl advice and see her happy with Master Ness. Though
not so easy to deal with the likes of a once charming, now vin-
dictive gentleman of Wiltshire.

Aware of the improvement in Charlotte's condition, the gravel-
voiced Sophia invited her niece downstairs. "I've a neighbour
coming by, a certain Lady Scane and her companion—though
I think I'll keep the description of them secret. Suffice it to
say, my dear, I doubt if you've seen their like before." She
gazed quizzically at her niece, then nodded when Charlotte
said yes, she would be happy to meet the visitors. "How could
I refuse, Aunt Sophia, when you lure me with talk of a secret?"

An hour later she was ready, Sophia escorting her from the
room and down the polished sweep of the staircase. They were
near the foot of the steps when Charlotte said, "Would you

mind if it was Mistress Cannaway? I would rather be known by that name than any other."

Sophia said nothing until they reached the doorway of the withdrawing room. Then, in her deep rasping tones, she announced, "How nice to see you again, Lady Scane, you and your companion. May I present my niece, Mistress Charlotte Cannaway. Her father is the best coachmaker in England, a fact which still eludes us here in Bristol."

Her elbow gripped by Sophia, Charlotte entered the room. She noticed the array of furniture: an elmwood dresser, three and four and five delicate chairs, a mirror framed with leaves and grapes, all of them shiny with gilt. A trysting couch, its serpentine back allowing a young lady and her suitor to sit side by side, though each facing in the opposite direction. Impossible for their bodies to touch. Impossible for the lovers to hold hands without being seen. And difficult, though not quite impossible, for the young pair to exchange an occasional amorous glance.

Red velvet curtains flanked the three tall windows. Coal knobs—expensive city fuel—glowed with a deeper red in the grate. There were other furnishings, a Turkish carpet intricate in its design, a brass fire stand with its irons, a glass-fronted bookcase and a second matching cabinet, this containing porcelain and pewter.

For a moment, as she gazed about her, Charlotte imagined the scene superimposed on the chipped, scarred objects that passed as furniture at Wintersill Hall. Perhaps there'd been chairs and cabinets like this in Sir Henry's day. It would have fitted with the man who'd built his wife a Moorish Palace.

But not with Brook or his cronies. The embroidered chairs would not have survived the onslaught of their raucous games. Though neither, and it comforted her to think it, would Brook himself last long amid the well-chosen elegance of Aunt Sophia's house. His first clumsy movement, and he'd find himself sprawling on The Biss.

She turned her attention to the visitors—and immediately

wondered how she could ever have overlooked them. True, they were shadowed, the light from the windows streaming past them. Even so, they were remarkable, the Lady Scane and her companion.

The woman, Charlotte guessed, was the churchyard side of sixty, though how to tell when her face was powdered white, her cheeks rouged red, and her lips dabbed across with a garish cinnamon yellow? A small mouseskin patch was glued beside her left eye, another, in the shape of a heart, decorated the right extremity of her mouth. Her hair was caught up into a beehive, then held in place by a cage of twisted silver. She wore fingerless gloves, her hands curled on the chair arms, her fingers weighty with a jeweller's tray of rings.

Lady Scane's companion stood beside her, and it was he who left Charlotte speechless. Dressed in a livery of pink and grey and violet, his uniform made all the more splendid with frogging and epaulettes of gold. His head was capped with a short bleached wig. He grinned cheerfully, *his teeth so white against the blackness of his face!*

He was black! Not polished or sooted or powdered black, though was he dyed black perhaps, stained black, as though to contrast with the whiteness of his mistress?

Charlotte found her tongue and said, "Lady Scane." The visitor inclined her head, mouthed something that approximated, "Mistress Cannaway," then squinted up at Sophia.

"Well," she demanded, "what d'you think of his suiting? He's well enough pleased with it himself. Are you not well pleased with it, Elijah, all them pretty colours?"

The Negro servant, and Charlotte supposed him to be no more than ten years old, grinned again and said, "Yes'm."

Sophia and Charlotte seated themselves as Lady Scane continued, "Bawled at first, when I got him. Had to whip you for that, eh, Elijah?" and the boy said, "Yes'm." His mistress went on to describe how he was coming along with his English— "Yes'm"—and getting to be more talkative by the day. "Isn't that so, Elijah? Don't you now chatter lively as a parrot?" And the black and white and gold and pink and grey and violet servant set his clean young teeth in a grin and expounded, "Yes'm."

SIXTEEN

Squawking in alarm, Waylen Cannaway was ousted from the office in the stoneyard. "Leave the account book where it is," William told him. "Find something to do elsewhere. I need this place to myself for a while."

The young man scowled in protest as he was evicted. Never before had he been treated so brusquely by his father. By God, he thought, he is going to check my additions! All these years he has trusted me, and now he casts doubt on my sums!

Waylen retreated from the clapboard hut, sulking his way between piles of brick and finished stone to the house. He thought it harsh and unfair of his father to pounce like that, as if eager to catch him out.

"I really don't see why I'm excluded," he told his mother. "I am as good at figures as he is any day of the week!"

Margaret Cannaway looked at her indignant, tight-buttoned son. "Your knowledge of figures is not in question," she retorted, "though I am none too pleased by your manners. You will do as your father tells you, Master Waylen, and may Heaven help you if you come whining again to me. Besides which, I very much doubt you can yet match your father at anything."

Scalded again, Waylen kicked his disconsolate way around the yard.

*

Alone in the hut, the bearlike William drew a crumpled paper from his pocket. Edging the account book aside, he heaved himself into a chair and spread the stock receipt on the wide plank desk.

For a while he did nothing, save to smooth the sheet beneath the repetitive sweep of his hand.

Things were not as his brother-in-law had supposed.

"I know you for a sensible fellow," Nathan had told him. Though the quarry master had been mistaken. William Cannaway had been anything but sensible in the matter of his fluctuating stock.

He had borrowed £2,000, seen his stock rise like a feather in a chimney draught, *but had not troubled to pay the interest on his loan.*

Why bother, he'd decided, when they know me and trust me and hold my certificates in their vaults? The Curative and Medicinal Essence Society had prospered from the start and had seemed—an appropriate phrase for William Cannaway— as safe as strong-built houses.

The money had been advanced to him by a branch of the Western Counties and City of Bristol Bank. The transaction had taken place in mid-March, William agreeing to the ten per cent generative interest they'd imposed. Thus he had owed immediately—payable by mid-April—£2,200. But by then his stock was rising, so why take time from work and dress in his Sunday best and waste half the day to-ing and fro-ing into town?

By mid-May he'd owed the bank £2,420. Though why bother with the repaying of a pittance when his stock was worth more than £7,000?

And by mid-June—to be exact, June 14—William Cannaway was in debt to the Western Counties and City of Bristol
Bank for the sum of £2,662. Though why pester the clerks
when, the last time he'd looked, his shares were valued at
£120 each?

Since then, *and now*, he owed—payable by mid-July—
£2,928. A reasonable rate of interest for someone who'd
made a fourfold profit on his loan. Reasonable, anyway, until
the morning Nathan Reed had charged in.

Yet not so reasonable now, ten days later, when Nathan had
called by to tell his brother-in-law that the shares were down to
twenty and as leaky as a boat without a keel.

Whatever William did now, however much or little he
could recoup from the sale of his stock, he would owe the bank
more than he could lay hands on, and sat hunched over a desk
that might itself soon have to be sold.

✳

Aware of the rumours that circulated in the Kennett Vale,
Brook Wintersill had turned neither mad nor to religion.

The defeat and humiliation he had suffered had driven him
inward upon himself, his expression set in a grey, waxen
mould. He did not utter a single word for three days, leaving
Lucas to see that Venn was buried, the grave no more than a
shallow ditch in the grounds.

The hired keepers kicked their heels and talked of desertion.
They'd been promised more than this—a headlong gallop to
Faxforge, hours of near suffocation in a shed, then a miserable
ten-mile retreat on foot to the Hall. It was Venn himself
who'd promised them good money, but all they'd seen so far
was the man get his head shot to splinters. And the inside of a
hut. And the wheel-scarred track that had curved its endless
blasted way across the downs.

With Brook Wintersill unapproachable, they cornered Eldon
Sith. "We've done what was ordered. No fault of ours if things

went wrong. We're finished 'ere, Master Sith, and we now wants payin'."

Crowded by them, Eldon said, "I shall see what Master Wintersill—"

"No need. *You* can pay us, then get it off 'im later. An' there'll be extra, eh, Master Sith, on account of the discomforts we've been put to?"

Helpless, he paid them, then watched as they took horses from the stables.

It was late the next day when Brook Wintersill broke the mould. His first words were inaudible, ugly dry raspings in his throat. Eldon exclaimed, "It's good to see you're recovered, Brooksy!" But his further well-wishes were silenced by Ripnall's angry "It's him I want to hear, not you!"

"I said"—and the words were clearer now—"I shall not let it rest at this."

"The keepers have gone," Lucas told him. "Everyone's gone except us. We'd be hard put to attack Faxforge again, if that's what—"

"To hell with Faxforge! I'll see Faxforge dealt with later. I am talking about *her!* The cause of it all!" His eyes reddened by lack of sleep, he glared at his two remaining allies. "We are going to search for her. It is all we are going to do from now on. Search for her and find her. And we will. Oh, Christ, so we will! We'll find sweet Charlotte yet!"

In the weeks that followed her recovery, Charlotte was introduced to a score of Sophia's eccentric friends. Some of these called by at The Biss, whilst others were visited in their own elegant homes.

Charlotte had at first been hesitant to leave the house, frightened that her husband might have somehow tracked her to the city. Though how could he, when he'd not known in which direction she had fled? During her time at Wintersill

Hall she had told him little about Sophia and, so far as she knew, Brook had never visited Bristol. His favourite stamping ground was London, and it cheered her to know that the capital was more than a hundred miles away. . . .

She took to strolling along The Biss as far as St. Stephen's Church, then watched the modern drawbridge being raised for the passage of ships along the Frome. She made friends with a port official, the grizzled old man supplying her with a tide table, so she'd know when the water was due to ebb or flow in the river. It was a sight to see, the running of the tide, a sight around which she would happily organize her day.

Low tide, and the brick-walled river glistened with its slick black mud. The vessels leaned over, their hulls half buried, the tops of their masts not much higher than the quays. Then with the turn of the tide the water swirled in to cover the mud and lift the ships clear and go on lifting them by ten feet and twenty and thirty, and by forty if the wind was from the west. The masts and rigging sprouted like plants, the frigates and cutters and traders pulling tight at their mooring ropes, the dirty, droughted channel flooded into life.

The captains and their crews appeared, whilst teams of horses dragged sleds stacked high with boxes, drums and bales, chests and wickerwork containers, long or bulbous, whitened with salt or stained by the transport of wine. It was then that the yelling started, and the steady monotonous cursing as the sailors lifted and roped the cargoes. The chorus of invective would be pierced from time to time by a scream. A man's hand had been trapped, the bones of a foot crushed by the runners of a sled, an arm entangled in the taut, vibrating hawsers of a crane.

And all the while the captains snapped their orders and the mates relayed them, bellowing at the crews. "Load, God nudge you, load! Can't you see the river's full! Another hour and— Get that blasted box aboard! Well, swing it then! Swing it, you vermin!" Their shouts were matched by the seething curses of the crew. The sailors knew full well what the tide was doing. Swirling the current to a halt and about to draw breath before sucking the water from the Frome and along the Severn and down the estuary, then back into the throat of the sea.

Day after day the fascinated Charlotte watched the theatre of life on the quay. The Biss itself was but one of many wharves that flanked the Frome, as the river was but a tributary of the Avon. Along it were other moorings, other quays and slipways, a longer fence of cranes. Yet even these were just part of the tidal network, running as they did toward the Severn, with its anchorages for the greater, deep-water traders.

As often as she followed the tides, she accompanied Sophia into town. She came to know her way around Marsh Street and Corn Street, Broad Street and High Street, Wine Street and The Pithay and The Shambles. She grew used to the dinning of the smithies, the acrid smell of the soap boilers' shops, the screeching cries of the street traders, the stench of the tanneries and dye vats. She was agile enough to avoid the gutter filth and piles of garbage, the clawing hands of the beggars, the skidding metal runners of the sleds. Warned and guided by Sophia, she picked and dodged her way through the markets and past the pillories and mounting blocks, stooping beneath the myriad shop signs that darkened the streets and swung like bludgeons in the wind.

She immersed herself in the noise and colour, in the dangerous, hard-edged movements of the city.

She wrote a detailed letter to her family, almost daring them to believe the description she gave of Lady Scane and her companion, of the way the ships sprouted in the very heart of Bristol, of the fashions and fabrics and fantasies that left her, as she put it, "eyes wide and mouth agape, and in danger of being run over by a sled. They allow no carts or wagons on the main streets. It has something to do with Bristol's position as the storehouse of port and sherry. There are too many vaults, so I'm told, the roofs of which might collapse beneath the vibrations of a wheeled conveyance. So these massive sleds grind along in the grooves they've cut in the stones. As Aunt Sophia has often remarked to me, it's a shame the city is too insubstantial to support a 'Cannaway Carrier'."

*

Night after night Margaret fed William his dinner, then watched him produce a tattered handbill of the Curative and Medicinal Essence Society and read it line by line. He no longer accompanied her when she wearily climbed to bed. A few more minutes; he'd follow her soon; a final pipe of tobacco or a last breath of air. Whatever reason he gave, she accepted it, knowing he'd be slumped at the table downstairs, the handbill falling apart along its folds.

Alone beneath the coverlet, she knew what he owed to the Western Counties and City of Bristol Bank.

Before the fourteenth of July, £2,928.

On and after the fourteenth of July, £3,220.

And she knew he couldn't pay it, unless he sold his business and his house.

In those lonely hours before William toiled to bed, Margaret struggled with the problem, *their* problem, and realised how slight were their chances of salvation.

William would never again borrow money, be it from another bank or from Nathan Reed or Brydd Cannaway or—No, not from anyone, least of all from those who believed him a success.

Time and again he would ask himself if he'd been wrong to buy the stock. Then time and again he'd assure himself he had not. Proud and stubborn, he would keep his worthless shares a secret, turning the tattered handbill and reading into it some miraculous recovery, a universal acceptance of that splashing Spanish spring.

With less than two weeks to go before the punitive payment of July 14, Margaret Cannaway told lies to her children and a lie to William, then paid a driver all he demanded, to take her—"Yes, if need be, at breakneck pace"—to Faxforge.

It was not that she expected Brydd Cannaway to hand her

£2,928. It was just that he might know of someone she could go to and beg from, without William shredding his pride.

✳

Sophia conducted her niece to a shop in the High Street, the most fashionable and expensive dressmakers in Bristol. It was owned and run by the spinster sisters Emma and Lettie Trove. They were, for the most part, timid, whispering women, though tart in their rejoinder if a customer chivvied them along.

"I'd present my niece, Mistress Charlotte Cannaway, who's come to grace this city for a while."

The sempstresses eyed and weighed and measured Charlotte with their first welcoming glance. Ah, they thought, if ever she was free! With such a tall, slim figure as that! If that elegant young lady could somehow be enticed on to the pinning stand! Just for an hour, then we could tack-stitch half the dresses we are making! My goodness, she has a pretty build, the stark Sophia's niece!

"She needs some gowns for the evenings. And shawls of course. And gloves. And something striking by way of a cloak. And a cape and jacket and pinner and garters and— Well, if you've a moment to spare, here and there, perhaps you would see her fitted out. I know how busy you are—"

"My, that's true." Lettie nodded. "There are not enough hours in the day."

"We are run almost ragged," Emma said, smiling shyly at her joke. "I just don't know how we'll *ever* find the time."

The sisters glanced at Charlotte again and asked if she'd care to step by tomorrow, they were sure they could set an hour aside tomorrow. And would she be offended if they remarked on the fineness of her figure?

On the way back to The Biss Sophia said, "They'll want you as the model for their clothes. They will fashion you the most elegant garments in the city, though they'll keep you pinned on their platform half the day." She linked arms with Charlotte and drew her close. "My fault," Sophia rasped. "Should have brought you to Bristol before now."

"Before I met Brook Wintersill?"

"Let's say before he tipped the scales, with the other dish still empty. Every girl should have the chance to weigh this young fellow against that. Not that one can weigh their true nature. All I am saying is—"

"All you are saying is right, Aunt Sophia, though it's not your fault I married Master Brook." She stopped as they crossed into Marsh Street, then continued, "Nor entirely mine, I think, that it failed."

Sophia glanced shrewdly at her niece, looked away again and said, "There's a gathering. Some kind of late-night soirée at a house near the drawbridge. Should you wish to call in on it, there'll be some youngish people and—"

"Young fellows?" Charlotte grinned. "Young men I might balance in the scales? Are you parading me, Aunt Sophia? Are you putting me back on the market?"

"I'm saying what's on the calendar," she dismissed. "Go or not, it's no concern of mine."

"And if I did go? Would you act as my chaperone and effect the introductions and—"

"Tide's out," Sophia remarked as they turned along the quay. "Lost a bracelet once. Saw it fall in the mud. It's somewhere there, though sunk beyond reclaiming." Then she murmured something that sounded like, "Have to see you're met with proper style."

Charlotte turned and embraced her. It has been a long time, she thought, since I was greeted by young fellows and complimented on my looks. Pray God they'll still think me worth the flattering.

SEVENTEEN

In a manor house near the wool centre of Swindon, Brydd Cannaway asked a rubicund apple of a man for three thousand guineas in coin. Then he waited, his request acknowledged by no more than a bouncing of the man's jowls and dewlap.

Happy beyond measure to have learned that Charlotte was safe in Bristol, Brydd now faced a problem of a different complexion. He knew the menace of Brook Wintersill was by no means over and done with. The man was unlikely to again pose a threat to Faxforge, yet he would surely one day seek to avenge his defeat. For the moment, however, Charlotte was beyond Brook's reach, her whereabouts unknown to him. And Brydd could now turn his attentions to the raising of three thousand guineas.

His host, and friend for almost twenty years, was the paunchy Edward Flowerdewe. By his own modest description a merchant of Swindon, his interests ranged from banking to property, from transport to an alphabet of trades. He owned and controlled a score of profitable companies, mixed freely with the commercial 'fraternities of London and Bristol, and had all the appearance of a roseate, small-town mayor.

But Brydd knew that Edward's jovial manner concealed a mind like a whetted sickle, a butcher's slicer, a surgeon's tapered scalpel. Even so, it surprised him when Flowerdewe said, "A loan of three thousand guineas for your brother, to help him settle his debts at the bank? I rather think not, Brydd. I think I'll not lend William such a sum."

Nineteen years earlier—to be exact, in April 1701—the rubicund merchant had organized and put up the money for a coach race, the object being to link Swindon with Devizes on a roundabout, sixty-mile circuit. Brydd Cannaway had built and entered a vehicle, shared the driving of it with Step Cotter— and lost the race by a matter of yards. But Flowerdewe's offer had called for more than just the winning, and the contract had been granted to Faxforge. Two coaches now, another two later, and after that . . . Since when the yard at Faxforge had constructed some eighteen "Cannaway Carriers" for Edward Flowerdewe, thirty or so for transport companies in East Anglia and the Netherlands and France.

They were not tied together by written agreement, the lean Brydd Cannaway and the dimpled merchant of Swindon. They met a few times a year, discussed further extensions to the route, the need for larger Carriers, the general progress and direction of the business. Their mutual respect had grown into a liking for each other, and Brydd now voiced his surprise at Edward's refusal to help.

"My brother's debt aside, his prospects today are as good as they've ever been. In some ways far better, for as I told you he has undertaken to build a crescent of houses in Devizes."

"Twenty of them. Yes, so you did. I've seen William's workmanship before. It's excellent. He stands to make a good profit when they're done. But when will that be, I wonder? A year from now? A year and a half, if not two?"

"Never will be a surer date if he cannot repay what he owes. With your permission, Edward, I'll repeat what I told you this morning. My brother must raise the money *now*, or at least before the fourteenth of this month, else the interest alone will add—"

"Damnable things, these generative rates. But it's too long to wait, that's the trouble. A year and maybe two. If the scheme's to work at all . . ." He was speaking to himself now, moving about the room, his paunch straining the embroidered fabric of his waistcoat. Brydd waited, bemused by Edward's mutterings. If the merchant chose to deny William the money, well, it was Edward's decision, Edward's money to do with as he wished. Yet why, if he thought so highly of William's skills as a builder and agreed there'd be a profit when the crescent was finished, had he so quickly indicated no?

"Are you turning him down because he was fool enough to buy shares? I can see no other reason—"

"No, you can't, Master Brydd, because I've not yet explained it. And anyway, did I say I have turned him down?"

"I'm in a fog, Edward, and it's thickening around me. I've asked you for three thousand guineas as a loan for my brother—"

"And I have said I'll not lend him such a sum. Or any other, come to that. And you take that to mean he's turned down?"

"I must admit I do. Unless"—he smiled dryly—"you intend to make him a gift of it."

The corpulent Flowerdewe blinked and ignored the remark. He crossed to a cabinet, returned with a bottle of fine dark port and topped Brydd's long-stemmed glass. "There is a third solution. Beyond lending or, well, that joke you made. I shall advance your brother what he needs."

"Advance it against what, Edward? The profits of William's crescent in Devizes?"

"No, for there will be no profits. Nor, indeed, a crescent built by William. It's part of the understanding we must come to. However, I shall first need your agreement in this, or there'll be no understanding at all."

"The fog," Brydd told him, "has thickened to a soup. Sit

down, Edward, and, with all the clarity you can muster, tell me
what the hell you mean."

❋

"I made this visit to London. Got off the coach there at the
'Black Boar' tavern and was met by—by a lady of my ac-
quaintance.

"Dismal day. Sky clouded over. Mud to the boot tops in the
streets. However, we found ourselves a conveyance and were
rumbled off from the coachyard on as miserable a journey as I
ever underwent. A perfectly monstrous vehicle! The wheels too
wide! The springs designed as a nightmare! The driver ducking
on his bench to avoid being brained by the shop signs! The
most dreadful passage between the coachyard and the house
where my companion—well, never mind that—but it certainly
banged an idea into my head."

The fog, Brydd thought, is thinning. . . .

"I kept the bruises of that journey for a week. Though before I left London I sought out some friends of mine, councillors and the like. Told them how painful and unwelcoming I
found it, being jarred through the streets of their city. Made
quite a fuss, so I did, and put up my idea to them. I told them
what London needed was a special-made vehicle. One as would
conform to the proportions of the streets."

A brisk wind blowing, the fog scudding away . . .

"And how I knew of a fellow who could fashion such a vehicle. And make as many as were needed. And had a yard—"

That might be enlarged . . .

"—that could be stretched and built up by—"

William . . .

"—a reliable builder I knew of, and how I'd be willing to
finance the scheme—"

Which is why William must abandon his houses. . . .

"—and have something ready for their approval by October.
I had to put a date on it, you see that, don't you, Brydd? Once
the idea was out, I had to secure us the first chance at the con-

tract. If we have the thing ready by October and the councillors accept it, they'll grant us the concession we're after. Special ranks for the vehicles. The sole right to ply within the coachyards. An immediate order for fifty of these, what should I call them—"

"You should call them," Brydd told him, " 'Cannaway Conductors', since that's to be their purpose."

Edward Flowerdewe drummed chubby fingers on the swell of his vivid waistcoat. He thought back the all but twenty years to Brydd's insistence that their first road vehicle be known as the "Cannaway Carrier".

"It occurred to me," he said mildly, "you might this time see it as—the 'Flowerdewe Flyer'?"

"So I might," Brydd nodded, "if you were the one to design and build it, then put it through its paces. Now tell me, though I think I've guessed. What's to be my brother's part in this?"

"Simple enough. He's to make Faxforge ready as a manufactory for our vehicles. Our Conductors."

"And you'd like him to start without delay. And that's why he must surrender his contract to build houses in Devizes? So he can turn his efforts to Faxforge?"

"That's it," Flowerdewe agreed. "He must concentrate his skills and abilities upon Faxforge, in return for which I'll be happy to advance him what he needs." Leaning forward, he said, "I have already obtained the measurements they require. How narrow they want the vehicle; how tight the lock; how the canopy must be waterproof and braced against— But you'll have to read the Specific for yourself, it's a welter of limits and precisions."

"I will," Brydd said. "Though before I take it—what will happen if I fail to meet their demands?"

"It goes quite beyond my belief that either you or your brother *will* fail, Master Brydd. However, if that should happen, I'll be the poorer by quite a sizeable amount. Though you, respected as you are, will lose more, I think, than can be purchased with ready coins." He shook his head, his jowls quivering agreement. "But this is unproductive talk, my dear friend. Let's finish our port in comfort, then set the clerks to work in my bank. I shall have them prepare a letter of transfer, which Master William may submit to his bank in Melksham. Two thousand guineas by way of the letter, the remaining thousand to be conveyed in coin by you to your overreached brother. A basic tenet of business, so I've found; nothing calms creditors so quick as the visible presence of coins."

Brydd rose from his chair and offered the merchant his hand. "My profoundest gratitude, Edward. I am almost inclined to let the vehicle be known as your Flyer. You really should have insisted on it. If only as a tenet of business."

✳

Brydd and William came near to blows.

"Who told you of my debt? It is a personal thing, and of the greatest privacy to me. I'll know who's spread it around! Let's hear you come out with it, Brydd! I demand to know who told you!"

The bulky, shambling William was now hollow-eyed and gaunt. A big man still, though robbed of sleep, denying himself his food.

Brydd had not yet offered him the money, or told him what it would cost. He had already greeted Margaret and lied with conviction, pretending they'd not seen each other for months. If William ever learned that his own wife had been the one to disclose his secret— But he wouldn't. The chapter was closed, the door locked and the key tossed away.

Brydd said, "There's an offer been made to us by Master Flowerdewe of Swindon. Though I wonder, since you bellow to know who told me of your debt, if you've the mind or desire to hear it."

William managed a final belligerent glare. Then he nodded wearily at his brother. Very well, he would hear what Master Flowerdewe had to offer.

"First though," Brydd told him, "I have obtained the means by which you can settle your debt. Two thousand guineas in a letter of transfer, and a thousand more in coin." Gesturing at the satchel he'd brought with him, he said, "Which is why my right arm feels longer than my left."

"But how?" William asked dully. "How could you possibly have raised such a sum on my behalf? And even if I were to accept it, it would take years, God alone knows how many years to repay."

"Oh, there *is* a price to be paid," Brydd agreed, "but not in the currency of the realm. You are instead to abandon all thoughts of those buildings in Devizes. Rescind your agreement; do it how you will. Then come and help me tear up Faxforge by its roots."

It was a well-chosen phrase, intriguing enough to shake William from his despair. Tear up his brother's coachyard? But why? And what did that have to do with the surrender of the crescent in Devizes?

"Edward Flowerdewe has lumped us together, old William; the Cannaway brothers, win or lose. The word is out and spreading. There's to be a manufactory built at Faxforge, and a new kind of runner for the capital."

"And my houses?" William murmured. "I had always hoped to extend the range of my houses."

To which Brydd could only say, "So you will, one day," then let the buckled leather bag settle, its contents chinking, on the ground.

✳

With Peter Seal still in Paris, Brook could count on no one but Lucas and Eldon to assist him in his search for Charlotte. It was a hopeless quest, though they roamed the streets of Marlborough and Devizes, as far west as Chippenham, as far south as Pewsey.

They visited Markis Mayman, knowing he would by now have heard of their humiliating defeat. He greeted them cautiously, offering them a single measured sherry. Then he told them he knew nothing of Charlotte's whereabouts. "However, Brooksy, I must add this. If I *were* privy to such information, I should not impart it to you. Not any more. Not when you fly the flag of brigandage and murder. You've become a rough-shod fellow these days, old Brooksy. Or maybe distance has sharpened my sight."

"Oh no," Brook told him, "there is nothing sharp about you. You're the fat and squeamish creature you ever were, Master Mayman. And still with a taste for thin gruel." He nodded at the sherry, then sent the bottle crashing into a trayload of twine-stem glasses. Markis reddened with anger, stammering as his visitors left him, "You'll raise your flag too high, so you will! And there'll be someone who'll cut it down!"

They rode to Grand Park, to learn if Charlotte had taken refuge with Theo and Simeon Taylor. The brothers had also heard of the events at Faxforge, and had expected Brook to call.

Once again he attempted to browbeat them, yelling that Charlotte was *his* wife, *his* damned property, and the Devil help anyone who barred his rightful path! With Lucas Ripnall at his shoulder, he menaced the courteous young men.

Theo Taylor said, "I'd come no closer if I were you, Master Wintersill," then whistled in Brook's face. There was a sound of padding on the floor, a chorus of guttural growls. Three black, sinewy dogs appeared in the doorway, their lips curled with far more menace than Brook or Lucas could manage. The visitors withdrew, breaking nothing, touching nothing but the stirrups and saddles of their mounts.

In the weeks that followed they continued their hopeless search. It suited Brook to be absent from the Hall, since a score of creditors had all but laid siege to the place. Writs had been issued and, finally, in an attempt to stem the tide, Brook sold off an extensive part of his estate. Gone was the woodland behind the house, and with it Venn's derelict cottage. Gone was the ground to the east of the lake, the purchaser tearing the unburned boards from the walls of the Moorish Palace.

And gone of course was the money, though even this left half the creditors unsatisfied, demanding he sell the rest of his property, the Hall itself if need be.

They had never liked Master Wintersill when he'd been buying. And they despised him now, this arrogant gentleman who could neither keep his wife nor pay his bills. If this was what the gentry had come to, then England was in a parlous state indeed.

EIGHTEEN

The sisters had stripped Charlotte to her underclothes, dressed her in an unfinished garment, then directed her up the three shallow steps to the platform. "Just until the storm goes past," Emma Trove encouraged. "We are ever so grateful, aren't we, Lettie?" To which Lettie mumbled, "Ever so," around a mouthful of pins.

It was well into July now, a summer storm thrashing its way across Bristol, Charlotte a willing prisoner in the dress shop in High Street. She had come there earlier, on her own account, to collect a pair of open-seam gloves and a pouch of campanulate buttons. And then she'd stayed chatting with the Trove sisters and the storm had rattled the bottle-end windows and Emma had said, "I hope you'll not be offended, Mistress Cannaway, but might we call on your assistance whilst you're waiting out the storm? You do have ever so neat a waist, doesn't she, Lettie? And the roundest of hips. And, I know you'll not mind my saying it, my dear, but the perfect breasts for dressing. Only until the storm blows by. Though of course if you'd rather not . . ." Then Emma had sighed and Lettie had shaken her head at the difficult problems they'd be faced with.

"Certainly I'll help, if I can."

The sempstresses had smiled at her and promptly led her to the back of the shop. They'd an unfinished gown, they told her, designed for the wife of a wealthy tradesman—"though she's somewhat older than you, my dear, and more fleshed out on the hips. But you're both of a height, and if you wouldn't mind standing whilst we fit it . . ."

The garment was of quilted satin, embroidered with birds on branches. Its underskirts had been steamed and pressed, its sleeves puffed out to make the wearer's wrists and hands seem slim. It was Emma Trove who'd chosen the colours, taking liberties with them, yet showing a fine eye for what should be crimson, then daring the contrast of emerald with indigo, the marriage of ochre and orange. Emma was the painter, Lettie the mistress of the pins.

For the next hour they circled their patient prisoner, telling her they were almost finished, just one more tuck and nip. And then—though Charlotte could not remember how the subject had arisen—Emma Trove said, "Ah, yes . . . Men . . . Not much better on the whole than the plague . . ."

"Poison for the most part," Lettie mouthed around her pins. "Corrupt and offensive vermin. Do stand still, there's a dear."

Charlotte said, "No doubt there are some like that—"

"Ten in every dozen."

"Nineteen to the score."

"Like the one who fell in love with us."

"The cruel and— Do keep still, or we'll never get it done."

"It was a long time ago now," Emma Trove introduced. "I was the prettiest thing in those days, though I will admit my sister had more sparkle to her eyes. Still and however, it was my eyes that caught him, this *man*, and I wondered how I'd ever break the news to Lettie that I might soon be married. It was what you might call a pleasurable agony, waiting for him

to kneel at my feet and take my hand and . . . and ask that I
be his wife. . . ."

Emma's voice faded and for a while there was nothing but
the spatter and rattle of the storm. Then she coughed dis-
creetly and Charlotte heard her say, ". . . been to the market
and came back to find him seated with Lettie, close as could
be to her, and their fingers all entwined. . . . The best week of
the year for fruit, isn't it silly to remember that, such a trivial
thing, every kind of produce a person could wish for . . ."

The gentle spinster's voice faded again, and it was Lettie
now, her mouth free of pins, who quietly took up the tale.

"Odd that we ever spoke together after that, Emma and me.
And we didn't, of course, not for quite a few days. We were
very young and very selfish and ever so enchanted by this—
man. I'd made sure he was beside me on the settle when
Emma returned from shopping. I'd waited my chance, d'you
see, and that was my victory, and I did so want my sister to
witness her loss. Now I would be the one to enjoy the delicious
agonies, the one he'd kneel to and ask for in marriage. . . ."

She nodded at the memory of it, then glanced across the cluttered dress shop, inviting Emma to catch up the thread.

Sympathetic toward them both, Charlotte started as the elderly, small-boned Emma Trove snapped, "Lied to us both, he
did, the poxilated vermin! Ditched me in favour of Lettie—"

"And two weeks later he threw *me* over as well! Ran out on
both of us, and with a— But would you rather tell it, my dear
Emma?"

"No, Lettie, I think you should, seeing as how you were
more recent in his affections."

Charlotte glanced from one to the other, her eyes resting on
Lettie as the woman stabbed pins into a cushion. It was not
done in anger, though steadily, steadily, as if to ensure the victim's sufferings, and extend them. . . .

"Ran out on both of us, how's that, Mistress Charlotte?
Though worse, and we still find it hard to believe—*with a
woman who was not even English!* With a woman who was

alien to these shores! With a—well, I'll not sully my lips by naming the country she came from—but suffice it to say *with a foreigner.*"

"He certainly had a way with English," Emma Trove said wryly. "Let's hope he'd the gift of tongues." Then Lettie drove a pin clean through the lavender-filled cushion, a *coup de grâce* for their victim. Perhaps, somewhere far away, a smiling silky-voiced man would clutch his chest and topple forward, with breath enough to cry, "Ah, Emma! Sweet Emma! Oh, my dearest, treasured Lettie!" Then, as he deserved to, die.

＊

The storm abated and Charlotte was released from the pinning stand. She exchanged the birds-on-branches gown for her own, collected her gloves and the pouch of bell-shaped buttons, then embraced the delightful sisters. "I'll be happy to assist you again, Mistress Emma, Mistress Lettie, though I'd best be getting home. These storms have a habit of going around in circles and Aunt Sophia might soon send Master Chapman out to find me."

"We've met him," they told her. "Terrible stern he is, the butler Chapman."

Charlotte nodded, remembering how he'd frightened her when she first came across him in the house. And then how she'd stopped to talk with him, listening to his stories of the old Bristol, the old times always better than the new. And how she'd first dared to tease him—though lightly, inoffensively—and how his lips had been stretched into a grim, unpractised smile. "Very dull, no doubt, my stories," he'd admitted. "Old brass, and rubbed too often, you might think."

"Not at all, Master Chapman. Far from being dull, I'd say you've rubbed them to a shine."

After that she had only to imagine what she wanted, and Chapman made sure she got it. Strict and stern in his service of Sophia Biss—and there was no finer mistress, not in the old times or the new—the correct and demanding Chapman found a softness in his heart for Charlotte Cannaway. She was, he convinced himself, the way young ladies *used* to be, when Bristol was less raucous and crowded, less given over to the hurly-burly of traffic and catchpenny trades. Another fifty years and the city would crumble and fall into the Avon, or subside into the Frome. Thirty years beyond that and, by the turn of the century, the stench of the place would have killed the population, if the noise had not already driven them mad.

Though by then he'd be in heaven—there would always be work for a well-mannered butler in heaven—and free of the city-port's choke and clangour.

Waiting in the dress-shop doorway, Charlotte glanced at the sky and decided she would splash back to The Biss. It was not so far; High Street, Corn Street, Marsh Street and out through the city gate . . . Not far at all in distance, though the rain would have flooded the open central gutters, the wind blocked the thoroughfares with fallen shop signs, toppled stalls, the debris of a stormed-over city. She would need to pick her way with care, and hope the evening sky stayed light.

※

There was a grumble of thunder as she turned beside the Cross. A flash of lightning at the entry to Corn Street. Ten steps on and a second flash that blinded her, this followed within seconds by a split, a crack, a pounding of sound, the fisting of thunder giving way to the drumbeat of the rain.

She ran the length of Corn Street, saw Marsh Street blocked by the fallen face of a building, the snake of fractured bricks from a chimney, the whole of the street a litter of beams and laths, a cloud of rain-dampened smoke. And behind it the cries and shouts of those who'd been made homeless by the storm.

Brushing aside the spit and drip of water, she turned along Fish Lane. If the lightning flashed—well, all the better, it might illuminate the path. And if not—then she'd do best to hurry on, knowing the passageway led to the quay, from where it would be a safe if soaking journey to The Biss.

Charlotte was not quite half the way along when an arm was thrust in front of her and a rusty razor of a voice said, "Who's this then, if not a sweet'n come to call?"

She squirmed and dodged, sensing the stink of his breath. It blew closer as the voice intruded. "Who'd this be but a pretty, venturing out for fun! Don't rush off now, pretty!"

But by then Charlotte was running. Not only from the malodorous caller and the ruined blade of his voice. Not only from the threat that reached for her here in the muddy darkness of this Bristol side street, but from the sudden gusting memories of Brook Wintersill and the way he'd barged in and torn at her and done what he wished, making *her* do what he wished. . . .

The lightning struck again, somewhere to the west. Its brilliance showed the entrance to an alley and she turned into it, hoping to confound her pursuer. The floor of the alley ran with water, flooding down across the rough-set cobbles. She heard the voice say, "Slow up, sweet'n. Don't go upsetting me —or you'll make me handle you rough!" She fled stumbling down the slope, the hem of her skirt to her knees. The man splashed after her, his broad flat shoes better suited to the course. With every expulsion of breath he said this was what she was—this is what he would do. But not just this—she shouldn't think so—but this as well—she seemed sprightly enough—and this—"my hectic little sweet'n!"

Her feet bruised, her legs spattered high with mud, Charlotte spilled from the alleyway, twisting left, and ran headlong into four cloaked figures. She cried out at the shock of their presence, their broad-brimmed hats tipped forward, concealing their faces in the rain. For an instant they were just black looming shapes, the embodiment of her unseen pursuer.

Then one of the men said, "Take no part in this!" His head raised, he gazed hard at Charlotte, whilst two of his companions hurried obediently away, to be swallowed by the shadows and the rain.

The man's face seemed carved from the tight skin of his

cheekbones to the tight skin of his jaw. It was a face she would later remember, though no sooner had she met his piercing gaze than he had caught her by the arm, urging her toward the fourth member of the group. "Do what you must with her. We'll meet up later." Then, with a final glance at Charlotte, the third man strode in the direction of the others. Before she could turn, he too had been swallowed by the dark.

Weak from the chase, she allowed the remaining anonymous figure to draw her aside. He was shorter than the one who'd snapped the commands, a brief glimpse revealing a more compassionate face. "What's to do now, young lady? What's so urgent as to make you— Ah, yes, I can see him for myself."

The footpad who had chased her along Fish Lane and down the alleyway scrabbled to a halt near the entrance. "Leave be," he warned, "she's mine." He backed his claim by producing a wicked, short-handled axe, then came slowly, flat-footed, along the street. Charlotte wanted to tell the young man yes, leave be! This was no affair of his! Yet she prayed he would *not* abandon her to the mercies of this skulker and his axe!

"Stay by the wall," he murmured. "I'll just see this fellow on his way." Then, as she gaped in disbelief, he moved toward the footpad, dipped a hand inside his cloak and in a single fluid movement drew a Navy cutlass, cutting the air within an inch of the footpad's eyes. "It's you, sir, as might wish to leave things be. Or not?"

The man stumbled backward, wheeled and ran for the alley. There were plenty of sweet'ns to be laid for, though none worth the risk of a blinding.

✳

Charlotte's protector sheathed his sword. "World's become a menagerie," he remarked. "More wild beasts about than people. But you've nothing to fear from me, young lady. The name's Forby Kimber." He lifted the wide-brimmed tricorn from his head, ignoring the rain that pattered against his wig.

Hatless, he revealed himself as a cheerful, somewhat innocuous-looking fellow, with a pleasant curve to his lips, a clarity in his gaze. Charlotte supposed him to be about twenty-five. And, had it not been for his display with the cutlass, she would have taken him for a bookseller, a purveyor perhaps of fine art.

She said, "Cover your head, Master Kimber. My name is Charlotte Cannaway, and I am most deeply indebted to you. Who knows but you've saved my life?"

"Then you'd best pay up," he told her. "Confide to me where you live, Mistress Cannaway, and I'll be happy to see you home. And yes, I believe I will cover over; a wig's never the same once it's shrunk and been restretched. Your address then, to square the debt?"

"I am staying with my aunt, Mistress Sophia Biss, whose house is on the river front of the Frome." Her voice was unsteady, the double shock of pursuit and rescue now giving way to more commonplace discomforts. She had managed to retain the bag containing her gloves and campanulate buttons. But her shoes were ruined, her feet bruised, her legs and skirt besmirched by the filth of the alley. The feathered, roll-edge hat she had worn for her outing to the Trove sisters was as limp and lacklustre as her hair. She wanted to be home now, in the warmth and privacy of her bedroom, left alone there with a bowl of scented water, brick-heated towels and her aunt's extensive range of curling irons and combs.

The brisk and courteous Forby Kimber seemed to understand this. Without further ado he escorted her from the alley mouth, along the side of a tree-lined square and, in far less time than she'd expected, to The Biss. He chatted as they made their way through the gloom, his remarks sparing Charlotte the need to respond. She managed a smile at something he said, glancing across at him, and saw his eyes darting this way and that—a young Daniel alert for the prowling of lions. As the thought occurred to her, she murmured, "Such forwardness may not appeal to you, Master Kimber, but I hope you will call on me before long, so I may properly thank you for—"

"Tomorrow is what I had in mind, Mistress Cannaway. I'd already decided to present my card tomorrow and trust you'd be willing to receive me." Then he grinned and said, "How's *that* for forwardness?"

✳

Sometime before dawn—though no way of knowing the hour; no cord-wound clock in her bedroom here in Bristol— Charlotte awoke and remembered the four men with whom she had collided near the alley. The only one she'd seen clearly was Master Kimber, yet she wondered who the first two had been, the cloaked and clandestine figures who had hurried away into the rain. And beyond *them,* commanding them, so it seemed, the man who'd possessed such a hard, implacable glare. Brave enough when it came to thrusting *her* aside, he had nevertheless been quick to follow his friends. For all his height and the menace of his expression, he'd left the far less belligerent Forby Kimber to draw his cutlass in her defence. A fine performance—"Do what you must with her"—then vanishing from the scene!

So why, as the dark took the brush strokes of dawn, did she keep his hard-planed image in her mind?

NINETEEN

Sophia Biss regarded Charlotte's caller as a pleasant and unpretentious gentleman, easy company and a welcome companion for her niece. He had a lively sense of humour, a willingness to tell a tale against himself, a wide-ranging knowledge of Bristol and the world. Neither his dress sense nor his manners could be faulted. He was a credit to himself, the young Master Kimber.

And, she was sure, a liar of considerable proportions.

Not that what he said rang untrue. "I manage—*attempt* to manage—a shipping office on the Redcliffe Quay. And take every advantage of my petty title to escape from the office when I can. Fortunately, it's a family concern. Anywhere else I'd be a clerk, and called a clerk. But here I'm the manager, a position I abuse to the utmost."

"It is unusual," Sophia had observed, "to find office managers quite so adept with a cutlass. Yet, from what Charlotte tells me . . ."

"A skill born of necessity, Mistress Biss. As you see, I am somewhat lacking in height, and was always rather nervous by nature. So, if I am ever to go anywhere in this city, I need something to set between me and the beasts who prowl about. And the reason I carry a cutlass? Well, quite frankly, the short blade suits my size. And it *looks* so wicked. Would you not agree, Mistress Cannaway? Don't you think I looked devilish wicked out there last evening, the cutlass flashing in the rain?" He frowned, as if seeking her agreement, then cleared his brow and sat back in his chair, laughing to ridicule his claim.

It was not what Forby Kimber said that rang untrue. It was what he chose *not* to say, leaving Sophia Biss convinced he was more than he announced himself to be. The often absent manager of a shipping office? Quite likely he was. And with family connections in the maritime business? Again, quite possibly so. But she doubted that he was just a manager, just an easygoing gentleman who'd been found a desk by his family. He had irons in other fires, she suspected, though it was anyone's guess as to what he might be forging.

He called at The Biss again that week, inviting Charlotte to a horse-race meeting in the park near Brandon Hill. She accepted, dressed in a skirt-and-jacket outfit, the russet velvet tailored to perfection by Emma and Lettie Trove. One of the neatest garments they'd stitched up in years; as it should be when Mistress Cannaway had been so patient on the stand.

And there, on the summer green of the park, Charlotte found herself besieged by admirers, only breaking free of them to watch Forby ride in a race.

He had told her of his intention, then bowed when she said she'd risk a guinea or so on the outcome.

"Yes," he'd told her, "do so because it flatters me. Though, I warn you, it's money down the drain."

"We'll see," she'd said equably. "You make such a fuss of your height, Master Kimber, but your so-called lack of it will lighten you in the saddle. I'd say you're worth the risk."

Using money pressed upon her by Sophia, she wagered a five-guinea piece.

There were twelve horses in this, the seventh race of the day. And with nothing more than a flag to start them. And Forby still fiddling with his stirrups at the off . . .

At the quarter marker he was well down the field. . . .

At the halfway stage he was lost from Charlotte's sight among the pack. . . .

The three-quarter mark and he'd forced his way through, his determined jockeying bringing him up with the leaders. . . .

Five or six horses pounded together past the finish post, and it was a while before the stewards announced, "Master Kimber of this city first across!"

Charlotte collected her winnings, her attention so distracted by her milling escorts that she left the betting agent's booth before counting what she had won. Twenty-five guineas— *Twenty-five guineas! No wonder the man had acted churlish!*

Walking home on that still warm summer evening, she asked Forby Kimber, swordsman and jockey, who the third man had been—"the day you came to my defence. The one, as I remember, who told the others to take no part in things, then pushed me across to you. A forbidding, lean-featured man. Not the sort I would have expected to run off."

Forby grinned, assembling his expression. "Him? The hard-faced one? Oh, he's just a captain among the many here in Bristol. One of those who come to get their forms signed and sealed in the office."

"With so many," she murmured, "I doubt you remember his name."

"I am sure I do not, Mistress Cannaway. I had scarcely met him before you came tumbling from the alley. Hammond, is it? Or Cox?"

It was then, for reasons of her own, that Charlotte also considered the young man a liar. She could not support her suspicion with facts. Nor did she wish to lose the friendship of the gallant and capable Master Kimber. She would say nothing more of the hard-planed man tonight, though she believed

Forby knew his name. Of one thing she was certain. It was neither Hammond nor Cox.

*

He took her again to Brandon Hill, though this time to the
summit. There, in the steady passage of an eastward breeze,
they watched a score of split-wood kites rise and dip above the
city. They cheered those who juggled their kites aloft, then
shared in the anguish if the vivid contraptions swerved and
came crashing to the ground.

Charlotte, her pleasure enhanced, was again surrounded by
admirers.

She suggested to Forby that it might be just the thing for
sailors to keep in a locker aboard ship. "A kite, I mean. Then if
their vessel was in danger of sinking they could launch it as a
signal of distress. It would only be of value in a breeze of
course, and of a colour that signified its message. Scarlet perhaps. Or whatever was approved by the Navy."

Forby Kimber glanced at her, then squinted at the long-
tailed kites.

"Not," she continued, "that our local captains would need
such signals, those who just ply the estuary of the Severn. The
Hammonds and, what was he called, that man who thrust me
aside?"

"You seem anxious to identify him, Mistress Cannaway."

"I think, Master Kimber, you might address me as Charlotte."

It was a nicely timed offer, an alluring offer, and made more
so as she slipped her arm in his. And it worked, since he told
her he thought the man was called Lodge, Matcham Lodge,
was it, something of the kind. "An evasive fellow, though he
was in the office this morning. It's the only reason I recollect
the name."

"I suggested scarlet because I thought it might show against
the sky. But I've no doubt the Navy will have their own prefer-
ence for the colour." Then she studied the kites, watching

them swoop and curve above the brick-kiln chimneys of Bristol.

She did not sense Forby Kimber sigh beside her; a gentle admission of his unrequited love.

✻

It would have heartened Brook Wintersill to see Faxforge so battered about. But he had kept his distance, believing what Brydd had told him: "Come within sight of this property and I shall shoot you, or call on a friend to shoot you, or have that friend call on someone else to shoot you for us all." A clear and comprehensive warning; not to be ignored.

There was now a gaping hole at the rear of the coach house, an entire row of outbuildings torn down. The path from the road gate had been widened, necessitating the loss of some fine old trees around the pond.

The vegetable plot had suffered. The small flower garden, Hester's pride and joy, now bore the scars of a clumsily manoeuvred wagon. Another vehicle, skidding for purchase, had sent a shower of stones against the window of Brydd's study-*cum*-parlour, cracking several of the panes. Overhead, a number of roof tiles had been dislodged by the constant vibrations of hammering, the passage of quarry wagons, the off-loading of stones and beams, supporting posts and lintels.

The challenge Brydd had issued to his brother had come unnervingly close to prophecy. They *were*, near as damn it, pulling Faxforge up by the roots.

Though with reason. The gap at the rear of the coach house would, before long, be an arched entrance, closed by double doors. The demolished outbuildings would be reconstructed, enlarging the area of the yard. Part of the hill that sloped upward to the Bellringers had been levelled as the site for a single shed not less than eighty feet long. This, in deference to the merchant of Swindon, Edward Flowerdewe, would be known as the Manufactory. It was here, God willing, that the "Cannaway Conductors" were to be assembled.

When—and if—the problems were overcome.

There were those that confronted Brydd Cannaway; the problems of designing the Conductor. There were the difficulties that faced his brother William; not least among them the construction of the eighty-foot Manufactory. There were the problems of accommodating and feeding the work force brought in from Melksham. And, inevitably, there was the clash of personalities, the heat of summer on their necks.

This too would have pleased the sullen Brook Wintersill, imagining those at Faxforge engaged on a Tower of Babel. . . .

It was William's son Waylen who struck the first discordant note. Officious and dissatisfied, he still grieved over the loss of the twenty town houses in Devizes. He had boasted of the contract—"My father's and mine"—to all those he knew at Melksham. "Quite a jump up," he'd told them, "our securing such an arrangement. Wouldn't surprise me if we're soon invited to build at the doorstep of London."

And then William's shares in the Medicinal and Curative Essence Society had collapsed. Brydd had gone to see Flowerdewe, who'd advanced William the money, though on condition the builder withdraw from his arrangement in Devizes.

After that Waylen Cannaway had lost respect for his father. The fine crescent of houses was gone forever, and now they were here, building sheds and workshops near an empty stretch of road that was not on the doorstep of anywhere!

So William's son paraded his grievance, reminding them all that "these careful cut stones and tiles and what have you, they were all destined for proper dwellings, not just common factory huts!"

The shambling William suffered the reprimands in silence. He should not have bought those shares, not clung to them anyway, or been so caught out when the medicine, the essence failed to cure. Even so, he wished his son would settle for one final outburst, then shut up.

Wrestling with problems of his own, Brydd was nevertheless

tempted to give Waylen the thrashing of his life. As was Giles, who glowered at his cousin in the yard, then argued with him at table in the evenings.

Elizabeth and Hester also dreamed of the things they wished to tell Waylen, though knew better than to interfere between other members of the family. The Cannaways had problems enough, without bickering amongst themselves.

A shipment of walling stones and slate arrived from Melksham. Waylen, who'd insisted on being given a desk in the corner of the yard, recorded it, remarking that it too had been destined for Devizes. "This will be the best-made factory in England, and no mistake! Keep it up and there'll be marble horse troughs in the yard."

"Oy! Master Cannaway. There's something as I'd like you to see over 'ere."

Waylen glanced up at the muscled and square-faced young man who called himself Jonas Jones. No longer flamboyant in his dress—and only Brydd knew he had once been a member of the Cherhill gang—Jonas jerked a thumb toward the cutaway slope beyond the coachyard.

"What is it, Jones?"

"Master Jones."

"Jones, Master Jones, what does it matter? Can't you see I'm busy recording what comes in here?"

"Won't take you long, Master Cannaway. An' you'll be all the better for seeing what I 'ave to show you."

Waylen laid his pen in the groove of his desk. Dressed as always in decent town clothes, he slapped at the dust stirred up by the incoming wagon, grunted his impatience at Jonas and followed him across the levelled area of ground. Matthew Ives looked away from his workbench and nodded at Waylen as he passed. Ben Waite interrupted the sawing of a plank. Two or three of William's work force smiled a greeting.

"Over 'ere," Jonas beckoned, guiding Waylen to a corner of the unfinished extension to the yard.

The accountant thought it odd that no one was working on

the sheds or the Manufactory. And odd that they'd smiled and grinned and nodded, the craftsmen so friendly toward him, though God knew he'd never encouraged such familiarities.

Then Jonas Jones removed his leather jerkin, folded it and set it on the ground. "Well now," he said, "'ere we are, nice and quiet. So let me show you what I've brought you along to see." He held up a calloused fist.

"Been a bit troublesome all around, you 'ave, Master Waylen. 'Eard you've been actin' spiteful toward your father. Shouldn't never say things against your father. Leastways not in public. Though I'm not 'ere to bandy words. That's *your* way, Master Waylen, but mine is—well, best put up your brawlers, for I plan to knock you about."

Waylen's sight grew blurred as Jonas thumped him between the eyes.

His ears rang as the onetime highwayman's knuckles were rounded on his skull.

His breath fled as his stomach was hollowed, his legs buckling beneath him.

Jonas Jones leaned down to assist Waylen Cannaway to his feet. He led the dazed young man back across the coachyard and propped him at his desk in the corner. "You take care now, Master Waylen. Don't want you topplin' off your stool." He awarded Waylen a friendly pat on the shoulder, then strode away, unconcerned that Brydd and William were watching nearby. Fellows such as them would understand.

PART THREE

MATCHAM

1720

TWENTY

Forby Kimber called again, this time to invite Charlotte to a ball.

"Friend of mine got married and is celebrating with a dance in the Wool Hall near Broad Street. Thing is, though, it's likely to go on until morning—with or without the happy couple. I'd best ask your aunt's permission, since you'll not be home before dawn."

"I'm sure you'll not need to," Charlotte smiled. "I am quite at liberty to come and go as I please. It would be different if I was un—" and she severed the word in time.

"Unworldly?" Forby suggested. "You are very far from that. But you *are* unmarried, and Mistress Biss is responsible for your welfare."

Evading a lie, Charlotte shrugged. "You must do as you think fit, Master Forby. My aunt will anyway appreciate the courtesy." And, she thought, it will strengthen the role I'm playing.

A day of indulgent preparation and she was ready. Forby Kimber arrived in a narrow-wheeled post chaise, alighted and came jauntily up the steps. He was greeted by Sophia, who caught him off balance by saying, "It's a break from the totting of stockage, eh, Master Kimber? And the filing of bills of lading?"

"Oh, yes indeed, Mistress Biss. A very welcome escape."

"You are prettily dressed for a manager, sir."

"It's a vanity," he admitted. "The kind that keeps me in debt."

She nodded her approval of his pinned satin stock, square-buckled shoes, brocade-trimmed frock coat and matching, pearl-buttoned waistcoat. And all on the salary of a clerk. Unless, of course, he was engaged in something more lucrative outside office hours. . . .

Charlotte descended to the hallway, her appearance rewarded by a courtly bow from Forby. Her pale hair was caught at the crown with a small Spanish comb, a single curl turned tight on her forehead, her ears concealed by intricate spirals, the attractive result of an afternoon's endeavours. And devilish hard work it had been, to get the effect she wanted.

Spoiled by the generous Sophia, Charlotte had finally eschewed the mouseskin patches, the circles of rouge, the brooches and bracelets and collars she'd been offered. Simplicity became her better, she believed, than splendour. Yet a striking simplicity it was, the full-length gown of deep bottle green, the shaped and pointed bodice of a gentler, more delicate viridity. Discreet buttons on the bodice. Her shoulders bare. An edging of lace at the gathered cuffs of the gown.

She glanced at Sophia, hoping her aunt would not be offended that her treasure chest of jewellery had been spurned.

"My taste," Sophia apologised, "is a sight more vulgar than yours. Though perhaps I'll offer you the box again—twenty years from now. *That's* when you'll be glad of those baubles, their sparkle outlasting our own. But for now? Tonight? They would suffer by comparison, my dear Charlotte. You'll be much in demand among the men at this ball. And fervently disliked by the women."

"I would have you know," Forby told them stiffly, "I am wearing my very best outfit. And now feel like a coal heaver coming back from his shift." His oblique and grouching compliment made them smile, and Charlotte went forward to link her arm in his and say, "There. Do you see? Not a trace of coal dust on my clothes."

The butler Chapman escorted them to the post chaise. "May I wish you, Master Kimber, and you, Mistress Cannaway, an enjoyable time at the revels."

At the revels, Forby thought. No one's attended revels in thirty years. He must have a damn fine memory for things, and it *is* a better word for it than ball or dance or whatever we call it today. "Yes, Master Chapman, and we'll keep your well-wishes with us. We'll tell you tomorrow how things were—at the revels."

"I'll be here to listen," Chapman said gravely, nursing his conviction that modern revels could not hold a candle to the bacchanals they had been. Now, in his day . . .

*

The narrow-wheeled vehicle bounced through Marsh Gate and along toward Broad Street. Forby reined in near the corner, tethered the horse in a rank with fifty others, tipped the senior watchman and conducted Charlotte through the portals of the Wool Hall. They were greeted by a number of young men and Charlotte realised that Forby Kimber was known to those who saw him. More than that, they exchanged what appeared to be a surreptitious sign, the discreet passing of an open hand across a tight-closed fist.

The juvenile game of old schoolmates, she supposed, remembering how she and Hester and Giles had, as children, invented elaborate signs and ceremonies, so the three of them might be privy to a secret. No matter that they were brother and sisters; they were members of the Faxforge Gang! The only members, though heaven help the one who ignored the elaborate ritual when they met. A single word misplaced, a gesture forgotten, and the offender would be banned for the day.

How many wonderful secrets did I miss, Charlotte thought, smiling at the memory as she was escorted into the Hall.

And then they were swamped by the shouts and laughter, the sawing of fiddles, the plangent music of a harpsichord. Pretty young women caught Forby by the hand, whilst elegant men, poised high on their heels, bowed to Charlotte, flattering her with phrases they had thought up for themselves or memorised from books.

She was led onto the floor and taught the gavotte and the minuet, the step-it-out and the jaunter. Forby came to her rescue and danced with her, then relinquished her to others. The music rose above the garlands that draped the room. Smoke spiralled upward from the candles, a heavier blanket puffed out from pipes to rise as quilting on the walls.

She was smothered with compliments by the men she partnered. Had she just arrived in Bristol? They hoped she had, or would think themselves blind for having failed to notice her before. Mistress Cannaway, was that the name? And you've known young Forby for a while? Well, there's a damn shame; hoped I might snatch you from him; I'm really a very nice fellow, Mistress Cannaway, and disgracefully wealthy, don't y'know?

The smoke and music and the colour of the clothes swirled around.

She withdrew to the wall and was surrounded by gentlemen who asked that she keep a dance free. Or would she rather take a breath of air—there were any number who invited her to take a breath of air. No? Then might they ask her to a soirée they'd be giving in October?

It was well past midnight when she saw Forby nodding in conversation with a tall, plain-dressed figure near one of the garlanded pillars.

She smiled her excuses, then went to join her escort.

As she neared the pair she heard the taller one say, "—safely set ashore near Bordeaux, where there'll be others to take them on." Then he saw her approach and all but stopped her with the harshness of his glare.

"I am not one for dancing," he dismissed. "Pray search out someone else."

Oh yes, she thought, this is the man who thrust me aside, then strode off to shepherd his friends. This is the one whose image I've had in mind, the one I've felt drawn to meet. Yet already he seems as lacking in manners as in courage.

"I am scarcely so impoverished," she retorted, "that I must go begging for partners around the room. And I assure you, sir, even if I were—"

"Captain Matcham Lodge," Forby hurried. "Mistress Charlotte Cannaway, whom I've the pleasure of escorting this evening. You're unwarranted brusque, you know, Matcham. I'm aware you dislike these gatherings—revels is how—"

"The end of the week," Matcham snapped. "I shall not want things to go wrong." Then he turned and was gone among the pillars of the Wool Hall, denying Charlotte even a perfunctory nod.

Forby gestured in helpless apology. "It is often their way, I'm afraid, these captains who traffic the Channel. Too much their own masters perhaps. Out of touch with common politeness. It's to do, I suppose, with their being so often at sea. Though Captain Lodge is not always so—"

"Spare your defence of him, Forby! He's just a crude and stamping man who'd be impolite regardless of his trade. He may, as you say, be often at sea, strutting the decks of his dominion. But on land he's no more than a noisy and unhandsome bully. It cheers me that he's gone. Did I hear him mention Bordeaux? Then my pity's for the French!"

Forby nodded, aware that Charlotte protested too vehemently to be indifferent to Matcham Lodge. Once again he blanketed a sigh. Then, smiling as a shield for his feelings, he escorted her out onto the floor.

✳

"I am not one for dancing. Pray search out someone else."
She lay awake in her room, willing herself to recapture the scenes and chatter of the evening. But the compliments faded, the noise and colour ebbing away to leave Matcham Lodge like some tall, forbidding rock upon the beach.

Less than a dozen words, she thought, yet what a masterpiece of self-delusion and downright bad manners! "I am not one for dancing." Well, that's plain enough to see, Captain Lodge. You look altogether too raw and unschooled for such pastimes. I did not for a moment suppose you capable of dancing. Except perhaps in a tavern.

You've a sharp tongue, Mistress Cannaway.

Not as a rule, sir. Though I will admit, you're the type who sets it on edge.

He smiled and said she must forgive him; he too was somewhat on edge. Even so, Mistress Cannaway, I owe you an apology. I am, as you say, somewhat raw and unschooled—

I withdraw the remark, Captain Lodge. It was hasty of me. I am in no position to judge.

He shrugged and said she was nonetheless correct. There is not much call for common courtesies aboard ship. But I do apologise, Mistress Cannaway. Not that that, I'm afraid, makes me any the more capable of dancing.

There is little enough to it, she told him. One need not attempt the more intricate patterns of step.

In that case, Mistress Cannaway, may I request the pleasure of a dance?

The other women pretended not to watch. But they were looking, Charlotte could see they were looking. And the men were gazing openly as the handsome couple moved in unison around the floor.

There was a sudden cacophony of noise along The Biss. Street sellers emerged to shout their wares, traders pushing their handcarts, all of them aware that it was now precisely five in the morning, the hour at which they might shatter the silence of the quay.

Charlotte moved, restless in the bed. Her imagined pleasures were swept away, reality once again seizing hold.

"*I am not one for dancing. Pray search out someone else.*"

✳

There were further clashes at Faxforge, a steady exchange of curses as the men worked to prepare the yard. Masons and carpenters, joiners and drivers and the Cannaways themselves struggled to solve their own particular problems.

The pivot of it all was Brydd. It was he who must deal with the Specific, the binding list of instructions drawn up by the councillors in London. He had read and reread the document, believed he understood their commands and restrictions, then attempted to visualise what they wanted.

And what they wanted, so it seemed, was impossible.

A vehicle this narrow? Impossible. And no higher than the pricked-up ears of a horse? Impossible. And with comfortable seats for two passengers, a bench for the driver, a weatherproof canopy, a thiefproof trunk, a wheel lock that would take the Conductor through almost a quarter of the compass? Impossible. All of it impossible.

He told Elizabeth point-blank, "I do not think I can meet their demands. They go beyond reason. What they're asking for is some magical machine—"

"Which is why you've been given the task. There are plenty of yards that can turn out commonplace runners. But they don't want a runner. They want a 'Cannaway Conductor'."

"Read the Specific and you'll see what they want is a miracle! A gig that can navigate alleys no wider than my arms? And turn within the radius of a cartwheel? And with the passengers sheltered and the driver sat lower than a signboard? I tell you, sweet Elizabeth, what they've set is a problem beyond solution!"

"The way you describe it," she murmured, "it does sound rather beyond us. Maybe you should visit Edward Flowerdewe. Tell him we're not in tune with city gigs. Let him know such things are too difficult for us, stuck out here in the country."

Then she concealed her smile as Brydd said, "I wouldn't go so far as . . . It's really a question of the wheel lock and the bench. . . . Another hour or so in the parlour and . . . Just let me scratch out some ideas . . ."

Elizabeth nodded, aware that her husband would claw at the problems until dawn. He would again say it was madness, then again sit hunched in the candlelight, the ritual to be repeated throughout the nights and weeks to come.

She did not think Brydd Cannaway incapable of failure. But she doubted if she would ever meet a man so willing to catch up the gauntlet of a challenge.

※

Peter Seal had enjoyed himself in Paris, though he was happy, he admitted, to be back in his native country, hearing a language he understood.

Yet in some ways the difficulties stayed with him, had been *encouraged* to stay with him, for he had returned to England with a most vivacious souvenir.

Her name was Anne-Marie, her nature affectionate, her command of English abysmal. She said little, preferring to work wonders with her eyes. It suited Peter Seal very well; he would talk and she would listen, neither of them needing to venture out of their depth.

Yawning behind the coffeehouse window, he stroked the girl's neck and said, "First time I've been to this city in an age. It's a busy place, I'll say that for it. Busy as Paris, eh, *ma chérie? Il y a beaucoup de monde ici, n'est-ce pas? Beaucoup de bruit?*"

Surprised by his lapse into her language, the girl chattered agreement. There were many people, yes, and much noise. But the air smelled different, had he noticed how much sharper the air was here than in Paris?

Peter Seal couldn't say, for not only had he lost the thread of her chatter, but he was now leaning forward, staring intently through the window.

The girl stared with him, then swung away, pouting her displeasure. If he wished to watch other women—

But he was not watching other women. He was staring with interest at one particular woman, her graceful stride taking her along the far side of the street. More than six months had passed since he'd seen her. She had changed beyond—but no, not quite beyond recognition. She was still Charlotte Wintersill.

And wouldn't Brooksy be pleased to learn that his wife, his hedgerow bitch, was parading the streets of Bristol.

✳

Forby Kimber continued to call at The Biss. He knew Charlotte found him amusing and was fond of him, a courteous and undemanding friend. But he also knew their relationship was just that, one of friendship, and that he stirred no deep emotion within her, caused no quickening of her heart.

He wished to tell her he was in love with her, yet feared that if he did so she would shy away, in an effort to spare him the cruelty of truth. He'd gain nothing by his declaration, upsetting the tenor of their friendship and forcing her to weigh the implications of each affectionate gesture. In short, he would probably lose her, having overplayed his hand.

It was, and he accepted it, a game for three, the third player yet to show his cards. After that? Well, yes, if the other player continued to snap and snarl, Charlotte might dismiss him from her thoughts. Forby hoped so, though he realised that Matcham Lodge must first be brought to the table.

Meanwhile, Forby and Charlotte went together to parties

and dinners and the sort of gatherings the butler Chapman regarded as revels. He took her around Bristol in his post chaise or, if the address was nearby, they walked in the warm summer air.

It was late in August, early in the evening, when they returned from a supper by way of the quay that formed the northern bank of the Avon. They were on the cheese wedge of the city, their heads bowed against a gusting westerly wind. Their homeward route led out toward the point of the wedge, then across to the Frome and The Biss. A refreshing walk, and safe from the footpads who haunted the central alleys. They would not crouch in ambush out here, in the broad thoroughfares of Queen Square or on the open, cobbled wharves.

Charlotte clung to Forby's arm, her free hand raised to keep her bonnet in place, her petticoats billowing at the knee. They made their way along Risers Wharf and around a curve of the river. She glanced ahead and asked, "What's the cause of the excitement there? Those uniformed men, swarming about the quay."

Forby Kimber raised his head. She felt his grip tighten on her arm. She heard him mutter, "God and damnation!" then protested as he pulled her against the shadowed clapboards of a warehouse.

"What is it, Forby? Are they customs officials on a raid?"

"Be quiet. Let me think. Damnation, but he'll have them aboard tonight. . . . There's an hour or more until the tide. . . . And they won't yet have seen . . ."

"Forby? You're tearing my cloak on the wall. Master Forby!"

He turned the way they'd come, his head thrust forward as he peered at the line of masts and close-furled sails.

"Do you see that ship? The fourth—no, the fifth along. The *Nereid,* that vessel with the drab red hull. Well, do you see it?" He gripped her more tightly, the urgent growl of his voice out of keeping with the Forby Kimber she knew.

Confused and indignant, she twisted in his grasp and said, "Yes! Yes, I see it! And you're still set on tearing—"

"Damn your cloak. I'll buy you another, a dozen others. Now listen to me, Charlotte. You're to go aboard that ship and warn them there's government agents on the scour."

"I? And why not you? I don't know what's so alarmed you, Forby, but I'll need a fuller explanation of things before I—"

"No, you won't. Not when I tell you it's Matcham Lodge you'll be warning. And his neck in a rope if you refuse. Believe me, my dear Charlotte, I myself must keep out of it, and the explanations must wait. But you—you can get across there, and not be put at risk." Then, with a weight of sadness in his words and an easing of his grasp, he said, "I know Captain Lodge and—well, he'll see you come to no harm. Though you *must* get aboard there and tell him of the men on the scour! I implore you! *Go and warn him now!*" He urged her out and along the wharf, hissing from the shadows as though to drive her. "Quickly, Charlotte, or he hangs!" She glanced back in consternation, but by then he'd disappeared along the side of the pitch-daubed warehouse.

They have a gift, Charlotte thought furiously, for slinking away from trouble. From the alley mouth the night I was chased. Oh, Forby stood his ground then, and it was Matcham Lodge who fled. But now it's Master Kimber's turn to make himself scarce. The one, it seems, is after all as bad as the other.

Yet Forby's words had shocked her—"his neck in a rope if you refuse"—and she hurried onward, the wind now blowing in pursuit. Whatever Matcham Lodge was up to, however heinous his crime, she could not through her own inaction let him hang. Though she might tomorrow, if he ran like a rat again tonight.

TWENTY-ONE

A narrow, unrailed plank linked Risers Wharf with the stern of the *Nereid*. Charlotte hesitated, her skirts blowing, her cloak whipped tight around her. Then the wind drew breath and she ran along the plank, aware that if she missed her step there'd be the deep black ditch of water . . .

The vessel moved, and was jerked by its stern lines. Charlotte stumbled, twisting desperately in an effort to reach the deck. Better the injuries from a hard fall there than—

But she was caught and held upright by a man who said, "Can't have no women aboard now, my lovely. Away you go and try your luck further on." A powerful man, his broad head covered by a traditional striped woollen cap. His voice low, his expression impassive, he was already turning her to send her back to the quay. She remembered what Forby had told her— *"Go aboard that ship and warn them . . ."* Them, he had said. Not just the captain.

So she blurted, "I've been sent by Master Kimber! There's government agents on the scour! You must warn Captain Lodge that—" But by then the man had swung her around and toward the companionway, his boot heel rapping a signal on the deck. "Down you go, and tell it to him quick!" He leaned forward, slid back the hatch cover, opened the waist-high doors.

She was all but propelled down the oak-wood steps to the cabin. As she entered it she saw a table, half covered by a chart; a white silk handkerchief; a money pouch; a lantern with the wick turned low . . .

And at one side of the table she saw two bearded men, massive broad-shouldered men, their gaze pitiless. And each with a pistol levelled at her face. . . .

Across from them she saw Matcham Lodge, his right arm extended toward her, halving the distance between the muzzle of his own heavy pistol and her head. "Well," he said curtly. "Master Kimber's lady. And what brings you tumbling aboard?"

Ignoring his ill grace, she told him, "There are uniformed men on the quay. Government agents. Master Forby sent me to warn you. He's managed to keep himself clear of things, though he says there'll be a rope for you if—"

"Stop gabbling. How many are there?"

"The agents? I don't know. I glimpsed twenty or so. Though if I'd stopped to count them—"

"Very well. Stand over there." He brushed past her and called quietly to the man who'd stamped the alarm. "I want someone playing a fiddle, Master Cope! Get the crew grouped around him by the gangplank! And for God's sake impede our visitors!" He turned to his bearded companions, the men waiting calmly and in silence, their pistols now laid within reach on the table.

It was then that Charlotte said, "I've no need to be part of this, Captain Lodge. Nor wish to be. You've heard what I was sent to tell you, and even that was against my better judgement."

She moved to climb the companionway, halting as Matcham warned her, "You'll be questioned on the quay. You have no answers to give them, and they'll know it. They'll take you away and slap the truth from you, and your whimperings will see these men hanged, and Forby and I and Master Cope along with them. Unless that's what you intend for us, *stand over there and keep shut!*"

From above came the sudden, jaunty, out-of-place sawing of a fiddle. Then the rhythmic clapping of men in time with the music. Then the voice of Master Cope—"You've only a few moments, Cap'n. The searchers are on the next ship. And they're led by Mason Tagg."

Charlotte saw Matcham stiffen at the name, then mouth it in silence, as though his worst fears were confirmed. He nodded at his companions. "There's concealed bunks below the deck here. Pull the table toward you. I'll see to the pistols and the rest of it."

They heard the first mate say, "Tagg's hurryin' them along, Cap'n. Best be sharp."

The silent, broad-shouldered men hauled the table across, kicked aside the worn rush matting, stooped to raise the trap. They lowered themselves awkwardly into the canvas hammocks slung below the deck. Matcham said, "Quick!" and there were sounds of scuffling from above, the music silenced in mid-tune. And the trap was still raised, the matting rolled back, the table off centre when a man's black boots and dark grey hose and the hem of his long black frock coat appeared on the steps.

Charlotte's eyes darted between the companionway and the cabin. She remembered Forby's words, "his neck in a rope." She knew she must do something—*something*—to save Matcham and the others. And not only them but herself.

A series of images flashed across her mind. Gaudy, vivid fragments that brought with them the sounds of merriment, the shrieks and banter of the women from Mistress De Rue's Seminary in Swindon.

Ignoring Matcham, she pulled the bonnet from her head and shrugged herself free of her cloak. She tore downward at the row of campanulate buttons she'd so carefully sewn on her bodice. By doing so she revealed the upper curve of her breasts, the scalloped edge and drawstring of her shift. The display, though not yet especially daring, would be a clear indication of her business aboard this ship.

She moved to bar the visitor's descent.

In as broad a Wiltshire accent as she could manage, she protested, "Our good cap'n 'ere didn't say as 'ow I'd be expected to please a friend. Couldn't you jus' take a turn about the deck, sir, till me and the cap'n—"

"One more word, you bloody little doxy, and I'll see you before the magistrates, and have you whipped from Bristol to your birthplace." He stamped on down, his left hand ready to push Charlotte away, his eyes already flicking to search the cabin. Charlotte retreated beyond reach, seeing now that the table was in place, the worn rush mat across the trap. There was no sign of the chart or pouch, the handkerchief or pistols. Matcham was at the far end of the cabin, filling two thick tumblers with rum.

He turned, held out one of the tumblers to Charlotte, then ignored her as he gazed at Mason Tagg.

The man's waistcoat, with its ebony buttons, was a match with his frock coat, his stock the same dark fabric as his hose. Yet his hands and face were paper pale, his wig chalked as white as a playhouse ghost, his short stovepipe hat as black as the lining of a chimney. He kept pinching at the side brim of the hat, unaware perhaps that the habit had worn it threadbare and greasy in the light.

But Mason Tagg had chosen his dress with care. After all, what would blue or green do for someone who was an officer, a servant of the Crown? It was black that spoke of authority, black that brought suspicious types to attention, black that told them the colour of their future if they lied.

"You know me, I believe, Captain Lodge."

"Well enough, Master Tagg, to bet a guinea you'll decline my rum."

"Pray bet it, Captain, and prove to me you're as stupid as I

think. I should certainly take your guinea, then leave your rum
on the table to trap the flies. It'd be the first time a tavern-
room sailor ever paid me to take his slop."

"You're in your usual vile humour tonight, Master Tagg.
Can't you find anyone to hang?"

"I am looking at someone, Captain Lodge. Someone I would
pay a guinea to see hanged. And this, I take it, is your present
comfort, when you're not engaged in treason against the
King." He gestured with a practised disgust toward Charlotte,
nodding as she noisily sucked at her drink. "What a miserable
life you do lead; in the shadow of the gibbet, and diseased by
the likes of this."

Charlotte Cannaway blinked and held tight to her glass. Her
hand shook involuntarily and she wanted to tell this foul-
minded creature who she was—Mistress Charlotte Cannaway
of Faxforge, the decent, ordinary daughter of fine and honest
parents! Or, if you prefer, Mistress Charlotte Wintersill of
Wintersill Hall, my husband being a gentleman of the county,
in name if not by nature! And you! How dare you hurl your
filthy insults? How dare you—

But she forced herself to stay silent, guessing what Master
Tagg would think of her outburst. A whore with her bodice
three quarters open, and a glass of rum unstable in her hand.
Oh, he'd love the claim that she was decent and ordinary, her
parents honest and fine. And better than that—the secret she'd
kept from Forby, the secret she intended to keep from Matcham—better than that would Mason Tagg love her claim that
she was really a lady of Wiltshire! He would probably toss *her*
a guinea as payment for the laughter she had caused.

She heard Matcham say, "I choose carefully the women I
bring aboard, Master Tagg. It's only certain men who get
down here uninvited."

"You're a traitor to the Crown, you slap-jack sailor. I know
it and shall prove it, as you will know whose boots are the ones
that kick you away on the gallows! You've been running
Jacobites to France, and you think because you're not caught

yet you can do it until the Day of Judgement claims us all. But I'll tell you this. I'll be fair with you. I shall have you strangling in a hempen cord before the closing of this year. And here! *Here's a coin of mine that says I will!*" His eyes blazed with an unnerving kinship to madness. He held up the piece he'd dragged from his pocket, then hurled it in fury at the table. The coin spun off, forcing Charlotte to duck, rum spilling from her glass as she did so.

It amused Mason Tagg to see her cringe, splashed by the drink. But it also amused the unsmiling Matcham Lodge, since the coin came to rest behind a horsehair cushion of the bench. Behind the back rest of which, in a hollow compartment, were the chart and white silk handkerchief, this last an identification among Jacobites; those who would see King George unthroned, and the likes of Mason Tagg entertained on the gallows he so much loved.

But he'd not quite finished, the pinkness of his anger still suffusing the limpid white. "We've let you slip in and out of this port too easily, Captain Lodge. But it won't happen again, I assure you. You'll be watched from now on, night and day. You'll be weighed in and measured out, your vessel stripped from its masthead to the keel. I *know* you're a traitor. I know it as the fit of my shoes."

"I 'ope that coin you tossed will be comin' to me. All this time you gen'lemen 'ave been stood 'ere discoursin', I could've 'ad quite a time ashore with me friends. Quite a merry time." She spoke with a laboured dignity, and kept her head nodding in support of the claim until Tagg had stormed from the cabin.

Then she gazed across in silence at Matcham Lodge.

✳

He held her gaze, knowing how far she had gone on his behalf. Her clothes torn, the woman accused of—well, of being things she was evidently not. The accent she'd adopted, in order to be convincing in her role. The way she'd let Tagg drive her backward, whilst he, Matcham, had thrust the rum at her as though it was her drink by habit. And the way she'd sucked at it. And the way she'd laid claim to the coin, her pathetic attempt at dignity gathered around her like the torn-apart loops of her bodice.

They heard the sound of the fiddle again, played low and easy near the gangplank.

"That was a generous performance, Mistress Cannaway."

"I am pleased you remember my name, Captain Lodge. Are you all the things he says you are, that most dreadful Mason Tagg?"

"Well, I may be a tavern-room sailor, and slap-jack, and—"

"But a traitor to the Crown?"

"Not as I see it, no."

"Will you tell me who they are, these Jacobites? I'm ashamed to say I've no knowledge of politics at all."

"When I get back from—when I return, I promise you I shall tell you who they are. Not *who* they are, but what they are and why."

"That night," she said quietly, closing the untorn loops and buttons of her bodice. "You may not remember, but I was chased from an alley—"

"And I left you to the mercy of Forby Kimber? And his cutlass? Why ever should I not remember deserting a lady in distress? It will have to remain a shameful episode in my life, Mistress Cannaway. However—"

"The men you were with—they were Jacobites?"

"And are now in Rome."

"Yes," she murmured, "yes. I never did really believe you'd slunk away that night—" Then she saw his shadow move across the lantern and felt herself caught up by him, his lips pressing tight on hers, his hands demanding she stay where she was, as long as he desired. He was quite the fellow for telling her to stand or stay where she was.

But this time Charlotte was willing to obey, and it was afterward she convinced herself that *she'd* been the one to first draw apart, then direct his attention to the men concealed below the deck. Working together, they drew back the matting, raised the trap and assisted the Jacobite leaders from their shallow, premature graves. The men flexed their shoulders, far too wide for the hammocks, then glanced at Matcham and nodded their respect for his whore.

He took her on deck, where she murmured, "Is Forby your ally in what you do?"

"When I get back. You must go ashore now; the tide will be turning soon."

"Has Forby told you where I live? On The Biss. I'm the niece of Mistress Sophia Biss. It's the house—"

"I'll not come there. The less there is to link us the better. You'll have to come to the ship. If you will."

"And be seen by Tagg? And regarded as—"

Matcham stood over her and grinned. It was something he did badly, though it seemed all the better that he tried. "You're too sensitive, Mistress Cannaway. I was insulted too, you know, though it's you who deserve his coin. I'll have it for you in a week or so. Take my hand and I'll see you ashore."

He led her across, the gangplank springing beneath their weight. Then he called to a man on the next ship in line. "I'll be out of here on the tide, Master Fisk. Will you walk a young lady to The Biss for me?"

"Pleased to do so, Captain. And fair sail if you're slipped before I'm back."

And Charlotte said quickly, "Yes, Captain Lodge. As your friend remarks. Fair sail."

Matcham stooped to kiss her again, this time lightly, almost hesitantly, as if they had now constructed a spell that any forcefulness might break. A gentle kiss, interrupted by Master Fisk, who was armed for Charlotte's protection with a plaited, tar-stiffened rope.

"Off we go then, lady. I'm known as 'Celibate' Fisk. Though I can't say as I've never been married, 'cause I have. Twice, tell the truth. Twice, that is, in England. And once in Italy. And once on the island of Corsicay, what's down in the Mediterranean Sea. And another time, though it didn't last, in a port on the coast of Africa. But you mustn't think me fickle, my lady, it's simply that I get myself about. Ah, yes, and there was a girl I got wed to, pretty young thing in Dublin."

Politely measuring his pace to hers, Master Fisk strolled along, the plaited cudgel on his shoulder, leaving Charlotte to arrange the puzzle of her thoughts. The most colourful piece portrayed Forby Kimber, the most sombre showing a likeness of Mason Tagg. Whilst the third, the shadowy centrepiece . . .

✻

In the week during which Charlotte waited for Matcham to return to Risers Wharf, her family grew desperate at Faxforge.

For all Brydd's efforts, the support he received from Giles and Jonas Jones, the care with which Ben Waite and Matthew Ives crafted their work, the skills shown by William and his masons, the endless hours of cooking and serving by Elizabeth and Hester—for all they had done, the "Cannaway Conductor" failed to meet the Specific.

The impish Step Cotter had driven it around the yard. Then been forced to duck, or snap the cords that were set at the height of city signboards. He had taken the vehicle through a street of barrels, the tubs positioned in accordance with the twenty-page instructions. And clipped the barrels whenever he made his turn.

Sam Gilmore had been brought from the "Blazing Rag" to take a seat alongside William, so the Conductor could be tested with two heavyweight passengers aboard. And the vehicle had tipped off balance, almost throwing the men to the ground.

Ben and Matthew hastened to assure Brydd these were all minor setbacks, nothing that couldn't be corrected by the time Edward Flowerdewe arrived. And Brydd said, "Perhaps so," knowing his craftsmen would not accuse him of outright failure. Though failure it was, the design just a mimicry of others, a patched and brazed imitation, devoid of original thought.

✳

He was irritable now, the master of Faxforge, his eyes bloodshot, his shoulders hunched as if to darken the pallor of his face. He worked on in his study by candlelight, penning his designs, then skidding the sheets away, his back to the wind that hissed its derision through the broken panes of glass.

How to make the wheels turn sharper . . . How to seat the driver below the swing of the signs . . . And keep the passengers balanced, with or without their baggage . . .

Giles had offered to mend the windows, and been told to get on with the work he'd been given in the yard. Then, when his son had limped away, Brydd sat staring across the cluttered corner room, ashamed that he saw fit to bark at others because he himself had lost his bite.

Yet how to bring the wheels close in, the trunk further forward, the brake positioned just so . . .

Stiff and bleary at his desk, Brydd turned to blink at another encroaching dawn. How many days and pots of ink and sheets of paper and sprinkles of drying-sand had he wasted, scratching his unoriginal designs? He'd not always been this slow, this glutinous. After all, it was he who'd invented the "Cannaway Carrier"—a vehicle still in demand after twenty years. And he who'd improved the draw-brake system on heavy running wagons. And the folding step by which passengers might alight from a coach. And the intricate springing that—

But enough, he derided, of my brilliant former achievements! It's what I accomplish now that matters—what I might accomplish if my brain stops running to soup.

He heard a wagon turn in at the road gate and went yawning from the house to meet it. He saw William on the high, unsprung bench, and beside him William's brother-in-law, the quarry master Nathan Reed. A welcome visitor, Nathan, even though his greeting was country blunt. "By God, but you look worn to the bone."

"And feel it," Brydd admitted. "You and William get your cart to the yard, then we'll breakfast in the kitchen." He stood at the path edge, watching listlessly as William struggled to manoeuvre the wagon. He got the four-horse team safely around, then cursed as the prow of the massive quarry wagon became entangled with the cut-back wall of trees beside the pond.

Too tired to be of value, Brydd thought how much better it would be if the bench had turned in concert with the wheels. Not that it was possible with a lumberer like that. But with something lighter . . .

A passenger carriage . . .

A conveyance expressly designed for the streets and alleyways of a city. Have the driving bench low above the forward axle, the bolster and kingpin *behind* it, the driver turning as the front wheels turned, then no matter how narrow the gauge . . .

He deserted William and Nathan, shouting as he strode toward the house. "Giles! Rouse yourself and get down, sir! I need your assistance in the study! There's a sketch I have in mind. Do you hear me, sir? Are you dressed and clattering down?"

Elizabeth and Hester were already in the kitchen, cutting slices of cheese and bread and cold meats for the twenty-strong work force. And setting out salted pickles for Step Cotter. And a small dish of plums for Waylen. And a dozen pitchers of ale.

Brydd greeted his wife and daughter, told them William and Nathan Reed had arrived, then smiled as he added, "Or are struggling to do so." And with that he crossed to the littered corner room, convinced his idea was worth the further expenditure of ink and paper and the sprinklings of sand.

TWENTY-TWO

The message was delivered by a sooty young urchin who thrust it at Chapman and raced off. Folded in from the corners, the sealed square of parchment was addressed quite simply, "Mistress Charlotte Cannaway."

Chapman requested a polished silver tray from the maidservant Tilly, "Preferably without your finger marks around it," then laid the parchment on the centre of the tray. He tutted his disapproval as he noticed a smudge on the letter itself. Doubtless the urchin's handiwork. Grubby little monster. But just another example of the way the world was going.

He carried the tray upstairs and presented the message to Charlotte. It was midmorning and she too was engaged in correspondence, completing a close-written, five-page letter to her family. She took the parchment from the tray, then gazed in unspoken question at the butler.

"Just a brat, Mistress Charlotte. Scampered away before I could collar him. And—here's an odd thing—before I could tip him his farthing. Must have been paid aforehand, I suppose, and well enough not to want more." He withdrew, once again confused by the changing values of life. A messenger boy who spurned the chance of a coin? That would never have happened in his day. People knew better than to pass up a farthing in his day. They'd a proper sense of values in his day.

Enjoying the suspense, Charlotte slid a thumbnail around the green wax seal. The folded-in corners opened slowly and she read, "This evening at dusk. If you will."

That, in its entirety, was it. No endearment, no signature, not even an initial. Though there wouldn't be of course, since "the less there is to link us the better."

However, there was nothing to prevent her saying the name quietly to herself. Or imagining the tide that had swirled along the Avon, bearing upon it the dark red ship.

✳

Common sense told her to dress with all the vulgarity of a whore. It was what the hideous Mason Tagg had supposed her to be—what she'd wanted him to believe—and he'd made it clear he'd be keeping a watch on the vessel. So the brightest skirt and bodice in her wardrobe. A hat with an extra plumage of feathers pinned around the brim. And powder today. And rouge on her cheekbones. And buttoned, calf-length boots.

She paraded for the amusement of it in front of Aunt Sophia.

"Most attractive," Sophia managed. "Delightful, my dear. A dance and charade, is it, with everyone dressed from the vibrant pages of history? And who have you chosen to portray, may I ask? A courtesan of France?"

"A courtesan of sorts," Charlotte nodded, "though perhaps not so refined."

"Well, you are certainly, ah, costumed for the part." She silently gave thanks that neither Brydd nor Elizabeth was here to see how their daughter was dressed tonight. No matter that Charlotte was a married woman. *Worse* that she was a married woman. And as for her being a courtesan, the young lady would pass just as well as a fresh-to-the-business whore!

Avoiding the butler, Charlotte slipped quietly from the

house. The sun was setting now, though the blush of light was enough to guide her along the elm-fringed border of Queen Square. She smiled at the way her marvellous Aunt Sophia had stifled all criticism, inventing a charade and finding a role for her niece to play. And she was still smiling as she left the square and turned east toward Risers Wharf. But the smile died quickly as Mason Tagg came across the quay and called out, "Wait!"

He peered at her, his hand reaching for her arm. "You've a face that's familiar. Say something, doxy. My ears are as sharp as my eyes."

Again attempting a broad Wiltshire accent, Charlotte protested, "I'm sure I'm not 'customed to bein' intruded on like this, though *you've* a face as *I* find familiar, Master Jason Flag!"

"Oh yes. I've placed you now. Captain Lodge's comfort, when he's not too busy with treason. And it's Mason Tagg, you daubed little harlot. You'll never get far, you won't, unless you remember the names of the gentlemen you meet. Very important, so I'm told, that a doxy should recollect her clients. On your way to his ship, are you? On your way to comfort the captain?"

His pale, almost bloodless fingers stroked her arm.

"Cap'n Lodge is just one of several friends I 'appen to know in Bristol. An' what's wrong with that? Can't a girl 'ave friends in this city, Master Tagg? Agin the law is it now for a lady to 'ave companions among our honest seafarin'—"

"I'll walk along with you." His hand stopped stroking and he held her above the elbow. Then, the tone of his voice softened and sugared, he told her he had nothing personal against her. She was only a girl, and prettier than most, though somewhat lost to temptation. "But you've got yourself in with a bad un in Captain Lodge. You've been with him a while, I dare say, and think him quite the lover. And exciting the way he sneaks his Jacobites in and out of port. The number of times he's got past us! And left us at a loss on the quay! He's a real fox is

Master Matcham! I tell you, girl, I could almost admire him, if he wasn't running Jacobites but gin. A regular sleek fox, our slippery captain."

Oh yes, Charlotte thought, shake your head and smile, Master Tagg, and pretend your admiration. She told him, "Maybe I 'ave got meself misguided. Though I promise you, sir, I don't know what you mean by—Jacobites is it you call 'em? And treason, you say? Well, I'm not a treasonous woman. Mind the puddle, sir. Wouldn't do to soil your boots."

Tagg nodded and led her around the mud. He said, "The Crown has always been generous toward those who stand for England. And if you were to help us—"

"I'd do so willingly. I know my duty. 'Ow generous?"

"That would depend on the value of what you could tell us. But there's every chance you'd be richer by fifty guineas."

"Fifty?" Charlotte warbled. Then with what she trusted was a proper sense of cunning, "An' 'ow do I know I'll get it? Maybe I can find out what you're after, an' I'll come to you an' tell it, an' all you'll give me is a glass of rum an' a stingin' slap on me arse. 'Ow can I be sure, Master Tagg? Fifty guineas is an 'efty sum to toss around."

He stopped her then, close to the warehouse where Forby Kimber had torn her cloak on the wall; close to the spot where he'd urged her to save Matcham Lodge from a hanging.

"The Crown," Tagg snarled, "does not break agreements, even with the likes of whores! You'll get the money, girl, the day you make me the wiser! Now then"—and again he sugared his tone—"now, my young lady, where's the need for such suspicion? I tell you in all honesty, I do not really wish to see your captain hang. I know I said different the other night, but that was just to scare him to his senses. You come to me when you next know of strangers on his ship. They'll be burly, tight-lipped men most likely. As soon as we've caught them I'll count you out your money. They're the real traitors, not the adventuresome Captain Lodge."

"An' what will 'appen to 'im, to Master Matcham?"

"Well," Tagg pondered, "let's see. He's a personable fellow, and if he made a nice speech of repentance to the magistrates, he'd probably serve a sixmonth in the gaol. Though you'd have to go gentle with him when he came out, the prison diet being somewhat meanish with meat." He squeezed her arm and let his pink lips widen in a smile. "Keep in mind what I tell you. And remember. I'm not without influence in the courts. Many's the culprit I've helped. Or hindered."

Charlotte babbled something and got away from him, fearing she would vomit her disgust within his sight. She could still feel the touch of his stroking, limpid hand. And hear the things he'd called her, the sugar-sweet lies he'd told her, the valueless offers and promises he had made.

She did not look back, fearing the Jacobite hunter would still be there. Instead she forced herself to walk briskly across the quay, her hips swinging as Tagg would have expected of Captain Lodge's comfort.

❅

The hatches were closed across the cabin ports, the cabin illuminated as before by candles and lanterns. There was a black bottle on the table, an inexpert arrangement of flowers in a jar. Master Cope called down, "Lady's come aboard, Cap'n," and Matcham Lodge stepped forward to greet his guest.

He was dressed in jacket and breeches, the coat resplendent with its bordered cuffs and lapels, its scattering of buttons, the glint of metal turned from brass to gold in the mellow, flickering lights. He was not the type to wear a wig. Nor, it seemed, to do more than comb his fingers through the twists and tangles of his hair. He nodded at Charlotte as she reached the foot of the companionway, his welcoming smile drawn tight by the immediate anger in her voice.

"Is there anyone concealed below the deck here tonight, Captain Lodge?"

"Not to my knowledge, Mistress Charlotte."

"I ask, d'you see, because the learning of it could be money in the bank for me! Fifty guineas if I go back up there and tell Master Tagg—and tell that man—that hideous, slimy creature —if I inform him of what I know! Now that's a sizeable reward, you'd agree, for the tattles of a harlot!" Then she stood rigid and wept in silence because it was no longer amusing, this dressing up as a whore and strolling through Queen Square, her outfit as vivid as she could make it, her hat weighed down with its plumage, her accent as broad as the swing of her rounded hips. It had started amusing, though it had now turned sour and ugly. Her pretence—her charade—had taken her too far. Mason Tagg had accepted her as a doxy, a waterfront comfort, and because of it he'd thought fit to snarl at her and threaten her and bribe her with his bag of government coins. And with the lie that Matcham would spend no more than a sixmonth in gaol . . .

He frowned and approached her, stopping as she raised a hand in arrest. He listened whilst she told him what had happened, her voice growing firmer as she acknowledged that the fault had been hers.

"Yes," he said quietly, "you've played the part too well, and it upsets you that the audience applauds. But it shouldn't, Mistress Charlotte, it shouldn't upset you at all. You've fooled Master Tagg, and wasn't that your intention when you painted and powdered your face? He's insulted you, and I'm sorry for that, though every word he levelled against you makes him all the more of a fool. He's many other things, and worse, but he'd squirm like an eel to be recognised as a fool."

She nodded and turned away to dry her tears. Then she faced him again and shrugged aside her memories of Tagg. She asked what the flowers were, "And is that another bottle of your dreadful, scorching rum?"

She already regretted the distance she'd set between them. How much better, she wished, how much more in tune with her dreams if she'd come in all her chosen vulgarity, and been welcomed by Matcham and embraced by him in the mellow light of the lanterns. To have been caught up by him as before and held in his arms and praised for the effort she'd made on his behalf, her pretty pretence a game they could both enjoy.

But with Master Mason Tagg taking part, the game could yet end on the gallows.

"I am ignorant of flowers," Matcham told her. "As for the bottle, it holds something a good deal better than the stuff I forced upon you the other night. Which reminds me. Here's the token I promised you the last time we met." He reached in a pocket and produced a small, polished leather box. "When you see what it is," he warned, "you might well prefer to throw it in the river." Then he passed it to her and she raised the lid, lifting out the coin Mason Tagg had hurled in his madness at the table.

The coin was no longer just a worn and isolated piece. It was rimmed with silver now and suspended from a delicate silver chain. And although King George stared blankly from one side of the coin, the other was neatly engraved with the words, "From a Slap-Jack Sailor to his Comfort."

Slowly, twisting it in her fingers, Charlotte turned the pendant over and over. Then she smiled at Matcham and said, "It is not even a guinea. He said he'd wager a guinea to see you hanged before Christmas. But this is just a crown! He's not only a fool, but the cheapest kind of fool I ever saw. Or maybe he is shrewder than we think. Why should he wager a guinea after all, if he knows he is bound to lose?

"But I thank you for this, Captain Matcham. And for the inscription, though God forbid my aunt Sophia should ever read it." The box and pendant spilled on the table as Matcham gently held Charlotte to him, her trembling caused in part by her happiness here, in part by the memory of the sinister figure who waited above them on the quay.

✳

They sat across from each other and she agreed the Canary wine was a good deal better than the rum. She touched the pendant, making idle shapes with the intricate silver chain.

"You know," she told him, "this only settles half the debt you owe me. You also promised an explanation of these Jacobites. It's a word you use with caution, though it seems to bring a froth to the lips of Master Tagg. Are they really the traitors he claims them to be?"

"Traitors? Patriots? The country's true monarchists? Enemies of the State and Crown? I can only tell you they are men —Scots for the most part, though by no means the Scots alone —who believe we've been deprived of our proper English king. They regard the present monarch, German George, as simply a usurper. A leaden creature who decries our way of life and is as sorry he came from Hanover as are we—as are the Jacobites— that he came. He has no more than a smattering of our language, so it's said. And imports fat mistresses from Germany to his court. And spends half his days cross-legged on the carpet, cutting out paper toys."

"Talk like that," Charlotte murmured, "and I can see why Tagg would have you hanged. But you've not yet explained—"

"Nor do I think I can." Matcham shrugged. "It's a question of lineage, Mistress Charlotte, the Jacobites believing that the true and royal line has been diverted. King James was forced from the throne some thirty years ago, the crown taken then by the Dutchman William and his wife—"

"A Dutchman, a German, the English and the Scots!"

"And a Spanish fleet," Matcham added, "and a Polish princess, and the French King Louis, and King James's court in exile in Rome. And an uprising that failed, an invasion that came to nought, the hopes of the future growing in the belly of a certain Clementina Sobieski. And a slap-jack captain who will, if you insist, attempt to make things clear. Though his own knowledge being riddled with faults—"

"Tell me this instead, Captain Matcham. Tell me instead why you risk your life to aid these rootless Jacobites. Because, from the little you do understand, you believe in the rightness of their cause?"

"In an English king for England? You may say I believe in that."

"Tagg called you adventuresome. Is that part of the lure?"

"My father," Matcham told her, "was the registrar of graves for the city of Bath and a number of villages in the district. He knew his Bible from Genesis to Malachi. And swindled widows. And resold gravestones. And died in bed with a smile of piety on his lips. Is adventure part of the lure, Mistress Charlotte? I think it would have to be, don't you?"

"Nigella," she said. "It's come to me now. That's what those flowers are called. Nigella, or mist-on-the-downs." She gazed at him and said, "I've no right to ask what prompts you, Master Matcham. But there is one more question."

"Do I risk my neck for the money?"

"No, it's not that. I merely wish to know if there's anything *I* might be allowed to do."

"For the adventure of it, Mistress Charlotte? For the rightness of the cause?"

She moved her head, then traced patterns with the silver-link chain. "No," she whispered, her voice scarcely audible. "For you."

Better at explaining this than the complexities of lineage and alliance, Matcham grasped her hand briefly as he told her he would not allow her to be endangered by his ventures. "The other night, when we buried those fellows for a time below the deck, you saved us all by the quickness and daring of your actions. And fooled the black and white Tagg again this evening. And that's enough, my dear Charlotte. I'll not see you mauled about by that ill-minded servant of the Crown."

She nodded acceptance, then listened as he recounted tales of the coast of Africa, of the Spanish peninsula, of the corsair ship he'd encountered—"Did we fight them? With nothing more than pistols aboard? No, Mistress Charlotte; we put about as quick as we could and fled!" He told her how different the houses were in Africa and Spain, how brilliant the

costumes of the people, how strange the languages they spoke.
He did not force his presence or his drink upon Charlotte, or
oil his stories with claims she'd be encouraged to believe.
When he told her of a storm he'd survived near Corsica—"the
water curling above us, our vessel attached like an ikon to a
wall"—she sat forward enthralled, watching as his hands
moved to illustrate the scene. And when he told her he'd been
invited to ride a camel—"Beyond doubt the world's most vile-
tempered beast, and mine the one that chose to spit at me, accurate as a fountain in the face!"—she laughed aloud at the
image he'd created. And, listening, she stretched her hand to
catch at his, at ease within the warmth and glow of the cabin,
the sweetness of Canary a cinnamon curtain drawn around
them.

The clatter of feet on deck came as hail at a window.
Charlotte was telling of her life and the coachyard at Faxforge,
though she stopped in mid-sentence, gazing at Matcham as he
turned to the stairway of the cabin.

They heard a rap on the hatch, and Matcham was already
on his feet and moving as Master Cope called down, "A word
with you, Cap'n. Soon as you please, sir." The mate did not
apologise for his intrusion; why would he, since he'd not have
banged the hatch unless it was urgent?

Charlotte waited for the fox to return. She examined the
coin he had given her. The profile of King George, a blunt-
nosed monarch with laurels in his hair; then, turning the
crown, Matcham's clean-etched message, "From a Slap-Jack
Sailor to his Comfort." She wondered if it ever could be so.

The Matcham Lodge who returned to the cabin was no
longer the one who'd sprawled at the far side of the table, his
legs stretched out, his expression relaxed as he told her of
camels and corsairs. He was once again the hard-faced man
she'd collided with near the alley mouth, the one who'd
stalked away from her in the Wool Hall.

And unwilling, it seemed, to tell her what was what.

So Charlotte took the reins and asked, "Are we due for another visit from Mason Tagg? Give me some warning, Master Matcham, and I won't have to damage the button loops of my bodice."

He stared at her, looked away to think things out for himself, then settled his gaze on her again. She started to speak and he gestured at her to stay silent. A moment passed, the ship creaking as it was dragged by the current, jerked by its forelines and by the ropes that held it tethered at the stern. Someone moved above them on the deck. Someone shouted orders on the quay.

Then Matcham said, "There's been a setback, Mistress Charlotte. I am expecting a man to come aboard before long— a Jacobite as you'll have guessed—though Master Cope informs me all the entries to the wharf have been sealed. Tagg's agents are questioning anyone who leaves or approaches the area." He hesitated before adding, "Anyone, that is, except—"

"Daubed-up women?" she queried. "Doxies plying their trade?"

He nodded. "So it seems."

She came to her feet, laid the silver-rimmed pendant in its box and placed the box in a drawstring purse. Then she told him, "I have acted the part with some success, you'll agree, so trust me to continue with it now. Where can he be found, this Jacobite of yours, and what would you have me tell him to keep him from being trapped? I promise you, Captain Matcham, I relish the chance to make a further fool of Master Tagg."

He stood silent for a moment, then asked, "Do you know the streets called Bankside and The Stray?"

"They are near the City Bridge, are they not?"

"That's right. And there's a house on the corner. It has a plain black door, with a lantern above the portal. Will you go there and tell the man who answers you've a message for Master Clark. He'll conduct you upstairs, where Master Clark will make himself known to you. Explain to him that the quay's ringed around and he must get his passenger to the anchorage downriver. I'll expect him between midnight and a quarter past the hour."

Charlotte repeated the instructions, careful to recite them word for word. Matcham nodded and said, "It's unlikely you'll be followed, though if you suspect there's someone—"

"Don't worry, my dear Captain. I'll take care." She smiled as he came forward to embrace her, then asked him how long he'd be away. He told her, "No more than a week. Bristol seems to hold a special charm for me these days. It's something to do with the freshness of the girls who parade the quay."

"Oh, it's *girls* for the greedy cap'n!" she exclaimed, her accent shifting to fit the role. "You must tell me who the others are, Master Matcham, so's I'll know which ones to send splashin' in the river!" Then she clung lightly to him and, no longer needing a prism for her feelings, murmured in her own gentle tone, "Fair sail to you, dear Matcham. And a following breeze for your return."

✳

Uniformed agents detained her at the eastern end of the wharf. They'd admired the swing of her hips as she approached them, ogling her now as she tossed her head and demanded, "What's this then, this arrestin' of a decent young woman?"

They liked that, the claim that she was decent. And the way she stood, arms akimbo, with all the indignation of a whore. And the sulkiness of her pout. And the knowledge of men in her eyes.

"You're not being arrested, missy. Unless of course you've gone against the law."

"Well, I ain't." She gestured vaguely at the ships and said, "I've come from one of them vessels and I'm on me way to meet a friend. An important friend."

"And who might he be, this friend of yours?"

"None of your business."

"Withholding information from His Majesty's agents? Showing disrespect toward officers of the Crown? You'd do best to go careful, so you would, and there's fair warning." They stared at her, enjoying their power, stripping her with their gaze. It was dull, uncomfortable duty, stuck there half the night on the open quay. They welcomed the chance to tease these frisky young harlots. Scare them enough and they'd likely as not say, "We could settle matters, if you wanted. In that alley, between them buildings?" And, one at a time, the men would leave their post.

So they asked her again, "Who are you trotting to meet, eh, missy? And no more impudence, else we'll have you taken away."

A dozen names had already come to her mind. Aldermen of the city. Magistrates. Merchants and businessmen. She'd met them at Sophia's house, or in their own elegant homes. She could name one of them now, confident that the agents would accept what she said. What else could they do, especially if she added, "Married, of course, an' afeared of any scandal."

Then she thought of another name and asked the senior agent if she might speak with him alone. Scare them enough, he acknowledged, leading her to the gap between the buildings. The rest of the detail grinned among themselves. They'd take their turn in order of seniority, little Billy Buchan going last.

But a moment later they saw Charlotte emerge from the alley, her inquisitor all but bowing her on her way. Then he turned and snapped at the men to look sharp. "You are in the King's service, damn you, not wash hags huddled round a tub!" He ignored their questions—"Why let her go? Who's her important friend?"—and peered nervously along the wharf.

It'd be a fine thing, he told himself, if Master Tagg ever knew that I knew he had a doxy on the side. Let *that* get out and he'd have me chipping ice from the decks of a whaler.

She reached the corner of Bankside and The Stray. In terms of distance, it was no more than a half mile from Risers Wharf.

Though a close-built, alley-cut, indirect journey it was. Some of it was lighted by lanterns, the rest a maze of side streets, thin dark veins that threaded their way between the brighter, safer arteries of the city. A tremulous and uncertain half mile for Charlotte Cannaway.

She rapped on the plain black door.

She told the man who opened it, "I have a message for Master Clark."

She was led up broad mahogany stairs that curved within velvet-railed balustrades.

She entered a well-furnished chamber, reminiscent of the withdrawing room in Aunt Sophia's house. The man who'd conducted her there bowed and left her to wait.

She moved to a window and stood looking down at The Stray. I must explain that the quay's been ringed around. . . . And he must get his passenger to the anchorage downriver. . . . Where Matcham will expect him between midnight and—

She turned, sensing someone in the doorway. The man's face was in shadow, the candlelight absorbed by the heavy damask on the walls. She heard him say, "I am Master Clark. I believe you have a message— Well, hell in ferment, so it's you! Bound to happen, I suppose, though I must admit— Doubtless he has his reasons, old Matcham, though it was never intended that *you* should be a part of this, Mistress Charlotte." Then he strode forward, shrugging in apology.

"Master Clark," she measured. "Well, of course. The master clerk. Or should you now be addressed as the master conspirator, my dear and deceitful Forby Kimber?"

TWENTY-THREE

Once again the spring-heeled urchin; the delivery of a folded parchment message. Though this time the contents ran to several lines.

"I am safely returned," Charlotte read, "and beg that we may meet at noon tomorrow on the common near Temple Gate. Pray do not feel discomforted if I ask that you be more yourself."

It was easy enough for Charlotte to decipher the meaning of his words. She was no longer to play the harlot, the captain's comfort. So she need no longer dress the part. She would, as he'd asked, be herself, or at least the woman Matcham knew as Charlotte Cannaway.

He had hired a trap and took her out to the forest that formed a mile-thick hedge beyond the southern wall of the city. They alighted there and walked in the woodland, Charlotte boasting of the way she had fooled Tagg's agents, Matcham wryly amused by her account. The two of them were at ease with each other, the young woman's humour quick and inventive, her remarks tossed as pollen on the wind. Matcham

Lodge was more measured in what he told her, his occasional jokes annealed by the absurdities of life.

Later, in a more serious mood, she asked, "How long will it go on, Master Matcham, this transporting of Jacobites to France?"

"Until their king can return from exile, I suppose. Until they're assured of an English monarch on the throne of England."

"And will you continue to carry them? I mean, with Mason Tagg tightening his net? He regards you as a slippery fox, you know, though I doubt there's anyone as sly as that unctuous servant of the Crown."

"Are you concerned about me, Charlotte? The fox run to earth? The slap-jack sailor netted by Master Tagg?" He glanced cheerfully at her, in time to see her nod, or maybe just dip her head below the overhanging branches that roofed the path.

＊

It became their favourite haunt, this curving expanse of forest. They ventured deeper into the shadowed privacy of the trees, Charlotte carrying a picnic basket stocked with meat and bread, pewter mugs and ale. They found dappled clearings, believing themselves the first to have ever set foot there. They engaged in a happy foolishness, referring to the various paths and clearings by names that would be meaningless to others. "The Snag Path"—where Charlotte had twice left her hat on a briar. "The Track Where We Saw the Deer"—though in fact they had merely heard an animal plunging ahead of them through the undergrowth. And of course there had to be a "Cannaway Clearing" and "The Captain's Clearing," and a swampy area they avoided, dismissing it as "Mason's Marsh."

Today, in the warm final week of September, they'd discovered yet another open patch among the trees. Their meal over, Charlotte was seated, her back to an oak, responding to a challenge from Matcham Lodge. He stood a few feet from her, out in the clearing, intoning in a way he knew would infuriate her. "You might as well admit it. Own to it now. You cannot. There's nothing for it but to accept your defeat with good grace."

"It depends what you mean by colourful."

"Ah-hah! So the lady plays for time. I mean exciting. Unusual. Out of the ordinary. I mean—"

"Very well then, how's this? Two miles north of Faxforge is the Beckhampton Crossing."

"Nothing very colourful—"

"Just be patient, my dear Matcham. And west of Beckhampton is the village of Cherhill. And *there*, in that village, is a band of highwaymen who prey upon travellers and—" She stopped, then glowered for effect at the world-weary shaking of his head.

"There are highwaymen everywhere," he told her, "and it's their nature to prey on passers-by. I regret to say it, Mistress Charlotte, but you have still to convince me that Wiltshire is as colourful as you claim."

"I've seen snakes in the Kennett River. Some of them as long as—that branch over there."

"Tut, tut," he said, "you surely mean as short. If I were to tell you of the sea serpents—"

"There's a hill; you can see it from Faxforge. A steep conical mound called Silbury Hill. In the base of it lives a devil— Don't trouble shaking your head again, Captain Dubious—it's true! A devil inhabits the base of that hill, and he's been seen by, I don't know, by coachmen and riders, by doctors and reverend gentlemen, by travellers of every stripe. And what's more, let me tell you, there've been bones found in the ditch that encircles Silbury Hill! Human bones. Gnawed clean, then scattered about. And what have you to say to that, eh, Master Matcham? Human bones crunched apart and thrown around!"

Smiling with pleasure at the game, Charlotte came to her feet and advanced on him. Her arm extended, her finger pointing, she issued a challenge of her own. "Still too commonplace for you, these tales of Wiltshire? Then perhaps you'd care to spend a night near Silbury Hill. Though I'd not advise it, my dear Matcham, for I like you better with the flesh intact on your bones."

She expected him to laugh, or at least admit she'd recounted a colourful tale. But he seemed suddenly ill at ease, turning from her and moving away to snap leaves from a nearby bush. For an instant Charlotte wondered if the hard-eyed captain was, after all, a believer in devils and demons. She had heard somewhere—at The Biss? from Sophia? from Forby Kimber?—that sailors often lived and died by their superstitions. Though surely not Matcham Lodge.

Then he turned back and without preamble said, "I am in love with you, Charlotte. I have been so for long enough to know it as the truth. I wish us to be married, before which I shall finish with this Jacobite business—"

"Matcham. Please, Matcham—"

"—and make arrangements whereby we may sail—"

"—you must listen to me. I too am in love. I prize you above all else in this world—"

"—for the island of Jamaica, a place, so I'm told, where much can be achieved. I would have you go with me, Charlotte—"

"—and if it were possible, God knows if it were possible, I'd go wherever you chose it to be."

"—as my wife. I believe the two of us—" And only then did he falter, only then truly hearing what she'd said. "What's all this; if it were possible? It is not only possible, my dear Charlotte, it is something we can turn to a fact by Sunday! Most of my crew will stay with me. You say you prize me—quite high the way you put it—and we can be married in your aunt Sophia's house, or at Faxforge, or even at the base of Silbury Hill, though for that I'd bring a double brace of pistols! So what's impossible about it? Don't you know I would have to be gnawed and chewed to nothing before I'd ever let harm

befall you? I am near drowned in love with you, and not likely
to countenance the impossible."

He moved forward to kiss her, his heart opened to her and
made joyous by what she'd told him, the man she prized above
all else in the world. . . .

But she retreated, her tears spilling as she moaned her con-
fession and sank to her knees; not caring, even wishing perhaps
that Matcham Lodge would strike her as reward for the way
she had led him so dishonestly along their shadowed summer
paths. . . .

"You are *what!* Do I hear you aright! Do I hear you saying
you are already married! Turn to me; damn you, woman, turn
and face me and— Oh yes, I hear you now— You are married
to a man named Wintersill and are ashamed to have led me
along. Yes, I see. The lady playing the harlot, and the lady a
would-be harlot all the while." Then he stamped toward her,
his eyes hard, the planes of his face never so drawn as now. He
reached down and Charlotte flinched away. His broad hand
thrust past her as he snatched at the wicker basket with its
stone jar of ale and pewter mugs, its knives and platters and
napkins, everything sent to break and shatter on the farthest
side of the glade.

She scrambled to keep pace with him through the forest,
and they rode back in silence to the city. He took her to the
head of The Biss, waited for her to step from the trap, then
lashed the reins and left her.

She entered the house, brushed Chapman aside, ignored
Aunt Sophia, turned the key in the lock of her door. Then she
lay face down on the bed, sobbing because the best she had
hoped for had happened. And, at that instant, been destroyed.

*

Four days later, solitary days during which Sophia refrained
from questioning her niece, Charlotte left the house. She had
made her decision. If Matcham would still accept her, she'd be

his woman, his mistress, whatever he chose to call her. She would ignore the disciplines of her upbringing, bear the brand of adultery, travel with him to the island of Jamaica or wherever else the *Nereid* might carry them. If—and she repeated it for the hundredth time—if the slap-jack sailor would still allow her aboard.

Avoiding Tagg's agents, she crossed to the south bank of the Avon. From there she could look back across the river at Risers Wharf. And see "Celibate" Fisk on the stern of his ship. And the water lapping beside it, in the space where Matcham's vessel should have been. . . .

She thought of taking her miseries to Forby Kimber. He would probably know where Matcham had gone, and when he was most likely to return. But he might also know the rest of it by now—that the Charlotte Cannaway he'd escorted to the races and the revels was a married woman, young enough to entice both Forby and Matcham Lodge.

It was one thing to be Master Clark, supporter of the Jacobite cause; quite another to be Charlotte Wintersill, an errant wife who thought it clever to pretend she was free.

More critical of herself than Forby might have been, she walked disconsolate along the quay. Then back and across the bridge and aimlessly through the city, returning with the dusk to The Biss.

The house door was open, a carriage left unattended near the steps. She wondered which of her aunt's eccentric friends had called by this evening, forced herself to show a semblance of interest, then entered the hall and, to the left of it, the elegant soft-lit withdrawing room.

Behind her the house door was slammed shut.

✳

Ahead she saw Sophia, her aunt's expression a pallid mask of disgust. And there, the object of Sophia's bitter gaze, was a blotchy, high-heeled man it took Charlotte a moment to recog-

nise as her husband, the run-to-seed Brook Wintersill, gentleman of Wiltshire.

Beside him, though deeper in the shadows, was Lucas Ripnall, a pistol hanging from his hand.

The butler Chapman was sprawled on the trysting couch,
blood seeping from a bruise above his closed and congealed left
eye.

And then, to make the poison perfect, came the shrilling
Eldon Sith, his complaint that he'd been left an unconsciona-
ble long time behind the door out there and would much appreciate a glass. "I'll serve it meself," he told Chapman. "You
just indicate where it is."

"We keep a special stock," the butler murmured. "It runs in
the ditch below the quay. Drink as deep of it as you like."

Eldon sprang at him and Charlotte slapped the attacker full
in the face. As Eldon stumbled, hissing with pain, Brook Wintersill came forward, catching at his wife and pushing her back
against the wall. "Bad habits!" he charged. "Is this how ladies
behave in the sink of Bristol?" They struggled for a moment,
then Charlotte stood silent, her neck pinched in the claw of
his hand.

Lucas said, "Time enough for that later. Tell 'em what
we've come for, Brooksy. Tell 'em why we're here, then let's
be off. There might be others coming by and—"

"And what?" Brook railed. "Am I the husband of this hedgerow bitch, or am I not? Do I have the right to reclaim my
wife, this tiresome runaway woman who thinks she can make a
mockery of the Wintersill name—"

"Just say it," Lucas snapped. "Just say it and we'll be gone."

Small comfort to Charlotte, though it seemed that even the
strutting Ripnall was weary of Brook's complaints.

She asked him, "How did you learn of my whereabouts?"

"Pure good fortune," he told her, relaxing his hold on her
neck. "You were spotted by Peter Seal a month ago, though
the damned fool had some foreign girl with him and he lost

you in the street. But it gave us a starting point. He remarked that he'd seen you, so with Eldon and Lucas I took lodgings near Broad Street. From then on it was just a matter of time. With all your smart new clothes, you were bound to parade about the city."

"Very well. So you've found me. And will you now say what you're here for?"

The harsh, husky voice of Aunt Sophia. "Master Wintersill has already told me what he's here for, Charlotte. He is here to extort a considerable sum of money. Though perhaps you should spell it out yourself, Master Wintersill, so your wife might hear the pretty way you put it."

Lucas Ripnall urged, "Yes, Brook, for God's sake tell it and let's be off." Standing within the safety of Ripnall's pistol, Eldon Sith nodded agreement.

The women gazed unblinking at Brook Wintersill as he said he'd been forced to sell off half his property. Yet, if the Hall itself was to be saved, he needed more.

"A justified recompense is how you termed it."

"If it pleases you, Mistress Biss—"

"It does not please me at all," she rasped. "I am merely reminding you of your words. A justified recompense—"

"And so it is!" Brook shouted. "It is owed to me for having searched this far to find my wife, and now discover her as a gilded city bitch! I am owed for her absence, damn you! I am owed for it, and shall be paid to keep away. Ten thousand pounds, or I'll snatch Charlotte back and have you—*you*, Mistress Biss, arraigned as a woman who markets girls on the streets." He pushed his brandied face close to her as he said, "I *can* have it done, and I shall. There's plenty who'll back me in court. It might surprise you what men will say for the price of an evening's pleasure. It might even more surprise you when the magistrates find you at fault."

He rocked toward her, then recovered his balance, saying again, "Ten thousand pounds, and I'll have it called for in a week. Or I'll come as a husband has the right to do and make sure my wife's led home. And you, Mistress Biss—oh, be sure I shall see you labelled as the procuress of infants, the purveyor of innocents for evil."

Her expression unwavering, Sophia said, "It will not be an easy amount to raise, Master Wintersill. And certainly not within the stretch of a single week. I might by then have a quarter of it, enough perhaps to lessen the pangs of your greed. Send your errand boy to me then. Though preferably not this one"—her gaze stinging Eldon—"or that one"—a similar whiplash for Lucas. "And, if you hope to see so much as a penny of your so-called recompense, do not you, Master Wintersill, ever come here again. Today being the first time we've met, I quite lack the stomach for a second." Then she waited, Charlotte at her side, the injured Chapman across from them, as the gentlemen of Wiltshire took their leave.

They heard the carriage rattle away along The Biss. They listened for the fading of its departure. And for another full moment beyond the final vestiges of sound.

* * *

✳

His wound washed and dressed, the butler was ordered to bed. He maintained he was as right as rain, though his voice trembled and he grasped at a chair back for support. "Disgraceful," he said, "being caught unawares like that. It'd never have happened in the old days. I'd have seen to 'em then. Upon my word I would." He managed a final defiant glance before turning unsteadily from the room.

The women stayed where they were, hearing Tilly's voice in the hallway. "'Ere, Master Chapman, take me arm an'—"

"I'll thank you to be about your business, girl. Tomorrow, early, I shall be holding an inspection of the silver. Sugar casters. Chocolate pots. The salvers and dishes. Cutlery and candlesticks. The tankards and jugs and basins. The sauceboats and sweet trays . . ."

Sophia smiled briefly. "I am not at all sure," she said, "that our sympathies would not be better directed toward Tilly."

But the moment passed and the women revived the terror of Brook's visit, talking on together through the night. Charlotte was adamant that her husband—how unreal the word sounded—should be thwarted in his demands.

"I agree," Sophia said, "though if we send his errand boy back empty-handed, Master Wintersill will hurry to reclaim you. As for his threats against me, a procuress of infants, a purveyor of innocents for evil, I can only suppose he got those phrases from some highly seasoned tract. But the fact remains, my dear, you are still that man's wife and should, in law, be dwelling under his roof. If we deny him what he claims, he'll be here, and with justification, to take you back."

"And what if I am not here when he comes?"

"Where else would you be? You dare not return to Faxforge. I've a score of friends who'd be happy to shelter you, though it would perforce be a temporary measure."

"I'd be at sea. That is, if . . ." Then, her hand extended, needing Sophia's firm grasp, she told her aunt about Matcham Lodge, about the odious Mason Tagg, about the way she'd played the whore and learned the identity of a certain Master Clark. And, the heart of the matter, about Matcham's declaration in the forest and how, only then, had she admitted to him the truth. "Since when his ship has been absent from the port."

Sophia sighed, then pushed away the sorrow she felt for her niece. Nothing constructive would come from grieving.

"The way you describe this Captain Lodge, it seems you've rather diminished your chances. But you say Master Kimber will most likely know where he's gone. Then you'd best get along to him in the morning and tell him what's to do. We still have seven days' grace before the errand boy's due to call. I myself will make a thousand pounds ready, just in case. It's less than Brook Wintersill expects, though I doubt—and forgive me, my dear—if he'll reject that sum in favour of having you home." Then she murmured, "Jamaica, was it? Well, let's hope not. Not yet."

TWENTY-FOUR

The vehicle in the Cannaway yard was a thief, a composite, a hybrid—and as neat an oddity as any conveyance in the country. It was a four-wheeled carriage, more properly known as the "Cannaway Conductor", its rear wheels almost four feet in height, its front wheels less than three. The major problem—the one Brydd had been struggling with when he'd seen his brother's wagon stuck near the road gate—had been overcome by the hinging of passenger seat to driving bench. Thus, when the driver guided his horse to the left or right, the bench turned in concert with the shafts.

There'd been under-pivoted carts before; though not, so far as Brydd Cannaway knew, vehicles that could be twisted in the middle.

Anyway, the Conductor could now round the corners of all but the meanest alleys, its hinging so designed to accommodate the rise or dip of a hill. And, since the need for the under pivot was gone, the driving bench was set far lower, almost above the forward axle, its height determined by the stretch and resilience of the springs.

The driver would not now crack his skull on a signboard.

Nor would he have to shout that the way was too narrow. Nor would his passengers be lurched and jounced in a weighty, broad-wheeled wagon.

Oddity though it might seem to the citizens of London, there were many who'd clamber aboard it, delighted by its neatness and soothed by its intricate springs.

Or so they hoped at Faxforge as they waited for Edward Flowerdewe and the councillors from the capital to arrive.

✳

Brydd Cannaway made a final inspection of the yard. He carried with him the thumbed and tattered Specific, the demands and measurements set out by the councillors. So many feet and this many inches for the free-swinging height of a shop board. So many feet and this many inches for the width of a main street; a foot and a quarter less for the breadth of an alley.

Barrels had been positioned about the yard, to represent a network of city streets. Posts had been erected, with cords strung tight between them, marking the lower edge of the absent shop signs. A boarded ramp sloped upward, levelled off, then descended in a steep downward gradient to the yard. Another demand of the Specific.

Well, Brydd thought, we have followed their instructions to the letter. The Conductor meets their every specification; the barrels are set as wide apart—as close together!—as they demanded. The skein of cords is as low as they claim the signboards hang in London. He rapped a fist against the edge of the steep, board ramp, then continued his tour of the simulated streets.

A while later, and Giles shouted from the road gate, "Coach coming down! It's a great gilt thing; it's—" But his message was lost amid the drumming of hoofbeats and the rumble of the wheels.

The bulbous mayoral carriage slowed, turned between the gate posts and came swaying up the drive. It was drawn—unnecessarily so, Brydd thought—by six plumed and tasselled horses, the springs of its driving bench depressed by not one, nor two, but three liveried coachmen.

London, Brydd decided, come to spend a day in the country. He welcomed the paunchy and rubicund Edward Flowerdewe.

"Now listen," Flowerdewe offered. "If you're not yet ready for us—"

"I believe we are, Edward. According to the Specific."

"Oh? Well, that's wonderful, Master Brydd. Couldn't be happier. The journey's not been wasted then. Truly ready, and up to the mark? Then perhaps you'd care to meet—"

"Perhaps you and your friends would care to meet my wife."

Flowerdewe cleared his throat and beamed, though Brydd sensed an awkwardness about him, almost as if the jowled merchant regretted coming here today. Yet how could that be, when Edward had insisted on the date and the day, his frequent messages reminding Faxforge he'd have the councillors in tow?

But Elizabeth and Hester had appeared by then, Elizabeth curtseying as the visitors bowed their greeting. She took care to memorise who was who, pleasing them as she answered each by name. And Hester pleased them simply by being Hester, the most delightful young girl they'd seen this side of Park Lane. Most delightful. An advertisement for the country life. Pretty a thing as a man could wish to—

"—the test first," Brydd was telling Flowerdewe, "after which we've some good red port."

"Always was your favourite, eh, Brydd? It was always your favourite, was it not, a glass or two of dark ruby?"

Edward Flowerdewe's questions seemed as out of place as his bluster. He knew full well what Brydd Cannaway liked, so why this pressing enthusiasm, as though they might altogether dispense with the testing of the Conductor?

"It strikes me," Brydd said quietly, "that something is amiss. If it's to do with the carriage—"

"Oh, dear me, no! Nothing whatsoever! I'm jumping like a puppet to see what you've got for us. Jumping like a puppet, Master Brydd. And so are the councillors. So off you go now, and we'll find all the faults we can!" He laughed, showing his threat was unintended. Yet Brydd did not anyway believe in the threat; only that the laughter concealed something Flowerdewe was frightened to admit.

But why should Edward be a mass of false jollity when the feather-hatted councillors of London were here, debouched from their six-horse coach? Why should the merchant of Swindon act so nervous when he'd handed out thousands of pounds in the expectation that the Cannaway brothers would design him a Conductor and the sheds in which to make it? Yet now seemed more keen that they broach the dark red port?

Brydd walked away to join Step Cotter. It was Step who would drive the Conductor; Giles and Jonas who would see that the ramp was held firm; William and Waylen who would ride as passengers; the craftsmen and workmen ranged around the perimeter, willing the vehicle on.

Chairs and benches had been brought out for the councillors. They scratched at their wigs, settled their hats, and smiled at Hester as she offered mint cordial from a tray. Then one of them glanced at Flowerdewe, who called across to Brydd, "At your convenience, Master Cannaway!"

Step Cotter mounted the driving bench. He turned to look down at Brydd. "Easy as spitting," he remarked. "They'll order up a hundred after this." Then he clucked in his special and private language at the horse and took the "Cannaway Conductor" among the casks that stood as the buildings and byways of the city.

❋

Neither mount nor driver nor vehicle missed a move. Step took the Conductor cleanly between the barrels, turned the horse and the shafts and the driving seat round a corner, then again round a corner, then up the incline and along the level, braking as he descended to the yard. He navigated the carriage through a series of snakeways, never once clipping wheel hub to barrel stave. He showed that the Conductor could be tilted, reversed without trouble, its springs leaving the passengers unbruised as it was raced across the cobbles. He did not at any time catch his head on the taut-drawn cords that marked the signboards and, as he turned the Conductor through its final series of bends, the craftsmen of Faxforge and the workmen from Melksham roared and applauded his triumph.

Brydd Cannaway shared a smile with his family. He turned to see Flowerdewe and the councillors beaming at the show, though with their hats in their hands or their hands in their pockets.

He called across to them, "After all you have seen here, gentlemen, is it not worth a slap of your palms?" And to Flowerdewe, "Should I ask Master Cotter to make the rounds again?" There *was* something amiss, sorely amiss, and it showed in Edward Flowerdewe's all too hasty denial.

"Be assured," the merchant told him, "it's just what we're after, the very thing London needs." Then he bobbed his excuses at the councillors, clutched Brydd by the arm and steered him toward a corner of the yard.

The triumph of the run already soured by suspicion, Brydd shook free of Edward's grasp. "It's time you made yourself clear, Master Flowerdewe. It's just what you're after, so you say? The very thing London needs? Then tell me why such an evident success should leave you and your companions twisting their hats in ill-disguised embarrassment. Is there something you disapprove of in the carriage?"

"On my oath, Master Brydd, it's the best thing—"

"Then *what?* If the runner suits you—and William's efforts have constructed your Manufactory—why are you all so hesitant to applaud?"

Flowerdewe chewed his lips for a moment, searching for a

response he knew was not there. As best he could he explained to Brydd Cannaway that the idea of a newly designed conveyance was being resisted by the chair-men and drivers of London. "They're the long-established porters of sedan chairs and the drivers of the existing, unwieldy carts. They are a powerful force, and all but govern the streets. I never expected them to be so resistant in their ways. But it seems the word's got out—"

"As you said it would," Brydd murmured. "You yourself promised to put the word around."

In a failing effort to defend himself, the merchant exclaimed, "To extend your reputation, my dear Brydd! To let London know what Wiltshire knows already!" Then the final ditch of his defence was overrun as Brydd demanded, "So where have we come to now, Master Edward?" and listened, his face impassive, as Flowerdewe admitted that the councillors could not find space for the "Cannaway Conductors" anywhere in the city.

"There'd be riots, don't you see! The chair-men and drivers would refuse to carry anyone in the face of such competition!"

"So you're withdrawing your support, is that it, Edward? And expect my brother to repay what you advanced him? And think it well to leave us now, with a proven carriage and Faxforge extended as the Manufactory you wanted?"

"The money is nothing," Flowerdewe hastened. "And you may rely on me, Brydd, I'll have orders for curricles and wagons pouring in! I shall not see you short of work. There are fellows I know of—well, even perhaps these councillors— who'd regard it as a privilege to order up a runner from your yard. You will be swamped, let me promise you! Inundated! Flooded with offers between now and—"

"Spare your efforts," Brydd levelled. "Your intentions are well meant, though I doubt that we'll have much time down here for the individual clients you recommend. We'll be busy enough, I think, turning out Conductors. I have a limited sense of geography, Master Edward, though I know for a fact there are other cities in England, and even a few in more distant parts of the world."

∗

Two days from now and Brook Wintersill's errand boy was due at the house on The Biss.

Charlotte had been to see Forby Kimber, a painful meeting for both of them, though Forby had said, "It always did strike strange with me, the idea of so attractive a woman going around unmarried."

"I should have told you, long ago."

"Was there," he said quietly, "ever a long ago for you and me? Wasn't it always you and Matcham, I dare say from the moment you came spilling from that alley in the storm?"

"I never met a man more kind or courteous than you, my dear Forby. I was never granted so fine a friend as you."

"That's right." He nodded slowly. "We are the best and finest of friends." He smiled, not telling her his feelings transcended mere friendship, since what would be the point of it, when she'd already confided to him her love for Matcham Lodge?

She had also told him Brook Wintersill had tracked her to The Biss and was demanding money from Aunt Sophia. "Which is why I must know when Matcham will be back. Did he come to you after—after that last time I was with him in the forest?"

"He, ah, blew in, shall we say? Stormed around for a while. Then said he'd business in Bordeaux." Bordeaux, she thought. Bordeaux, thank God, so not yet the island of Jamaica.

"Then he might return—"

"Any time now," the gentle Forby encouraged. "Tonight. Tomorrow. It depends on the mood of the winds." Moving about the room at the corner of Bankside and The Stray, he peered at Charlotte and said, "Ignore it as an intrusion if you will, but he does seem the most vexatious type of fellow, this Master Wintersill you married."

"Oh yes," Charlotte echoed. "He is indeed the most vexatious type of fellow. Though I doubt he'd find anyone to speak as highly of him as that."

Four days had elapsed since her meeting with Forby Kimber. Since then, morning and evening, she had gone to see if the red-hulled vessel was at its moorings off Risers Wharf.

She wondered if Matcham had decided to stay clear of Mason Tagg, the *Nereid* anchored far along the Severn, or out in the estuary, or in a port on the other side of England.

And now there were only two days to go before the errand boy was due.

*

No matter that the councillors of London had failed to applaud the merits of the Conductor, the Cannaways closed ranks at Faxforge.

William went to collect his wife and daughter from Melksham, Margaret happy to be reunited with her husband, Louisa whining that her special naval-tip hat was left behind. "*And,* now I think of it, my second mirror. Oh, this is all quite intolerable! I will not have it! There's shoes—my favourite and best-preserved shoes! The ones with the heels curved inward and the beading—" And with that she reached over and jerked angrily at the reins. "Turn this thing around," she said imperiously. "I'm sorry if we're close to Faxforge, but I'll not stand for the likes of that goading little Hester making out the clothes I've brought are my best ones, when I know full well they are not."

"I've told you before," William murmured. "Never pull at a horse's mouth like that."

"Well, I'm sorry. I'm *sorry!* But I want the carriage turned around."

Margaret leaned forward, her patience with Louisa snapped apart. But the bulk of William's body was between them, and he guided the vehicle in an arc.

Louisa Cannaway nodded, celebrating her victory with a smile.

"Out!"

"Father? What are you nudging me for? You'll have me tumbling—"

"Out! Off! Down from this seat. You've said it yourself. We're close enough to Faxforge."

The girl half fell, half clambered to the grass. William glanced at his wife, who said quietly, "Take the vehicle on, if you will, please, William."

Behind them Louisa opened her mouth, her piteous wail soaring above the downs. Abandoned, and with nothing to do but bring the wailing to a choked and whimpered silence, she was left to hoist her nine cambric petticoats and trudge the three miles in pursuit of her parents.

When Hester learned her cousin "would be along in a while" she went to lean on the road gate, ready to wave the moment Louisa came in sight.

＊

The man's patience seemed limitless. Hour upon hour he waited; watching, studying the house. As evening approached he saw candlelight bloom in the ground-floor windows, to the left of the wide, pillared steps. A figure appeared, silhouetted against the light. For a while he too stood watching, as if returning the other man's gaze. But they were too far apart, the mullioned windows turned to mirrors by the lights.

Inside the room, Brook Wintersill gave a sudden bark of laughter. Tomorrow, he thought. By this time tomorrow I'll be a damnsight heavier than now. Unavoidable, since I'll be holding a bagful of coin. He moved to pour himself a drink, downed it quickly and recharged his glass to the brim. It was halfway to his lips when he heard someone at the outside door.

A friend?

A pertinacious creditor?

The money perhaps, Mistress Biss preferring to send it rather than have Wintersill's errand boy in her oh, so precious house? It's the sort of thing she would do, Brook decided, mimicking Sophia as he started toward the door.

Then he stopped, retraced his steps and busied himself at a drawer in the long, scarred sideboard. When he left the room a second time, he already weighed heavier than before.

TWENTY-FIVE

The servant girl felt the sickness of terror rise and bubble in her throat. She pressed a hand to her mouth, her body squirming, her bare knees scratched by the boards. *But it wasn't my fault! Not really, it wasn't. I was only trying to whisk the dust and—*

She scooped blindly at the shattered porcelain figures. Then despair took hold of her and she cowered on the floor, the bile running from her mouth.

Innocent and ignorant, her speech unintelligible, the simple-minded Fern was lost in confusion. She had done what Mistress Dench had said she must do. Go up to Master Wintersill's rooms. Set the candle nice and steady on the table. Then clear the grate. Then lay the fire, kindling under and the twice-split logs above. Then go around, dusting. Careful as can be, mind. Then arrange his bed, as tidy as you've been taught. Then bring the candle with you and come nice and steady down the staircase to the kitchen. Everything nice and steady, young Fern. And a slice of apple biscuit when you're done.

The girl had been entrusted with these tasks before. She could not say how often she had cleaned Brook Wintersill's rooms, for she had no sense of time, no reckoning of numbers. But she knew she had performed these tasks and been rewarded with a sweetmeat. And that she had never done so bad a thing as the thing she had done tonight.

By pure mischance, a gust of air had extinguished the solitary candle. The room had been plunged into darkness and the startled Fern had touched the whisk to one of Brook's favourite possessions. It was a rare and expensive statuette—a tableau of incredible obscenities. It had cost him dear, though he had never tired of its lewd and inventive variety.

But now it was smashed beyond repair.

The girl again scooped at the fragments. She tipped them in the pocket of her apron, convinced that if Master Wintersill didn't see them he'd forget they had ever been there. Then, forgetting the candle, she edged in terror from the room.

Three uncertain steps along the gallery and she heard the sudden rap of a caller at the door. She shrank back, heard Brook in the hall, approaching the entranceway, retracing his steps, emerging at last to see who'd come by at such an hour.

Fern moved, and the shards of porcelain grated in her pocket. She stiffened, her face contorted, her eyes clenched shut as if, by seeing no one, she herself would not be seen.

She heard voices, the first flat exchange erupting with Brook Wintersill's bellow of anger. The words were too loud, too fast, too angry for the girl to understand. She pressed her head to the wall, wondering if she couldn't somehow, if Mistress Dench was to help her, if they couldn't in some way mend the figures with a paste.

Suddenly, below, the shouting stopped. It has gone on for such a long time, Fern thought. I hope I won't be so shouted at as that. Whatever has he done, this caller, to so displease Master Brook?

In desperate need of a friend, a fellow victim, the servant girl squinted down through the gallery rail.

She saw the top of a tricorn, the skirt of a cloak, a hand extended, offering a paper to Brook. "Sign this, I advise you, and be satisfied."

"A twentieth part of what I asked for? And you a bloody intruder on this scene? By Christ, there is anyone as could raise a sum like that! *Anyone!*"

"Fair enough then. I withdraw the offer and leave you free to find your anyone."

The paper vanished below the shadow of the tricorn. The man nodded and turned toward the door. Squinting from the gallery, Fern saw the caller move away, saw Brook step after him, saw her master draw a brassbound pistol from his coat, raise it and level it and make the weapon flash with flame.

The door jumped with the impact of the ball. Splinters were torn from the grain, dust puffing from the hinges, the wave of sound bringing plaster thirty feet from the ceiling. Fern blinked with the shock of it, aware in her own simple mind that what had happened wasn't fair. The caller, her fellow victim, had already turned his back on Brook Wintersill when the pistol was fired.

But by then the caller had wheeled and stamped firm, a pistol of his own thrust forward, its muzzle eyeing Brook Wintersill's chest.

"In character to the last," the caller murmured. "Treacherous and deceitful to the last. But you've had your shot now, you'll agree. So you're bound to allow me mine." His arm snapped rigid, the nose of his pistol sniffing the sweat of Brook's fear. Fern watched, her mouth hanging open, her mind unable to grasp why this was happening, though thinking it only fair that it should. She did not understand what her fellow victim had meant by treacherous or deceitful. But she thought it right that the caller be given his chance to bring plaster from the roof. And make the staircase shake. And brighten the entrance with flame.

"It was an accident," Brook pleaded. "I misfired it by accident, I swear to you I did." He clutched at the newel post, his heels against the lowest riser of the stairs.

"Yes, indeed," the man told him. "Accident's the word. An accident that you missed me, yet one that will now allow me to aim with all the purpose I possess. Pray quick, Master Wintersill. Though you may find heaven on holiday tonight!"

Incredibly, Brook Wintersill sank to his knees, his palms pressed together, his face glistening as he mumbled obedience to the man he had failed to kill. "Lord God, forgive me for my sins, which have been multiple and evil. Lord God, forgive me for the life I have led astray. I heartily renounce my wickedness and— Oh, please, God, forgive me for my weakness, oh, please, sweet God, allow me to dry my eyes." He rocked forward, fumbling for a handkerchief, then produced a grey, flat-barrelled shooter. He fired on the instant, the sound of the weapon drowned by the boom of the caller's pistol. Both men flinched, though it was Brook Wintersill who parted his lips in a smile, a strictured smile, a final tensing of the muscles before he fell back against the stairs and slipped down to the base of them, his eyes rolled upward as though to greet another caller, though this one already lodged within his skull.

Unseen on the gallery, the servant girl smothered her giggles. She'd seen dogs shot before, and rabbits, and foxes, and she had now seen Brook Wintersill shot dead.

So he wouldn't much care what had happened to his statue.

But Mistress Dench might care. Mistress Dench might say she'd been clumsy.

Which was why the girl kept a hand on the pocket of her apron, ignoring the man who sighed and walked quietly from the Hall.

✳

The planks of the bar glistening under his washcloth, Sam Gilmore glanced up to see Jarvis Cannaway enter the tavern. Every inch the doctor, Sam approved, though why should our young physician look so uncommonly ill at ease?

He set the question aside as Jarvis crossed the sawdust carpet to the bar. There was none of the intrusive landlord about Sam. Questions, he accepted, had a habit of getting themselves answered in the flowering fullness of time. So he settled for a nod and a courteous "Master Jarvis."

"It's good to see you, Master Gilmore."

"Oh, it's Gilmore, is it? So formal, when you used to climb the bar to reach the sugar twists?"

"I apologise. It is good to see you, Sam."

"Aye, that's more friendly. And what do wool-town doctors drink these days?"

"Later, if you will." Visibly nervous, the nineteen-year-old Jarvis glanced at the doorway to the kitchen. "Might I have a word with you, Sam? Through there?"

"You might," Sam responded, then called to his potboy, the fearless and diminutive John Whitten. "Take charge here, John. I've business with Dr. Cannaway."

"You ailin', Master Gilmore?"

"No, you cheeky young whelp! Though you'll be ailing if you get within reach of my hand."

"So you're a doctor, eh?" the potboy queried. "Tell you what, Dr. Cannaway. I've got this terrible fear of spiders. 'Orrible scuttly things they are. I don't s'pose—"

"The bar!" Sam threatened. "*The bar!*"

John grinned and turned to his duties, leaving Sam to usher Jarvis through to the kitchen. "He's a law to himself," the innkeeper muttered. "I swear he's more at liberty here than I am. Do you know, Master Jarvis, we had a party of travellers come by last week—"

"Sam? My sister's husband has been murdered. Someone has gone to the Hall and shot Brook Wintersill dead. I'm on my way to tell my parents, though I thought to call in on you first. I have seen the body. And—Sam—I have heard things that cause me deep concern."

The burly landlord filled his belly and chest with air. Then he expelled it slowly and said, "That for a fact, eh? Gone and got himself killed at last. Well, Master Jarvis, since you'll not disclose what doctors drink in Marlborough, you'll have to make do with the best French wine I possess. Suffered, did he, afore he died?"

"Dear God, Sam, this is not a matter for—"

"For what? Not a cause for celebration? Not a reason for the breaking of a seal? The man who made your own sister's marriage a hell upon the earth? The man who led his bloody-handed friends against Faxforge and left a decent young sapling named Lewis Plant dead from a knife stab in the back? The man who saw your father injured, your brother all but crippled? *You* say what you like, Master Jarvis! But *I* say it's the best news I've heard in many a long day. And yes, I hope he suffered. And yes, I shall drink to his perdition. So tell me, Master Jarvis, do I fetch one glass or two?"

Swamped by Sam Gilmore's outburst, the young Jarvis Cannaway said two. Then he waited as the landlord rummaged in a lead-lined chest, produced a bottle and cut away the seal. He wiped two blemished glasses on his sleeve, filled them with the dark red wine of Cahors, then handed one to Jarvis, almost daring him not to drink.

They celebrated in silence.

Then Jarvis said, "It may displease you, but Master Winter-sill died before he knew it. The ball passed clean through the centre of his forehead."

"Was he armed?"

"Doubly so, it appears. There's a gash in the door from a pistol shot and a mark above it that was made by a small-bore shooter. The pistol was near the body, the shooter still in his hand."

"So he fired twice," Sam mused. "And his killer? How many other gouges did you find?"

"Just the one. The wound to Wintersill's head."

The landlord sipped contentedly at his wine. "We may differ in our opinions," he growled, "though frankly you must be as heartened as I that he's dead. So why be nervous, Master Jarvis? Or is it—oh, Lord, I'm growing slow in my old age—is it because you suspect it was me?"

"No, Sam. Not really. For all your happiness, not you."

"Master Whitten then?"

Ignoring the question, Jarvis said, "You were at Faxforge, I believe, on the night of Wintersill's attack."

"The second attack, to be precise. I wish to God I had been there for the first."

"And did you hear what my father said to Brook Wintersill? How he would shoot him, or ask a friend to shoot him, or have someone shoot him for them all? It seems to be something of a motto in the valley."

Sam Gilmore glared in disbelief. "There is not much point," he told Jarvis, "in learning a poem if you don't get the damn thing right. What Brydd Cannaway said was that he'd shoot Master Wintersill if he came within sight of Faxforge. *If he came within sight of Faxforge, Master Jarvis! Not in Wintersill Hall!*"

"Then who?" the young man blurted. "Who else if not my father?"

The landlord turned away, rubbing his eyes with his hand. "Who else?" he echoed. "You ask who else if not Brydd? Well, my worried Jarvis, how's this for a list of runners? How about Jonas Jones? Or Step Cotter? Or Matthew Ives? Or Ben Waite? Or any of the fellows here at Beckhampton? Or any of Wintersill's own friends? Or maybe one of the tradesmen he owed, the farmers he angered, the neighbours he's insulted all these years? Maybe it was me after all, or the insolent young Whitten. And maybe, and why not, Master Jarvis, it was you! Good God, man, there's a hundred of us who might have killed him, and most of us who should!" He turned then, his pale grey eyes unblinking. "As a point of fact it was not me who killed him, though I take no credit for saying it. But if you really suspect your own father, then ask him face to face.

And if he tells you yes, then embrace him and toss the knowledge in the pond." Peering at Jarvis, Sam queried, "Died afore he knew it? You sure he didn't suffer, just a while?"

*

Jarvis took the news of Brook's death to Faxforge. "I cannot be sorry," Brydd told him. "In all conscience I think it's a loss the world can bear. And from what you say—at least two shots fired by Wintersill himself—it's a long way off being murder. Have you any idea who killed him?"

Jarvis Cannaway shrugged awkwardly. "It was witnessed by a servant girl, though she suffers from an impediment of the mind. She was anyway crouched above the intruder, unable to see his face. I've spoken to Sam Gilmore about it, and he seems to think there is half of Wiltshire to choose from." The young man hesitated, and it was Brydd himself who said, "Do you fear it was me, my dear Jarvis? If I was to say, and I *do* say, I am glad the killer went unseen, would that turn your fears to suspicions? Is that why you're so ill at ease tonight? Because you think I have killed my own son-in-law?"

"No, sir. I do not think you killed him. But I'm concerned that there's others who will."

"True enough," Brydd acknowledged. "I shall probably head the list. And between you and me, my dear Jarvis, I'd be offended if I didn't. I'll be straight with you, sir. If Master Wintersill had ventured on this property, or even come close to doing so, I would most likely have shot him. But to put your mind at rest— No. I did not go up there and kill him. Nor did anyone else from Faxforge. But I'd take issue with those who say there is half of Wiltshire to choose from. I myself would extend the borders to half of England."

Jarvis let his shoulders sag with relief. He told himself he had not really suspected his father. It was just that, well, the name Cannaway did belong at the head of the list.

Brydd explained to his wife he'd be leaving for Bristol in the morning. "I failed Charlotte before, when her husband was alive. I will not now have her learn of his death in a letter."

By midnight the news was the topic of conversation along the length of the Kennett Vale. By morning there were a dozen men who claimed credit for the killing.

※

He spent two days with his sister and his daughter at The Biss. They'd welcomed him with an urgency he'd not expected, Sophia explaining that Brook had tracked down Charlotte, burst in and demanded ten thousand pounds, or he'd—

"No more," Brydd told them. "He has no further need of menace or of money." He'd gone on, as gently as possible, to tell them Brook Wintersill was dead, killed in an exchange of shots in the entranceway of the Hall. "We have no idea who it was, though an investigation is already under way."

Charlotte had come to him, curling both her hands in his. "I hope," she murmured, "that the men engaged on this investigation do not look too far, or dig too deep. There are some things to which Heaven itself, I believe, would be blind."

Even so, later, she had wept. Her tears were not for her husband, not for Brook directly, but more for the waste he had made of his life, the chances he had squandered, the brandy-sweetened pleasures he'd thought so real. He'd been noisy with drink, made breathless by the cruelties of his passion. But had he ever, she wondered, been happy beyond the cutting of a thick wax seal, or the shudder of satisfaction in her bed?

It was Brook who had sold off Lady Wintersill's pictures, Brook who'd reduced the Hall to its sparsely furnished state. And, at the last, it was Brook who had paid his creditors with all he had left, the property that ringed his house.

It did not take Charlotte long to still her tears for Brook Wintersill. But they brimmed in her eyes again as she thought of her own mistakes, her own squandered chances, the deceitful way she had led Matcham Lodge along.

Forby had told her Matcham was in Bordeaux. Yet he should have been back by now. Well, perhaps he was out there tonight, his dark red vessel dipping its way across the Channel, Master Cope in the bows, the crew at their stations, Captain Matcham Lodge at the wheel.

So why then did the tears spring anew, her mind obsessed by the fear that the *Nereid* was thrusting south-by-west toward the far distant island of Jamaica?

❋

Next morning Sophia busied herself in the city. Charlotte spent the day in quiet conversation with her father. They talked of the Wintersill estate, or what little would be left of it when the creditors had been paid.

"God knows, I want nothing from it," Charlotte stated, "though I must see a decent allowance settled on Mistress Dench and Fern. And, if possible, some annuity paid to that excellent Ephram Toll."

They talked of Faxforge and the "Cannaway Conductor", Brydd describing how the yard had been enlarged, and how well Step Cotter had driven the vehicle, and how—smiling at his daughter's indignation—Edward Flowerdewe had admitted there was no place yet in London for the runner.

"But that is shameful of him! He and his fainthearted councillors! Why are they elected, if all they can do is grovel to the bullies who monopolise the streets!"

"Things are bound to improve in time. Meanwhile, there are other cities, other countries to be approached."

I wonder, she thought, if there are cities in Jamaica?

She told him then about a man she had met, a certain Captain Matcham Lodge. "I won't say he's the most sociable of fellows; rather comes and goes as he likes. If you were ever to meet him, Father, you would probably think him selfish and arrogant, and it's true to say—"

"One moment," Brydd queried. "Is this by any chance the same Captain Matcham Lodge that Sophia assures me holds

your heart? Oh, don't look so alarmed. She may be your un-
bending aunt, my dear Charlotte, but remember she's also my
sister. Will you bring him to Faxforge, this unsociable and
arrogant Captain Lodge?"

"I am awaiting his return from Bordeaux." She left it at
that, and Brydd nodded and said he'd be staging home in the
morning. "Visit us when you can. There's quite a gathering of
Cannaways there now. Though if you do bring Captain Lodge
with you, he'd best be warned of the dangers. They're called
Hester and Louisa."

TWENTY-SIX

The vessel was in the estuary mouth when the Navy cutters closed in. Charlotte had guessed correctly when she'd put Master Cope in the bows, the crew ranged amidships, the captain at the wheel. But neither she nor Matcham had supposed there'd be cutters waiting for the *Nereid*, or that Mason Tagg would demand to be in at the kill.

The journey from Bordeaux had been slow and uncertain, a light swell running, fog hanging low on the water. The fog had thinned in time for Master Cope to recognise landmarks along the reed-fringed estuary: a derelict windmill, a cluster of fishermen's cottages, the ribs of a Portuguese trader that had drifted —or had it been lured?—onto the mud.

And then, soundlessly, the fog had again closed in.

The *Nereid* had crept forward, the crewmen peering from the rails. Soundings had been taken, the depth relayed quietly, man by man. It was not yet dusk, though the fog cast a gloomy, greenish hue across the water. There was no real sense of movement, the vessel just an unlit wick within the bottle-green chimney of a lamp.

Then the wind had gusted toward them, blowing the fog down the estuary, pressing the sails to the masts. And, as the *Nereid* lost way, so the sloop-rigged cutters emerged from a channel in the reeds.

Master Cope yelled a warning. But Matcham was already turning the wheel, desperate to get the wind behind the sails. He heard other voices, rapped out commands, his own name screamed across the water. "I know it, Captain Lodge! As the fit of my shoes! I know you for a traitor!"

There were further shouts, a warning to drop anchor and be boarded. The *Nereid* continued to come about, but slowly, sluggishly, whilst the Navy boats closed in.

Within a moment of the warning came the crackle of musket fire, then the bark of a deck gun. The *Nereid* was swept with case shot, its foresail riddled, two of the crew killed by the hail of fragments. Master Cope staggered backward, his left arm all but torn away at the elbow. There was a second blast of case shot and Matcham too was sent reeling, blood filling the wound in his side.

The cutters were less than a hundred yards off now. But the *Nereid* was still turning, the flap-flap of its sails giving way to a shiver as they filled before the wind. Mason Tagg continued screaming, his words drowned by the crackle of the muskets, the steady bark of the deck guns. He had seen Matcham fall, and was yelling at him not to die, not until he'd been measured for a rope. "I paid you money! I wagered a coin I'd have you strangling this year! Do you hear me, traitor? You *owe* me, Matcham Lodge! *You owe me!*"

The wind shifted, streamers of fog drifting across from the west. Spitting their fury, the cutters slid in pursuit of their bloodied prey.

✳

Five days later, though the sky was still dark above the city, the maidservant Tilly was startled from her sleep. She had been dreaming of the butcher Broadrip Ness, casting him as a nobleman in ermine, a romantic intruder in her chamber.

She herself was in strawberry silk; her nightgown of silk, the bedclothes of silk, her silk-pillowed couch curtained in pink, as were the windows and walls of the room. Shapes had altered within the dream, though there was no shortage whatever of strawberry silk.

She heard the tap of Broadrip's knuckles on the door. Then the tap of his heels on the blushing marble tiles. Then the tap of his rings on the bedpost, the tap of his buckle as he removed his sword belt, a confident half-smile on his lips as the lady gasped in insincere alarm. "Lord Broadrip! For shame, sir!" She moved to hold him at bay—then awoke, scowling furiously, the tapping revealed as an insistent pounding on the door that admitted to The Biss.

Dressed in a linen shift and plain woollen wrap, the maidservant shuffled yawning along the hallway. "Who's out there? What you want?"

"Is that Tilly? It's Forby Kimber. Let me in, Tilly, quick as you can, or you may hear the soldiers get me yet!"

Angry though she was that her dream had been shattered, the girl had a fondness for Master Kimber. She slipped the bolts, urged him inside, then bolted the door behind him. As she did so the glow of a lantern filled the passage beside the stairs. Chapman appeared, dressed in slippers and an old-fashioned *banian*, an antiquated pistol at the ready. He peered at Forby, grunted to himself, "Likely have blown my hand off anyway," and dropped the weapon in a pocket of the long Indian robe.

Above them, smudges of candlelight merged on the landing as Sophia and Charlotte ventured from their rooms. Recognising the caller, Sophia said, "You are here on a matter of some urgency, I would guess. Say your piece, Master Forby. We shall not obstruct you with questions."

Forby nodded, advanced toward the light of Chapman's

lantern, then told them the Jacobite hunter Mason Tagg had drawn in the strings of his net.

✳

"He raided my house an hour ago. Thank God the locks held him until we'd got clear through an alley. We went to another house, where we learned he'd scooped half the sailors from Risers Wharf. I've not been followed here, I can promise you, though I thought it as well to alert you, Mistress Charlotte, and make sure your address is not known to Mason Tagg."

"Where is Matcham? Where is Captain Lodge?"

"I'll come to that in a moment. Let's first be certain that no one Tagg's arrested could direct him here to The Biss."

"Only you and Matcham would know where to find me." Then, the chill of the hour made colder by a half-remembered name, she came close to the landing rail and told him, "Though I was once escorted home by a man called Fisk. Only the once. He told me of the myriad women—"

"'Celibate' Fisk?"

"Yes. The much-married—"

"Then indeed it's a matter of urgency," Forby hastened. "Master Fisk is among those who've been arrested." Turning to Sophia, he said, "You may count on a visit, Mistress Biss. The government agents will be along here before dawn. And if Mason Tagg sets eyes on your niece—" The lift of Forby's shoulders, the movement of his hands, and his message was as clear as it was damning. Charlotte would be recognised. The house torn apart. The household taken for questioning. Their very lives at the mercy of a man not widely noted for his compassion.

Charlotte asked Sophia if a carriage could be hired at such an hour. "I've a skill with the reins, as you know. I'll be away from here—"

"Chapman?"

"Aye, Mistress Biss?"

"Will you hurry to find us a vehicle, then have it ready behind the house?"

"I'll do that," he nodded, "and I'll see the young lady safe to her father's yard." He turned to the maidservant. "Get you some clothes on, Tilly. You're in for the busiest time of your layabout life."

The girl scampered to her quarters. Chapman stood his lantern on a half-moon table in the hallway. Sophia said, "*Sauve qui peut*, Master Forby. You have ever been the gentleman, and we're indebted that you risked yourself to warn us."

Not wishing to delay him, yet needing an answer to the question that filled and spilled over in her mind, Charlotte raised the hem of her shift and ran down to join Forby in the hallway.

"You said you would come to it, the whereabouts of Matcham. I only need to know he is still in Bordeaux. Tell me that and—"

"It is only a rumour. You must understand. Nothing has yet been proved."

She stared at him, her apprehension again more chilly than the air. "What must I understand? What is it that's still not proved? *What is it, Forby? What?*"

"It's just something that's being put about by the Navy. By Tagg. Some wild claim that cutters intercepted the *Nereid*, their deck guns holding the vessel as she turned to escape them in the fog."

"When—When was all this supposed to be?"

"A few days ago. I thought it best not to alarm you. It *is* only a rumour, Charlotte. You must not suppose it for the truth."

Her voice scarcely audible, though rising, she asked him, "Exactly how many days ago? Two, would you say? Or four? Or a week? *When* did it happen, Master Kimber, this glorious action by the Navy?"

"It is now rather less than a week," Forby murmured, then nodded in reluctant agreement as Charlotte said, "Long enough for word to have reached you. From Matcham. Or from any of his crew who survived."

He repeated, "It is only a rumour," though it drained him to put conviction behind the words.

He raised his head in farewell to Sophia, leaned forward to kiss Charlotte, then told her he'd send news to Faxforge—"the instant I hear that Matcham is safe ashore." He seemed on the point of saying something else, but Tilly beckoned to him from beside the stairs and he followed the girl toward the unlighted rear door of the house. Sophia descended to the hallway and they stood together for a moment, the pepper-haired widow and the pale-haired widow, the image of the red-hulled ship lost amid the running of the sea. . . .

✳

Two hours later, confirming Forby's fears, Sophia and Tilly heard the slam of a musket butt on the door.

Forby Kimber had fled to a hideout, a safe house, whilst Charlotte and Chapman were by now, God willing, clear of the city and on the Bristol–London road.

"You know your instructions," Sophia told the girl. "Down you go then and let our visitors in." Then she turned to her dressing glass and continued making ready for her meeting with Mason Tagg.

"In the name of the King! Open to the servants of the King!" A furious battering on the door, and Tilly's courageous rejoinder, "An' is the king going to pay if you knock it off its 'inges? Just a minute! The bolts is tight in their rings. Just 'old on an'—there we are."

Tagg entered the hallway, followed by armed marines and his own dark-uniformed agents. He demanded to know who was present in the house, not at all amused when Tilly said, "Afore you all come burstin' in, or now?"

"Have a care, girl. Such remarks are ill advised. You'd do better to answer me straight."

"Well, there's me and the mistress. An' the cook, though she never leaves the kitchen."

"And another young woman, so I've heard."

"There *was* another," Tilly corrected, "but she's been gone since—wait a minute—what month is it now?"

Tagg nodded at the doorway to his left. "Have your mistress come down." Then he strode into the withdrawing room, snapping his fingers in command to one of the soldiers, who went around with flint and tinderbox, the trooper cursing as he elbowed a vase from a table. It was on the tip of the maidservant's tongue to ask if King George would pay for that, but she thought better of it and hurried up the stairs to Sophia.

Mason Tagg fingered the side brim of his hat. He checked with a captain of marines that the alley behind The Biss was sealed off tight. A man who took his pleasures as he found them, Tagg ran the edge of his muddy boots along the border of a Turkish rug.

Stooped and wheezing, her face a mask of cinnamon and pink, Sophia hobbled into the room, leaning for support on Tilly's arm. She stopped to fiddle with the pinnings of her badly arranged lace cap, then peered about her, saying, "Messenger come from the king? A message from His Gracious Majesty, may God in His wisdom grant him health and protection all his days? Where is he, then, this envoy from the monarch? What?"

Tilly saw her mistress to a chair. Sophia continued to peer around, deaf, it seemed, as the maidservant explained, "Mistress Sophia Biss; though you'd best talk slow an' clear to 'er, sir. And be patient, on account of she tends to wander."

Tagg stepped forward, measuring his words as with a spoon. "I am Mason Tagg, Mistress Biss. I have reason to believe there is a woman here. Or she was, as your slattern tells me. A young woman who's been seen keeping company with a certain Captain Lodge."

"Never met him . . ."

"I am not suggesting—"

". . . so why should he send me a message, our gracious and beloved King George?"

"We are not speaking of King George, Mistress Biss! There is no message from the throne! We are speaking of the woman who I know was brought here by Master Fisk, sailor of this port. A woman who came ashore from that traitor Lodge's vessel and was escorted to your door. A slender woman? With fair hair? Don't dither with me, I pray you! She was here and you will tell me who she was!"

With a flash of clarity—undisturbed valleys in the ruined landscape of the grey and senile mind—the grotesque and querulous Sophia snapped, "Mary Rush. Religious, so she claimed to be. Loyal, or so she avowed. Took her in, did I not, sir? Fed and clothed her, and was pleased of her company, her being considerably more bright than this creature you rightly call my slattern. A companion for my overburdened years. Or so I thought. The eyes of my eyes. Her hearing enough to get me safely across the streets of this dangerous town. And then what?"

"Where is she now, Mistress Biss?"

"Where was she ever?" the harridan retorted. "Out and selling herself, *selling herself*, along the quays and river fronts of Bristol! You ask me where she is now, Master Tagg, and I tell you, as I'd tell our beloved King George—"

"I am empowered to search this house, Mistress Biss."

"Then do so," Sophia encouraged, rocking in agony at the waywardness of her own weak-minded sex. "Do so, Master Mason Tagg, and I'll commend you to Admiral Norton. And to Admiral Stamford. And to the Customs commissioners and the Board of the Treasury, and to all those others who have dined here in this house. They will surely wish to see you rewarded as a conscientious servant of the Crown. Do so. Leave your warrant on the table. Sign your name to it. Was it you who smashed that vase, eh, Tilly? What?"

Without the warrant to back him, Mason Tagg led his men from the house. Tilly said nothing as she bolted the door, then went to stand in the withdrawing room, her respect for Mistress Biss beyond all bounds.

Releasing her long, bony body from the chair, Sophia slipped the pins from her cap and prowled, stretching, around the room. "I have a suggestion," she told Tilly. "Bring me some water and a cloth, so I can wipe this rainbow of powder from my face. Then we'll sit here together with a bottle of wine between us and invent the kind of hell we think most appropriate for Master Mason Tagg. For a start I'd make him burn his treasured hat."

✻

The butler Chapman all but brought Faxforge to attention. His faultless good manners left Elizabeth and Margaret bobbing their approval, whilst Louisa mimicked the precision of his speech. Hester merely smiled at him, acknowledging that Master Chapman was as genuine as he seemed.

"Weren't you terrified," she asked him, "coming all this way from the city? And with my sister to be guarded? And the highwaymen of the Cherhill gang behind every hedgerow on the downs?"

"It was, I admit, a besetting fear, Mistress Hester. Though I hoped to protect Mistress Charlotte with— But perhaps you'd care to see the gig for yourself." And with that he'd escorted her to the vehicle and shown her the pistols in their holsters, the loaded blunderbuss under the bench, the cudgel and bayonet and the leather-bulb alarm horn.

Delighted, the girl reached across and squeezed it. The moan, the bleat, the howl of noise rose above Faxforge, the sound still drifting as Hester flinched away.

"Clumsy of me," Chapman apologised, as men came running to the source of the alarm. "Fell against the bulb."

From then on Hester Cannaway was the devoted friend of Aunt Sophia's devoted butler. And it was Hester who walked farther and waved longer as Chapman took his gig along the road to Beckhampton, from where he would guide it west toward the noisy and noisome city-port of Bristol.

＊

Safe now at Faxforge and reunited with her family, Charlotte nevertheless sought sanctuary in silence. She wandered for hours at a time on the downs, or stood alone among the Bellringers, not caring that the October wind gusted around her, or that a sudden rainstorm penetrated to the lining of her cloak.

At night she lay in the room that had been hers before she'd accepted the promise, the broken promise, of a married life with Brook. And there in the darkness, as on the wind-swept downs, the words Forby Kimber had intended should cheer her came as an ever more mocking litany—"It is only a rumour . . . only a rumour . . ."

She decided to pay one final visit to Wintersill Hall. The reason, so she told herself, was that Mistress Dench and Fern might still be there. If the estate was to be sold—and it seemed inevitable—the housekeeper and her innocent, simpleminded charge would most likely be forced to leave.

Charlotte took the problem to her father. It was agreed that she and Giles would ride up there, with a sufficient sum of money to assist Mistress Dench whilst she looked for another situation. It was in Brydd's mind to ask if Charlotte would rather he went in her place. Sensing his concern, she said quietly, "Any anguish God deems fitting will be caused by more recent events than those that occurred at the Hall. And I shall have Giles with me, to bellow at the ghosts."

＊

It was the first time he had seen the place. Small in comparison with many a country house, it was large enough to make Giles whistle through his teeth. "There was just you and— him, and the three or four servants? We could do with a house like this down at Faxforge."

Remaining for a moment in the gig, she murmured, "There were others. It seems there were always others. Lucas and Eldon. Peter and Markis. Brook's friends and their friends. And the women of course. And the man who injured you so cruelly, and then killed Lewis, that monstrous Keeper Venn. I tell you, Giles, there was never a shortage of others." She gazed at the building. At the hall where Brook and his cronies had followed their raucous pursuits, sliding coins along the table to be caught between the breasts of their women. At the parlour, the scene of many a long and vicious card game. And then, above the parlour, at the corner room, the chamber that had so often been her refuge, so often no more than a furnished prison cell.

Giles asked, "Be all right if I look around? Or maybe you'd prefer me to stay with you."

"To shout away the ghosts?" She smiled, then told him to be off. She would call him when she was ready to leave.

She debated whether to rap on the main door or walk through the stable arch and across the coachyard to the kitchen. She chose the latter route, skirting the building, fresh memories assailing her as she glanced toward the stables, at the rear of which was the tack room where she'd hidden on the night of her escape. How furious Keeper Venn would be to learn that Charlotte had been standing not a dozen feet from him, shaking with terror behind the web of straps and bridles. He was in hell now of course, Victor Venn. Though perhaps one of the demons had told him, before consigning him to the flames.

She turned from the memory, then frowned as she saw that the kitchen door was open, no firelight or candlelight in the windows. Inside, the range was cold, the table filmed with dust, the air devoid of the normal smells of stew and soup, ripe English cheeses, aromatic herbs. The clothes hooks on the wall were empty.

Charlotte called out, already knowing there'd be no answer.

She made her way to the foot of the staircase, looked upward at the portraits that flanked the upper, divided flights,
then let her gaze travel slowly along the gallery to the door of
her corner room.

Not wanting anything from this place, she suddenly remembered an item she'd admired. But it would mean going up
there, to her room. She hesitated and was on the point of sum-
moning Giles for his support, when the picture came to her of
the three of them, long ago, the children of Faxforge incanting
a spell as they ventured across the downland after dark.

Their voices uncertain, they had murmured together, Charlotte and Hester hand in hand, Giles growling in pretence that
he was Brydd.

"Hecate or Caliban, *monstrum horrendum*,
Blackguard or skulker, rapscallion or knave,
Off and begone with you! We're not afeared of you!
Charlotte and Hester and Giles the brave!"

She recited it softly as she climbed the stairs to the landing.
Its power held good, though she was saying it faster as she
walked the length of the gallery.

"Hecate or Caliban, *monstrum horrendum*,
Blackguard or skulker, rapscallion or knave . . ."

The door to her room was shut.

She raised the latch and let the heavy oak panel swing inward.

Her bed had been torn to ribbons. The coverlets, pillows,
mattress, even the mahogany bedframe. All had been slashed
again and again, over and over, the strips of material themselves cut across, as if the important thing was not merely the
act of vengeance but the continued shredding of where the
hedgerow bitch had lain.

Trembling now, the power of the spell dissolved by what she
had seen, Charlotte ran into the room, snatched what she was

after, then fled again, this final time, down the stairs and across the entranceway, struggling to turn the key in the locked main door.

She shouted for her brother. He came limping toward her from the direction of the lake.

"I want to leave now."

"Did you see the housekeeper?"

"She's gone."

"Ah, well. What's that you've got there?"

"It's a clock," she said simply. "A cord-wound clock. It is mine."

∗

No word came from Forby.

Sophia wrote with a full and vainglorious account of how she and Tilly had outwitted Mason Tagg. But she made no mention of the missing Captain Lodge.

Charlotte continued her solitary walks across the downs. From the treeless ridges she watched the traffic that ran south from Beckhampton, or north as it came from Devizes, willing each cart and carriage to turn in at the road gate, or to stop and let a passenger alight. The occasional vehicle *did* turn in, though only to bring a customer to the yard.

Work was progressing with the "Cannaway Conductor", its future uncertain, its suitability beyond doubt. And, alongside it, regardless of what Brydd had told Flowerdewe, the family and their craftsmen continued with the everyday making and mending of wagons and drays, traps and harrows, whatever was needed by way of haulage or transport. Loyal though they were to the farmers and merchants of the Kennett Vale, they had anyway little choice in the matter. Until someone showed an interest in the Conductor, it would be work as usual at Fax-forge—or starve.

Charlotte watched from a distance as a tinker's cart made its perilous, lopsided way along the road from the "Blazing Rag". Muffled against the weather, the itinerant pedlar hauled in near the road gate, then sat, wondering perhaps if it was worth his while to hawk his shoddy goods. He glanced toward Charlotte. Good luck to you, she thought. You'll be a clever fellow if you can palm off your stuff on Elizabeth and Margaret.

She turned to resume her walk, then stopped as the man lashed with his reins. She stared down at him from the ridge as he steered the cart, not left through the road gate, or onward toward Devizes, *but determinedly across the verge of the road and up the shallow slope toward her!*

He was yelling as he came, pans and colanders founting from the cart. A group of riders appeared from the direction of Devizes, some of them rising in their stirrups as they stared in disbelief at the hell-bent scene. Charlotte retreated to where a low outcrop of rock would at least prevent the man from running her down. What in God's name was he yelling? If *what?* If you *what?*

"*If you will!*"

The horsemen on the road saw the lunatic pedlar jump from his cart and send his shapeless leather hat spinning in the wind. They saw the woman run toward him, reaching, it seemed, to be taken in his arms. Country ways, they decided, settling back in their saddles. Or maybe the man's been drinking his own concoctions.

✳

They stood together, holding each other, eager to speak yet unwilling to move apart. Then, eventually, they walked beyond the outcrop of rock and along a shallow valley, from where they climbed to a crest of the downs.

"Always did keep a lookout," Matcham told her, "for Navy vessels, and attractive young comforts on the quay. But sharp-eyed or no, we were given the devil of a pounding by their guns. I lost two of my crew, and Master Cope lost an arm. I myself was hit, though not gravely. But a few more brisk rounds and we'd *all* have been lost."

"Yes," Charlotte murmured, "so we would."

"Anyway, we got free of them in the fog and made port near St. Brieuc. A tiring business, trying to make oneself clear to the Frenchies. I assumed—and with a shell-shot vessel for evidence —that things had gone sour in Bristol. It was a while before I could get back there—"

"Why *did* you go back?"

"Forby," Matcham said, his friendship for the gallant Master Kimber needing no more explanation than that. "He told me your husband had been killed and that Tagg would likely have come sniffing along The Biss. Did you hear what I was shouting from the cart?"

There was something odd in what Matcham had told her. He had heard from Forby that Brook Wintersill was dead. Though how could that be, when she herself had not seen Forby between the time her father had brought the news and the morning Master Kimber had come hammering on the door? So how could he have known? And, come to think of it, why had he shown no surprise when he'd learned, there in the hallway at The Biss, that Charlotte would flee to Faxforge? Forby Kimber had not heard of Brook's death from Charlotte. Or from Sophia. Yet it was Forby who'd told Matcham.

So Forby had known it because—

Because Forby had learned it first.

It was Master Kimber, Master Clark, who'd killed Brook Wintersill.

"Did you, my dear Charlotte?"

"I'm sorry, Matcham. Did I— Yes. Oh yes."

"It was relevant to the subject I broached in the forest. You might need time to think it over. I imagine I could put up for a while at, what was that place I passed, the 'Blazing Rag'?"

"Your hearing's less sharp than your eyesight, Master Matcham. I have already said yes to you twice." She kissed him, the lovers outlined clear and bold on the horizon.

And they would doubtless have enjoyed their freedom

longer, had Charlotte not seen Brydd and William, Giles and Jonas Jones, spread out and moving purposefully toward them, to have a word with the lunatic pedlar who had Mistress Cannaway pinned in his embrace.

GRAHAM SHELBY is the author of several critically acclaimed historical novels and has lived in Europe, Africa and Scandinavia. He is a former copywriter and book reviewer, and his other works include *The Devil Is Loose* and *The Wolf at the Door*.

The Cannaway Concern is the second in a sweeping family saga set in eighteenth-century England. The first, *The Cannaways*, was published by Doubleday in 1978.

Graham Shelby is married and lives in an isolated farmhouse in Southern France.